THE JOURNEY

Pilgrimage of Faith

Tales of the Pistolero Padre

G. Terrell Cotter

21stCENTURY PRESS

READING YOU LOUD AND CLEAR.

The Journey, Pilgrimage of Faith
Tales of the Pistolero Padre

Copyright © 2010 G. Terrell Cotter

Published by 21st Century Press

21st Century Press
2131 W. Republic Rd.
PMB 41
Springfield, MO 65807

Contact the author at:
George Terrell Cotter
3204 Saint Ives Court
Plano, TX 75075
214/213-2399
gterrellcotter@yahoo.com

ISBN 978-0-9824428-5-2

Cover: Keith Locke
Book Design: Lee Fredrickson

Visit our website at: www.21stcenturypress.com

2131 W. Republic Rd., PMB 41,
Springfield, MO 65807

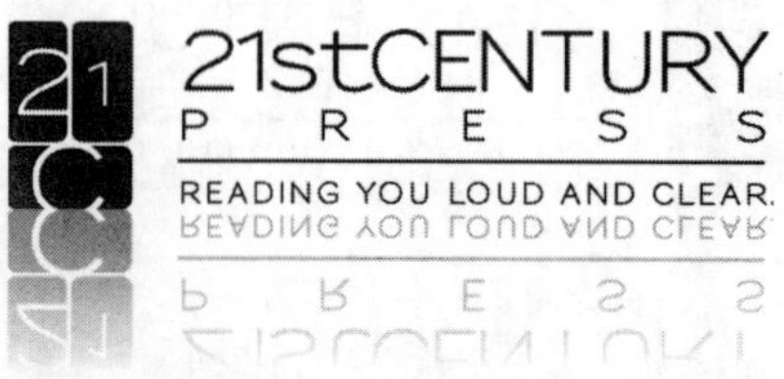

DEDICATION

To my beloved wife Jean,
faithful companion in the ministry of the Word,
without whom I would have never understood the journey,
this book is lovingly dedicated.

Contents

INTRODUCTION

For forty years I lived life on my own terms apart from knowing God or understanding any relevance the Bible had to my life. Frankly, I saw no practical purpose for the Bible other than as a table decoration or a book used by lying politicians swearing to act truthfully and in good faith. But God, through divine intervention placed a humble little country preacher in my path who taught the Word as if it was real and had application to my life. The first Sunday I attended that church the pastor said something that I will never forget: "God wants you (first person singular) to know Him face to face just like Abraham, Moses, David, Peter and Paul." Well, I had never considered that to be possible. However, I wanted to find out if such a personal encounter with God could be a realization. But where and how was I to meet The Almighty "face to face?"

I wrote these stories in the hope of encouraging you to glean the riches from the mind of God found in the Bible which are practical for enriching our lives in every way. More importantly, within the pages of the Bible is an unfolding of knowing God "face to face." West Texas is the setting with a list of fictional characters with some of the personality traits of people I have known, loved, respected, and sometimes tried to avoid as they interacted in everyday circumstances.

I have something fantastic to share with you; God wants you to know Him face to face just like Abraham, Moses, David, Peter, and Paul. I can assure you that if you will humble yourself and seek His face, He will find you (Psalm 27:8; 2 Chronicles 15:4). This is a neverending journey which I hope in some small way to share with you.

Yours in Christ,
G. Terrell Cotter

PROLOGUE – THE JOURNEY

A little over a quarter century earlier Philip Cole had set forth on a journey to know God face to face. Not just to know about Him, or worship Him, but what some had called the audacity of hoping to experience first hand the living presence of El Shaddai (God Almighty) this side of eternity. His expectations were of an intense spiritual journey experiencing the depths and heights of 'me and my God,' a personal conquest, perhaps rivaling the adventures of Cyrano de Bergerac, Don Quixote de la Mancha, or some other heroic, comical, or somewhat less than perfect figure. But God (the divine initiative) had an entirely different plan for Philip, which was not at all the journey this loner from West Texas would have chosen.

After retirement from a business career in Dallas, Philip and his wife Emma moved back to his West Texas family farm. Spanning more than forty years, their marriage had been a discovery of the journey together; the depths, heights, length, and width of the bonds of love, and the weaving of two souls into one. Then again, as many a friend has said, "Philip married up."

Emma came from strong Dutch-German stock where her dad had been a successful business executive and her mom a homemaker. She was still a strikingly handsome woman with azure blue eyes, having lost none of the personality and zest for life that made her so attractive from the first moment Philip had laid eyes on her. But much more, she possessed something transcendent, with principled goodness. Her diction and speech were sophisticatedly elegant; Philip's having degenerated into one of the boys. She would have been perfectly happy with a vegetable plate. Philip insisted on some sort of dead animal on his. Her taste in music ran towards classical, leaving room for the old Christian Hymns. Emma was every bit Philip's match in knowing the Bible, having been in leadership as part of an international woman's Bible study for twenty plus years.

Philip on the other hand was a cat of a different stripe. He was in many ways a solitary being, a textbook introvert, who may have been a little schizophrenic, beset by shadowy bouts of depression. As a child raised in a 'good' home, his mother battled mental illness all of her life. That was well over half a century ago, and everyone knows one needs to 'get over it.' Most of us don't —not on this side of eternity.

As a boy, Philip had done well in sports but poorly in academics, being told by his high school math teacher not to plan on higher education. But his one strength was tenacity, finishing undergraduate work by more effort than talent. In seminary, an eccentric Greek professor uncovered a profound learning disability. He once thought that the languages of Greek and Hebrew were combination works of the deepest pit of hell, mixed generously with God's merciful grace. To this day, Philip couldn't spell cat if you spotted him the "c" and the "t". But overlying an otherwise cantankerous, impatient, somber old man was an abiding trust that the Almighty could, and would, make all things right.

The old man had a habit of carrying a well-worn Colt Commander 38 Super. Thus, the locals tagged him with the handle 'Pistolero Padre.' However, he knew he wasn't a real pistolero. That esteemed title was reserved for such legendary gunmen as Texas Ranger Capt. Jack Hayes and his entire company of men (more recently—Jordan, Keith, and Askins). There is no need to justify carrying a gun to those who will never understand, but in West Texas a gun is a tool like any other. Just as meaningful to those who do understand, it tied one to the history of the land and the people who lived and died there.

Philip had three hobbies, four if you include trying to keep Emma happy. He loved Bible study, his dog, shooting, and Emma (not necessarily in that order). Since becoming a believer late in life, Philip had developed almost an addiction to studying the Word. In the early days, Philip had been influenced by 'real' theologians like C.H. Spurgeon, Aiden W. Tozer, C.F. Keil and F. Delitzsch, Louis Berkhof, Donald Barnhouse, J.I. Packer, Watchman Nee, and more recently, James Montgomery Boice, R.C. Sproul, Stanley Toussaint, John Walvoord, and Charles Caldwell Ryrie.

Dr. Ryrie had written, "The Bible is the greatest of all books; to study it is the noblest of all pursuits; to understand it, the highest of all goals."[1] Philip had more than his share of shortcomings, but he took those words to heart, and studying the Word was a daily part of his early morning discipline when the spirit and the mind seemed to be a little clearer. But the journey was the goal. His old Prof in seminary used to say, "Transformation is the name of the game, not information." So this journey would require lots of transformation in body, soul, and spirit.

CHAPTER 1

Jonah and the Turkey Hunt
The Book of Jonah

The old Chevy pickup rumbled down the winding gravel road, heading into town well before sunup. During the night a dusting of snow had begun, but by now had turned into a storm with the wind driving white flakes sideways and sometime up. Inside, warm and cozy Philip Cole (alias the Pistolero Padre) along with his dog Coco sitting alert in the front seat, watched for game and took note of how even the mesquite trees and cactus looked frozen and parched. There is something indefinable about living in the country which is more than just being laid back. An early winter morning feels, looks, and smells fresh like the first day of creation.

Philip inhaled deeply, enjoying the peace of the morning, his mind drifting back over the last twenty-five years. Oh how much his life had changed. His journey to know the Lord had not turned out like he had expected. Philip had hoped to stay in his comfort zone, which would have been a solo journey with the Lord, perhaps leading to a cloistered monastic life. But the good Lord apparently had a different agenda. Philip certainly was never able to anticipate the immediate future. It seemed like the more he tried to reach up to the Lord, the more the Lord put him in circumstances to reach out to others—that old troublesome 'one another' stuff in the Bible. *"In his heart a man plans his course, but the LORD determines his steps"* (Proverbs 16:9).

Anyone who has never been part of a small country town might not appreciate the familiarity that is part of that culture. Philip drove an old blue Chevy pickup, so if someone saw it from a distance, they knew it was Philip or his wife Emma. Bill Stackhouse, the banker, had a black Lexus. Rusty Warns, the sheriff, a white Chevy Suburban. Charlie Marsh, Philip's pastor, a white Ford pickup, and so forth. Heaven forbid one would change cars every three or four years, which would upset the social order to no end. If you pass another vehicle on the road, you lift one or two fingers off the steering wheel (not the same finger as was often used in Dallas) as an informal passing sign of "howdy." If you passed someone walking, you always looked them straight in the eyes and acknowledged their presence with a "howdy." In West Texas, it still wasn't unusual to reply "yes ma'am" or "no sir," a carryover expression of respect from bygone days. It is a kinder, gentler style of life, but as Dr. Phil is known to say, "Just because I am from Texas doesn't mean I think as slow as I talk."

Philip pulled to a stop at Andy's Café and Domino Emporium, a tin-roof, wood-framed converted feed store that was the early morning hangout for the elder statesmen social crowd. On opening the pickup door, a fog of bacon grease envelops you. Andy's was the real thing when it came to an old-fashioned throwback to the '50s café. There were formica tables with red and white checked tablecloths, straight-back chairs, a bar no one ever sat at, the kitchen with a see through framed cutout, waitresses wearing pink bib dresses over white blouses, and no less than Andy as head cook strapped in a white apron and wearing a 'gimme' cap from the local feed store. As far as anyone could tell, everything was fried on the huge griddle except the coffee, and that sometimes came into question. Most of the 'old guys' only ordered coffee, having eaten breakfast hours earlier. But Andy did a brisk business of eggs any way you wanted them, as long as they were fried. The rest of the meal consisted of fried ham, bacon or sausage, fried hash-browns, biscuits (about a quarter pound each), along with thick sawmill gravy.

Philip had managed to become just one of the boys as he sipped a cup of piping hot black coffee, with two packets of brown raw granular sugar (a bad habit left over from Africa trips), while catching up on the news. The normal complaints included stock tanks running dry, feed prices too high, the price of a new set of tires, and the cost of a new pickup (not that any of this crowd was about to buy one).

There are few secrets in small towns, and the gossip that morning was about a confrontation the day before between Bill Stackhouse (the banker and a pillar of local society) and Jeff Mc-Clintock, a local handyman-contractor who was more than just a little rough around the edges. Jeff was a jack-of-all-trades including masonry, framing, roofing, septic tanks, water lines, and demolition. The two men couldn't look more different, with Bill having a short banker's haircut and a face as smooth as a baby's behind, while Jeff had long hair in a pony tail, sporting about three days of unshaven beard. Bill had contracted to have Jeff remove an old outbuilding on his property, but Bill wasn't satisfied with the cleanup afterwards.

"I happened to be driving by Bill's place and saw the whole thing," Johnny Smith gave his first hand account while vigorously pantomiming the action. "Bill looked like a windmill, flailing his arms in animated dispute, while Jeff stood closed fisted, his arms crossed tight as an old Indian chief. Jeff's voice was about three pitches above normal explaining he expected to be paid, then he would handle any 'call backs,' but Bill was rattling off a list of items he wanted cleaned up first. I thought for sure Jeff was going to pop him. Finally Bill threw up his arms one last time and stomped off in a cloud of dust. Jeff just stood there staring a hole in Bill's back."

The coffee was hot, the fellowship acceptable, and the temperatures outside hovered around freezing, making no one in a hurry to get about the day's chores. The entrance of Sheriff Rusty Warns broke the conversation. Sheriff Warns was from the old school; khaki slacks and a long sleeve white western shirt, old polished boots, Stetson hat, and a black tie that only came two-thirds of the way to his cowboy belt buckle. He was one of those types that if you didn't look quick you missed him, almost a nervous personality but long on common sense. He wore his handgun on a second belt at a slight angle favoring the holstered pistol, Texas Ranger style. The Sheriff, not one to waste time with formalities, headed straight for Philip's table.

"How about a cup of coffee, Sheriff," Philip offered, pushing a chair out with his boot.

The Sheriff didn't bother to sit down but leaned on the chair, "Can't right now, but since I saw your pickup out front I dropped in to see if you might have a cylinder release for my model 66 in your spare parts box. Lost mine, and I'm carrying a semi until the parts come in."

"That's called a thumb piece and thumb piece nut," Philip responded, having done a quick mental inventory of his spare parts box. "I think I've got one, but if I don't, I've got a model 19 we can get the parts off of until yours get here." It was agreed that the Sheriff would drop by Philip's place to pick up the parts.

Later that afternoon the Sheriff arrived at the Cole homestead, as rough a three hundred fifty acres as you've ever seen. Most of the land was hilly. It was covered in scrub-oak, and mesquite with one small hay pasture, all fenced and cross fenced, a nice fifteen acre lake Philip had built, and a medium size barn with a small corral. The house wasn't much either. Some of Philip's friends joked you could throw a cat through the walls and not hurt the cat, but it was paid for and it was home. Philip met Sheriff Warns at the front door, "I've got your parts, but how about that cup of coffee now?"

"That'd be good; I've had a full day."

"Problems, sheriff?" Philip asked while pouring the coffee.

"No, just taking care of business." One of the things that made Rusty such a good Sheriff was that he paid attention to the little things so they didn't turn into big things. The Sheriff took a sip of coffee, "Padre, there's one thing you could help me with. You probably know Bill Stackhouse had that little altercation with Jeff yesterday. Bill won't cut Jeff any slack at all. Jeff's an okay guy, but he's madder'n a 'wet hen,' and I don't want nothing to turn into something."

Philip didn't have to think for long, "I don't usually look for an argument to get in the middle of." The Sheriff came about as close as he was likely to in asking a favor, "I was thinking, Jeff's so angry he's closed-up pretty good, but Bill considers himself a religious man, and he might listen to you. Anyway, if there's one thing Bill loves its bird hunting; maybe you could invite him over." At that Sheriff Warns was up, "Thanks for the parts and the hospitality. Quote him something out of the Bible. I just don't want this thing to get outa hand. I'd be beholden to you." The Sheriff drove off and Philip began to think that a little prayer couldn't hurt this situation.

The next morning Philip dropped by the bank, where he found Bill who was in none too good a mood. Banker Bill was a little on the heavy set side. He wore a typical dark suit with a white shirt and tie and smelled like drug store aftershave. The right approach never hurts, Philip thought. "Bill, I was thinking we might go dust a couple of turkeys Saturday." Bill's expression changed from a grimace to a hint of a smile, "That might just be what I need. How about me coming by your house about five so we can listen and set up before sunup?" Philip nodded in agreement but thought, "Sounds cold to me, but I've been known to do more foolish things, and it is bird hunting." Philip added one last thought, "Oh, leave the aftershave at home."

After arriving back home, Philip checked on the horses in the barn then settled into his office for a little Bible study. At the present time, Philip was studying the minor prophet Jonah, a short book of only four chapters, about a ten minute read if you take your time. Jonah is the only book in the Bible that ends with a question. You're happily reading along, taking in all the action, and then it abruptly ends with God Himself asking a question. The curtain comes down, and you're left to ponder God's question. The central character is Jonah, but it is written to the descendants of Abraham, so the question is to them. God's purpose is to help them understand His character (part of the journey).

After deliberating on his study, Philip thought about how Jonah is so misunderstood. The message isn't about a fish or whale or even Jonah. However, Philip chuckled to himself that the second chapter is the first recorded submariner's prayer. The book is simple: God said go, Jonah said no. God made Jonah an offer he couldn't refuse. Jonah reconsidered his options, and then God revealed His character to both Jews and Gentiles. But, within that simple story is revealed God's sovereign work as the Lord of all. Jonah may be misunderstood, but Philip had another situation on his hands. How could he possibly help with the misunderstanding between Bill Stackhouse and Jeff McClintock?

Early Saturday morning was cold but clear, with the stars standing out as if the Creator had just sprinkled the heavens anew. Philip was finishing a little time with the Lord when Bill's black Lexus rolled down the driveway. After the usual formalities of 'Howdy' and a firm handshake, Bill noted how he was looking forward to an overdue day in the woods. Bill pulled a gun case out of the back seat, then unsheathed a Benelli Super Black Eagle, which to Philip's traditional preference was as ugly as a mud fence. Philip walked back into his study to slip his L. C. Smith side by side off the shelf and grabbed a handful of No. 6's.

Fallen leaves and brush covered the ground, making the approach in the dark slow and deliberate, but after listening for the roosting birds, the two managed to 'Indian up' to their chosen spot. Philip set up to call with Bill about twenty yards ahead. The early morning had just a touch of dew from the rotting vegetation, but the air was cold and crisp, bringing a slight sting to any exposed skin, but refreshing the spirit. Waiting for daylight, Philip took a deep breath, enjoying the smell of the forest.

The turkey crop that year was good. Some toms gobbled, first in one place and then another. But it looked like they had set up their ambush in the wrong spot. However, any day in the woods is a fine time to restore peace to the soul. Over the following few hours, the two visitors enjoyed communion with the forest creatures. A couple of squirrels chased each other through a patch of hardwoods in the creek bottom. A Great Blue Heron glided to a soft landing at a neighbor's stock pond. A couple of does with one yearling wandered by, nibbling on some honeysuckle in a thicket, while cardinals darted in and out of the same underbrush. Off in the distance, following a fence line, a coyote tracked the scent of what hopefully would become breakfast. In the opposite direction an armadillo moseyed through, looking like some prehistoric rodent. Just being out in God's creation is a big part of what hunting is all about.

Along towards late morning, Philip signaled Bill to head towards the house for a little down time and lunch, but Bill very slowly pointed off to their left. Bill was twisting while coming up with his shotgun in ultra slow motion. It took Philip a minute for his eyes to distinguish between the gray birds and the fallen foliage, but sure enough a small flock of turkeys were making their way towards them while working over the acorn crop. On further inspection, there was one Tom in the group, which Philip spotted about the same time Bill blazed away. The Tom went down, and Bill was up in an instant to recover his trophy. The morning hunt was successful.

Emma, anticipating two hungry hunters, served them turkey and smoked ham sandwiches on the front porch. Texas can be nice this time of year, not staying cold long. By noon the temperature had warmed to shirt sleeve weather. Bill was a straight-laced formal type of guy, but the country pace relaxes a fella. Pretty soon Bill got around to what was bothering him, "I appreciate the offer to hunt because I needed to clear my head. You probably heard about my little set-to with Jeff McClintock. I know as a Christian I'm supposed to turn the other cheek and forgive, but with McClintock's temper, he won't listen to reason. I don't see how this thing can be resolved because it's gotten to the point where I won't talk to him. Padre, you got any advice?"

Silence held for quite a while, and there might have even been a prayer for wisdom shot straight up. Phillip finally offered, "Bill, believe it or not I get a lot of my everyday direction from the Bible, and it just so happens I've been reading Jonah." Bill leaned back with a pained look on his face, interrupting, "Jonah? That's the fishy story. I don't know if I can buy that one. Anyway, those prophets were just for the Old Testament." Philip, not one to play the fool lightly responded in a not too patient tone, "Do you want my advise or not?" Bill nodded affirmatively.

"Well, the Bible, both Old and New Testaments, says Jonah was a real person. Over in 2 Kings it says Jonah was an accredited prophet from a town near Nazareth. And in Matthew, Jesus treated Jonah's experience 'in the fish' as factual. So I tend to accept it as fact too. But the main point of the book isn't the fish, or even Jonah's disobedience. Everywhere you look in the book of Jonah you see God revealed as sovereign over His servants, nature, sea creatures, and other nations. Everything from a fierce storm to a tiny worm, as the sovereign God He treats everyone with grace and mercy." Bill's body language had changed from skepticism to inquisitive; not sold but at least listening.

"The story goes, God commissioned Jonah to go tell their ancient enemy, located in the city of Nineveh, that He was aware of their wicked ways and wanted them to repent. Well, you might say the Ninevites tended to be a pretty rough group, maybe a little like Jeff. Jonah didn't want to go because he knew God's character, a God of grace and mercy. Jonah feared that even as evil as the Ninevites were, they might still accept God's warning to repent. So he hopped a ship heading in the opposite direction. You know the part about the fish swallowing Jonah, so I'll just cut to the chase. God displayed His character of grace and mercy by forgiving the Ninevites when they repented after hearing Jonah's warning. Jonah's fear had become reality, so Jonah was deeply depressed. Then God asked the final question, 'Shouldn't I have compassion on Nineveh too?'"

Bill thought about the story for a while. "You said grace and mercy, but they seem like the same thing?" Philip swallowed his last bit of sandwich, washed down with a little coffee. "I once had an old pastor friend tell me the difference: grace is getting something good you don't deserve; mercy is not getting something bad you do deserve.

But that isn't the most important lesson. The first clue is, God's sovereignty flavors every part of Jonah, and I think what it is telling us is that grace and mercy aren't just something God does; they are part of who God is. In other words, authentic grace and mercy only exist because God exists. And second, the book is really unusual in that it ends asking us the question: If you believe God is sovereign, and if He is grace and mercy, and if we consider ourselves to be His children, then shouldn't we conform our life to be like His and treat others the same way?"

There was silence for a long while. Bill's countenance changed from one of bewilderment to a look on his face like the light just came on. Then he whispered, "This thing with Jeff and me is kinda like your story. Maybe I'm a little like that Jonah fella, expecting God to bless me, but thinking of Jeff like Jonah did

Nineveh, as outsiders. Maybe if I know God cares about everyone, I should treat Jeff the same way." After another very long silence, Bill literally jumped to his feet. "Come on Padre, let's run into town and see if Jeff's a bird hunter. He's been standing on the outside of God's grace and mercy too long."

Philip's Study Notes, Jonah

One interesting and very important distinction is that in the Hebrew text of Jonah there is a consistent interplay between the different names for God. For those who knew Him personally (i.e. Jonah, the Jewish people), the name is the four consonant letters YHWH (the so-called tetragrammaton consisting of four Hebrew consonants, Yod, He, Waw, He: the Hebrew name of the self-existent covenant God), pronounced *Yah-weh* when you add a couple of vowels. However, for those who didn't know Him personally the name used in Jonah is Elohim, meaning "Lord."

One of the keys to understanding the book of Jonah is in observing the interplay between those who know God experientially and those who only know of another god. Consequently, if you are blessed to know Him personally you just might ought to know His character also. Knowing His character should influence your character, which is what Jonah is all about.

Please allow one small rabbit trail off our beaten path. When a devout Jew reading the Hebrew text comes to the name Yahweh, they pronounce it *Adoni* (master), because to even pronounce the personal holy name would be to "take the name of God in vain." In your English translation you can tell when the name is Yahweh by it being printed LORD (all caps); while Elohim is translated and printed God or Lord. Jehovah is the German pronunciation of the tetragrammaton. So unless you are German, you would use the more proper Hebrew "Yahweh."

CHAPTER 1, Jonah's Disobedience

The first three verses foreshadow what is to come. This story isn't about a fish or a prophet; it's about the revelation of God's character to the nation Israel. In verses 1-2, it is the LORD (Yahweh, the self-existent "I Am that I Am") who spoke His command to the prophet Jonah; it was He who heard the great cry against the wickedness of Nineveh. But in verse 3, Jonah *"flees from the presence of the LORD"* as though the Creator of the universe was so provincial that His only dominion was Israel, and His only concern was the Jewish people.

Jonah refused God's commission by hopping a ship going in the opposite direction, and God had plenty of other prophets He could have used. But God's sovereign will was for Jonah to do this job. When God caused a great storm on the sea, the sailors discovered their problems were caused by Jonah's disobedience. The interesting thing is that the conversation between the sailors and Jonah starts off with the sailors talking about their gods, then transitions to Jonah's God (Elohim), but ends up with them believing in Yahweh.

Jonah convinced the sailors everyone would be lost if they didn't do something, so reluctantly they pitched him overboard. It looks like he is going to drown for sure, but then something worse happens. He gets swallowed by a fish, which is an even more terrible death. But if you think about it, the fish that God caused to swallow Jonah was a result of God's grace and mercy, because it turned out to be Jonah's salvation from drowning.

CHAPTER 2, Jonah's Prayer of Faith

Before Jonah is swallowed by the fish, he is dejected and disobedient. Then inexplicably at the darkest moment in the fish's belly, Jonah prays a beautiful prayer of confidence in the God of his salvation; faith in Yahweh (read chapter 2 for Jonah's prayer of faith).

"Then Jonah prayed to Yahweh his God from the stomach of the fish." Jonah could no more run from the presence of Yahweh than he could run from his own shadow. God was present in Israel, in the boat, in the sea and in the fish. Jonah changed from lack of faith to faith in God's salvation: *"I called out of my distress to Yahweh, and He answered me,"* (v2) *"I will look again toward Thy holy temple,"* (v4) *"Thou hast brought up my life from the pit,"* (v6) *"I will sacrifice to Thee with the voice of thanksgiving."* (v9) God's providence caused the fish to spit him out, on dry ground no less. By this time God had Jonah's attention, causing him to high tail it about 500 miles to Nineveh.

CHAPTER 3, Jonah Delivers Yahweh's Message

Then comes the funny part. The action of the whole first half of the book is about Jonah going to preach, but when he gets to Nineveh, he walks through the city for three days, proclaiming only one short sentence: *"Forty more days and Nineveh will be overturned."* Have you ever heard of a preacher who limited his sermon to one sentence? Can't you just imagine how bitter those eight caustic words must have stuck in Jonah's throat, and how halfhearted he must have delivered the message?

But, God's grace and mercy was working in the Ninevites' hearts. Sure enough, for the very reason Jonah feared, those heathens did repent, which made Jonah so mad he wanted to die. The contradiction is this: Jonah wanted to have the benefit of God's grace and mercy, having just been saved from the belly of the fish, but Jonah didn't want God to treat others the same way.

It isn't incidental, by the way, that both Jonah and the Ninevites' salvation happened after they repented and believed God in faith. Repentance means to change your mind about something, and that's what Jonah did in his prayer while in the fish, and that's what the Ninevites did when they heard God's warning. But true repentance always has an affect, which is to believe what God said in faith. The king of Nineveh said, "*God may turn and relent*" (v9; the Hebrew word '*nacham*' which is the idea of breathing deeply from compassion or comfort). The Bible then says, "*They turned from their wicked ways, then God relented*" (v10). The Hebrew language expressing 'breathing deeply' out of compassion and comfort reveals the heart of God even towards wicked people.

CHAPTER 4, Yahweh's Character

In the last chapter, God put Jonah through a grace and mercy curriculum to teach Israel a lesson about what His character is like. Jonah went out of the city and hunkered down on a hill overlooking the great city to see if God would condemn or forgive the Ninevites. God caused a vine to grow to give Jonah shade, which made Jonah very happy. But God caused a worm to attack the vine, withering it. Afterwards, God caused a scorching east wind. Jonah's attitude changed, and he wanted to die again. If one had any question about the consistency of God's sovereign action, understand that the same Hebrew verb is used before the fish, the vine, the worm and the wind, which proves God's Divine initiative and sovereignty.

But Jonah was living by the flesh, where self-centered circumstances, not truth, were the root of his attitude. Then the most amazing thing happens. The curtain falls at the end, and God leaves Jonah with a question: "*You had compassion on the plant which you didn't even cause to grow, which came up overnight and perished overnight. And should I not have compassion on Nineveh, the great city in which there are more then 120,000 persons who do not know the difference between their right and left hand, as well as many animals?*"

Conclusion:

Yahweh's character, His very being, is to have compassion and mercy on all. For those of us who know God personally, we are to be more than just recipients of His lovingkindness; we are to reflect His compassion to the world. God's character was most completely revealed in His Son Jesus, the Christ. For a Christian, the journey is one of being progressively conformed to the image of Christ.

CHAPTER 2

RAHAB AND THE RED DRESS
MATTHEW 1:5 AND
JOSHUA 2:1-24; 6:17

(Cathy Felder, single mother of one, had recently returned to her West Texas hometown to raise her daughter.)

Struggling for consciousness in the middle of the night, Kathy Felder is vaguely aware of a strange noise coming from the kitchen. Kathy's first thought is of her daughter Kim in an upstairs bedroom. She and Kim were alone, living on a farm miles from town and no neighbors within half a mile. The shimmering full moon is so bright that there is no need for a light. Kathy reached for a baseball bat she kept next to the bed, which she realized now was little more than a false sense of security. Occasionally, a muffled racket came from the kitchen, but Kathy's first priority was her daughter. She eased up the steps to Kim's upstairs bedroom, quietly opened the door, and seeing her daughter asleep turned her attention to the intruder.

The young single mother, with the determination of a mamma grizzly, moved barefooted in slow deliberate steps down the stairs and across the living room to the kitchen door. The bat was cocked over her shoulder, ready for immediate action. Trembling with fear, she peeked around the open door to locate the un-welcomed intruder. There he was, on the breakfast table—about a 20 pound raccoon, helping himself to homemade blueberry muffins which she had asked Kim to put in the refrigerator. Sliding the outside screen door open with the bat, Kathy flicks on the light. Realizing the jig is up, the little bandit makes a break for the open door.

The excitement was over, but her heart still pounded in her throat. Sleep clearly wasn't an option; anyway she would have to get up in about an hour to go to work at Andy's Café where she had just hired on as a waitress. Kathy ended up on the front porch, enjoying the solitude and peace of her West Texas farm as she sat in the cool night breeze and contemplated her situation.

Kathy was the youngest of three children by ten years. All three had eventually moved to the big city for jobs. She had gotten into some minor trouble as a teenager, dropped out of high school, and had left the farm for the city where she could live on her own terms. She was young and didn't know you can't do that—if you are a teenage girl and all alone, the world system sets the terms because it is bigger, and meaner, and stronger than you. In the meantime, and it was a 'mean' time after Kathy begat a daughter out of wedlock and her parents had passed on, she decided to move back to the abandoned family farm because they had no place else to go.

Andy's Café and Domino Emporium was the normal morning beehive of activity. Philip Cole hadn't been in for a few days, so he noticed there was a new waitress. She was very attractive —not beautiful, but strikingly attractive. She was tall and thin, with a tiny waist, short reddish blond hair, fair complexion, radiant brown eyes, and as he was about to find out, very determined. Kathy walked up to Philip's table and without so much as a 'howdy,' bluntly stated her intent: "I understand they call you the Pistolero Padre—I need a gun!" Philip was taken aback, but he felt like this young stranger must be desperate. "Maybe we could talk about this when you're not so busy." Kathy smiled then nodded, "Things slow down around here about ten. Would that be okay?"

Mid-morning, Philip made his way back to the café where the two of them could sit and reason together. Kathy, noticing Philip's presence, walked over and invited him to have a seat at one of the tables. Then before he could get a word in edgewise, she started right in. "My parents have passed on, and my seven year old daughter Kim and I are living out on the old Felder place. I have to pay some back taxes but thank goodness Sheriff Warns wouldn't let the county sell the farm out from under me. We're all alone out there, and I don't feel comfortable without some protection."

Philip reflected for a moment as she tapped her fingernails on the table, and then worked through out loud her situation. "You were raised on a farm around guns, so you know to respect them." Kathy nodded in the affirmative. Philip wanted to make a point about being safe. "Clearheaded thinking is the only thing that's going to keep the two of you safe and make you feel at ease, and for what you're talking about a gun is a last resort when you can't get away. But it is true that living on a farm you may need a gun for rattlesnakes or rabid skunks, not to mention a two-legged critter. You also have to ask yourself, do you have time to teach your daughter about gun safety?" Kathy interrupted, "Kim is blind, I guess that's the reason I feel more need for protection." Philip couldn't help but show a surprised look on his face, but the revelation of Kim being blind also made him all the more committed to helping if he could. "Maybe you and Kim could drop by the house to see Emma and me. My wife is more than a fair hand with a gun, and she's got a little pump 20 gauge she keeps around the house just for such a purpose."

It was deep in summer, so Philip took care of some chores in town so that he would have time in the heat of the day to do some Bible study. Having the habit of alternating between Old and New Testament books, he had just finished a long study in Isaiah. For no particular reason, Philip opened his well worn Bible to the first Gospel, Matthew, which he had read and taught dozens of times before.

Matthew starts out, *"The record of the genealogy of Jesus the Messiah, the son of David, the son of Abraham."* He would have skipped the genealogy except past experience had taught him that every word could have great significance. Matthew's genealogy is just what you might anticipate from the Jewish culture of that day. It starts with a list of only the male descendents, but then unexpectedly in the middle inserting a selection of female names: Tamar, Rahab, Ruth, and Bathsheba. The old man thought to himself out loud, "That's funny; they didn't mention the great matriarchs Sarah, Rebecca, or Leah. But Matthew lists these four, all of whom had what you might call serious personality flaws. I wonder why the Lord chose these four to be listed for all time in the line of Messiah." Even though Matthew was a Jew writing to the Jews, starting with the genealogy including two Gentile women, Rahab and Ruth, there is this hint that Messiah was to be more than the Jewish Savior only.

This woman Rahab fascinated Philip. Over the years he had collected a fine reference library, and with a little research discovered Rahab was highly regarded by both Jews and Christians. Yet in her past she had been a prostitute, a Gentile and an outcast. One of his old reference books tells about an ancient Jewish writing, called the *Tal Megillah*, where Rahab is said to have married Joshua. Their descendents produced eight priests. But this same Rahab is also mentioned in the New Testament where the book of Hebrews has enshrined her for all time in the hall of faith. The old man often talked to himself, this time framing what he knew about faith, hoping to understand this mysterious person Rahab. "*'Faith is the assurance of things hoped for, the conviction of things not seen'* (Hebrews 11:1). '*Without faith it is impossible to please Him, for he who comes to God must believe that He is, and that He is a rewarder of those who seek Him'* (Hebrews 11:6). Faith is the glue that connects all of the Old and New Testament stories of Rahab. Why is faith bound so carefully to the accounts of this woman in the genealogy of the Messiah, and why don't I understand it? I know the story, but this lesson on faith hasn't gone from my head to my heart."

Philip decided a little time spent looking over the verses in Joshua 2 related to Rahab couldn't hurt. Rahab's faith was expressed in her willingness to hide Israelites sent to Jericho to spy out the city, believing that the God of the Hebrews was about to give the city and eventually the land to them. She cut a deal with the spies to spare her family when the attack came, the condition being that she hang a scarlet cord from her window.

Sunday afternoon found Philip and Emma having a visit on their front porch over homemade peach ice cream with their pastor and his wife, Charlie and Peggy Marsh. Charlie was a mountain of a man, but he had the heart of a humble shepherd. Charlie looked more like a pro football tackle, while Peggy would do well to stretch to five-two. He was blond headed; almost white, with very light complexion and deep pale blue eyes. Big as he was, Charlie had one other characteristic that stood out above everything else, he stuttered. As Charlie said, "It isn't a handicap unless I t-t-talk!" Not being one to let this handicap hold him back from the appointed task the Lord had called him to, Charlie had developed a humorous way of dealing with it, "Not only am I a s-s-stutterer, I'm a g-g-great stutterer. I may be the b-b-best stutterer y-you have ever heard." Charlie and Peggy dated in college and for a long time she was afraid to tell him her major, speech therapy. God does have a sense of humor. Peggy was what Philip might call "cute as a duck with a hat on;" with short dark brown hair, sparkling brown eyes, and with an outgoing personality that complemented her pixie persona.

As fate would have it, up drives Kathy and Kim. After the normal 'Howdies' and introductions, Emma and Kathy excused themselves to discuss handling a pump shotgun, while Kim agreed to share a generous bowl of ice cream. Kim was wearing a bright red dress, which went with her enthusiastic personality. At the same time there was something a little reserved, maybe sad, something in her soul Philip couldn't put his finger on. She was the spitting image of her mom, tall for her age and thin with long bright blond hair put up in twin pony tails that bounced like coiled springs as she walked. "Kim," Philip said, "you're as cute as a speckled pup under a wagon." Kim had a way of squinting which caused her little nose to wrinkle, which gave her a precocious ambiance. "I'm blind you know. Can I feel your face so that I will know you?" Philip took Kim by the hand and placed her before him as he sat in his rocker. Kim slowly felt Philip's face and said, "You are old, and you are not always happy." Kid or no kid, Philip unintentionally squinted to match Kim's face, and then set his jaw. "I may be old and maybe a little grouchy occasionally, but I made the ice cream you're eating." Kim let Philip's response pass and moved to Peggy. "You have a kind face." Next was Pastor Marsh's turn as he lifted Kim to sit on his knee. "You are a big man! How big are you?" His voice was gentle. "On a good d-d-day, before I get b-b-beat down by some of the flock like Mr. Cole, I'll go about s-s-six-six and 250 pounds." "I like you Pastor Marsh," Kim said as she returned to her ice cream.

"Kim," Pastor Marsh paused from his ice cream. "Mr. Cole was about to t-tell us of a woman named Rahab in the Bible. Would y-you like to hear the story?" "Can I keep eating my ice cream?"

Philip set his ice cream bowl aside, holding his hands together to warm them. He considered for a moment what he had been studying. "Well, the story goes, after the death of Moses, Joshua was appointed leader of the Israelites. God told Joshua to cross the river Jordan and possess the land, which God had promised to give them many years before. Israel was camped on the east side of the river Jordan, but on the west side just a couple of miles off was the great walled city of Jericho. Joshua sent two spies to check it out, and they ended up at the house of a woman by the name of Rahab. When the king of Jericho heard about the spies, he commanded Rahab to hand them over. But she hid them on her roof, telling the king the spies had already escaped. Later she went up on her roof to talk to the spies, during which time she confessed her faith in their God and her belief that their God had given the city and land to the sons of Israel. Rahab asked the spies to see to it that her household would be spared when the attack came. The spies agreed, with the condition that she must mark her house by hanging a scarlet cord out the window. When the walls fell and the attack came, because the Israelites saw the scarlet cord, the only people saved in the whole city were Rahab's family." Philip paused for a moment. "That's the story, but there is something more about Rahab's faith and that scarlet cord that I don't fully understand." Charlie took a last spoonful of ice cream. "We m-m-might need to think a-about that one for a w-while."

Emma and Kathy came back to the front porch for some ice cream. "How'd it go?" Philip inquired. Emma's smile reassured him that Kathy would be responsible and was teachable. "Kathy's a natural with a shotgun, so the main thing we went over was how to safely handle one. When season opens, I think Kathy and I might fix up a batch of dove for you." Emma wanted to see for herself that Kim would also be responsible around a firearm. "Kim, would you be willing to treat a gun in the house with due respect?" "Yes ma'am, mama's already talked with me about that."

As can happen during the summer, dark clouds had banked up in the northwest, and it looked like an afternoon thunderstorm was brewing. "Thanks for the ice cream, but we'd better be 'gittin' home," Kathy said as she buckled Kim into her seat. Kathy's family farm was only about a mile south, but storms can come up fast this time of year.

The wind picked up a bit, but the outflow breeze from the thunderstorm was cool. The women decided they had been blown around enough, so they excused themselves to the kitchen for a cup of tea while Philip and Charlie continued their visit over a fresh cup of coffee. Ten minutes couldn't have gone by when a tremendous bolt of lightning struck a live oak on the far hill off to the south. There seemed to be no concern until Philip noticed the lightning had started a grass fire, and in only a few moments the wind had whipped it into a furious wall of flames.

Philip jumped to his feet. "That's heading right for Kathy's place, get in the pickup Charlie." Philip's old pickup roared down the gravel road as their worst fears were realized. The wind was leapfrogging the fire as it raced along the prairie. An inferno, spawning little blazing whirlwinds out front, was now very near Kathy's two-story house. Time seemed to go in slow motion. "I'm going 70 and that fire's going to get there before we do."

Philip slid the pickup to a stop as Kathy ran for them. The old wooden lapboard house was on fire and smoke was billowing out. When Philip saw the look of desperation and fear on Kathy's face, he knew they were in trouble. "Kim's in her bedroom on the second floor, and I can't get to her. Help me, oh God please help me!"

The smoke was so dense there was no way to go inside, so Kathy led Philip and Charlie around the backside where Kim's bedroom was located. The window was open and Kim was standing there in her red dress. Charlie took control. "Kim, this is Pastor Marsh. I'm right under your window. J-j-jump and I will c-c-catch you." Kim screamed, "I'm afraid to jump." Charlie calmly reminded her, "Kim you k-k-know me, you know I am big enough and strong enough to s-s-save you. Trust me and jump. I will c-c-catch you." Slowly Kim climbed into a sitting position in the window; she hesitated for a moment, and then jumped.

In the split second that Kim was in the air, Philip had a revelation to beat all revelations. Seeing Kim's red dress, and her desperate need of being saved from the fire, incandescent pictures flashed in Philip's mind. He saw snapshots of the blood on the door lintel at the first Passover when the Jews were saved from the death angel, the rivers of blood of the sacrificed animals at holy convocations, the scarlet cord Rahab hung out the window, the obedience by faith of Jesus shedding His blood for the sins of the world, and just then, the faith of Kim wearing the red dress trusting Charlie to catch her. She believed that what Charlie said was true, even though she could not see it. That's saving faith in action.

Everything continued in slow motion as Kim, in a splash of red, fell towards Charlie's outstretched arms. Those huge arms gathered her in like a feather pillow, and he gave her a big hug as Kathy raced to their side. By this time Emma and Peggy had arrived with the volunteer fire department.

Just as Emma got to Philip's side he was mumbling to himself, "That's why Rahab with the scarlet cord is in the genealogy of the Messiah, the scarlet thread through the Bible, a foreshadowing of the blood of the Lamb! That's what God was trying to tell me about faith; they all needed a Savior and their salvation was through faith in the blood." Emma wasn't much surprised by Philip mumbling incoherently, but she sometimes worried at what must be going on in the old man's head. Emma pulled on Philip's arm. "Rahab, blood, Savior, what are you talking about?" Philip smiled, "Oh nothing Sweetheart, something just went from my head to my heart."

After the fire was out, Charlie gathered everyone out front for a prayer of thanksgiving that no one was hurt. One of the older couples from Charlie's church had already approached Kathy about staying with them for a while. Since most of the community was present, Charlie also added, "I'll talk with the other pastors to organize a house raising out here in a week or so. Looking forward to seeing all of you back here at that time." Charlie led the prayer and Kim closed it with an "Amen."

Philip's Study Notes on Rahab
Matthew 1, The Genealogy of Yeshua, the Messiah

The Gospel According to Matthew is written from a distinctly Jewish perspective so that they, the descendents of Abraham, might know that Yeshua (Jesus) was the Anointed One, their Messiah, the Lamb of God. The Gospel starts with a genealogy of the line which produced Messiah.

It is interesting that Matthew inverted the chronological order, putting David before Abraham. One of Philip's professors had written, "Matthew has a definite purpose in inverting the chronological order of the names. The promises given to David were restricted; that is, they were Jewish, national, and royal in character. To David was promised an eternal throne, an eternal king, and an eternal kingdom (2 Samuel 7:12-17; Psalm 89). On the other hand, the promises given to Abraham were more comprehensive, being personal, national, and universal (Genesis 12:1-3; 13:14-17; 15:13-21; 17:1-8; 22:16-19). Abraham was given the promise among others that in him should all the nations of the earth be blessed."[2] The genealogy in Matthew is important because it outlines the family line from which Messiah will come, and the promises given to Messiah's ancestors are to be fulfilled in and through the Anointed One.

David Stern is a Messianic Jew who made the following observation about the women mentioned in Matthew's genealogy: "Women, especially those born Gentiles, were rarely included in biblical genealogies. The first four were Gentile women whom

God honored by including them among the recorded ancestors of Yeshua the Jewish Messiah—through whom Gentiles, women and slaves are saved equally with Jews, men and free."[3]

Joshua 2, Rahab's Faith in the God of Israel

The walled citadel of Jericho controlled the west bank of the Jordan and therefore the primary passage to the central highlands of the Promised Land. Even today the old road from the Jordan valley goes from Jericho along the Wadi Kelt up to Jerusalem.

(2:1-7) Joshua's plan was to send spies to gather intel on the city such as fortified towers, thickness of the walls, gates, opposing forces, morale of the people, etc. But God seemed to have a parallel plan to save a sinful woman who believed in Him. Rahab is called a "*zonah*" (harlot), not an innkeeper as Josephus proposed. In some mysterious way, we are not told how, God brought the spies and the harlot Rahab together. The spies were observed in the city. Word was sent to the king, and officers of the court went to Rahab's home to arrest them. Rahab had hidden the spies on her roof under flax stalks. She told the soldiers that the spies had been there but had escaped before the city gates were closed for the evening.

(2:8-11) After the soldiers left, Rahab went up on the roof to talk with the spies, at which time a most remarkable conversation occurs. Rahab refers to the God of Israel by His personal, covenant name 'Yahweh' (the self-existent One). But even more amazing is her confession of faith in Yahweh: "*I know Yahweh has given you the land, For we have heard how Yahweh dried up the water of the Red Sea . . . and what you did to the two kings of the Amorites, for Yahweh your God, He is God in heaven above and on earth beneath* " (vv 9-11).

(2:12-21) Rahab's concern was for her family as well as herself. She was most probably concerned for their spiritual conversion to what she knew to be the one true God, as well as their physical safety. Rahab asked, "*Since I have dealt kindly with you,* *will you also deal kindly with my father's household?"* (v12) Rahab used the Hebrew word *"hesed"* which can be translated kindness but has the meaning of steadfast loyalty and faithful love based on a covenant. *Hesed* is often translated more broadly as loving-kindness. The spies agreed to keep the *hesed* covenant, but Rahab must do three things: her house must be identified with a scarlet cord; during the attack, her family must not venture out of her home; and all her family must keep this a secret. Otherwise the covenant was invalidated.

Hebrews 11, The Triumph of Faith

In the book of Hebrews, Rahab is singled out for her faith along with such notables as Noah, Abraham, Sarah, and Moses; pretty tall cotton for a Gentile woman with a tarnished reputation. Hebrews 11 says, *"Now faith is the assurance of things hoped for, the conviction of things not seen. For by it the men of old gained approval"* (vv 1-2). *"And without faith it is impossible to please Him, for he who comes to God must believe that He is, and that He is a rewarder of those who seek Him"* (v6). *"By faith Rahab the harlot did not perish along with those who were disobedient"* (v31).

Conclusion

By faith Rahab did not perish. She believed in the one true God, and she believed that He was the rewarder of those who seek Him. The journey begins by grace through faith. Salvation to all is by faith in Christ's atoning work, apart from all human merit whatsoever. The Gospel is that God, in a righteous act, "gave His only begotten Son," which was sufficient to appease His wrath and at the same time reconcile sinful man to Himself. This was an act of grace, received on the principle of faith. Will you trust that Jesus' death on the cross was sufficient for your sin-debt and receive God's unmerited gift of eternal life with Him today?

CHAPTER 3

RUTH, A LOVE STORY
THE BOOK OF RUTH

Drought makes for hard times on game, livestock, and people. This thought came to Philip Cole's mind as the 747 prepared for final approach to Nairobi International Airport. From the air, the parched landscape below looked just like his West Texas home, but this was the Dark Continent, Sub-Sahara East Africa. Philip stretched his tired back while still buckled in, then observed to his wife Emma, "Well Dorothy, we're not in Kansas any more."

Philip, Emma, and Frank Nogery had arranged a teaching missionary trip to Rwanda and Eastern Congo through ALARM Ministries (African Leadership and Reconciliation Ministries headquartered in Nairobi and Dallas). Frank, a recent graduate from seminary in Dallas, wanted to visit for the first time his ancestral home in Goma, Congo. Many years before, his parents had immigrated to the United States with the help of a missionary doctor, Frank's dad having gone on to become an M.D. himself.

With a thud, the 747 touched down at Nairobi International, and all attention turned to gathering the luggage before catching a connecting flight to Kigali, Rwanda. Arriving in Kigali ended a

27 hour journey from Dallas to Rwanda, via Paris and Nairobi. This trip was on their own nickel to meet an urgent need, and there's no extra time or money for overnight layovers and fancy hotels.

Rwanda and Congo are a contradiction in reality, a real life oxymoron. The landscape must be what the Garden of Eden would have looked like. The Central African highlands are tropical, located very near the equator, but at an altitude from about 5000 up to 15,000 feet. Fences are made of tropical hibiscus and bougainvillea. Avocado trees are used for shade. Ficus trees are the size of the largest pecan trees back home, and bananas trees are everywhere. Yet in this horticultural paradise, tribal wars have gone on for generations, encouraged by power brokers from Europe who finance warlords so the financiers can rape the natural resources. How many lives is a diamond worth? Apparently quiet a few, including children. If the European financiers had spent half as much money on education as automatic weapons, we would all be outsourcing our work through Africa, instead of sending them aid that is stolen by the warlords.

Man can be the cruelest creature. To watch a trio of lionesses take down a wildebeest isn't pretty, but it's nature's way. But man is capable of blood lust. In 1994 the president of Rwanda was assassinated by a bomb placed on his airplane. Before the debris hit the ground the majority Hutu tribe started a campaign of murder to eradicate the minority ruling Tutsi tribe. To add a little more personal touch, the leaders of the genocide that followed thought it would be a good idea to kill all the educated as well, so there would be no voice of reason left. Out of a population of six million, over seven hundred thousand were murdered, mostly by being hacked to death with machetes. In an act characteristic of their organization, the United Nations pulled out its troops protecting hundreds of women and children in Kigali, and the United States was equally useless. Nobel Peace Prize winner Kofi Annan ordered the UN troops pulled out that were protecting a couple hundred women and children who were subsequently hacked to death. Most of the pastors, being among the educated, were murdered. Thus, there was the urgent need and reason for our journey—to equip untrained church leaders to teach the Bible.

But now the situation had momentarily stabilized by African standards, and it was moderately safe. The hardcore Hutu rebels had been driven into the area of east Congo where Rwanda, Congo and Uganda meet. In the two weeks before our trip, our host Obed had gone missing, arrested by the local military. No one knew where, or if, he was being held. Obed is diabetic, and there was no way for his family to get medicine to him. It turned out he had been beaten up and pitched in a cell for three days, then released. From Texas, Philip communicated with Obed to ask if he was up to being our guide. He responded, "My resolve is greater now than before. If they kill us, they kill us. But we go feed pastors who wait for us!" Now don't get me wrong, no one is keen on "if they kill us, they kill us." But the truth be told, the only reason they didn't back out was they couldn't fail a man like Obed. A select few men or women of God you might follow into the enemy's camp just to spit in the devil's eye. Obed was one of those, but it wasn't bravado that made them step off that plane in Kigali.

After processing through passport control at Kigali, the half comatose group was glad to see Obed Surkura, our host and a friend of Philip's from past trips. Obed is somewhat of a living legend as a church planter. He is a small, stoutly built man (the same height as Emma). He had a countenance fortified with steel that Philip imagined must have been like the apostle Paul. In some ways Obed's grit reminded Philip of a Texas Ranger; confident, resolute, bold, steady, faithful. At Obed's side is a lovely young lady by the name of Ruth Bamolek. The luggage is secured on top of Obed's well used Suzuki SUV, and the rough half paved road to his home is a fitting end to a long hard journey.

Early the next morning, with heads beginning to clear, they shared their type of coffee. It was instant coffee mixed with instant cocoa, with a generous spoon full of brown granular sugar and real milk—ah, back in Africa. Ruth emerges from the back porch, where all the cooking is done. Fried eggs from Obed's chickens are served atop white bread. A bowl full of tiny bananas is served on the plain wooden table. A little later, Ruth reappears with boiling water for more coffee, and Obed takes the opportunity to properly introduce her. She is light-skinned, with strikingly beautiful features. She is slim, with dark, almost black searching eyes. Ruth extends her hand, the usual custom of greeting. She bows at the waist while shaking hands. Out of the corner of Philip's eye he noticed Frank sits up a little taller.

To the Christian community in this part of Africa, Obed is close to folklore. Back home we have a saying: "You play the hand that's dealt you." But that has a different significance if you have witnessed genocide, famine, poverty, and continuous tribal wars. You think a little differently when your living room has a plaster patch covering where an artillery round had exploded through the wall during the 1994 genocide. To share Obed's food and home is a special honor that humbles a soul.

Philip's attention turned to the young lady serving them, and he could constrain himself no longer. "Obed, fill us in on Ruth. I don't remember ever meeting her before." In broken English, Obed explained: "Ruth came to us from Goma, Congo where we go today. You remember volcano with lava flow from vents went through middle town. Not recognize it from last time you there. Two year ago her family killed by exiled Rwanda bandits live in bush. She escape, but then year or so later lava flow destroy home. Believe or not, young lady walk 350 kilometers, Goma to Kigali. She remembered me, my visits to missionaries there. Ruth show up at front gate one morning with little bundle of all worldly possessions wrapped in cloth under her arm. Nothing for her to return to, but ask go along with us, help prepare food at conference this week."

The trip from Kigali to Goma, Congo took most of the day. The roads are paved with potholes the size of small cars, but the country is beautiful with hills, valleys, and volcanic mountains. The hills are patch-worked with individual food crops where the farmer's only equipment is a hoe and shovel. If you were lucky, you had both. Being on the equator they could produce three crops a year. The mountains just off to the north are where the highland gorillas live, protected only by happenchance from the ignorance of man. Along the road, some local entrepreneurs had gone into the transportation business, building something that looked like what we used to call scooters (two wheeled toys with one foot place on the platform between the wheels with an upright hand rail), but much larger and made of wood. A load was placed on the magnum-scooter to be coasted down the hills.

Driving along the road is so rough that you have to support yourself by holding on with your arms. Philip's mind turned to the book of Ruth, brought about by having a real live Ruth traveling with them. There was something extraordinary about her; maybe gentle grace mixed with a type of peace that had so often eluded Philip.

He and Frank would be teaching Bible Study Methods. This study was right out of Traina's book and Prof's seminary class, using the book of Galatians as the study text. Considering many, if not most of the pastors were relatively unprepared to teach the Word, Philip and Frank thought it would be good to nail down the basics of salvation as explained in Galatians. Emma had prepared a study on the seven feasts out of Leviticus 23 for the women. At first glance, you might think these "under educated" pastors might not understand seminary level work, but most of them spoke their native language (French, Swahili, Kinyarwanda, and some English). They lacked opportunity and resources, not ability.

Obed's old Suzuki was a 'holy car' (that is, much prayed

over). There is no such thing as road repair in this part of Africa, and the journey had been rough on everyone. But as they came near the Congo border, it was obvious the old car's engine was missing badly. In the states, this would be inconvenient but not a big deal. Here, it is your lifeline home. Passing through passport control was relatively uneventful. One would simply insert a twenty dollar bill in the passport to accelerate the otherwise long process. The car sputtered and chocked into Goma, completely dying when they stopped at the prearranged meeting place. Philip gave Obed a 'do you have a plan to get us out of here' look. Obed must have wondered about Philip's faith. "We here with week for Lord's work; no good worry about other things. As you say, 'stay on task.' Two men who come to conference good mechanics, they look at car in Lord's time."

About that time a man in a relatively modern Toyota Land Cruiser arrived. He and Obed shook hands, and then Obed introduced the man as the only missionary left in town, whose home we would be sharing during our stay. Obed said he had many friends in Goma, so he would wait with the car until someone came by that recognized him (I don't know if life is really that different in Africa or if it is really that different if you are Obed Surkura). The luggage was transferred into the Toyota, then Emma, Ruth, Frank and Philip left for the missionary's home.

The missionary couple rented out rooms to supplement their income; Phil and Emma together, Obed and Frank together, with Ruth on the couch in the living room. The missionaries had recently returned to Goma after some rebel fighting in the area had driven them out. The bandits would come into town, shoot up the place and take what they wanted. The local merchants, being considerably more resourceful than the politicians or the UN, made a deal with the rebels. "Leave us a list of what you want, and if it is in the town, we will set it out at the south road for you to pick up." For whatever reason, the deal worked, but it still wasn't safe to travel the interior roads which our pastors would have to use to get to the conference.

The missionaries were glad for the company, and we talked into the night about their work. Philip had momentarily mellowed into a false sense of security by being with the missionary couple, which one should not do. Then they instructed, "If we say get in the Toyota, don't pick up anything. Just get in the car because we are going to try to make it to the border." 'Try to make it' was the real eye opener.

Ruth was up early the next morning helping with breakfast. There isn't a lot of opportunity for a homeless single woman in that part of the world, but there was something special about Ruth which back home we call 'character.' Her existence was literally day to day, yet she had a peace about her that the God she had accepted while living with Obed would provide what she needed. This gives real meaning to the song "Great Is Thy Faithfulness."

Philip couldn't help but think about the book of Ruth, and he was envious of the peace both our Ruth and the Ruth of the Bible brandished. There were many similarities; the Ruth of the Bible was a heathen girl from Moab who married into a Jewish family, and our Ruth had worshiped a form of ancestor religion, only recently accepting by faith Jesus as her Savior. Our Ruth had lost her family. Naomi (the mother-in-law of Ruth in the Bible) had lost her husband and two sons. So when Naomi decided to return to Israel, Ruth determined to go with her, saying those famous lines, "*Do not urge me to leave you or turn back from following you; for where you go, I will go, and where you lodge, I will lodge. Your people shall be my people, and your God, my God*" (1:16). That confession of faith not only changed Ruth's life, but also placed her in the line which would produce the long awaited Messiah.

As the story goes, when Naomi and Ruth reached Bethlehem

(Naomi's ancestral home), Ruth would glean at the edges of the field for food. It turned out one of the big land owners was a fella named Boaz, in whose field Ruth just happened to be gleaning. Boaz also just happened to be a once removed relative of Naomi. In the Jewish culture, a relative could act as a *go'el*, a kinsman-redeemer to ensure the continuation of the family. Sure enough, Boaz fell head over heels in love with Ruth (poetic license) and took her to be his wife. He redeemed Ruth and Naomi out of poverty and into his family. Boaz's mother was Rahab. Ruth and Boaz's son was Obed who fathered Jesse who fathered King David, all in the genealogy of Yeshua—you get the idea. God is faithful!

The pastor's conference was full, with over 100 men and women risking life and limb to take advantage of much needed training. Spiritual hunger is a funny thing, for in the churches back home it is hard to get someone to sit still for an hour Bible study. But here the pastors sat on wooden planks from eight o'clock in the morning until six in the afternoon, with an occasional break. Emma had prepared training for the women, but when the men found out it was from the Old Testament, they wanted to hear it also since most had never been taught out of those books. Of course, Leviticus was a mystery. Emma's preparation and presentation was so good, she was able to show how the seven feasts are a picture of Jesus Christ's work: past, present and future. It was one of those 'aha' moments when the pastors realized the relevance and application of Old Testament writings.

The food was no problem for Philip and Emma. They had rice and pinto beans just like back home. Cornbread would have rounded out the meal nicely, but they had a paste like dough for bread. This would have required an acquired taste, one that Philip and Emma never acquired. From previous trips, Philip learned to bring along a big bottle of Tabasco to give those beans and rice a little personality. Boil the water and have a cup of African coffee—life is good. There is nothing like the taste of vegetables fresh from the garden, grown in fertile volcanic soil—to die for. Ruth was right in the middle of the action, cooking and ministering to the other women. What did the writer of Proverbs say? *"An excellent wife, who can find? For her worth is far above jewels. The heart of her husband trusts in her, and he will have no lack of gain. She does him good and not evil all the days of her life"* (31:10-12). Frank stayed busy teaching, but it would be an understatement to say he noticed Ruth.

Philip was keenly aware that faith must course through these people's veins, but along towards the end of the week he couldn't help but ask Obed about the condition of the car. Obed's patience must have been tested, but he understood how Philip's life didn't include daily situations where the Lord was the only answer. "Two mechanics, good brother in Christ. Found two of three leads on alternator broken off, probably from the rough road. They soldered leads back on and the car now good as new." Philip said a silent pray of thanksgiving to the Lord, but decided it wouldn't hurt to continue to pray for a safe trip back over those same rough roads.

There was one serious problem that turned into a fateful permanent one. In some strange way, the cooks ended up with a large fish out of the lake and cooked it into a kind of fish soup with vegetables. Philip decided to stay with the beans and rice, but Emma wanted to try the soup. Whatever bacteria or bug that was in the soup infected Emma to the point that she was unable to eat, and she turned whiter than a sheet. Somehow that lady continued to teach, living mostly on bottled water. Emma later received temporary medical help in Nairobi, but the doctors back home said it had either caused or activated a dormant condition, and she would suffer with it the remainder of her life. Philip felt responsible. The first trip to Africa he went alone, and afterwards Emma told him that was the last time for her to stay home; she had as much right to serve the Lord as he did. Emma was right, and she certainly carried her own weight teaching, but that didn't make Philip feel any less responsible.

The week in Goma flew by. The party had to leave their new friends, truly brothers and sisters in Christ, to return to Kigali for another pastor's conference (Emma still sick as a dog). During the two weeks, Frank and Ruth had time to get to know each other. Oh, to be young again. Ruth was an extraordinary woman, and it's no reason to get married. However, what good is a seminary degree if you're still single. You know how churches think; we'll get two for the price of one. A short week later in Kigali our work was finished, and it was time for the long trip home. The people are what you remember; everyone with more faith and obedience to their Lord than we will ever know.

There was one other small incidence at the airport caused by Philip's momentary lapse of judgment. When traveling, Philip usually took pictures to use as part of a 'dog and pony' show back home for the generous folks in Dallas who had helped finance the teaching trip. Philip stepped just outside the door to the waiting room to snap a picture of the plane they would fly out on, but the second the camera clicked he felt a tap on his shoulder. A stern looking young man in a suit and tie flashed some sort of identification and said one word, "Passport," sticking his hand out. Philip handed him his passport, at which time the man pivoted saying, "follow me," as he headed back into the waiting room. Emma was reading, innocently assuming Philip would stay out of trouble. The man in the suit didn't stop, but proceeded past two security checks and one passport station, down to the main floor. He then went down stairs into the basement, with Philip right behind questioning their destination.

The next thing Philip knew he was standing in the middle of a whole bunch of men, all wearing suits and ties, and not a single one smiling. He found out later from Obed that this was the secret police. The head man was given Philip's passport. He looked over the passport in detail, noting earlier stamps from different African countries, plus Israel, Jordan, and a few locations in Europe. He too seemed to lack a sense of humor. Finally he looked up, holding the passport in one hand while tapping on the table with the other. "You must take film out!" Philip was using one of those throw away cameras that you send in to have the film developed. "You can't take the film out." The man either didn't understand about the camera or was used to his orders being followed. Philip suspected the latter. "You must take film out!" "You can't take the film out," Philip replied. Realizing this conversation wasn't going to resolve the situation, he asked if the man read English. The top man nodded his head. Philip handed him the camera, pointing to the instructions on the back. If this guy had a congenial personality, he never let on. This time he made the situation a little more definite. "You stay or camera stay!" "Why didn't you say so, I would love for you to have this camera."

The head man handed Philip his passport with an expression of his hand that he was dismissed. It was time for the plane to leave, and there was no way Philip was going to make it back through two security checks plus passport control. "My plane is due to take off now, would you have your man escort me through the check points?" The head man looked at Philip with an expression that didn't require a translator, but he finally smiled at the stupid tourist and motioned for his man to get me upstairs. The two shot through each check point as the secret policeman flashed identification. Everyone was on board, but the plane was still on the tarmac with the stairs at the back door. An unhappy attendant ushered Philip aboard. He closed the door, instructed him to buckle up, and then signaled to the pilot that the idiot was on board.

Back in West Texas things settled down into the old routine for Philip and Emma. It turned out Frank and Ruth started emailing, from which a long distance romance blossomed. Sure enough, one night Philip got a call from Frank. "Put Emma on the line with you." After an appropriate pause, Frank bubbled over. "I've got one ticket to Kigali and two tickets to come home. We've finished the paperwork so I'm going to get Ruth and marry her." Philip and Emma acted all surprised. They didn't know who was the luckier; Ruth to have Frank or Frank to have Ruth. One other irritating thing happened from Philip's perspective. He kept getting emails from Goma and Kigali. They were all the same: "Send Emma back to teach us about the Old Testament."

Philip's Study Notes, Ruth

The book of Ruth, like most of the Bible, is the revelation of God's lovingkindness towards mankind. Our Lord, in the most loving act possible, provided a *go'el* (kinsman-redeemer) to redeem both Jew and Gentile. The journey is one of exploring the depths of God's love in the mountains of happiness, by the springs of refreshment, or in the deserts of despair. God's love is always there.

Chapter 1, Naomi Is Empty

The events recorded in Ruth took place during the time of the Judges. There was a famine in the land, most probably due to Yahweh's judgment for Israel following after other gods. Naomi's husband decided to move his family from Bethlehem to Moab, about 50 miles away on the east side of the Dead Sea, where subsequently their two sons took Moabite women as wives. This was three strikes against an Israeli: 1) Israel was in rebellion with their God; 2) They moved from the promised land; and 3) They married outside the descendents of Abraham. The depressed situation continued as Naomi's husband and her two sons died.

Naomi, burdened by grief, decided to return home to Bethlehem. The daughter-in-laws would have no place in Israel, so she counseled them to stay with their people. But Ruth could not be dissuaded, insisting that she would not only return with Naomi, but that Naomi's people were now her people, and Naomi's God was her God. The Hebrew word order emphatically contrasts the choice of the two daughter-in-laws when Ruth clung to Naomi. The Hebrew, related to Ruth's choice, is also very direct: "*your people my people, your God my God.*" God, in providential sovereignty still allows (or it might be said requires) us to make a choice to follow Him. The fall of Adam and Eve in the garden was a choice to 'go independent' from God. Salvation is a choice to be dependent on God. Following God may not be easy, but it is simple. Near the end of chapter 1, Naomi would make a prophetic statement that typified the events of this book: "*I went out full, but Yahweh has brought me back empty*" (v 21a). She went out with a husband and two sons. Should you find yourself 'empty,' the choice of whom to follow is yours.

There are two key words in this first chapter. The Hebrew word translated 'return' indicates that their salvation was to be in returning to their land, people, and God. The other key word is the Hebrew word '*hesed*' (one of the key words of the Old Testament) often translated lovingkindness, but the broad meaning is inclusive of Yahweh's covenant loyalty, care, grace, and mercy to His people.

In that culture, a woman without a husband was in a desperate predicament. Naomi was too old to marry, and the two daughters' only realistic hope was to marry another Moabite. Therefore, Ruth choosing to follow Naomi was most unusual. Ruth's actions of self-giving love to one who could offer nothing in return must have touched God's heart.

Chapter 2, Ruth Reaps God's Blessings

Three persons dominate the scene: Ruth, Naomi, and Boaz. Each person's character was revealed. Ruth acted in self-giving love. Naomi remained depressed by grief. Boaz was a close relative of

Naomi's deceased husband and was obviously a successful farmer along with being a person of great personal integrity. He was called in the Hebrew, 'a mighty man of valor.'

God had made allowances for the poor (Lev 19:9-10) in that the corners of the fields were to be left for the poor to glean. A square or rectangular field was to be reaped in a circle, leaving a triangle of grain at each corner for the poor to harvest.

Boaz, moved by Ruth's compassion and selfless care for Naomi, prayed that Yahweh would richly reward Ruth. Here we see a lesson that all should pay close attention to: beware of what you pray because God may use you to be the instrument of His blessing. In other words, don't pray it unless you mean it, which apparently Boaz did.

Chapter 3, Naomi's Kinsman-Redeemer

You might imagine that persistence could be a trait of a Jewish mother-in-law. Naomi recognized the possibility that Boaz might act as Ruth's kinsman-redeemer, or *go'el*. As we might say today, Naomi told Ruth to wash-up, with just a touch of perfume, and put on your best Sunday-go-to-meetin clothes, and then go sleep at Boaz's feet. In that culture, there was nothing inappropriate in Ruth's actions. Rather it was an assertion that he was a kinsman. Boaz recognized the meaning of Ruth's honorable and rightful act, but there was another kinsman who had the first right of refusal.

Chapter 4, Boaz Acts as Redeemer

Boaz, probably with a little extra skip in his get-along, took the initiative by going to the city gate where most business was transacted. Sure enough, the kinsman with first rights happened by, so Boaz called together 10 witnesses. To make a long story short, the other kinsman was offered the right to redeem Naomi's land, but ultimately refused because part of the deal included also being responsible for Ruth. He refused, fearing that the arrangement might endanger his estate. Boaz, like all good redeemers, immediately closed the deal to take Ruth as his wife. The text completes the cycle of 'full then empty' by revealing that Naomi helped raise her grandson. She could have said, "I went out full, and Yahweh brought me back empty, but now by His grace I am made full again," This is God's redemption plan.

This love story ends in such a manner that no one could miss the meaning; the two became grandparents to David, Israel's greatest king. But by God's testimony, even more importantly, from this union would come the Anointed One to occupy David's throne. He would be the King of the Jews and Gentiles, for eternity.

Word Study "Redemption"

The common concept of redemption comes from the freeing of slaves by the paying of a ransom. In this concept it is important to note that the price was paid to free the slave, not to purchase them in order to sell them to another.

The Old Testament is full of events which are visual aids of spiritual realities (most to be fulfilled at a future time). Job, after losing everything except his life, looking forward confesses, *"And as for me, I know that my Redeemer lives, and at the last He will take His stand on the earth"* (Job 19:25). David worships Yahweh, *"Let the words of my mouth and the meditation of my heart be acceptable in Thy sight, O Yahweh, my rock and my Redeemer"* (Psalm 19:14). Note that to both Job and David, redemption wasn't just an event, it was a person.

Isaiah, which says more about Messiah than any other book of the Old Testament, uses Redeemer as the name of God thirteen times: *"And all flesh will know that I, Yahweh, am your Savior, and your Redeemer, the Mighty One of Jacob"* (49:26b) Redeemer is primarily an Old Testament concept fulfilled in Christ who paid the price for all mankind who were in bondage to sin—*"the wages of sin is death"* (Romans 6:23a). He paid this debt in His death. Paul describes the relationship between sinful man and the Redeemer Christ Jesus: …*"for all have sinned and fall short of the glory of God, being justified as a gift by His grace through the <u>redemption</u> which is in Christ Jesus"* (Romans 3:23-24).

Perhaps the most famous Old Testament passage about redemption is from the book of Ruth. Ruth was redeemed by Boaz, acting as her *go'el* (kinsman-redeemer). According to Jewish Law (Leviticus 25:25-28 and Deuteronomy 25:5-10) a relative was permitted to marry a widow if the husband died without a male heir. This was permitted for two reasons: to produce a male child to carry on the family name, and to retain family ownership of property. Remember, property wasn't just land; it was the promise of God to Abram. Boaz was a close relative; therefore he could act as *go'el* in her behalf. Twenty-three times some form of the Hebrew word *go'el* (redeem, redeemer, redemption, kinsman-redeemer) is used in the book of Ruth.

Conclusion

How important was Boaz's redemption of Ruth? Ruth was a Gentile redeemed into the family of Boaz whose marriage produced a son (Obed) who fathered Jesse, who fathered King David. A Gentile was taken into the royal Davidic line (Messianic line). Jesus Christ, as our *Go'el* (kinsman-redeemer) paid the price to redeem you and me out of bondage to sin in order to set us free into the family of God.

CHAPTER 4

SATAN TEMPTS, GOD TESTS
JAMES 1:2-18

Someone has said, "God loves you just the way you are, but He loves you too much to let you stay that way." Part of the journey stated in two-bit theological terms is called "progressive sanctification." The Almighty didn't ask my advice, but when He saves a person the "old man" is co-crucified with Christ, and raised to a new spiritual creation (Galatians 2:20). However, He left something in us called the "flesh" through which sin can operate. Good spiritual attributes like faith, endurance, and wisdom are a part of the way God deals with the flesh within us. Apparently, those spiritual attributes are actualized in 'tests,' which seems like a lot of trouble to me. But I think I'll defer to God's providence.

Crackling from the wood stove in Philip Cole's office turned his attention away from his study to the fact that the fire needed stoking, and a chill suggested another stick of oak wouldn't hurt either. Coco was sound asleep on his rug by the stove, so Philip would have to be extra careful; Lord forbid he should wake Coco and get that disapproving look the dog was prone to have. The present study was in the Epistle of James, probably written by the half-brother of Jesus. (You know what an Epistle is, don't you? An Epistle was the wife of an Apostle. . . It's a joke.) The Epistle of

James is the most Jewish book in the New Testament and would fit right in with the wisdom literature of the Old Testament. As wisdom literature, the outline of the book might be found in chapter 1, verse 19: "*Let everyone be quick to hear, slow to speak and slow to anger*" (chapters 1 and 2, Quick to Hear; chapter 3, Slow to Speak; and chapters 4 and 5, Slow to Anger).

Philip's converted study was odd by any standard. An old oak desk occupied one corner and a pot bellied stove was in the other. There were homemade book shelves to the ceiling, and a couple of stacks of recently used books on the floor by the desk resembling mini-skyscrapers. There was also a well outfitted loading bench with a 1950's style single stage loading press for handgun-rifle shells, plus a shotgun shell press. Lying on the loading bench is his partially disassembled L.C. Smith side by side shotgun, cleaned but needing to be put back in working order.

The desk is covered with half a dozen books including Aland's third edition Greek New Testament, Bauer's Lexicon, Ryrie's Study Bible, and several commentaries. The books on the shelves are diverse, with one and a half walls full of theological books. There was a well used section on Texas Rangers, and another on historical figures such a Winston Churchill, Theodore Roosevelt, Thomas Jefferson, Abraham Lincoln, Stonewall Jackson and so forth. Another section was about Africa, along with a reinforced shelf with boxes of every caliber and weight of bullet and a dozen loading manuals, all of it interspersed with pictures of family, friends and travels. The only open space on the wall was reserved for a modest glass gun case. Most of the rifles Philip made when he lived in Dallas, having access to a complete gun repair shop. The only one not made by him was his favorite, a 1939 Model 70 in Government '06.

Six AM straight up, and the telephone rings. Philip stretches, and then walks into the kitchen, answering with his typical "howdy." From the other end comes the voice of a friend Philip hadn't heard from in several years. "Philip, the company made a new shotgun they want tested, and I've got a couple of fairly new handguns that need wringing out too. If you've got time for some extended shooting for a couple of days, I'll pick up several cases of ammo and drive out to see you." The voice was that of Jerry Wright, a representative of one of the larger gun manufacturers. Jerry was on their shooting team and a full time salesman. He was also responsible for some testing. "Jerry, you old hound dog, I had no idea you were still sucking air. Sure I'll help you out in a pinch, since no one else will shoot with you. However, I ain't working for free. I'll do it if you'll buy shotgun shells that are reloadable, and oh, don't bring any of those aluminum handgun shells either." Jerry responded, "You old cuss, you always did have an angle, but if Emma will feed me her home cooking, you've got a deal. Maybe you could mention some red beans and jalapeño cornbread, and I'm figuring I've got the better end of the deal. One last thing, I've got a little bit of a situation maybe we could talk about." Philip didn't have any idea what Jerry's "situation" was, but the appointment was set. Philip added, "What if I invite Sheriff Warns and Frank Criswell? I don't think you've met Frank. He's a retired Ranger who lives out this way. I think you two would get along real well, and maybe he can straighten you out on your handgun technique, if that's possible."

"Okay, you set up your group for next Wednesday. With the four of us, I think we can finish the test in about two days." Jerry's job sounded like a dream, but he came by it honestly. He was a competitive shooter, who had actually been on the Olympic shotgun team years before. He was well respected in the gun industry, and was a conscientious, hard worker representing his company.

The week flew by. Philip caught up on chores so that he could take off a couple of days for undisturbed enjoyment. Jerry arrived early evening Tuesday, just in time for dinner. Jerry is one of those people everyone likes, with a wholesome, unpretentious personality.

Emma put out a spread of home cooking with fresh vegetables out of her garden, while three old friends got caught up on family things. Emma waited for a break in the conversation, and then mentioned, "I hoped you would bring Ann along. I haven't talked with her in a long time." Jerry looked down, causing a pause in his response: "Ann is busy this week." But there was something wrong in his voice. Not one to pry, Philip changed the subject, and the three continued their visit over coffee and home-made blackberry cobbler, with just a small scoop of ice cream melting on the steaming cobbler.

The following day, Rusty Warns and Frank Criswell were at Philip's house early. Emma had breakfast ready, which made for a perfect time for introductions and getting to know each other. Afterwards, Jerry talked about the tests, which would amount to "proving acceptability." The company had come out with a new mid-priced, light-weight semi-automatic shotgun which would be a tough market considering the competition. There was also an ultralite 357 revolver and a 1911 type variation, which was Philip's favorite type of pistol. "We will clean the shotgun every two hundred rounds and the handguns every thousand rounds. In addition to the number of rounds fired, we will pattern the shotgun. We also need to fire the handguns for accuracy." Philip's target range amounted to a four position covered shooting area with benches, so the testing progressed rapidly. Everyone shared in the duties, but Frank was the only one willing to put that many full power rounds through the 357 ultralite. But other than the recoil, it would be a fine trail gun. You don't have to shoot full power loads if it's your personal revolver. Philip was particularly taken with the 1911 variation, but Emma would never put up with him buying another pistol when "he had more than he could shoot."

The fellowship was great, the guns performed up to expectation, and Emma's cooking was enough to founder a fella. Friday evening the foursome had met their goal, and having had enough shooting to last them for a week or two, it was time to shake hands with "thank you" all around. Jerry agreed to stay over one last night because Emma had promised him smoked ham, pinto beans, jalapeño cornbread, homemade Chow-chow, and pickled green tomatoes, along with the last of the cobbler.

After dinner Jerry and Philip retired to the front porch with a fresh cup of coffee. Jerry seemed lost in thought for a while but finally got to what was troubling him. "Philip, can I discuss something personal with you?" There was a part of Philip that would just as soon not get involved in someone else's problems, but he nodded and Jerry went on. "After 20 years of marriage, a real problem has come up between Ann and me. But the problem isn't Ann, it's me. About six months ago we went to a college reunion, and I saw an old girlfriend. Now I can't get her out of my head. Nothing inappropriate happened, but I'll tell you, I think about her constantly. I don't even know if she's available, but I sure do want to find out. At first I enjoyed day-dreaming about her, but now thoughts just come into my head. I know that's wrong, but my mind keeps going there. I don't know how to fight this."

Philip rubbed his brow, running Jerry's situation through what he called a Bible filter. Then after a long pause, offered: "Jerry, you are describing a spiritual battle, so you are going to have to face a hard thing to do. You are going to have to stand on the truth of the Word and deny the lie of the flesh. The journey for a Christian isn't easy, so you are going to have to decide if you are committed to living by the Word. I've been there, so let me warn you. There will come a point when your flesh is going to say to you, 'who are you going to believe, me or your lying eyes?' Your flesh is going to say it in your head—first person singular with a Texas accent." Jerry looked whipped, but he said with resolve, "I'm in, I don't have anywhere else to turn before this addiction damages my marriage. I'll stand on the truth of the Word."

Philip went to his study and brought out his study notes and a couple of Bibles. Turning to the book of James, he looked Jerry square in the eye and said straight forward to him, "You are going to have to steel your heart towards God because no one has enough strength to fight this battle against the flesh in their own power. We deceive ourselves if we think the flesh isn't strong because one on one, it will whip you every time. You know this desire you feel is not God's best for you. You and Ann have been faithful to each other for 20 years. As the Lord told Jeremiah, "*The heart is more deceitful than all else and is desperately sick; who can understand it? I the Lord search the heart, I test the mind*" (17:9-10a). This brings us to the book of James and the subject of testing. We have been testing guns to prove they are good, but there is another kind of test. James talks about two kinds of spiritual tests. You are in a time of testing, so the first step is to recognize that.

I'm going to cut to the chase, and then we can study the book of James in detail. You have to make a definite decision— unwavering, unchanging. God will test you for approval, with the intent of strengthening your faith. In all these tests you need to ask God for the strength to persevere. Faith, or lack of faith, is the condition that determines who will receive this type of help to sustain you. God wants you to be approved, which is to be progressively transformed into the likeness of Christ. Satan has another kind of test, which is to test you to failure. God tests for approval, Satan tests for failure.

My granddad used to say, 'It takes a strong man to eat boiled owl,' which is what your tests are going to seem like. Make up your mind now to trust God in your spiritual trials, and He will help you. God saved you and gave you a faithful wife. If you are in a right relationship with God, your only thought of that other lady should be that she is saved and living a Christian life apart from you." Jerry and Philip sat together for a long time and didn't say anything. That may be the mark of real friendship. Emma came out with the coffee pot to see if they wanted refills. Jerry looked over at Emma. "I've made up my mind. Emma, you got any of that boiled owl in the frig?"

Philip chuckled, partly from Jerry's sense of humor but also from having been there. "Okay, now let's look over James."

Philip's Study Notes, James 1:2-18

Remember, James is wisdom literature. The best way to understand the wisdom of these 17 verses is if we examine the Greek verb tense and do a couple of word studies. You will note that there is somewhat of a formula to success or failure when confronted with spiritual trials.

(2-4) *"Consider it all joy, my brethren, when you encounter various trials, knowing that the testing of your faith produces endurance. And let endurance have its perfect result, that you may be perfect and complete, lacking in nothing."* When it says 'consider,' that is an Aorist Imperative verb which calls for a specific and definite decision on your part; not just think about it but make up your mind—unwavering, unchanging. The Greek word translated 'trials' has the meaning of a test. Some of these tests come from outward circumstances and some are inward moral tests. Some are from God and some are from Satan.

The words 'various trials' literally means 'falling into the midst of people or circumstances.' For right now, just remember that this word 'testing' is a particular kind of test (Gr. *dokimion*, testing for approval), and it is contrasted with another kind of test later on in verse 13. The reason these trials are grounds for joy is they are capable of developing your faith in perseverance which produces good results. The word translated 'perseverance' is not to passively endure or to just hold on, but the quality that enables you to stand in the storm, squared up to the gale.

(5) *"But if any of you lacks wisdom, let him ask of God, who gives to all generously and without reproach, and it will be given to him."* The verb 'ask' is Present Imperative which means to follow this command as often as the situation or need arises. So what does that mean? It is telling you this test is likely to continue, and you will need to ask of God over and over for His grace to endure.

(6) "*But, he must ask in faith without any doubting, for the one who doubts is like the surf of the sea, driven and tossed by the wind.*" Faith, or lack of faith, is the condition that determines who will receive this type of help from God. When tested, you are going to have to stand steadfast on that truth, which is why resolve at the very first is so important.

(7-8) These next two verses give you a picture of a person who lacks faith: "*For that man ought not to expect (negative present imperative) that he will receive anything from the Lord, being a double-minded man, unstable in all his ways.*" The verb 'not to expect' (Negative Present) means don't do this over and over; don't come to God and ask for help if you don't truly believe He can and will help you. The word 'double-minded' literally means double-souled; one mind says trust, another mind says cave in to the flesh's desires. 'Unstable in <u>all</u> his ways' marks everything he does: personal, business, social, and spiritual; indecisiveness negates his effectiveness.

(9-11) If it is any consolation, verses 9-11 indicate these kinds of trials level the playing field for everyone; rich or poor, smart or stupid, all of us are the same in spiritual tests.

(12) "*Blessed is a man who perseveres under trial; for once he has been approved, he will receive the crown of life which the Lord has promised to those who love Him.*" 'Blessed' means worthy to be spoken well of, which indicates the state of the believer in Christ. The verb 'approved' describes the successful testing of precious metals such as having removed the dross. The 'crown of life' is the crown given to a victorious athlete such as the Greek's wreath of laurel in the Olympics.

Do you know how the metalsmith knows the silver has all the dross removed? He keeps the fire to it, removing the dross, until he can see his face in the liquid metal. God wants to transform you until He can see His face in you. He wants to transform you into the image of Christ, and that means passing through the fire. No, being a Christian is not for the fainthearted!

(13) Now we get to the other type of testing I told you about earlier. James uses several Greek words which are translated 'test,' 'trials,' or 'temptation'; they all could be translated 'test.' Verse 13 says: *"Let no one say when he is tempted, I am being tempted by God; for God cannot be tempted by evil, and He Himself does not tempt anyone."* First, let's get the 'being tempted by God' part out of the way. There is no moral depravity to which temptation may appeal to God. Therefore, it is inconsistent to think that God could be the author of temptation.

The word translated 'tempted' in verse 13 is the Greek word *'pei-ra-zo,'* which is in contrast to *'do-ki-mi-on'* back in verse 3, where I told you just to remember that it was a form or type of test. *Dokimion,* back in verse 3 is a means of testing or proving in a good and acceptable sense, while *peirazo* is to test or prove in a failure sense. In verse 3 it says God will use tests *(dokinion),* which means He will test you in order for you to be approved. But in verse 13, *peirazo* is a temptation where Satan will test you to failure. God tests for approval, Satan tempts for failure."

(14) Being tempted isn't sin, but allowing it to mature into lust is. Verse 14 tells you about the trap of lust: *"But each one is tempted when he is carried away and enticed by his own lust."* Someone has said, 'Lust is the craving for salt of a man who is dying of thirst.' The two verbs, 'carried away' and 'enticed' are taken from hunting and fishing, where you lure the prey to come out from safety. You know what it's like to cast that plug out there next to the lily pads, hoping to entice that big mouth bass to come out and take it. In the case of lust, you are caught by Satan's lure, and enticed by your own desires.

Conclusion:

God tests to strengthen your faith, but you are going to have to ask over and over for His help for the strength to prove your faith. Ask in genuine faith, and He will strengthen you. But double-minded faith is not faith at all. What you decide will affect everything you do: personal, business, family, everything. God is like a silversmith removing your dross, molding you into the image of Christ. Being tempted isn't sin, but taking the lure is. However, there is always forgiveness for a Christian. God tests to approval, Satan tests to failure. God's tests are God-centered. Satan's temptations are self-centered. Don't be surprised if your journey has a few detours by way of testing.

CHAPTER 5

LITTLE MISS MEPHIBOSHETH,
2 SAMUEL 9

Andy's Café and Domino Emporium was a beehive of activity. The normal crowd of slackers sipped coffee while discussing the latest local events. Cattle were bringing top dollar, so the local ranchers were in a particularly good mood. Rain had been adequate so the hay crop was in good shape. Feed and diesel prices were up, but nothing new there except something to complain about. Andy was doing a booming business with the breakfast customers, serving enough cholesterol to keep the cardiologists in Houston, San Antonio and Dallas in new Mercedes.

Frank Criswell was at the bar talking with Cathy Felder, one of the waitresses Philip and Emma had come to know well. Frank was a retired Texas Ranger, but still young compared with the other slackers at Philip Cole's table. Philip and Frank had hunted and fished some together, becoming fairly good friends. Philip had a profound respect for the Texas Ranger organization, having studied their history in some detail. Frank was what Philip called the 'old school' where a Ranger did what was right. However, now the judges and lawyers had made the job tedious, so when Frank had his twenty years in he retired. There was no bitterness. It was just time to let a new generation, who knew more about criminal rights (the definition of an oxymoron) than how to handle a 45, have their turn.

After a while, Frank walked over to Philip. "Padre, we've got a little problem. Any chance you will have time to talk with me and Cathy?" Philip's countenance turned to one of puzzlement, thinking that is the first time he had ever heard Frank say "me and Cathy." He nodded, "At your convenience." Frank walked back to the bar. When Cathy had a moment, he asked her a question, and then came back to Philip's table. "This afternoon be good?" Philip smiled, nodding his head. "Emma made a carrot cake and I'll put on a pot of coffee. This afternoon it is."

Mid-afternoon Frank and Cathy drove up in Frank's sedan. Along with them was Kim, Cathy's daughter who was blind. Cathy and Kim had visited several times before, once just before her house burned down, and Emma was excited to see them. Kim was now nine years old, becoming a beautiful young lady. Because of her blindness, she was reserved. She liked Emma so the two got along well. Philip had cautioned Emma that Frank and Cathy might want to talk about something private, so she may need to keep Kim busy. After a couple minutes of casual conversation, Frank indicated he and Kathy needed to talk to Philip. So Emma invited Kim to have some leftover homemade peach ice cream. "Don't let that young whippersnapper eat all my ice cream," Philip called out. Emma and Kim went hand in hand into the kitchen, Kim giggling at the prospects of finishing off Philip's ice cream.

The three of them adjourned to the front porch table with a cup of coffee. Shortly thereafter, they were served slices of carrot cake by Emma and Kim, who excused themselves to return to their ice cream. Kathy clasped her hands together in a wringing motion. It was obvious she was more than just a little bewildered. "I am desperately concerned for Kim. She has always been self-conscious because of her blindness, but the other night I went to her room and she was crying. What she said just broke my heart. She said she prayed to God to let her die so that Frank and I could be normal. I held her and told her I could never be happy without my precious Kim. Then she looked at me and said, 'Mom, I know you will always love me and I love you, but I can't help what I feel.' Mr. Cole, what do we do?"

Philip remembered what his old professor used to say, "Great honks, stone the crows and starve the lizards." I'm not Solomon; I have no idea what to say. However inadequate he felt, they came here for help so he had to say something. "Well, that's interesting," he said, stalling for time to think. "Has this just come about or has Kim been like this before?" Cathy put her hand in Frank's, looking for help. "Padre, we have talked about this and we both think it has something to do with me. Plus the strange part is that it seems to be because Cathy is so happy. I know that doesn't make sense because we know Kim wants her mom to be happy, yet Cathy's happiness seems to be driving a wedge between Kim and us. I want Cathy to be my wife, but neither of us will do it at the expense of Kim."

Wow, thought Philip. This relationship has moved along a lot further than anyone knew, but Kathy and Frank were still expecting help. He took a sip of coffee and thought for a long while, looking directly into his cup. "Well, if I can separate my thinking from that precious little girl and just think clearly. I know one thing about this fallen world; it can be an equal opportunity grinding machine. Physically and emotionally life in this world can knock you down, take what should be yours, and cripple you. Reminds me of Mephibosheth." "Mephibo who?" Frank and Kathy said at the same time. Philip was as surprised as Frank and Kathy, bringing up Mephibosheth without really thinking about what he was saying. "It doesn't matter, but that gives me an idea. It's a long shot, but it's all I got. What are you two doing the rest of the afternoon?" Cathy indicated they had to make a grocery run, so Philip asked them to leave Kim and come back for dinner.

Philip went to the front door and called, "Emma, you and Kim come here." Presently, they both appeared through the door.

"Kim, when was the last time you went fishing?" Kim wrinkled up her nose as she was prone to do. "It's been a long time, but I really like to fish." Philip got this silly look on his face. "Good, then here's the plan: Frank, you and Cathy go get your groceries and come back for dinner. Kim and I are going to catch a mess of channel cat, and then Emma and Kim will whip up a dinner that will taste so good that you'll think you died and went to heaven." Philip had dammed up one of the gullies, making a fifteen acre stock pond which was just teeming with channel cat.

Emma fixed a thermos of cold water, and Philip got the fishing poles and bait. As they headed for the pond, Emma kept thinking that this was one of those Norman Rockwall moments. Here's an old man wearing a big straw hat with fishing poles on one shoulder, while holding hands with a pretty young girl, and walking down a dirt path towards a blue lake with a chocolate lab following close behind.

They were about halfway to the pond when Coco, the lab, ran to the front and barked, looking beside some brush next to the path. Philip called Coco back and told Kim, "Honey, I want you to stay with Coco. He only barks like that when there is danger." Philip 'Indianed up' to the brush, watching carefully. Sure enough, a rattlesnake was coiled up, waiting for lunch to come down the path. Philip kept his eye on the snake while warning, "Kim, there is a rattler here, so I am going to have to shoot my pistol. Don't be concerned because you are safe where you are with Coco." Philip eased his Colt 38 Super from its holster and shot the snake. Then the three of them proceeded to the pond. Philip found a shady spot, baited the lines, and the two of them began to catch fish. As with most pond fishing from the bank, there were times when both of them had a fish on the line. Sometimes they were interrupted with long waits in between, which gave Philip and Kim time to talk.

The conversation finally got around to Frank and Cathy, in which case Kim was excited for her mom. But Philip wanted to talk about how Kim felt, so he steered the conversation in that direction. Kim folded her hands, trying her best to sound like an adult. "Mr. Cole, you know that I am blind." Philip responded, "You couldn't tell by the way you keep catching bigger fish than me, but go on." Kim wrinkled her nose again and continued, "Well I am, and mom has a chance to be normal. I want her to be happy. Maybe I could come live with you and Mrs. Cole, and they could have a normal baby. My father left because I was blind, and in my entire life mom has done nothing but take care of me. Now she has a chance to be normal with Frank."

Philip thought about how this little girl was going to break his heart. "Who told you that your father left because you were blind?" "No one, but mom is so beautiful why else would he leave?" Philip thought now might be a good time for a serious arrow prayer. "Your mom is beautiful, but so are you." Hesitating for a moment, he fired one more prayer straight up, hoping for the best. "What do you feel God thinks about all this?" Kim had tried to logically think through her situation (as well as a nine year old could). "I think God wants me to let my mom be normal. I think if I really love my mom, I need to let her and Frank start over."

Philip fired a burst of arrow prayers upward, but also hoped Kim was old enough to understand reason. "Kim, there is something called covenant love, something like grace, that most people don't understand. In the Old Testament it is often expressed by the Hebrew word '*hesed*,' which we translate as lovingkindness. It means a heart attribute of love which contains mercy, loyalty, kindness and forgiveness—the whole package wrapped up in a covenant relationship. I know of a young man in the Bible called Mephibosheth which shows exactly what God thinks of you." Kim wrinkled her nose and laughed. "That's a funny name." Philip smiled and went on. "Well, I might just call you

Little Miss Mephibosheth because God wants you to believe in His lovingkindness."

The story is over in 2 Samuel (chapter 9 I think). Best I recall, there are two primary themes about grace: God's lovingkindness and eating at the King's table. But you don't care about primary themes so I will get back to my story. The first king of Israel, Saul, had died in battle along with his son Jonathan. Jonathan was David's closest friend, and they had made a covenant (or promise) to each other: If something should happen to one of them, the other one promised to take care of his family. David remembered the covenant he had made with Jonathan. So David called in one of Saul's servants and asked if there was anyone in Jonathan's family that had survived to whom he could 'show God's lovingkindness.' The servant said there was still a son, Mephibosheth, but he was crippled in both feet. David asked where he lived. The servant said he was in a town on the other side of the Jordan River. In other words, he's hiding out on the far side of nowhere. David commanded the servant to go get Mephibosheth and bring him to Jerusalem."

By this time both had stopped serious fishing, having caught enough for dinner. Kim had become best friends with Coco, loving on him to no end while she listened to Philip. "When Mephibosheth came to David, he bowed down to pay David honor. Now you have to understand that in those days Mephibosheth was the rightful heir to the throne. But he was crippled, meaning the people would not accept him as king. Under normal circumstances, the new king would kill the rightful heir so that he would not be challenged as to who was the rightful king, but David wasn't normal. David said to Mephibosheth, 'Don't be afraid! I will give back to you your father's land, and you will always eat at my table.' Now, having the land back was good, but eating at the king's table was the same thing as saying you are now part of my family.

Kim, I just thought of something. Maybe you shouldn't be

afraid to think you are keeping your mom from being normal." Kim took her attention off Coco momentarily, turning towards Philip with a precocious look. "I catch on Mr. Cole. You already said I was Little Miss Mephibosheth. I'm blind, not stupid." Philip hated it when he was talking down to someone, only to find out they were way ahead of him.

"Okay, you understand, let me get on with my story. Mephibosheth said to David that he couldn't understand his kindness, since he thought of himself as nothing more than a dead dog. But David had made a covenant with Jonathan to take care of his family. So deserve it or not, Mephibosheth was the beneficiary of David's lovingkindness." "Mr. Cole, what is beneficiary?" "A beneficiary is a person who benefits from a promise of some sort." "But no one made a promise to me." "Really good thinking Kim, because that brings up the real meaning of the story. You see, David's promise to Jonathan was a picture of what God's promise to His children is like. God made a promise to Himself to treat His children with lovingkindness, and that's called a unilateral covenant. I will guarantee you one thing, when you were born your mom made a promise to you and to herself; to always treat you with 'hesed' (lovingkindness)." Wrinkling her nose, Kim shook her head. "I understand."

"Now let's get to grace. Let me ask you a question, Kim. Why do you love on Coco when he hasn't done anything to deserve it?" Kim thought for a moment while stroking Coco's head. "Because I love him." Philip patted Kim on the head and said, "Well Kim, you love Coco because it is your character to love. It is God's character to love; in fact the apostle John wrote that 'God is love.' God has promised because of something called the New Covenant that He will have lovingkindness towards you, and it's how your mom and Frank feel about you too."

It was getting late, so the three of them headed to the house with a stringer of fish that Kim could barely carry. Pretty soon Cathy and Frank returned, so all sat down to a hardy dinner of fried catfish, fried potatoes, Emma's best ever cold slaw and steaming hot hush puppies. During dinner, Kim indicated she had something to show her mom. Reaching deep in a pocket, she produced an eight ring rattler, at which time Cathy gasped. Frank had to cover his face with the napkin to keep from laughing out loud. In such circumstances, and they happened way too often, Emma had a habit of folding her arms and giving Philip what could only be described as 'the look.'

Kim wrinkled her nose while smiling at her mom. "Mom, you can call me Little Miss Mephibosheth because of God's 'hesed' towards me even if I am blind. I don't want to be normal because then the king would have to kill me and I had much rather eat at his table." As if the rattler wasn't enough, Cathy looked at Philip as if to question what he had done to her daughter in the past three hours. Philip merely shrugged his shoulders. He looked at Kim and said, "See, its God's grace expressed in His lovingkindness." But Cathy had a serious, determined look on her face. "It may be God's grace, but somebody had better explain to me why my daughter thinks she's Little Miss What-Ever."

Philip was enjoying all the suspense but decided he had better explain before Emma kicked him under the table. "Well, we were talking about a story in 2 Samuel, about a boy named Mephibosheth. There was a great preacher named Adrian Rogers who has gone to be with the Lord. I think he said something that will explain it to you Cathy. I don't remember word for word, but the end of his sermon went something like this: Pastor Rogers said when he thought of Mephibosheth, a picture popped in his mind of this young crippled boy sitting at the king's table one day, feeling unworthy. David walks over and places a pure white napkin in Mephibosheth's lap, and it is large enough that it covers his crippled feet. Mephibosheth looks around and realizes he is at the king's table by grace, as a result of the king's covenant. The spiritual light came on that he deserves to be part of the king's family, not because of something he could do, but because of the king's promise. Ole' Mephibosheth sits up straight and said in a loud voice, "Pass me a second helping of those mashed potatoes because I live in the lovingkindness of the king!" Kim spoke up, "Pass me some more catfish and fried potatoes please, because I'm part of the family."

Philip's Study Notes
Covenant of Lovingkindness

One of the ways God relates to His children is through unilateral covenants—unilateral in the sense that He alone initiates and guarantees the covenant. God's covenant promises to those who trust in Him are that He will demonstrate lovingkindness (Heb. *khed-sed*): mercy, loyalty, forgiveness, grace and favor. Charles Ryrie said of lovingkindness (*hesed*): "Love and loyalty, the two essential aspects of a covenant relationship, are bound together in this word."[4] In many ways, the Bible is a love story of God for the crown of His creation.

The Davidic Covenant provides a builder from the house of David who will build God's house. Solomon pre-filled what Christ is fulfilling now in Christians and will fulfill in the future with the Jewish nation. God will establish His throne forever. God will be His Father, and He will be God's Son. God the Father will not take His lovingkindness away from Him.

David's covenant with Jonathan is like God's new covenant for us; God promises lovingkindness, plus we become a part of God's family. Usually a covenant is between two equal parties, but since no one is equal to God, he makes His covenant unilaterally. Mephibosheth was crippled. All of us have some sort of spiritual or emotional handicap, but Jesus came and found us, and made us part of His family. If you are very fortunate, you will realize somewhere along your journey that God's new covenant of lovingkindness in Christ Jesus is already yours to enjoy.

CHAPTER 6

THE ENGAGEMENT

Ateenage Jewish maiden looks at the cup before her. She picks it up with trembling hands, knowing that if she drinks from it her future life is tied to that decision. For better or worse, suffering or happiness, her life will be one with the young Jewish man who is proposing marriage. After what seems like an eternity to the young man, she smiles and lifts the cup to her lips. These events have happened countless times to Jewish couples over the last several thousand years.

With that sip of wine the couple is engaged, as binding as marriage. She of course wants to know when the wedding will take place, but the young man must go and prepare a house for them. Even then, only his father will determine when it is finished and he can return for his bride. In the meantime, she will purify herself and wear a veil symbolizing that she has been chosen. She will keep a lamp by her bed because he may come in the night, and the bridesmaids will do the same. The engagement will likely last a year or longer, and then when he comes for her it will probably be in the middle of the night. She must remain ready. She eagerly anticipates hearing the shofar (ram's horn), signifying that the young man has returned for his bride.

Philip Cole was busy around the homestead taking care of chores, mainly taking care of two overfed, underworked horses. Philip had a pretty good bay quarter horse thoroughbred mix, and Emma had a down right beautiful, jug-headed-step-on-your-boot-on-purpose, appaloosa. Cleaning out their hooves, brushing them down, and generally checking out their condition took the best part of an hour. Philip thought to himself out loud, "If a fella had a lot of spare time on his hands he could solve that right quick by getting a horse."

The busyness of that Saturday morning was so that Philip could spend the afternoon with a young couple intent on marriage. He had done pre-marital counseling many times before, but this one was complicated in that the bride-to-be was very apprehensive about their future. By this time the young man was beginning to wonder if she was right. By her nature she was a 'the glass is half empty and cracked' type personality. Philip reasoned that this should be the happiest time of their lives, and some things need to be resolved in the positive direction before this goes forward. Philip had a few simple ground rules about doing pre-marital counseling: if either party wanted to back out they could; no living together and no (further) sex until the wedding if they wanted to be married in a church and have God bless the union; both parties had to be believers; they had to be willing to accept Biblical counseling; Emma had to be part of the discussions; and they could not pay for the counseling sessions. In this case Philip had asked the couple not to set the wedding date until they had resolved some of the issues, because he was counseling for a lifetime together, not a wedding ceremony. All of this made perfect sense to Philip, but the mother of the bride to be was of another opinion. This was the mother's time to be front and center on stage, and she didn't appreciate marriage counseling getting in the way of her wedding planning. The joke around the café was that there was a contract out on Philip, and some guy named Guido from Chicago was in town.

That afternoon, Jodi Waddell and Johnny Smith (that common last name was another problem the mother had) drove up right on time. Jodi looked like the prototypical cheerleader, cute as a bug with an easy smile. Johnny was tall and lanky, a down-to-earth good ole boy but very bright intellectually. The two made a great looking couple, but there was something separating them.

Emma had lemonade and cookies ready, so the four of them got comfortable around a table on the front porch. A big covered front porch is a requirement of a country home in West Texas. This was their second meeting, so Philip wanted to get to the heart of the problem. "Let's get the formalities out of the way. Have you kept to our agreement?" Jodi and Johnny gave each other a loving look, and then nodded in the affirmative. "Okay, I would like to talk about your feelings about the future. The first time we met we talked about this being a one time thing, as in forever, until death do ye part. Think about ten years from now and tell me how you feel."

After a pause to see if Jodi wanted to go first, Johnny said, "I love Jodi, and ten years from now I hope to be married with a couple of kids running around the house. There is no one else for me." Jodi didn't offer a response, so Philip took another tack. "Jodi, tell me about when and how ya'll met." Jodie explained that they had known each other since high school; both went to Texas A&M and began seriously dating their junior year. Johnny had stayed in school to become a veterinarian, having continued to date Jodi long distance. Johnny had finished his schooling and had moved back to go into partnership with Doc Hayes, who was getting on up in years and wanted to sell his practice in the foreseeable future. During the last three years they had dated exclusively. Johnny wanted to get married while he was still in graduate school, but Jodi wanted him to wait until he graduated.

Now that Philip had Jodi talking, he returned to the subject at hand. "Jodi, how do you see yourself ten years from now?" Jodi looked down and spoke in a soft voice. "I totally love Johnny." Jodi's voice trailed off as she fidgeted with her lemonade. "But . . . I don't know how I will feel ten years from now. My family wouldn't be a good bet on long term relationships. My dad left when I was a baby, and this is my mom's third marriage. My sister got divorced two years ago, and they had problems from day one." There was a considerable pause while Jodi recovered her composure. "How long have you and Emma been married?" Emma felt like Jodi might respond better to another woman. "Forty-one long years this July, but when I finally got him housebroke I decided to keep him. I'm not real sure anyone else would have him anyway. Getting married is easy, but marriage isn't. But if you are both dedicated, it is worth it."

Philip took a bite of cookie while messing with his glass, giving Jodi time to think about what Emma had said, and then got back on track with the problem. "Well, maybe we can keep my shortcomings out of this. Jodi are you afraid you might end up divorced?" Jodi looked down but shook her head yes. "I think it is a reasonable concern, don't you?" "Maybe, I do think that is why we want to work these things through before you two get to the altar. Considering what you have experienced, I think you are very wise. But, one of the things we want to do is separate wisdom from fear."

Philip decided to try an arrow prayer (shoot one up when you're desperate) and a different approach. "I've got a possible solution. You know, you're not paying me for nothing. Come to think of it, you are paying me nothing. So my advice will be worth every penny I'm charging. Let's have an ancient Jewish Wedding!" Knowing her mom, it didn't take a second for Jodi to respond. "You're kidding, right? How do you think my mom is going to take that?" Philip looked Jodi right in the eyes to make sure she knew he was serious about this whole situation. "No, I'm serious as a heart attack. Jewish marriages generally last. For that matter, in the days when matchmakers were used the success rate, if you consider staying together a success, was astronomically high. But we're too late for a matchmaker. Let me do a little research to pull out the applicable scriptures, and then next time we can intelligently discuss an ancient Jewish wedding. Oh, and it might be best if you don't mention this to your mother for now."

The week went by quickly, with Jodi and Johnny back for another meeting with Emma and Philip. Emma served iced tea along with chocolate chip cookies, and everyone settled in. As promised, Philip opened his notes on the ancient Jewish wedding. "We almost know as much about the ancient Jewish wedding from the New Testament as the Old Testament. Jodi and Johnny, I think we should look at an ancient Jewish wedding to increase our wisdom and decrease the fear. But Jodi, I want you to be honest with yourself concerning your apprehension about the future. Don't rush into anything. There is always some fear of the unknown, but we want to see if there is any unreasonable fear.

I'm no expert on Jewish history, but I broke out several steps in the ancient engagement-wedding tradition. First is the selection of the bride. The father of the young man, or his trusted servant, would search for a suitable girl for his son. I say girl because she was usually in her early teens. As likely as not the young man had already found the girl of his dreams, but sometimes there was no acceptable Jewish girl living in that area. In that case, the father or his servant would find a suitable Jewish girl elsewhere. It's for a different reason in a Christian wedding, but I believe it is also important today that they both be believers, so that they will be what the Bible calls 'equally yoked.' Marriage is hard enough without one person thinking their faith in Christ is the most important thing in the world and the other person not understanding that commitment.

The covenant was next, which included the promise, the price and the cup. The young man and his father visited the home of the young girl. The young man took along a covenant, or contract, describing his promises and means to care for his bride, from which a written contract would be drawn up later. There must have been lots of Jewish lawyers in that day too, but I digress. A price, or love gift, was offered to the bride, showing how much he valued her. The father of the bride also provided a dowry to equip her for her new life. The young man had brought along a skin of wine. He would pour some wine in a cup and offer it to his bride-to-be. But, it was up to the girl to accept or reject the cup, accepting or rejecting the whole deal. If she drank the wine she was accepting the marriage proposal.

At that point the couple was engaged with all the rights and obligations of marriage—except physical consummation. You do know what physical consummation is, don't y__?" Before Philip could finish the sentence Emma gave him a swift kick under the table. "Da_ _ Emma." Jodi and Johnny ignored Philip's obvious pain while nodding a shy endearing confirmation. Philip, rubbing his shin, noted that Emma had crossed her arms, but he continued. "The bride was baptized in water which was a religious ritual of cleansing, signifying her changed state in the Jewish culture.

Next was the time of preparation. The groom would leave his bride to return to his father's house. Before he left, tradition has it that he would say, 'I go to prepare a place for you; if I go, I will return again unto you.'" Johnny interrupted, "I've read that before." "We'll get to that later. Back at his father's house he would prepare a 'wedding chamber' and a home of their own. The bride wore a white veil indicating she was holy, or set apart. During this time she would prepare herself to serve her husband. She would also gather her personal belongings to be ready when he would come for her, kinda like a hope chest. The bride, along with her bridesmaids, had to be ready at any time for the bridegroom to come and take her away. So they would keep a lamp lit and extra oil in case he came in the middle of the night." It was Jodi's turn to interrupt, "I know I have read that, but I didn't know anything about a Jewish wedding." "You will," Philip smiled.

"The father of the groom determined when the new home was finished. Then and only then would he release his son to go and get his bride. Often the groom would come with friends, secretly in the middle of the night, like a thief in the night. At this time he would shout 'behold the bridegroom comes' and blow the shofar. They would gather up the bride and her bridesmaids and take them all back to his father's house for the wedding ceremony.

The wedding day was one of the holiest days of the couple's life—a personal day of atonement when all their previous mistakes were forgiven. The marriage ceremony took place under a wedding canopy with the bridegroom coming first and the cantor singing, 'blessed is he who comes.' The bridegroom and bride retire to the wedding chamber seven days. Now if you want to put stress on a marriage that ought to do it." Philip quickly repositioned his legs in case Emma had a response. "Finally, at the end of the seven days there was the marriage supper for all the guests invited by the two families."

As already said, Johnny was a quick study. "Padre, I mean Mr. Cole, a lot of that sounds familiar from my Bible study." "It should because it is a picture of Yeshua and His bride." Jodi asked, "Who is Yeshua?" "Yeshua is the Hebrew pronunciation of Jesus; pronounce the 'J' like a 'Y' and the middle 'S' is the Hebrew letter that is pronounced 'sh.' The Bible talks about Yeshua's bride many times."

Philip put down his study notes, took a long drink of tea, and then looked at Jodi and Johnny. "Do either of you have any questions? You've got plenty to think about this week." Johnny was first to answer, "That's a load, Mr. Cole. Let Jodi and I talk about what you've said."

The following Saturday Jodi and Johnny were back for another visit. Hoping for a little less intense session, Philip asked about how their week had gone, and the four of them spent some time just being together. Jodi had gotten her teaching certificate and taken a job with the elementary school, teaching third grade mathematics and science. She had put up a poster in her room with one of the sayings Philip often quoted from his Prof in seminary: "IF THEY HAVEN'T LEARNED, YOU HAVEN'T TAUGHT." Johnny talked about wanting to make his first elk hunting trip next year and hoped Philip would go along.

When there was a break in the conversation, Jodi sat up straight, determined to end this conflict one way or the other. "Mr. Cole, Emma, what is the secret to spending a lifetime together?" For once Philip had enough sense to keep quiet and defer to his child bride. Emma let the question settle in everybody's mind. "Keeping Jesus at the center of your life. It's not easy, but it is simple. Last week Philip talked about how we, all believers, are His bride. He is preparing a place for us until His Father tells Him to come for us. Every prophecy has been fulfilled for His return; in fact my hope is so real, I listen for the shout and the shofar. We are to live in this age consecrated for Him, ready at all times.

If each of you keeps Jesus as the center of your life, there is no power on earth that can destroy your marriage. Marriage is hard; Lord knows Philip is hard to live with, but Jesus can keep what he has promised. If you remember that when you say those wedding vows they will really mean something. It's our faith in Him that keeps us together, and they have been the best years of my life." Philip nodded in agreement. "I'll tell you about hard. Try living together without having Jesus. You have to realize, I didn't become a believer until I was forty, so we were married for fifteen years without Jesus.

Johnny looked at Jodi, hoping she could dissuade her fears. Taking her hand in his, he kissed it. Jodi seemed to have a peace come over her. "Mr. Cole, I know where my trust rests. Do you think it would be alright if mamma went ahead with the wedding plans?" Philip extended his ice tea glass for a toast and said, "*Hava nagila*" (awake and rejoice).

Philip's Study Notes
Seeing Yeshua in the Ancient Jewish Wedding

The bride was chosen. "*You did not choose Me but I chose you*" (John 15:16);

The price was paid. "*knowing that you were not redeemed with perishable things like silver and gold from your futile way of life inherited from your forefathers, but with precious blood, as of a lamb unblemished and spotless, the blood of Christ*" (1 Peter 1:18-19);

The value of the bride was established. "*For God so loved the world that He gave His only begotten Son, that whoever believes in Him shall not perish, but have eternal life*" (John 3:16);

Eternal life is the engagement gift Yeshua gave. "*My sheep hear My voice, and I know them, and they follow Me; and I give eternal life to them, and they will never perish; and no one will snatch them out of My hand*" (John 10:27-28);

A dowry was given to the bride by her father. "*I will ask the Father, and He will give you another Helper, that He may be with you forever; that is the Spirit of Truth*" (John 14:16);

A covenant was drawn up. "*This cup which is poured out for you is the new covenant in My blood*" (Luke 22:20);

The bride was baptized. "*John (the baptizer) said to them, As for me, I baptize you with water; but One is coming who is mightier than I, and I am not fit to untie the thong of His sandals; He will baptize you with the Holy Spirit and fire*" (Luke 3:16);

The bridegroom departed to build their home. Jesus said, "*Do not let your heart be troubled; believe in God, believe also in Me. In My Father's house are many dwelling places; if it were not so, I would have told you; for I go to prepare a place for you. If I go and prepare a place for you, I will come again and receive you to Myself, that where I am, there you may be also"* (John 14:1-3);

The bridegroom did not know when his father would tell him to go get his bride. *"But of that day and hour no one knows, not even the angels of heaven, nor the Son, but the Father alone"* (Matthew 24:36);

The bridegroom will return with a shout. *"For the Lord Himself will descend from heaven with a shout, with the voice of the archangel and with the trumpet of God, and the dead in Christ will rise first. Then we who are alive and remain will be caught up together with them in the clouds to meet the Lord in the air, and so we shall always be with the Lord. Therefore comfort one another with these words"* (1 Thessalonians 4:16-18);

The wedding takes place under a canopy which symbolizes the descendents that would come from Abraham. Now this is pure conjecture on my part, but I always wondered why the Lord created the universe with untold numbers of galaxies and stars. Maybe Yeshua created the universe just to be a canopy for His bride—it fits with His extravagant kind of love.

The bride and groom will stay in the wedding chamber for 'seven'; that's what the Hebrew says. Conjecture again, but that 'seven' could be the seven years when the tribulation is going on down here on earth.

Finally, there is the marriage supper, or in this case the marriage supper of the Lamb. *"Then I heard something like the voice of a great multitude and like the sound of many waters and like the sound of mighty peals of thunder, saying, Hallelujah! For the Lord our God, the Almighty reigns. Let us rejoice and be glad and give the glory to Him, for the marriage of the Lamb has come and His bride has made herself ready. It was given to her to clothe herself in fine linen, bright and clean; for the fine linen is the righteous acts of the saints. Then he said to me, 'Write, Blessed are those who are invited to the marriage supper of the Lamb.' And he said to me, "These are the true words of God"* (Revelation 19:7-9).

CHAPTER 7

RED DUNCAN'S MARATHON,
2 CHRONICLES 14 – 16

Philip Cole didn't like spending time in Doc Blanchard's office, but he had gotten an infected leg from a cut when Emma's (dad-blamed, jug-headed) appaloosa had intentionally crowded him into the barbed wire fence while he was cleaning out her hooves. Philip's home remedy (or more correctly barn remedy) of washing it off in the horse trough with a little horse liniment followed by a smear of sulphur, hadn't worked this time for some reason. Doc's office smelled of alcohol and disinfectant. In the waiting room were several kids, spreading germs with obnoxious coughs. Old man Red Duncan was there, with his normal sour scowl on his face.

Philip had seen Red in Andy's earlier that morning. As usual, Red was sitting by himself in the corner, reading the local news rag. When he got up to leave he let out a groan, accompanied with a pained grimace. Charlie Marsh, the Methodist pastor, noticed Red's obvious pain. "Red are y-you okay? Maybe Philip could help, being that he is known to have f-f-fixed everything but a l-lovesick heart." Red tucked the paper under his arm, and didn't say a word. He just opened the door and left.

Red Duncan wasn't always that way. There was a time when he was the center of the community, always helping someone. It wasn't known if anyone outside of family knew his given name. Everyone just called him Red. He stood about five-eight and seemed two-thirds that wide in the shoulders; the strongest man Philip had ever met. Red must have been of Irish decent because he had a reddish-white complexion to go with his red hair. His forearms were as big as some men's legs, and his head rested on a neck that seemed to just be a continuation of his massive shoulders.

Philip, anxious to break the noise of the coughing looked over at Red. "Red, are you okay? Seriously, is there anything I can do?" Red grimaced from obvious pain as he repositioned himself in the chair. "Been better." Then the nurse called out, "Mr. Duncan," and ushered him into a patient room.

Finally it was Philip's time to move from waiting in the waiting room to waiting in the patient room. He always carried a small Bible in his pickup glove box, so at least he had something to read. What seemed like several lifetimes later, Doc Blanchard entered in a whirlwind of commotion; with his nurse assistant close behind.

Philip couldn't resist. "What's the hurry Doc? I've been waiting most of the day. By the way, who do I give my lunch order to?" Doc looked at his nurse and asked, "Do we still have some of those big rusty needles? Okay, Philip, don't give me any more trouble. What are you here for?" Philip pulled up his pants leg to reveal an inflamed, infected cut. "Emma said I had to come have you take a look at it." Doc let out a sigh. "You did wash this with soap, and then put an antibiotic on it with a clean bandage, right?" "Absolutely Doc, but speaking of trouble, I saw old Red Duncan in the waiting room. I can remember when he was the pillar of this community, the strongest man in the county. He was everything a man should be. He was a part time coach with the football team, an elder in his church, always in the middle of helping out in the community. But now he seems like a bitter old man."

Doc was working on Philip's leg, applying medication and bandages while talking. "Red has a really bad back from when a piece of tractor equipment fell on him, plus his leg was crushed in the wreck when the drunk driver ran into him a couple of years ago. He has his reasons, but I guess he is a bitter old man." Doc turned to his assistant and said, "Give Philip a shot for the infection, the kind that has to be given in his hip, and don't worry about how deep you stick it. Then give him a booster tetanus shot in the arm. If you'll do them both on one side, maybe he'll know a little of how Red feels." Doc left the room a minute, and then returned with a prescription and sample of medicine with instructions to apply a new bandage daily. "Your leg will heal up fine if you will do what I told you, but at your age I have one piece of advice. Don't buy any green bananas. You might not be around that long." Doc was walking out, and then stopped to look back. "Red is a good man; I hate to see him end up this way." Philip didn't offer any wisdom because he didn't have any to offer.

Several weeks went by with the normal activity for late spring in West Texas. Philip had a small hay pasture that he contracted out to have cut and baled. It was too small to own the necessary equipment, but just large enough to encourage him to try to grow his own top quality coastal Bermuda for the horses. With fertilizing and contracting costs, he could grow his own hay that couldn't have cost him more than buying alpha stacked in his barn. This way he had the privilege of gathering his own. Emma could drive the pickup with Philip loading the sixteen foot trailer. The work also gave Philip time to thank the good Lord that he had enough sense not to buy a milk cow to save on the cost of a gallon of milk.

One morning Philip was again at Andy's Café for coffee with the guys. Red Duncan was also there, but as usual sat at a corner table reading the newspaper. Charlie Marsh (sitting at Philip's table) dared to address Red again. "Red, how are y-you?" Red didn't bother to look up. "Not so well." "Well we are here to h-help if there is anything we c-can do." Philip thought to himself, "what's that 'we' stuff?" For some reason known only to God and little green apples, Red responded to Charlie's offer to see if Philip could help. "Well, I might could use a little advice from the Padre, but there is one ground rule. Tell me something that will help, but don't quote me anything out of the Bible. Me and the Lord ain't on the best of terms at the moment, and I don't need any religious garbage. Well, what do you say Padre?"

Philip had become particularly good at arrow prayers. He gave the prayer a few moments to make sure it had time to get there, and then said, "Phidippides." There was silence for a while, and then Red and Charlie said simultaneously, "What?" Any good story needs a moment to let the suspense build. Then Philip sat up and began to weave his tale. "About twenty-five hundred years ago the Persian Empire was spreading east into Macedonia, and the Greeks went out to meet them. At a battlefield on the plain near Marathon, the Greek army defeated the Persians. A courier named Phidippides ran 24 miles from the battlefield to Athens, bringing the news of the Greek victory. After Phidippides gave his report, he collapsed and died. The Olympic marathon race commemorates Phidippide's heroic act." After another long moment of silence to accent his point, Philip added: "The moral of the story is, 'life is a marathon' and we all need to finish well. It ain't much, but that's all I got."

Red was gracious enough to say "Thanks." He then took a last swig off his coffee, folded his paper under his arm and limped towards the door. Just as he got to the door, he turned around. "Padre, you still got that fat overfed underworked quarter horse?" "Well, I reckon that's a pretty good description of Cody." Red paused to think over what he was about to say, not being used to asking for help. "Padre, I need to break out about forty calves to give 'em shots. Two can get it done ten times easier than one. Would you be interested in giving that horse of yours a little work?" "Red, I don't have to think about that one, let's get her done." "Maybe tomorrow, about one?" "Red, I'll be there." Charlie watched as Red made his way out, and then looked over at Philip. "Red's a g-g-good man, but he's g-got to be in plenty of p-p-pain." "Yea Charlie, and it seems to be more than just physical."

The following morning Philip cleaned up Cody, checked him over, and found a sore spot on his right front hoof. Probably just a bruise, but this was a problem because he didn't want to back out on his appointment with Red. Philip looked over and there stood Emma's horse Porsche—fat, dumb, and happy. A sort of wicked grin came on his face. Philip had ridden Porsche many times, but neither Philip nor Porsche cared for it. Cody was half quarter horse, half thoroughbred, and standing fifteen-three which fit Philip's six-three frame. Porsche was purebred appaloosa and on her best day went about fourteen-two. The fact that Philip weighed twice what Emma did was not a factor in Porsche's ability to handle the weight. She was strong as a mule, but she tended to snort and complain a lot (which by the way was what that wicked grin was about).

Being as the afternoon was likely to turn into some serious work, Philip decided to walk Porsche over to Red's, and then back again to let her warm up and cool down properly. He went by the kitchen and got out some pinto beans from the frig. He mashed them and heated them in the microwave. He mixed in some picante sauce and sliced jalapenos, and then rolled the concoction in a couple floured tortillas. He grabbed a bottle of water, deciding to eat in the saddle as Porsche eased the three miles over to Red's place—life is good. Porsche snorted and shook her head, but Philip rubbed her neck and told her how special she was. Truth be known, she was enjoying the outing as much as he.

Red was waiting at the gate when Philip got there. He looked over the combination and couldn't help but grin. He wouldn't say anything about this six-three cowboy wanna-be riding a pony. Red's place was a little over four hundred acres. How those calves knew that someone wanted to gather them up that day no one will ever know, but they had gone to the roughest, most wooded place on the farm. Red was right! One person was never going to gather up this group. The plan was to drive all the momma cows up to the corral, hoping most of the calves would follow. For a while it looked like they were geniuses, but the count showed they were half a dozen short.

Now came the serious work, and Philip had to brag on Porsche. She was up to the task. First they tried to drive the six out one at a time, cutting one into the open, and then another. They kept going back to get a straggler, but with an hour's hard work, they still had all six in the brush. Red looked over and suggested the obvious, "I didn't want to, but it looks like we got to rope each one and lead them up to the corral." Philip agreed. By that time apparently Porsche was tired of fooling with these six outlaws, so she got right into the brush and brought one out in the open so Philip could drop a rope on it. Porsche earned her keep that day, cutting out four of the six while Red got the other two. In about an hour they had all the calves in the corral.

Philip and Red led their horses to the windmill watering trough for a well-earned drink. Porsche worked up a white foam lather and worked off about ten pounds of fat. Red offered to give the shots so Philip could go ahead home, but Philip figured if you're in for a penny you're in for a pound. This little operation still worked better as a team. About two hours later they had the caves checked out and shots finished. At the end of the day, Red had to admit that Emma had a pretty good pony. It was getting on towards evening, so Philip allowed Porsche to walk back slowly. When they got back to the barn, he washed her off and gave her a good rub. She always loves that (and a little extra sweet feed).

One evening the telephone rang and on the other end was none other than Red Duncan. "Padre, I wanted to thank you again for helping out, and I've been thinking about old Phidippides. Do you think it would be possible for us to talk, maybe get off alone somewhere?" Philip thought for a moment about an appropriate place, and then answered, "Red, I'd enjoy that. How about tomorrow afternoon? We can go down to the barn, sit on a bale of hay, and get caught up." Red agreed that would be a good place, so the appointed meeting was set. Philip hadn't contacted Red on purpose. He figured, roughly paraphrasing Lewis Sperry Chafer, "It would do more good to talk to God about Red than to talk to Red about God." So he had put in some time with God on the subject.

The following afternoon Red drove up in his old red pickup. He noticed that Philip's pickup was already at the barn, so he drove on down without stopping at the house. There were handshakes and 'howdies,' then Red and Philip each got comfortable on a bale of hay. Red commented that it looked like good hay this year. His yearling cattle were putting on good weight, and his wife was doing fine. Philip nodded, giving Red an opportunity to get to what was troubling him. Red moved a little spot of dirt back and forth with his boot for awhile, and then looked up at Philip and said, "Padre, I been thinking about the moral to that story you told, and I know I'm not running the end of this race to finish well. My back and leg hurt, but I can live with that; there is something else wrong and I can't put my finger on it."

In the country it's okay to let there be a pause in the conversation for time to think. "Red, I've never had the type of pain you have so I don't know what it's like, but one other thing you said back at the café concerned me. Are you angry with God?" Red looked a little exasperated, exhaled deeply and shook his head. "I know He is perfect. I know He will make all things to the good, but I am so angry with everything, including Him, that I could ride into hell just to spit in the devil's eye."

Emma brought down a pitcher of iced tea. She commented on how good it was to see Red again, and then went on back to her gardening. Philip appreciated the break in the tension, but felt like he had to give Red some sort of hope. "Red, there was a time when every man and boy in the county looked up to you, still do I guess. But something must have happened along the way. Tell me what was happening when your spirit was the best." Red let his mind drift back over the years. "Well, I was involved. I helped coach the football team, people needed help and I pitched in. I even worked with kids with their livestock at the county fair. Oh yeah, and I was an elder in my church." "That was what you did; I was thinking more about what was in your heart. Think back to an earlier time when you first got started. What was it like then?" Red thought for a long time before answering, "It never occurred to me, but I had just become a new Christian and I loved to sing the old hymns. I still remember the words to some of those old songs:

'Man of sorrows! What a name
For the Son of God who came
Ruined sinners to reclaim!
Hal-le-lu-jah, what a Savior!'[5]

If the doors were open I was at church. You probably won't believe this, but I was actually in the choir. I did as little damage as possible, you know, not so loud as to throw everyone off. I loved the words to those old hymns." Philip smiled because he shared Red's love for the lyrics to those old favorites. "Do you mind talking about how you became a Christian?" A look of peace settled over Red. "Must have been all grace and mercy from the Almighty because I was sure headed in the other direction. I used to have a temper that would scald paint off a moving freight train. One night I heard a traveling evangelist was coming to town, and for some reason I went to hear him. He didn't preach any fire and brimstone, but he said if anyone was burdened by their sin, God sent His Son to pay for the sins of the world, rendering all men savable if only they would believe. I didn't have much use for religion, but I wanted to get the weight of my sins off my back. The preacher told me I had to turn from who I was to Jesus. He said to trust in Jesus alone, and what Jesus did on the cross. For some reason that made perfect sense, so when the preacher gave the altar call the next thing I knew my legs were carrying me forward."

The answer to Red's problems popped into Philip's head, but he still had to figure out how to explain it because of Red's ground rules. "Red, do we still have the same ground rules that I can't use the Bible?" Red shifted his weight on the hay and said, "Shucks Padre, I never figured that would stand up for long with you so go ahead. I'm here because I want to hear what you have to say." "While you were talking about an earlier time, I kept thinking about one of Emma's favorite Bible characters, Asa. Let me grab my Bible out of the pickup." When he returned it took Philip a minute to find his place in 2 Chronicles. "Here it is! Asa was Solomon's great-grandson; he was one of the best kings of Judah. After Solomon died there was a disagreement between the tribes and they split in two. The ten tribes to the north created what was called Israel (later called Samaria), leaving the three tribes in the south; Judah, Benjamin and the Levites, as the southern kingdom called Judah. Asa's life is kinda divided up into three sections. First he did good, had opposition, and had victory. Second he did good, had opposition, and was spared but didn't have victory. Then last, he died a bitter old man estranged from God.

It says, '*Asa did good and right in the sight of Yahweh his God, for he removed the foreign altars and high places, tore down the sacred pillars, cut down the Asherim, and commanded Judah to seek Yahweh.*' One thing I have learned over the years and that is if you are doing God's will you can expect a spiritual counter-attack, and sure enough one came out of Ethiopia. Old Asa was outnumbered and outgunned. He didn't have a betting chance, so out of desperation he prayed, '*Yahweh, there is no one besides*

You to help in the battle between the powerful and those who have no strength; so help us, Yahweh our God, for we trust in You, and in Your name have come against this multitude.' Because of Asa's faith the Lord routed the enemy.

Time passed and Asa had a second reformation because the people had gone back to worshiping other gods. God called the prophet Azariah to go talk with Asa: *'Listen to me, Asa, and all Judah and Benjamin: Yahweh is with you when you are with Him, and if you seek Him, He will let you find Him; but if you forsake Him, He will forsake you.'* Asa listened to Azariah, but this time *'the high places were not removed from Israel.'* Nevertheless the Bible says: *'Asa's heart was blameless all his days.'* That sounds okay, but I think it might be the turning point of Asa's life because this time he let a little compromise leaven the bread, and things went downhill from then on.

Sure enough another adversary came against Judah, and this time it was the northern kingdom of Israel. But instead of trusting in God, this time the king brought out silver and gold from the treasuries of the House of the Lord to send them to the king living in Damascus. Asa said, *'Let there be a covenant between you and me. As between my father and your father. Behold I have sent you silver and gold; go, break your treaty with Baasha king of Israel so that he will withdraw from me.'*

God spared Judah, but there was no victory either. Asa's life spiraled downhill the remainder of his life. The story goes on that Asa became diseased in his feet. Yet even in his pain the king would not seek God. They buried Asa in his own tomb that *'he had cut out for himself.'*

Concerning this whole thing about finishing well, I want you to remember what God said, *'If you seek Me, I will let you find Me.'* It seems to me that finishing well is found in our daily dependence on seeking Him. Maybe somewhere along the way you lost your first love and traded it for doing good things. I've got a feeling that God appreciates all you did for Him, but He loves it when you sing to Him."

The two men just sat there for a long while. Finally Red got to his feet and said, "Thanks Padre, I really enjoyed seeing you and Emma again. Let me go home and think about old Asa." A couple of days went by, and then one evening the telephone rang. Emma answered, as usual, and then summoned Philip. On the other end of the line Philip heard Red say, "Padre, you know what I am going to do? If they'll have me I'm going to join the choir again and sing to the Lord!"

Philip's Study Notes, 2 Chronicles 14-16

Chapter 14, Asa Becomes King in Judah

(1-8) Asa's life is divided into three sections. The Bible says Asa became king and *"the land was undisturbed for ten years"* which means they had no wars. *"Asa did good and right in the sight of Yahweh his God, for he removed the foreign altars and high places, tore down the sacred pillars, cut down the Asherim, and commanded Judah to seek Yahweh"* (the Hebrew four consonant name of God, pronounced Yah-weh, the LORD). The Jews had started worshiping the gods who were in the Promised Land before they possessed it, but with Asa's leadership they obeyed the commands given about having no other god than Yahweh. Asa was God's representative first and the people's second.

(9-10) It seems to be an immutable fact of spiritual life that if you are doing God's will you can expect a counterattack, and sure enough one came out of Ethiopia. Asa had an army of five hundred eighty thousand well trained valiant warriors. But the Bible says; *"Now Zerah the Ethiopian came up against them with an army of one million men and three hundred chariots."* Let me put it like this, Zerah was a Mac truck and Asa was an armadillo trying to cross the road. To a foot soldier, those chariots were like a Sherman tank.

(11-15) The Hebrew gets a little difficult to translate, but generally Asa called out to his God and said, *"Yahweh, there is no one besides You to help in the battle between the powerful and those who have no strength; so help us, Yahweh our God, for we trust in You, and in Your name have come against this multitude."* The next short verse gives the results: *"So Yahweh routed the Ethiopians before Asa and before Judah, and the Ethiopians fled."* That wasn't blind faith. Asa believed that the God who took the people out of Egypt, parted the sea, provided for them in the desert forty years, caused the walls of Jericho to fall and put David on the throne, had the integrity of His Word to back it up.

Chapter 15, Azariah's Warning and Asa's Second Reform

(1-18) Time passed, and Asa had a second reformation because the people had gone back to worshiping other gods along with Yahweh. God called the prophet Azariah to go talk with Asa, and he said, *"Listen to me, Asa, and all Judah and Benjamin: Yahweh is with you when you are with Him, and if you seek Him, He will let you find Him; but if you forsake Him, He will forsake you."* That last part is too good not to read again, so I suggest you do. Asa took to heart what the prophet Azariah said, so he removed the idols from the land. So everyone went to Jerusalem and made a covenant with Yahweh to seek Him with all their heart. Asa went one step further and removed his mother from the position of Queen Mother because she had made an idol (don't you know things were a little chilly around the king's house). The story continues, *"But the high places were not removed from Israel; nevertheless Asa's heart was blameless all his days."*

Chapter 16, War Against Baasha and Aftermath

(1-6) Asa had compromised his spiritual leadership by leaving those high places (places to worship other gods), and about that time a second spiritual counterattack came. As is so often the case, this second trial could have been a curse or blessing, depending on Asa's reaction. This time the challenge came from Baasha, king of Israel, the ten northern tribes. Baasha's plan was to fortify a city just north of Jerusalem to cut off anyone traveling or trading the most direct route north.

Remember, when the Ethiopians came up against Judah, Asa prayed in total dependence on Yahweh. But this time the king brought out silver and gold from the treasuries of the House of the Lord to send them to the king living in Damascus. Asa said, *"Let there be a covenant between you and me. As between my father and your father. Behold I have sent you silver and gold; go, break your treaty with Baasha king of Israel so that he will withdraw from me."*

In Exodus 34, God renewed His covenant after the two broken tablets (Ten Commandments) were replaced. The following is part of what God said: *"Watch yourself that you make no covenant with the inhabitants of the land into which you are going, lest it become a snare in your midst. But rather, you are to tear down their altars and smash their sacred pillars and cut down their Asherim, for you shall not worship any other god, for Yahweh, whose name is Jealous, is a jealous God."* It seems that God feels that His relationship with us is like a marriage; our independence from Him is as if a spouse was having an affair. God says he is a jealous God. Just because times get tough, don't you go crawl into someone else's bed for comfort.

This time Asa wasn't defeated, but he didn't win either. If he had trusted God, Asa would have won all the land that Solomon had ruled over, including the northern ten tribes and Damascus. In the attack from Ethiopia, it was impossible for Asa to win. So he trusted in Yahweh. However, this time it looked like he could handle the problem himself, so he didn't trust in Yahweh. Yahweh is a jealous God, and He wants us to trust Him all the time.

(7-10) In God's mercy He sent Hanani, who was called a

seer, to confront Asa and condemn his loss of faith. Hanani went on to tell Asa that had he depended on God this time, like the first time, He would have expanded Judah's area to include both the northern kingdom and Damascus. This would have effectively returned his kingdom to the size Solomon ruled. Here are two more lessons: First, hard times may be your opportunity for the greatest blessing if you will only be faithful to God. Second, God is aware of every problem you have. He strongly desires to support you, but He will not accept a divided heart.

(11-14) Unfortunately, Asa illustrated the old axiom; if you are going in the wrong direction, just redouble your efforts. The seer's condemnation of Asa made him angry, so he threw the seer in jail and oppressed the people for good measure. The story goes on that Asa became diseased in his feet. Yet even in his pain the king would not seek God, but depended on physicians. They buried Asa in his own tomb that *"he had cut out for himself."* Asa ended up a self-made man, independent from God. That is the definition of sin—anything independent from God. Asa was one of the best kings, yet he did not finish well. Along the journey it is almost a certainty that opposition will come, but your safety is in daily dependence on the Lord. If you do that, then you can expect to finish well.

CHAPTER 8

BERSHITH –
THE HEAD OF THE TEXT
GENESIS 1:1-2

(An unknown pastor related this story)

Mt. Valley Cathedral was the most beautiful church in Bavaria, with its spires and stained glass windows, but its most famous attraction was an exquisite pipe organ. People from miles away, even from other countries came to hear this beautiful organ.

But all was not well. The church was still a marvelous work of architecture, and the light still sparkled through the stained glass windows—but there was an eerie silence in the Bavarian valley. The mountain valley no longer echoed the lovely, full melody of the organ. Experts from all over the world tried to repair it, but these things can be very temperamental—and even after their heroic efforts to fix the music piece, there were only sounds of disharmony.

One day an old man appeared at the door and spoke with the sexton. After some time the sexton reluctantly agreed to let the old man try his hand at repairing the instrument. For two full days the old man worked, and the sexton was becoming apprehensive, but then on the third day early in the morning the valley was filled with glorious music. Farmers dropped their plows, housewives stopped their work, shopkeepers locked their doors and all headed for the church. Even the trees seemed to respond as the glorious music echoed throughout the valley.

All listened and wondered how this miracle could have happened, but no one dared to speak for fear of interrupting the music. After the music had stopped, there was silence and finally a brave soul asked the old man how he could have fixed that complicated instrument when all the world's experts had failed. As you may have already guessed, the old man said it was an inside job. You see, the old man said he had created the instrument many years ago— "I created it, now I have restored it."

Thanksgiving had just passed and Christmas was around the corner. Philip had finished a visit with the boys at Andy's. Lester Hayes had been telling about his adventures of deer hunting, and how he fell out of a tree and broke his arm. It had rained the night before, and no sooner had he shinned up to his chosen spot to sit than he spotted a wall-hanger going away at a fast trot. In the excitement, while trying to operate his lever action Marlin, his foot slipped on the slick branch. Lester explained how this was a once in a lifetime buck (the one that got away always is), so he was trying to figure out how to load, aim, and fire in mid-air. He knew that gravity was about to end the opportunity, which it did.

Philip always enjoyed one of the group's yarns. Now, however, he had to take care of job number one. He must walk over to the hardware store to order Emma's Christmas present, a solar powered giant hummingbird. He could get her one of those nifty little rototillers so she wouldn't need him to cultivate, or a Bunn coffee maker for her kitchen (which was his first preference), but he had determined to go romantic this year. Philip figured that at the very least, one of those gigantic birds would look so imposing that it would keep the crows out of the garden.

Coming towards him on the sidewalk was Fred Garcia, a long time resident of the area. "Merry Christmas Fred," Philip greeted. "Howdy," replied Fred, but there wasn't much Christmas cheer in his voice. Philip is usually oblivious to the leading of the Spirit, but this time his heart was open, maybe because of the season. "Wow there Fred, it's almost Christmas. You sound like you could walk under a snake with your hat on." "Everything is fine Padre. I'm sorry for responding that way. I just had my mind on a problem in the past, but that is water under the bridge." "Fred, I don't mean to pry, but it sounds like you are the one under the bridge. Is there anything I can do to help?" Fred massaged the back of his neck, while he considered his situation. "I might just need someone to talk to, so maybe we could talk sometime." Philip didn't want to push, but he knew that long-term problems don't seem to resolve themselves with more time. "Do you have time for a cup of coffee?"

The two chose a corner table at Andy's where most of the crowd had moved out. Fred looked into his coffee cup, trying to decide where to start. "I'll just come right to the point. My sister and I haven't spoken in 12 years. We were raised in a close family where both our mom and dad created a good family, a good home, and a safe place to grow up. After our mom and dad passed, Elizabeth moved into our home while she finished two years at junior college. She met this slick older guy, fell in love, and decided to move in with him against our advice. I said some pretty hard things. As soon as the guy was finished toying with her, he dropped her like a hot skillet. But the separation between us remained. When you passed me on the street, I was thinking about Elizabeth. I am going through another Christmas apart from Elizabeth." Fred was silent, so it was Philip's turn to say something meaningful, but he didn't have a single thing that would help. "Fred, it sounds like your parents created something special when you and your sister were growing up. I don't know what to say about the situation with your sister, but I would like to pray about it if that would be acceptable to you." "Sure Padre, I appreciate you listening; that might be all I needed. Merry Christmas and tell Emma I said so."

After Fred left, Philip headed back to the hardware store to finish his Christmas shopping. As he walked, he said out loud, "I don't know why people complain about Christmas shopping."

The end of the year is a great time in West Texas, if you don't mind a little wind and dust. In the Middle East, the Aramaic word for a scorching summer wind is Sirocco; in West Texas they call it a normal summer day. The changing seasons reminds a person that God's creation has a beginning and an end. Winter is sometimes cold, and summer is always hot; but generally the temperature was agreeable. Winter doesn't last long anyway, so there is the rebirth of spring to look forward to.

This particular Saturday afternoon found Philip Cole relaxing at his gun range, shooting his Colt Commander. The smell of spent powder brings peace to a shooter's soul. The Commander was born as a 45, but many years ago Philip had seriously injured his right wrist, and the pounding of 230 grain bullets caused him to look for an acceptable alternative. Philip handloaded, or as he called it "rolled his own," so he could have created a tamer 45ACP round. But he liked to practice with what he was going to carry. Working through an old gunsmith friend, he was able to obtain a secondhand Commander slide that would accommodate a 38 Super barrel. A part here and a part there, and pretty soon Philip had a dandy little two slide Commander in both 45 and 38 Super. The process worked so well he bought a barrel, toggle, and spring for a 9mm to go with the 38 Super slide, and then a 10mm set of parts to go on the 45 slide. It seemed like a great idea at the time, but by the time Philip had bought three magazines for each caliber, he realized his theory had gotten ahead of common budget sense, which wasn't the first time and won't be the last.

Philip was working on his third box of reloads when up walks Charlie Marsh, the local pastor. "Emma said I could f-f-find you down here, so I c-came on down. Hope you don't m-mind me interrupting your t-t-target shooting." Philip dropped the magazine out, locked the slide back, set the pistol on a cloth, and pulled off his ear muffs before answering. "Charlie, it's good to see you. Sit down and rest a spell. I've got an extra set of ear protectors in my shooting bag if you want to shoot."

Shooting or chewing the fat didn't seem to be the purpose of Charlie's visit. "What brings you out this way on Saturday afternoon when you are supposed to be polishing off your sermon?" "Padre, I've g-got another three weeks on our present s-s-series, but after the end of the year I w-wanted to preach through Genesis. I might just have walked off in w-w-water over my head." Philip gave Charlie a sympathetic look, knowing the feeling. "Well Charlie, I've been working off and on for two years trying to get my arms around the first two verses, so don't feel lonesome. That first verse sets the tone for the remainder of the Bible, and it all comes down to a simple 'the.' So I just might be smart enough to confuse both of us. Frankly, in that white space between verses 1 and 2, I've got more questions than answers." Charlie had hoped for a more optimistic outlook for his Genesis series, but he was determined to teach all the Word, so he gave it one more shot. "Padre, are you w-willing to work on this s-study together? If nothing else, you have a b-b-better reference library than I do. I believe we'll b-both be blessed."

Philip respected Charlie more than Charlie would ever know because he was not only a fine teacher, but he put in practice what the church and community needed from a pastor. He quickly volunteered, "Charlie, I'd be honored to study with you. I've never studied the Word that I wasn't blessed." It was agreed they would get started Monday morning meeting at Charlie's office, and then each Monday thereafter. "I suggest we each read Genesis one or two times tomorrow after church, just to get grounded." The date was set with much anticipation and a big scoop of humility from both parties.

God created another glorious day in West Texas on Monday morning. Philip and Coco were headed for town by five-thirty. Charlie had arrived at his office early to prepare a pot of coffee. As Philip walked through the door, Charlie greeted Philip with "M-morning! This had b-better be productive because it's cutting into my p-p-prayer time." Philip thought to himself that a person who really believes in prayer is the rarest thing in the church, and Charlie's life was living proof of his dedication to spending the best time of his day with the Lord.

They both poured a cup of strong black coffee, and then got comfortable at the conference table in Charlie's study. Charlie offered that with a Sunday morning and evening sermon, he had not been able to study, but he had read Genesis through Sunday night. Philip on the other hand had discovered something that had been hiding in plain sight all the time. He was at the same time embarrassed by how obvious the answer should have been, but also amazed by the revelation.

"Charlie, my old Prof was right when he said, 'The first step in preparing to teach is to read the text six times. You will be amazed how much light the text shines on commentaries.'" Charlie interrupted, "I know about Prof. He also said, 'Reading my Bible spoils more good sermons than you'll ever know.'" Philip smiled, thinking back to seminary days and the daily chapel service. He then continued, "I only got through it twice, but reading Genesis yesterday gave me part of the answer I have been stumbling over for two years. I had isolated the first verse so long that I couldn't see the forest for the trees. The first verse is pivotal to the whole

Bible, and since I believe God is revealed in it as the Creator, I have been trying to resolve the issue of verse 2. This verse seems to describe a condition, formless and void, that doesn't sound like anything He would create.

Reading all of Genesis yesterday, I realized that Moses wasn't trying to prove that God was the Creator. He knew that because he knew God. Moses wrote with the presupposition that the reader would also know that God had revealed Himself in creation, as well as many other ways such as the covenants, the Law, and the sacrificial system that went along with the Tent of Meeting. Moses is not writing an apologetic for God's existence, or that He created all that is by speaking it into being; he simply asserts that God has always existed and therefore everything else that exists is by His cause. It was one of those 'when the light comes on moments.'"

Philip was wound up, so he took another big swig of coffee and got back on task. "The title of the book in Hebrew is *Bershith*, meaning 'the head of the text.' I'll just go ahead and give you my opinion that the ultimate meaning of verse 1 is the head of the Torah (the first five books of the Bible written by Moses). In the Hebrew, the text would literally read, '*In head created God the heavens and the earth.*' Okay Charlie, that's just seven words in Hebrew. Believe me, we have our work cut out for us, so let's go to roping and branding.

The prime root within the first word is *rosh*, meaning head or shake, as in *ro'sh hashshanah* (the head of the year or the Jewish New Year), so it might be translated in English as 'beginning.' I think it means the first in place, time, order, or rank; of a series of historical events. I looked up the other words in my Hebrew lexicon. Elohim (God) is in the plural form with the article which is to say 'supreme God,' not to be confused with 'other gods.' Next, '*bara*' is in the masculine tense. The prime root means 'to create,' no problem there. Next is '*shameh*,' translated 'heavens' from an unused Hebrew root meaning to be lofty, but also can mean where the stars abide. Next is '*erets*' from another unused root which means to be firm, or the earth. Now, if I give this an amplified translation, it might go something like, '*The head of the Torah, In the beginning there was a shaking, an historical event; the supreme God created the lofty spaces above and created a firm place, the earth.*' Charlie, if for the time being you can accept that translation, let's do some research and get back next week."

The boys at Andy's Café wanted to know how the two 'scholars' could make something so simple so complicated. Charlie thought to himself that they are right, because when Moses wrote Genesis, he intended the truth to be simple and straightforward. Charlie asked Frank Criswell, retired Texas Ranger, what he thought about the first verse in the Bible. "Frank it's j-just 10 words, 'In the b-beginning God created the heavens and the earth.' Is that complicated or s-s-simple, and what does it m-mean to you?" Frank was a no nonsense type of guy, so he thought for a moment before answering. "Charlie, to me it's simple and means just what it says. But, what I was thinking about when you asked the question was why I accept it as fact. As a Ranger I had to rely on my intuition to find the facts. I believe what it says because I know that God and I have ridden a lot of miles together. I don't just know about Him. I know Him, and therefore my gut tells me He is real. Common sense tells me there must have been a creator." Charlie responded, "W-wow, you just said w-w-what I've been trying to put into words. We have one scholar here, that's F-frank, and two s-students, the Padre and m-me."

Winter in West Texas is a breath of fresh air, with the early mornings usually cold but warming nicely by noon. There is also a little less work to do around the farm, with the exception of Emma's list of honey-dos which never runs out.

Emma wanted some work done in her garden to prepare it

for spring planting. I say her garden because she supervised every bit of it. She told Philip when to plow, when to disc and put it up in rows, when to cultivate and irrigate out of the lake, and so forth. In all fairness, they planted the garden together and she did most of the harvesting, unless it was something like okra or the higher fruit from the small orchard. Anyway, now was the time to plow the garden to allow the late winter rains to soak in deeply. Philip was about half way through when he heard a shotgun blast over the noise of the tractor. Taking the tractor out of gear, he hit the ground running. The blast had come from near the house, and that could only mean something serious. Philip cleared the corner of the house to find Emma holding her 870 pump shotgun while standing over a coyote. Emma always left taking care of predators up to Philip, but when he took a look, it was obvious why she had taken matters into her own hands. The coyote was rabid!

Mid-week found Philip at Andy's with the boys. Fred Garcia entered, and then looked around the room to locate Philip. Philip noticed and invited Fred to have a seat by sliding a chair out with his boot. Fred walked over but didn't take a seat. "Padre, I need to talk with you sometime when it is convenient." "Now's as good a time as any." The morning had turned really nice, so Philip suggested they might just take a walk if that was acceptable with Fred. The two set out with no particular destination in mind, walking slowly. Fred was thinking over what he wanted to say. Finally, looking up with what could only be described as a 'cry out for help' look on his face, he said: "Padre, I have heard how you helped others find the answer to their problems in the Bible. I need to know if there is an answer for Elizabeth and me?"

Philip didn't even try to answer Fred, knowing that all he could have said at the time was, "I got nothing." Rather, Philip put his hope in a quick-draw arrow prayer, and then looked over at Fred. "Fred, I don't know the answer, but I do know the One who has the answer, and so do you. I never thought of the Bible as a quick answer book, but I know God is working even now to redeem His fallen creation. You said your mom and dad created a near perfect home for you and your sister. Then when they passed on you took her in, but she went her own way. When you said that, I was thinking how it somewhat parallels the Genesis story. If I had to go with what I know now, it would be for us to pray that the Lord will help you and Elizabeth to recreate a family. I clearly don't know how to help, other than pray until the world looks flat." "Thanks Padre. I think that might be the best advice, because this might just have to be a 'God thing' to solve."

The following Monday morning Charlie and Philip were back working on their study of Genesis. Charlie had the week to study, along with about 60 hours of church duties as usual. So he went first this time: "I spent m-my time rereading Genesis and l-looking up general references to keep our s-s-study in context with the flow of the entire b-b-book. Genesis covers a time span of m-more than half of all human history; it is the seed of all r-revealed truth. I think Moses had t-t-two theological objectives: First to draw a l-line from creation through the patriarchs to the Sinai covenant; S-second to show that the call of the p-patriarchs and the g-giving of the Law at Sinai have as their ultimate g-g-goal to be part of the process of reestablishing God's original p-purpose in creation. In other w-w-words, part of the p-process is to tie all of God's revealed truth together, s-starting with the Genesis creation and ending with the new c-creation in Revelation, which by the w-way would connect both ends of the B-Bible together."

Philip let Charlie's comments sink in because he had brought up some profound issues. His understanding of what the Genesis creation is all about was finally beginning to take form. He had sometimes wondered if being endowed with average intellect had worked to his advantage. Instead of discerning the meaning of scripture immediately, he was forced to dig out one clue at a time (as if solving a mystery) until finally arriving at that golden 'ah ha' moment. "Charlie, I think this is what we had to get at, which is not isolating the first verse but keeping it in the context of Genesis, and for that matter, the whole of revealed truth. I found a quote about Genesis 1 from Matthew Henry that reminded me of what Frank said yesterday morning: 'The faith of humble Christians understand this better than the fancy of the most learned men. From what we see of heaven and earth, we learn the power of the great Creator. And let our make and place as men, remind us of our duty as Christians, always to keep heaven in our eye, and the earth under our feet.'

It seems to me that how you interpret the first verse has a lot to do with faith, and I don't mean blind faith, but faith that is established by your relationship with God. Well Charlie, what do you think?" Charlie sat there for a time, considering what they were learning. You could see in his eyes the excitement of knowing God through His Word. "I t-t-think we have begun to u-understand the first verse, but Padre, we have a long r-row to hoe ahead of us."

Charlie poured a fresh cup of coffee, and then moved on to verse 2. "Since the subject is c-creation, I found a quote from one of my f-f-favorite Christian writers, Aiden W. Tozer: 'However closely God may be identified with the w-w-work of His hands, they are and must eternally be other than He, and He is and m-must be antecedent to and independent of them. What d-d-does the divine immanence mean in direct Christian experience? It m-means simply that God is here. No point is nearer to God than any other point.'[6]"

Philip was organizing his study notes. "The Hebrew reads, *'And the earth was formless and void, and darkness was over the surface of the deep; and the Spirit of God was moving over the surface of the waters.'* Verse 2 tells us the state of things before God started the creation process described in the following six days (1:3-31). Charlie, let me just go ahead and confess. We are in over my head, but I keep going back to what we discussed yesterday. I know God, and I know His character. Therefore, when Moses writes, 'In the beginning God created,' I tend to take it as the only reasonable conclusion regardless of whether verse 2 follows verse one immediately, or if there is a time gap. The Hebrew word allows for creating out of existing material, but it isn't limited to that. It is one thing to study, but if you are going to teach this we ultimately have to come down on one side or the other. The Hebrew syntax is helpful, but it isn't like Greek where we might know for sure.

I guess the biggest problem I have is what the Bible doesn't say, that is finding another example of God creating anything formless and void. It seems to me more likely that the earth became formless and void someway. Now this is pure conjecture. The Bible doesn't tell us why the earth was formless and void, so this is just my theory. We know that at some point God created the angelic host, and some time after that there was a rebellion by Satan and one-third of the angels. My theory is that the battle in heaven between God's host and Satan's rebellious angels is what caused the chaos and darkness in verse 2, and words like "chaos" and "darkness" seem to me to describe sin (Ezekiel 28:11-19; Jude 6; 2 Peter 2:4). The book of Revelation describes an End Times battle in heaven, so the previous battle may have been something like that (Revelation 12:7-9).

Charlie, there comes a time when you either gotta fish or cut bait, so here goes my opinion. I want to put this in context. The most important thing about verse 1 is that it is one of the points along the way to the patriarchs, the promise, the Law and eventually Messiah. Verse 1 is traditionally taken as the first event in creation, the beginning of matter. Because of the Hebrew syntax, I am leaning towards saying verse 1 is a main clause. 'Beginning' is in fact absolute. Verse 1 describes the initial creation event, the beginning of matter. Now this is going to sound like double-talk, but the Hebrew syntax doesn't prevent it. I think verse 2 is an event that does not follow verse 1 immediately, meaning there is a time span between verse 1 and 2. Then verse 2 is describing a re-creation out of existing matter that resulted from a war between God's angels and Satan. Now there is one little problem with my theory. All of the theologians that I respect and trust disagree with my conclusion—go figure.

Having given my opinion on the first two verses, I think more importantly for our purposes, we should be asking how, or if, creation links to the Law. I'll kind of paint the bigger picture of what we are about to study. Chapters 1-11 form the introduction to the Pentateuch (the first five books of the Bible, which in the Hebrew text is the Torah). Moses sets the background for the theology connecting God's creation; interaction through the patriarchs and the Sinai covenant as part of God's plan to His original purpose in creation. The other important implication is that God's character is the basis of everything; creation, personal and corporate relationships, the Law, the Tabernacle, the sacrificial system leading to redemption and eventually new creation. Since God is the Creator, what standard other than His character could there be since He was before all things and created all things?" Philip inhaled deeply, and then took a long draw of coffee. Charlie took a sip of coffee, and then in a classic understatement intoned, "Well this is g-g-going to be e-easy. In two w-weeks we have finished t-two verses."

On Christmas Eve Philip made a run into town to pick up Emma's special gift at the hardware store. He exited the Best Value Hardware store with a three foot by four foot box in his arms and a big grin on his face, proud of himself for selecting such an original gift. He was about to get in his pickup when Fred and a young woman he didn't recognize drove up. "Padre!" Fred yelled out his window. "I was looking for your pickup, hoping to catch you. I want you to meet someone." Fred and his passenger got out and walked over to Philip. "I want you to meet Elizabeth, my baby sister. Elizabeth knows you have been praying for us, that we could get back to being family."

Elizabeth looked a little younger than Philip expected. She had short jet black hair and olive brown skin, and strikingly attractive. But the most noticeable thing about her was her warm smile. "You must be a powerful prayer warrior Mr., uh, I'm sorry, I only know you as Padre."

"It is so good to get to meet you Elizabeth that you can call me anything you want. What in the world has the good Lord done, and how did you get here?" Fred was so excited that he bubbled over and said, "I called her, and at first there was stone cold silence. Then at the same time, we both broke out crying like babies. We didn't say a thing for a long time, we just cried together. Padre, this is the greatest Christmas gift ever."

Elizabeth reached out and took Philip's hand and said, "I want to thank you with all my heart."

"Elizabeth, I didn't do anything more than pray. I will tell you this though; your reunion is meaningful to me because it affirms that God helped your mom and dad create a good family that would stand the test of time. You may have had a time of darkness in your lives, but God is faithful to help you recreate your family." Philip thought to himself, Tozer was right. 'God is here' and in the entire journey, and that is the meaning of Christmas.

Philip's Study Notes, Genesis 1:1-2

(1) The name Genesis found in the English translation comes from the title given by the Septuagint (the ancient translation of the Hebrew Old Testament into Greek). The Greek word means 'beginning.' The Hebrew title is Bereshith; literally 'head' or 'shacking.' The general consensus is that Moses is the author of the first five books of the Bible (the Pentateuch, but those five are also referred to as the Law or the Torah).

Keil and Delitzsch set the scene for verse 1: "Genesis commences with the creation of the world, because the heavens and the earth form the appointed sphere, so far as time and space are concerned, for the kingdom of God; because God, according to His eternal counsel, appointed the world to be the scene both for the revelation of His invisible essence, and also for the operations of His eternal love within and among His creatures; and because in the beginning He created the world to be and to become the kingdom of God."[7] Those are some profound observations. You might want to read that again.

There is a problem in verse 1 that theologians have argued over for ages. There is no article (the) before 'beginning,' so there has developed two primary theological arguments as to the meaning. The traditional reading considers 'beginning' as absolute (in the beginning), but the alternative reading considers 'beginning' as a construct (In the beginning of, or When God created). The alternative reading, a construct, allows for verse 1 to be describing a creation event subsequent to the initial event creating matter. Grammar does not resolve this problem one way or the other.

The dilemma of writing a commentary (study notes) is the knowledge that real theologians argue over these points, but the reader has the right to know what the commentator believes. With all due humility, even in the absence of an article (the), 'beginning' is in the absolute state describing the initial act of creating matter. However, it should be said that there is a difference between eternity past, which had no beginning, and the creation of matter. The God of the Bible dwells in eternity, not matter. As Tozer said, "He is antecedent to creation and independent from it."

The NET Bible has an excellent explanation of the opposing views: "The translation assumes that the form translated "beginning" is in the absolute state rather than the construct ("in the beginning of," or "when God created"). In other words, the clause in verse 1 is a main clause, verse 2 has three clauses that are descriptive and supply background information, and verse 3 begins the narrative sequence proper. The reference of the word "beginning" has to be defined from the context since there is no beginning or ending with God. *In the beginning.* The verse refers to the beginning of the world as we know it; it affirms that it is entirely the product of the creation of God. But there are two ways that this verse can be interpreted: (1) it may be taken to refer to the original act of creation with the rest of the events on the days of creation completing it. This would mean that the disjunctive clauses of verse 2 break the sequence of the creative work of the first day. (2) It may be taken as a summary statement of what the chapter will record, that is, verses 3-31 are about God's creating the world as we know it. If the first view is adopted, then we have a reference here to original creation; if the second view is taken, then Genesis itself does not account for the original creation of matter. To follow this view does not deny that the Bible teaches that God created everything out of nothing (cf. John 1:3)—it simply says that Genesis is not making that affirmation. This second view presupposes the existence of pre-existent matter, when God said, "Let there be light." The first view includes the description of the primordial state as part of the events of day one. The following narrative strongly favors the second view, for the "heavens/sky" did not exist prior to the second day of creation (see verse 8) and "earth/dry land" did not exist, at least as we know it, prior to the third day of creation (see verse 10)."[8]

The name of God in verse 1 is '*Elohim*' which means strong one. It is in the plural form which indicates the superlative such as the strongest one, but also leaves room for the doctrine of the

Trinity, even though that is not the point here. The Hebrew word 'bara' translated 'created' can mean the initial act of creation or can mean recreation out of preexisting material.

If there is a downside to dissecting the Hebrew in verse 1 as though it were New Testament Greek, it is that the primary meaning could be overlooked. Hebrew is very straight forward. What is being stated is that there was a moment in eternity (a beginning) when God caused things to exist leading to the obvious; if God created it, He is Sovereign Lord of all. Lordship, or what was later known as 'the Kingdom of God' is the theme of Genesis.

(2) One must reconcile the condition of the earth in verse 2. There is nothing that prevents there being a span of time between verse 1 and 2. During that time the earth became *"formless and void."*

Allen Ross comments on the chaos mentioned in verse 2: "But 1:2 describes a chaos: there was waste and void, and *darkness was over the surface of the deep.* The clauses in verse 2 are apparently circumstantial to verse 3, telling the world's condition when God began to renovate it. It was a chaos of emptiness, and darkness. Such conditions would not result from God's creative work (*bara*); rather, in the Bible they are symptomatic of sin and are coordinate with judgment. Moreover, God's creation by decree begins in verse 3, and the elements found in verse 2 are connected in creation, beginning with light to dispel the darkness. The expression *formless and empty* (*tohu wabohu*) seems also to provide an outline for chapter 1, which describes God's bringing shape and then fullness to the formless and empty earth."[9]

Conclusion: *"In the beginning God"*—STOP! There is no other! He created it, and He owns it! He is first in all things. He desires to be first in your life.

CHAPTER 9

A Burning Heart
Luke 24

Journalist James C. Hefley captured the life of Jesus beautifully in this piece entitled *One Solitary Life*:

> Here is a man who was born in an obscure village, the child of a peasant woman. He worked in a carpenter shop until He was thirty, and then for three years He was an itinerant preacher. He never wrote a book. He never held an office. He never owned a home. He never had a family. He never went to college. He never put His foot inside a big city. He never travelled two hundred miles from the place where He was born. He never did one of the things that usually accompany greatness. He had no credentials but Himself . . . While still a young man, the tide of popular opinion turned against Him. He was turned over to His enemies. He went through the mockery of a trial. He was nailed to a Cross between two thieves. His executioners gambled for the only piece of property He had on earth while He was dying—and that was His coat. When He was dead He was taken down and laid in a borrowed grave through the pity of a friend. Such was His human life. But, he rose from the dead. Nineteen wide centuries have come and gone and today He is the

Centerpiece of the human race and the Leader of the column of progress. I am within the mark when I say that all the armies that ever marched, and all the navies that ever were built, and all the parliaments that ever sat, and all the kings that ever reigned, put together, have not affected the life of man upon this earth as powerfully as has that One Solitary Life.

A few minutes past noon Easter Sunday found Emma and Philip leaving church service, Emma chit-chatting with everyone. Philip, with a slightly furrowed brow, was in the midst of a minor anxiety attack, trying to get away from the crowd. The definition of a crowd is relative, but for Philip it is anything more than Emma and Coco. With this flock it might be a hundred twenty-five on a normal Sunday, but this being Easter Sunday every seat was filled. Philip was encouraging Emma to "*vamenos su amigo,*" as usual speaking too loudly, since he was hard of hearing from not using ear protection as a child when hunting. From out of the crowd Emma heard the familiar voice of Kim (Felder) Criswell. "Mr. Cole, Mr. Cole!"

Emma had learned to answer for her slightly deaf husband. "Kim, we are over here." Kim headed straight for Emma's voice, pulling her mom like an over exuberant husky on a leash. On arriving, Kim all but shouted, "Mr. Cole, I have to tell you something. We have been studying about the meaning of Easter in Sunday school; you know that Jesus died but he is alive. My mom and I were talking about it last night and she got that little book you gave her to explain God's plan of salvation. And you know what? Mr. Cole, do you know what?" For once Philip was responsive to the leading of the Spirit. He knelt down on one knee and put his arm around Kim. "Yes dear, what happened?" Kim burst out, "I prayed for Jesus to come into my heart. I told

Him I knew I had done some things wrong, but that I was sure glad he paid for that, and that since he was alive I wanted Him to live in me." Philip was speechless. The crowd of humanity he had been trying to avoid didn't exist for a moment in time. There might have even been tears in his eyes, and so he simply gave Kim a big, long hug.

Driving home Emma took note that Philip had not said a word, which wasn't unusual except that this time he seemed to be lost in thought. On the CD was playing an old favorite by Gloria and Bill Gather.

They ate lunch, during which time Philip continued his moratorium against speech, except to compliment Emma on a fine meal. Philip adjourned to the front porch with a cup of coffee and his Bible, while Emma took advantage of the relative quiet of a Sunday afternoon to finish a biography of Amy Carmichael by Elizabeth Elliot. Having lost track of time while finishing her book, Emma glanced at the clock. She noticed it was six-thirty. Philip was not asking about dinner. She thought to herself as she laid the book aside, "Philip must be sick and I didn't even notice." She went to the kitchen, but he was not there. Next she looked out the window towards the barn, but his truck was not there either. Then she noticed his pickup was exactly where he had parked after church. She opened the refrigerator, glanced at the pie, and there was not a piece missing from the previous night. Now she was worried. She rushed to his study, but he was not there.

Philip was on blood thinners for an irregular heart beat ever since he had suffered a heart attack. The doctors warned the irregular beat could cause a stroke. Had he collapsed without being able to call out for help? Was he still alive? Emma felt the heat of white hot emotion swelling within, adrenaline coursing through her veins. Her face was flush. She had repressed the thought that something like this could happen without warning. But that's the way these things happen. Was she ready to face what she might discover in the next few moments? She rushed to the front door to call out for him, but before she could say a word she noticed Philip was sitting in his old wooden rocking chair staring at nothing in particular, the Bible open in his lap.

In an impatient voice she inquired, "What are you doing?" Philip looked up, still with a far off gaze in his eyes. With a nonchalant tone he answered, "I'm not doing anything, and I'm getting really good at it." Incredulously she responded, "It's after six-thirty. Don't you want supper?" In a somewhat unenthusiastic tone he replied, "I guess so." Emma could contain her concern no longer. "No, that's not good enough; what is wrong?" Philip, sitting up straight answered, "Emma, it's the same old thing. I told you forty years ago I love you, and if I change my mind I will tell you so." She sat down beside him. "That's nice to know, but that is not what I am talking about. It's six-thirty and you are not complaining about dinner, and worse yet there is no pie missing. Are you sick?" Finally noticing her sincere concern he said, "I am sick in my spirit, but that is too long a story before dinner. I am physically fine. Let's eat dinner, and then if you still want to talk about it we can come back out here. But it is something you cannot help with. I have to work through it myself."

After dinner Philip poured another cup of coffee while Emma fixed a cup of tea, settling beside each other on their swing on the front porch. Emma sipped her tea patiently waiting for Philip to explain. Philip began, "Emma, I honestly don't know what's wrong, but I saw something in Kim's eyes today that I have lost, and it made me sad. It felt like, if feelings mean anything, like I had wandered away from God. She may be blind, but there was something in her eyes that I can't explain; it was like there was a fire within her eyes. I think it was Immanuel Kant that said, 'the eyes are the window to your soul.' For some reason I thought about the two disciples on the road to Emmaus, and how they said their hearts were burning while Jesus explained to them how the Old Testament speaks of Him. During those forty days between Jesus' death on the cross and ascension, something happened to his followers that changed them from hopelessly wet rags into flaming torches that God used to ignite the gospel to the world. I actually walked into the bathroom to look into the mirror, and all I saw were tired eyes." Emma knew that there are some things that only God can fix. "Philip, I love you. Let me know if I can help."

Early the following morning, Philip was in his study, stoking the wood stove. Coco was in his place on the throw rug. Considering the burden he still felt, he decided to set aside his present study in Titus, deciding rather to do a survey of what the Old Testament had to say about Jesus' death and resurrection. He began with what Jesus had taught the two disciples on the Emmaus Road, *"And beginning with Moses and with all the prophets, He explained to them the things concerning Himself in the Scriptures"* (Luke 24:27, the risen Christ's encounter with two disciples on the road to Emmaus). Philip knew one thing for sure. He needed more than a dead savior. He needed to experience the living resurrected Christ.

Philip had one great advantage; early on in his Christian pilgrimage he was acutely aware of the Holy Spirit's help, and the knowledge of His presence. But he also had one great concern. Since becoming a believer he had consistently studied the Bible, yet for some unknown reason he found himself today coming up spiritually short of what he had seen in Kim's eyes. What had happened?

From the start, he never intended to just know 'about' God; he wanted to know God face to face, just like Paul had prayed for the Ephesians: *"that He would grant you, according to the riches of His glory, to be strengthened with power through His Spirit in the inner man; so that Christ may dwell in your hearts through faith; and that you, being rooted and grounded in love, may be able to comprehend with all the saints what is the breadth and length and height and depth, and* **to know** *the love of Christ which* *surpasses knowledge, that you may be filled up to all the fullness of God*" (Ephesians 3:16-19; the Greek word translated "to know" is *ginomi* from the verb *ginosko* which is to know experientially as contrasted with *oida* which is to know about).

Early on Jesus had told his disciples about what must happen, but they did not understand: "*But He warned them, and instructed them not to tell this to anyone, saying, 'The Son of Man must suffer many things, and be rejected by the elders and chief priests and scribes, and be killed, and be raised up on the third day'*" (Luke 8:21-22; also Matthew 16:21; Mark 8:31). Philip spent a considerable amount of time reading and reflecting on what the Old Testament said about the coming Messiah.

Years ago, sequestered at a Jesuit retreat house several days in prayer, meditating on the twenty-second Psalm, Phillip had written:

> "I watched the Lamb of God hanging between heaven
>   and earth,
> Death held back until His Father was satisfied,
> Those who loved Him helplessly watched,
> Others cast insults at the One dying for them.
> The Passover preparation underway inside the city walls,
> Our nostrils filled with the smell of the Passover meal
> But Your reproach is outside the walls,
> This place made holy by His presence
> Behold, behold, the Lamb of God,
> The self-sacrificing pain and suffering required of love,
>   *It is finished!*"

The old man turned in his study to the resurrection appearances, of which there were eleven. Jesus appeared to Mary Magdalene in Jerusalem when she went to the grave site (Mark 16:9-11; John 20:11-18). He also appeared to some other women that first Easter day (Matthew 28:9-10). He appeared to Peter in Jerusalem Easter Sunday (Luke 24:34; 1 Corinthians 15:5).

He walked with the two disciples on the Road to Emmaus (Luke 24:13-35). Later that same day He appeared to ten disciples in Jerusalem (Mark 16:14; Luke 24:26-43; John 20:19-25). A week later in Jerusalem He appeared to the eleven disciples (John 20:26-31; 1 Corinthians 15:5). He appeared in Galilee to seven disciples who were fishing (John 21:1-25). He appeared to five-hundred at one time (1 Corinthians 15:6). He appeared to His brother James (1 Corinthians 15:7) and to eleven disciples in Galilee (Matthew 28:16-20; Mark 16:15-18). Last, He appeared to His disciples in Jerusalem forty days after Easter Sunday, and then He ascended into heaven (Luke 24:44-53; Acts 1:3-12).

Jesus ate fish with them on two occasions which a disembodied spirit cannot do. His glorified body was different, but it still was a physical body with the marks left by the crucifixion. Philip thought out loud, "Even in His glorified body Jesus still has the nail holes in his hands and feet, and the wound in His side. The only glorified body anyone will ever have in heaven scarred for eternity will be the Lamb of God—what extravagant lovingkindness."

The question Philip always asked at the end of a lesson was, "So what?" Having been seen eleven times by hundreds of witnesses Philip had no question about the fact of the resurrection. His body was real. He needed some time to think these things through; maybe like the disciples; to let the truth of His resurrection sink in. Not realizing he may have been describing himself, several weeks prior Philip had told his pastor, "The problem with the church today is it is filled with people who don't get it. They are paralyzed just like the disciples immediately following Jesus' death. Whether they are believers, or people sitting in church (like Philip had been) who don't know they are unregenerate, they don't get it!" Now Philip was wondering if he was one of those who "didn't get it." All he had to offer was a humble prayer that the Lord might reignite his heart, now and always.

The following week was as busy as usual; taking care of the livestock, mending fences, working off the neverending list of honey-do's Emma always kept, and taking time to check the sights on his old Winchester Model 52D rifle. Philip had traded an old Unertl scope to a collector for the Winchester; obviously the collector was desperate to complete his vintage Marine sniper rifle. (The truth is, if a person could only have one gun on a farm, it would probably have to be a 22 rifle.) As much as Philip loved that old Winchester, he depended on his old Colt pistol for every day use, having it with him all the time. Philip rode the fence line on horseback, detesting the modern four wheel drive contraptions with their obnoxious noise. There is something refreshing about working from horseback. He thought out loud, "If I wanted to breathe in exhaust fumes and hear deafening noise, I would move back to Dallas."

As days rolled by some thoughts were on target concerning the resurrection; many others missed the mark. The women who were Jesus' disciples had gone to the tomb on the first day of the week to finish embalming His body with spices. The angels watching said something so provocative Philip could not get it out of his mind, *"Why do you seek the living One among the dead? He is not here, but He has risen"* (Luke 24:5b-6a).

Philip decided to take a second detailed look at the Emmaus Road story in Luke chapter 24. As the story goes, two disciples of Jesus are on their way home from Jerusalem, three days after Jesus' death on the cross. A stranger encounters them, and they walk together while the stranger explains all that the Old Testament had to say about Messiah, the Christ. While the stranger is explaining the Scriptures, the disciples felt an intense warming in their spirits. The three reach the two disciples home town, and they insist the stranger come in and stay with them. During dinner they realize the stranger is Jesus, the risen Christ.

Many years before, Emma and Philip had taken their first pilgrimage to Israel. Much to his surprise it had been a terribly difficult time of spiritual confusion. He was constantly bombarded with self-centered thoughts, maybe because he had not prepared spiritually. He might have treated this trip as just another vacation. This may have been an attack from demons. He did not know! The problem with demons is they can talk to you through your flesh in first person singular with a Texas accent. Israel was a life-changing experience, but it was also one of the most spiritually challenging times of Philip's life. Oh there were incredible high points like the first view of the Sea of Galilee, the first glimpse of Jerusalem, walking into Saint Ann's Cathedral and joining other groups singing hymns. But generally speaking, it was oppressive with bouts of deep depression.

Then on one of the last days the group went outside the Damascus gate to Gordon's Calvary, where there is a garden tomb much like Jesus would have been laid (First described as a possible burial site of Jesus by Major Gordon in 1887. The Bible says Jesus was crucified outside the city walls, but the present walls are much further north than they were two thousand years ago. The most likely place of burial and resurrection is the gaudy Church of the Holy Sepulcher—my comments). As with most of this trip, once again spiritual depression was oppressive. But then it happened; as Philip turned to leave the tomb, there was a carved inscription in the wooden door which was only visible as one turned to leave: "He isn't here, for He has risen." That inscription had been a God-send of relief from the spiritual depression.

The following Saturday Philip had planned on enjoying some target shooting with his 22 rifle, but he knew he did not have the peace of mind to concentrate. After lunch he told Emma he was going fishing in their lake. "Don't worry about me." He started the trolling motor and maneuvered to one of his favorite spots, but he never took the rod and reel out of the rack. Instead, he kept thinking about what the angels had told Mary, "*Why are you looking for the living One among the dead?*"

A preacher-evangelist friend whom Philip respected greatly had told him that repentance and cleansing always comes before revival in your heart. The truth be known, Philip had lost confidence in his Christian walk, but repentance was an old friend. "Has my spirit been paralyzed by looking for the living One among the dead? Have I made the Bible a substitute for the life-giving enablement of meeting with Him daily? Lord, You know my heart. I know that You have not, and will not withdraw your lovingkindness, but I also know my heart doesn't feel right. Like the two travelers on the Road to Emmaus, You changed lost hope into resurrection faith. I know You live, and I trust You to make that real in my heart."

About then, Philip realized something (or had a revelation, or just figured it out for himself). Feelings are important, but they should never override the truth. The 'truth' is, Jesus has risen from the grave and sits at the right hand of God the Father. The truth is, He is interceding for the Saints. The truth is, He will return in glory for His own, and after that He will return to fulfill the promises to the Jewish nation, ruling from Jerusalem as Lord of Lords and King of Kings. However, we should never treat those eminent truths with casual familiarity.

It is okay to question your feelings because you never want to lose that passion for God. But at the end of the day our hope is in God, not in our feelings. So even when we don't feel good, We can still trust in the Lord. That is enough for this part of the journey.

Philip's Study Notes

A Few Scriptures that Speak of Messiah:

"*He* (an individual from the woman's seed which would be the Anointed one, Jesus Christ) *shall bruise you on the head and you* (Satan; will cause the woman's seed to suffer) *shall bruise him on the heel*" (Genesis 3:15b/John 19:18).

Jesus told the scribes and Pharisees when asked for a sign, "*for just as Jonah was three days and three nights in the belly of the sea monster, so shall the Son of Man be three days and three nights in the heart of the earth*" (Jonah 1:17/Matthew 12:40).

In one of the most fearfully beautiful Psalms, "*For dogs have surrounded me; a band of evildoers has encompassed me; they pierced my hands and my feet. I can count all my bones. They look, they stare at me; they divide my garments among them, and for my clothing they cast lots*" (Psalm 22:16-18/John 19:34-37).

The prophet Isaiah wrote, "*He was despised and forsaken of men, a man of sorrows, and acquainted with grief; and like one from whom men hide their face, He was despised, and we did not esteem Him. Surely our griefs He Himself bore, and our sorrows He carried; yet we ourselves esteemed Him stricken, smitten of God, and afflicted. But He was pierced through for our transgressions, he was crushed for our iniquities; the chastening for our well-being fell upon Him, and by His scourging we are healed. All of us like sheep have gone astray, each of us has turned to his own way; but the Lord has caused the iniquity of us all to fall on Him. He was oppressed and He was afflicted, yet He did not open His mouth; like a lamb that is led to slaughter, and like a sheep that is silent before its shearers, so He did not open His mouth*" (Isaiah 53:2-7/Mark 15:27-32). "*But the* LORD (Yahweh, the self- existent One) *was pleased to crush Him, putting Him to grief; if He would render Himself as a guilt offering, He will prolong His days, and the good pleasure of Yahweh will prosper in His hand*" (Isaiah 53:10).

The Ryrie Study Bible on the significance of the Resurrection:
1. It proved Him to be the Son of God (Rom 1:4)
2. It confirmed the truth of all He said (Matt 28:6)
3. To all men:
    - It made certain the resurrection of all (1 Cor 15:20:22)
    - It made certain the coming judgment (Acts 17:31)
4. To believers:
    - It gives assurance of acceptance with God (Rom 4:25)
    - It guarantees power for service (Eph 1:19-22)
    - It guarantees the believer's resurrection (2 Cor 4:14)
    - It designates Christ as Head of the church
      (Eph 1:19-22)
    - It means a sympathetic High Priest in Heaven
      (Heb 4:14-16)[10]

Commentary on Luke 24:13-35

The Emmaus Disciples (you will need to read along in your Bible):

(13) The first word "*Behold*" or "*Now*" links this event to the Passover weekend which had just been celebrated in Jerusalem; "*that very day*" would have been resurrection Sunday. They were returning home to Emmaus. There were two of them; Jewish law required two witnesses.

Traveling is a major theme of Luke's writings, using it both in the gospel according to Luke and Acts to demonstrate the dynamic progress of the Good News. For instance, in 9:51, Luke stresses the beginning of these events which would tragically end in Jerusalem: "*And it came about, when the days were approaching for His ascension, that He resolutely set His face to go to Jerusalem.*" (In what was a total diversion from his study, Philip remembered that this section of Luke contains one of his favorite verses. Using the Greek text, Philip had translated the verse, "*Lord, how's about we Nuke em'!*" Now if any of you don't believe that is in there just read on. After Jesus "*set His face to go to Jerusalem*" (9:51), He sent messengers ahead to prepare a place to stay, but in Samaria they would not receive him (9:52-53). When James and John saw this they said, "*Lord, how's about we Nuke em'!*" Now read verse 54 for yourself, whatever your translation; but I digress).

(14-16) As they walked they were talking. In these two verses Luke uses two Greek verbs translated "*talking*" to set the scene for Jesus' entrance; "*talking*" *(homiloun)* repeated twice, and the second Greek word translated "*discussed*" *(syzetein)*. What they were talking about was "*all these things which had taken place*"(Passover week: triumphant entry or also known as lamb selection day, tension building in Jerusalem with the plot of the religious leaders, arrest, trials, crucifixion, burial, and three days later the women's report of seeing angels and an empty tomb). Luke introduces Jesus with the emphatic "*Jesus Himself.*" Why they were prevented from recognizing Him is pure conjecture, but perhaps it was because the shock of recognizing Him would have prevented the back and forth conversation where Jesus wanted to explain that all of these events were foretold in the Old Testament Scriptures, including His resurrection.

(17-18) A third Greek verb (*antiballete*) for talking, translated "*exchanging*" is used for their discussion which has the meaning of throwing something back and forth. Note that they are "*looking sad*"—shattered hope. There is a qualitative difference between hope and faith. In the rabbinic tradition, Jesus uses a question to draw out their thoughts and help them arrive at the proper conclusion.

(19-24) Here are some of the things that were being tossed back and forth: Jesus was a prophet in the sense of "telling forth" God's Word. But if only a prophet, He could not have also forgiven sin; He was "*mighty in deed and word*" as demonstrated in His ministry. "*Jesus returned to Galilee in the power of the Spirit*" (4:14); the resurrection affirmed Jesus as much more than just a prophet and teacher. Throughout the synoptic gospels (Matthew, Mark, and Luke) the writers draw the contrast between the people and the religious leaders as in these two verses (i.e., the people saw Jesus as a prophet, teacher, and healer, while the religious leaders saw Him as a threat to their political and religious hold on the people).

As commented on earlier, note that the two travelers *"were hoping that it was He who was going to redeem Israel"; hoping* rather than trusting in faith. The disciples clearly expected Jesus to redeem Israel from Roman rule and institute the kingdom at that time. One thing is clear; Israel, except for a few disciples, rejected Jesus as their Messiah. God wasn't switching from plan A to plan B. Therefore we don't know how He would have provided for the church age if the Jews had accepted Jesus as their Messiah. We do know that their rejection provided our opportunity to become part of the living body of Christ—today you can believe! The last pathetic part of the traveler's report was that they had heard the women's witness, and then also Peter and John's witness of an empty tomb. But they still had not believed.

(25-27) In the Greek text the pronoun *"and <u>he</u>"* (*kai autos*) is emphatic, although *"He"* remains unrecognized (*"him"* in the previous verse is also emphatic). Jesus tells them straight forward that all of these events were the divine plan from before creation. Note that He says their problem was they did not *"believe."* How convicting are our Lord's words to all of us when we lose hope? To Israel today, the Lord says, *"all the things which are written about Me in the Law of Moses and the prophets and the Psalms must be fulfilled."* Blindness on the part of the Jewish people by selective reasoning has led them to omit the foretold suffering servant (Isaiah 53). Walter Liefeld comments, "But 'the Christ' (Messiah, literally the 'Anointed One') did 'have to' (*edei*) suffer. The verb *dei*, meaning 'it is necessary,' is one of Luke's key words (cf. 2:49; 4:43; 13:16, 33; 15:32; 18:1; 19:5; 21:9; 22:7, 37; 24:7, 44) along with the basic passion prediction of 9:22 that occurs also in Matthew and Mark). The future glory of the Christ (v26) was mentioned in the context of the passion prediction, ascribed there to the 'Son of Man' (9:26; cf. 21:27)." [11]

(28-32) Did you know that in Alaska it is against the law to not stop and pick up someone stranded in the wintertime? Different circumstances require different reactions. In Emmaus there probably was not a Motel 6. In those days hospitality extended to travelers, so the two travelers "*urged Him*" (*parebiasanto*, could also be translated "*urged Him strongly*"). When Jesus broke the bread this action is probably not symbolic of celebrating the Last Supper. What is extraordinary was that the guest would break the bread, taking the role of the host. Why the disciples recognized Jesus at this time we are not told. It probably was divine timing, but it also was likely that in His hands they recognized the nail holes; either way it was at the time Jesus acted as host that they recognized Him.

Whatever the meaning of "*Were not our hearts burning within us while He was speaking to us*," their encounter with the risen Christ fundamentally changed their witness from lost hope to realized faith. The word "*burning*" (*kaiomene*) means to set alight, which is exactly what the risen Christ accomplished in the hearts of his disciples, changing their lives from paralyzed despair to faith that took the gospel to the world.

(33-35) So what did they do? Well, as Philip might say, their reaction (faith always causes action) was to "high tail it back to Jerusalem" that very hour to be witnesses to the risen Christ.

William Barclay says:

> The all-important and challenging question in this message is, 'Why do you seek the living One among the dead?'
>
> There are those who regard Him as the greatest man and the noblest hero who ever lived, as one who lived the loveliest life ever seen on earth; but who then died. That will not do. Jesus is not dead; He is alive.

There are those who regard Jesus simply as a man whose life must be studied, his words examined, his teaching analyzed. He is not only a figure in a book, even if that book is the greatest in the world; He is a living presence.

There are those who see in Jesus the perfect pattern and example. He is that; but a perfect example can be the most heartbreaking thing in the world. He is not simply a model for life; He is a living presence to help us to live.[12]

CHAPTER 10

BONDSERVANT OF JESUS CHRIST

Friday afternoon found Philip at the barn in a dust storm of commotion, something Emma described as a "huff of moseys," finishing up the week's chores before Frank Criswell arrived. Philip and Frank had volunteered (make that guaranteed) to provide the catfish fillets for a church fish fry, a gracious gesture for a noble cause. Out here, fifty people is a good turnout for a church dinner.

It just so happened that Philip's lake was full of nice, fat, two to five pound channel cat, perfect for filleting. The only drawback was that they were in the lake. However, considering that the alternative was a long drive to the fish market in San Antonio, Philip assured Frank they could run a trotline Friday night and have plenty of fish for the Saturday church dinner. Emma had dinner ready when Frank, Cathy and Kim arrived about six. After dinner Frank and Philip loaded the pickup with gear, while Emma, Cathy and Kim settled in for an evening of games.

After a short trip to the lake, with Coco running ahead, the men were ready to be fishermen for the Lord. Philip had a small johnboat equipped with a trolling motor, so working the trotlines was going to be easy. After a few minutes to seine for minnows along with a few perch, it was time to lay the trotlines. Philip reminded Frank that the lake has a goodly population of frogs (and where there are frogs there are cottonmouth water moccasins).

Both men carried sidearms, but carefully avoiding a confrontation is always desirable. "Just keep your eyes open Frank." Unfortunately, with night coming on the snakes were out looking for dinner. Philip was busy baiting a hook when Frank warned him what was about to happen, which postponed Philip doing his best demonstration of walking on water. Frank dispatched a big old cottonmouth with his 45. After that little bit of excitement, with Philip's heart still beating like a drum, things kinda settled down.

There were two natural channels in the lake, so the setup was ideal for two trotlines. Laying the lines only took about thirty minutes, so the two pulled out folding chairs for a comfortable night of fishing, with Coco at Philip's side. It was summertime, but in the country when the sun goes down you can depend on a cool gentle south breeze. Emma had made a thermos of hot coffee which Philip poured. A big blue heron across the lake had apparently finished dinner, so he gently lifted off to roost for the night. The two men sat there quietly sipping coffee and listening to the deafening croaking of the frogs. Then everything got quiet for a spell.

Philip had a special admiration for anyone in law enforcement work, considering Rangers the top of that profession. Frank had a whole bunch of good character qualities that Philip admired, but two stood out; his word was his bond, and he was a natural leader of men. He also happened to look the part; one or two inches over six feet with a slender wiry body, topped off with a mustache accenting his slim face. Like all Rangers he knew how to wear a hat, and in fact would have just as soon got caught dead as without his hat outside. Frank was one of those men who didn't take long to figure out what was right and what was wrong, and if it was wrong he was fixing to do something about it.

Frank broke the silence, "Philip how long have you been studying the Word?" For some reason known only to God and little green apples, men don't ask personal questions. But Philip and Frank had long since passed that point and in fact had become friends. Philip took a long sip of his coffee, thinking back on his introduction to understanding the Bible. "Well, other than as a table decoration I didn't care anything at all about the Bible until I became a believer, which didn't happen until I was forty. As far as I could see, the Bible wasn't relevant to my life."

Philip topped off their cups, and then settled back into his chair. "Along in my thirties we had a tree growing farm in East Texas, so we loaded up every Friday night and spent the weekend at the farm. It was a good time for everyone; we had horses, a couple of tractors, a lake stocked with fish, room to shoot, and more work than was possible to get done in two days. After spending the week in Dallas it was nice to wake up Saturday morning in the country."

Frank was surprised that Philip had been 40 before coming to Christ. "I became a believer when I was a teenager, and I can see how that would be easy because a young person is open to things at that age. But how in the world did you become a believer at forty?" Philip took another sip. "Why don't we check those lines and then we can talk some more."

The Lord must not have wanted Frank and Philip to make the long drive to San Antonio, not to mention the personal embarrassment of having to buy fish. They pulled eleven nice fish off the first line and nine off the second line. The fish were secured in a wire cage to keep malicious turtles from having a free meal. Kathy and Kim had gone home, so Emma came down with a refill for the coffee and a basket of oatmeal raisin cookies. It was getting along towards eleven o'clock, so the fresh coffee and cookies were much appreciated by all three, Coco included.

Frank walked to the pickup to get a light jacket, the evening breeze having developed a slight bite to it. Coco curled into a slightly tighter ball. Philip considered building a small fire, but it just wasn't that cold. Settling back into his chair, Frank wrapped both hands around his coffee cup for warmth. "Philip, you have never talked about how you became a believer." Philip's mind surveyed back a little over twenty-five years. "Well Frank, it wasn't very dramatic, you know. No bright light, no deep voice out of the storm cloud." Philip hesitated as he thought about earlier times. "I can remember in my late thirties that I was more or less invited by a few influential people into what I now realize was some pretty dark spiritual stuff that in fact appealed to my ego. However, I also remember a feeling somewhere in my soul that I can best describe as the Lord gently beckoning me to 'come home.' I remember being keenly aware of sin, and I knew it was separating me from God."

It had been a long time since Philip had thought about the events leading up to what turned out to be a life changing event. "It all started when Emma and I decided the kids needed a little religion to round out their experiences, so we visited the small Methodist church near our farm in East Texas. We were ready to go the first time when I got a telephone call early Sunday morning from a customer who wanted a semi-load of trees I already had heeled in on top of the ground. He said that he needed to pick them up that morning. I told Emma we had to stay home because I wanted the money a semi-load of trees would bring in. She understood, but said she and the kids were going on to church.

When church was over Emma went out to the car, only to discover a flat tire. On going back into the church to call me, the pastor and one of the elders overheard her and offered to change the tire. That seemed different to me that the pastor would take off his coat and change a tire, but that was only the beginning of things that were different about that pastor.

The following Sunday something happened that is as clear today as when it happened more than twenty-five years ago. In his sermon the preacher said, 'The Lord wants you to know God face-to-face just like Abraham, and Moses, and David, and John, and Peter, and Paul.' Well, I remember thinking that I didn't know that would be possible for an ordinary person to 'know God face-to-face.' I thought maybe special religious people like Billy Graham or the Pope might know God face-to-face, but not me!

That pastor's name was Charlie, the same as our Charlie here. He stopped us after church and asked where we lived. We told him about the weekend situation, so he asked if he could drop by that afternoon to meet us. I had lots of work to get done, and had no interest in meeting anyone. But only because he had changed that tire I said yes. Charlie showed up at the appointed time, and asked us a few general questions. I didn't know it at the time, but he immediately sized up that we were all lost as ducks.

One Saturday he stopped by again, so I asked him about what he had said about 'knowing God face-to-face.' He presented Emma and me with a proposal. The church had a Bible study every Wednesday night, but since we lived in Dallas he was willing to do something extra if we were serious about knowing God face-to-face. Charlie offered to come out Saturday and give Emma and me a private Bible study through the book of John, but only on the condition that we would read and study the material during the week.

As you know, the Gospel According to John is filled with event after event where Jesus is shown to be the Savior. It's a little embarrassing, but I'll tell you how slow I was. It wasn't until the fourteenth chapter before I finally put it all together, or better said, God finally got through to my hard heart.

I had an amusing experience almost immediately after receiving Christ that showed me the difference between religion and relationship. A new client in Dallas, a serious religious lady who obviously wore her halo entirely too tight, for some reason asked me if I was a Christian. I didn't know the proper passwords yet. As soon as she realized I didn't know how to phrase the answer correctly, she said that if I wasn't 'born-ed again' (intoned in a poisonous religious voice) that I was going to hell. This was one of those persons that could pronounce 'God' with three syl-lables; GU-OOD-D' with the accent on the last 'D.' I remember thinking, whatever you've got I don't want. But in my study of the Word I slowly began to know God face-to-face."

"Okay, then everything turned out good, right Philip?" Philip gave Frank an over the top of his glasses look. "Are you kidding, my business started slowly downhill and never recovered. The fire that I once had in my gut to make money was gone. Everything I had accumulated was now God's, and the fire in my belly was now to know and serve Him. You wouldn't know it now, but at the time we were fairly successful with two houses in Texas. We also had a place in Colorado, Emma was driving a Porsche, and I was in the fast lane out to shove my way ahead of everyone. Now don't get me wrong, I was only an average businessman, but if your heart is in it you can make a good living. But now my heart belonged to Jesus. Let's run that trot line again."

The Lord continued to bless with another eight nice cat on the first line and nine on the second. With the fish stored away and the lines re-baited, it was time to just enjoy the cool night breeze and look up at God's creation. In the country, there are so many stars it looks like a mist of light, with brighter ones stand-ing out, separated by the Milky Way across the middle. The two men just sat there enjoying the peace and each other's company. Coco begged for a second cookie, but other than that was not making himself a nuisance (such as a flying belly flop into the lake).

Frank stretched his legs and then topped off their cups. "Do you have a favorite between the Old and New Testaments?" Phil-ip had to think about that one for a while. "Maybe the Old Tes-tament. I'm not by nature an optimistic person, so it seems like the more I seek God the more often I end up in a desert experi-ence. There are times when just being with God is more neces-sary than theology, so sometimes I just crawl into the Psalms and rest there for a few months. When I am spiritually in the desert, the Hebrew language is so expressive and passionate that I need to know Him emotionally. On the other hand, I couldn't get along without the New Testament to understand what Christ's atoning righteousness has done for us. The two complement each other well because Hebrew is like a watercolor—passionate and expressive—while the Greek is like a pen and ink drawing, precise with each stroke defined. Time to check that trot line one last time." The Lord saw to it there would be an abundance of fried catfish fillets.

The night had turned off so nice that the two agreed to sit a while longer before preparing the fillets. There was still some coffee, so Frank topped off their cups one last time. The dawn was just beginning to break as a great blue heron glided to a landing on the other side of the lake. A coyote trotted by near the end of the lake, nose to the ground, following a scent. Off in the bottom a pack of crows were pestering something, probably the hoot owl that had kept them company earlier in the night. There were a few clouds and the sky was just beginning to turn pink.

"Philip, have you regretted what you've had to give up, you know, the houses, the Porsche, the fast lane, all that?" Philip sat there in silence for a long while, thinking back over the last twenty-five years. "You have no idea how dark my self-centered life was; if anything ever needed to be crucified it was my old self. My soul was blacker than a thousand midnights in a Louisiana swamp. If I had been really smart and successful, I would have been intolerable. I don't know how Emma stayed with me. What I got in exchange was Jesus' righteousness credited to my account and God the Father as my portion. My dad had a saying that fits my feelings about trusting God to make it turn out alright. Dad used to say, 'We'll just dance with who brung us!'"

CHAPTER 11

REBUILDING THE WALLS
NEHEMIAH 1-6

Emma and Philip had finished dinner, so Philip retired to the front porch with a fresh cup of coffee and a slice of Emma's pecan pie. Emma joined him a few minutes later with a cup of tea, foregoing the pie in deference to her waistline. It was turning out to be another beautiful sunset in West Texas, the sky bright blue with the clouds exploding into reds and pinks. The heat of the day was transitioning into a cool evening breeze.

Emma was sitting next to Philip in her rocker with a new novel. Philip had started a study in the book of Nehemiah, so in preparation his normal process was to read the book through two or three times. He was about half way through his second reading when he heard the phone ring. "Emma, it's your turn, can you get that?" Shortly Emma called out, "Philip, it's for you." On the other end of the line was a strange sounding voice with a definite 'big city Yankee' accent Philip did not recognize. "Mr. Cole, this is Lawrence Cohen. I have recently purchased some land in the area and the sheriff suggested I should talk with you." Philip shouldn't have responded in his normal way considering this was a stranger, but he did. "Well, the sheriff is known to sometimes jump to conclusions, and I want to say up front that I am innocent until proven guilty; unless of course you have pictures." There was stunned silence on the other end of the line. "Sorry

Mr. Cohen, you don't know me so I shouldn't have started in that way. What can I do for you?" There was another moment of silence. "The sheriff suggests it might be to my advantage to talk with you." Philip could not imagine what Rusty must have told Mr. Cohen, but he had to respond in some way. "If this isn't an emergency then I'm better at face-to-face, and since we haven't been introduced, I'd like to meet you. Would that be convenient for you? You are always welcome to come by the house, or I will meet you wherever you say." "Thank you for the invitation, I would love to visit your home. How do I get there and would tomorrow morning be too soon?" Philip gave his new acquaintance directions.

The following morning Mr. Cohen arrived driving a black sedan. The moment he exited his car Philip knew this was no native to West Texas. Mr. Cohen was dressed in a black suit, black tie, white shirt, black shoes and black fedora hat. For a moment Philip thought he was back in Jerusalem. Emma and Philip welcomed Mr. Cohen, and then they settled in on the front porch.

Of course Philip didn't know how Mr. Cohen would take his sarcasm, but with Philip what you see is what you get. "You know Mr. Cohen, anything Sheriff Warns says is totally unreliable, so I wouldn't put too much stock with recommending you talk with me. But it is good to meet you." It was only later that Philip figured out that Mr. Cohen was smart as a whip and could read a person before they even spoke. "Well, Sheriff Warns told me about you," he paused for a moment with a slight smile, "implying what you might say, so I thought a visit might be beneficial. I have a problem and I need some advice from someone who lives in the area. As I said last night, I have purchased a parcel of land north of town, intending to set up a retreat house for teachers." Philip interrupted, "What kind of teachers?" "Teachers of the Law, Rabbis. These men sometimes burn out, and they need a place to come to be refreshed. I am now retired. This has been a dream of mine for some time, but with work and all, I was never able to spare the time. Now I have the time and I believe it will be a good thing. I will come to the point. My problem is that my land is surrounded on all sides by a large ranch owned by a Mr. Jacobs from Houston. My deed indicates that I have an easement across Mr. Jacobs land for a driveway, but Mr. Jacobs' foreman came over and said in no uncertain terms that Mr. Jacobs did not want Jews crossing his land. To complicate matters, it turns out Mr. Jacobs is a partner in a large law firm in Houston and he has filed an injunction from using the easement. I have looked into the matter and I do have a legal easement, but by having a law firm supporting him Mr. Jacobs can tie this up in legal issues until I cannot afford to pay the legal fees to win. His foreman suggested I not even try to fight this because Mr. Jacobs has friends in the county and state government. Oh, and please call me Larry."

Anyone suggesting that it was useless to fight for what was right always irritated Philip. "Larry, do you know what they say about ten thousand lawyers at the bottom of the ocean?" Larry looked totally puzzled. Philip completed his thought, "It's a good start!"

Emma came out with a pitcher of iced tea. This gave Philip time to digest the situation. "Well Larry, I'd say you are between a rock and a hard place. I don't know what to tell you, but I do have one question." Larry was obviously an intense person sitting near the front of his chair, weighing each word Philip said. Philip took a sip of tea and continued, "The first thing that came to my mind is; where is God in all this?" "Mr. Cole, I don't understand what you are really asking." "Just call me Philip, but I'll cut to the chase. Is this retreat house God's idea, or is it your idea?" Larry was a thoughtful, straight forward type. He clasped his hands together giving due time to consider the question. "I honestly believe it is God's idea!" Philip smiled, responding immediately, "Well, that simplifies things. Now, what else can I do for you?" Mr. Cohen looked surprised, "I don't mean to seem ungrateful, but what do you mean that simplifies things? I still have the problem to solve." Philip looked up from his tea. "Larry, with all due respect it is not your problem to solve, it is God's problem to solve. It is your problem to be faithful while the Lord works it out.

If God can call Abram out of Ur, free His people from bondage in Egypt, give them the Law, and put up with that band of rebels for these three thousand five hundred years, certainly He can handle a Houston lawyer. After all, you said this is His plan." Larry positioned his right hand on his chin, a little like Rodin's Thinker, considering Philip's hypothesis. "Larry, the question is do you really believe this is God's idea? Let's you and I start praying about this, couldn't hurt. I would like to come out and see your place firsthand." Philip got directions and the two men agreed to meet the following morning at Mr. Cohen's place.

That evening Philip did some research on the internet. It turned out Mr. Lawrence Cohen was a very well respected Rabbi from Chicago, had written half-a-dozen books, and was an adjunct professor at the Jewish Theological School in New York as well as Merkaz Harav Seminary in Jerusalem. Plus he was a licensed tour guide in Israel. Philip thought to himself, "Being from Chicago it might simplify things if Larry would just call up one of the crooked politicians and have Guido fly into Houston and make Jacobs an offer he couldn't refuse!"

The following morning when Philip arrived, Larry was waiting at the locked gate just off the highway. The two men shook hands, and then Larry explained that they would need to walk in since Mr. Jacobs' foreman had chained and locked the gate. "Larry, are you sure this gate is the easement?" "This is it; I affirmed that the surveyor had marked the property boundaries and easement." Philip walked to the tool box in the bed of his truck, pulled out a hack saw and proceeded to cut the lock. Larry looked visibly concerned, after all Philip was still a relative stranger, and he had assumed half of what he had heard about Philip must not be true. Now he was reconsidering. "Is that illegal?" "Yea, probably. Do your best to look inconspicuously innocent." Philip sawed away as though he knew what he was doing. He incidentally commented as he worked, "The effect would be much more dramatic if I just shot it off. I have done that one time, but it's not like in the movies. Little hot metal pieces go everywhere, including back at you. Stings like heck, and you have to make up excuses how you got all those little red spots all over your face." The lock problem solved, the two men got in Philip's pickup and proceeded to drive the property.

There wasn't much conversation, as Philip concentrated on the good and bad features of Larry's property. Having driven out all four corners and one pass through the middle, Philip pulled to a stop on a little hill overlooking an old building site. In one corner they spooked four does and three fawns, in another place two pretty nice bucks, at which Larry was elated. "Philip, what do you think?" Philip removed his hat, wiped his brow with his handkerchief and took another look around. "Well Larry, if you had plans to grow anything except rocks on this place, I would say forget it. I don't see enough pasture to keep a goat alive. It does remind me of some parts of Israel's hill country with mesquite trees instead of olives and tamarisk; however, as a retreat center I think it will do just fine. You've got a good spot for about a twenty acre lake later which would spruce up the place considerably.

Let me ask you one more time about the injunction that the Houston lawyer filed. Do you have a copy with you?" "No, I have not received a copy yet." Philip looked puzzled. "Is it possible a certified letter is waiting for you at some other address?" "No, I am having all my mail forwarded to my post office box in town, and I have been getting mail regularly." Philip got a big grin on his face and said, "Well I'll be dad-gum! This is going to be more interesting than I had hoped. Let's look at your building site."

Larry directed Philip to what looked more like an archeological dig than a home site. There had been several rock buildings which were now in various states of collapse. All the wood roofs, windows and doors had either rotted or been burned. The two men dug around in the ruins for awhile with a stick exposing rusty nails and broken rock. "Do you know what you plan to do?" Larry was more than a little organized. His hand was accentuating his dream as though he was Moses parting the sea. He stepped off each building, explaining the master plan which included using the existing rock to rebuild the main house, and plans for a large combination building that included a meeting room, kitchen, dinning room plus a separate dorm. His plan was to accommodate up to twenty guests, each with private rooms.

Philip listened intently, amazed by the details of Larry's plan already developed. "If you don't have a rock man, Jeff McClintock is more than a fair hand and he is reasonable if you will clearly define your expectations ahead of time. He built our rock fireplace, so you can look at it and see for yourself. But first there needs to be a lot of cleanup, not to mention all those rocks must have the old mortar removed, then stacked in piles of equal thickness.

I'd like to talk to some of the boys and see if we can get a group to have a cleanup party out here." Now it was Larry's turn to look a little concerned, but he felt at ease to talk straight. "Philip, I need to know what I am getting into. Why would you do that?" Philip took off his hat again, wiping his brow while taking another look at the building site, picturing in his mind the completed facilities, and then turned his attention to Larry. "Well, several reasons. One, the Bible says, '*And I will bless those who bless you, and the one who curses you I will curse. And in you all the families of the earth shall be blessed*' (Genesis 12:3). Our Savior came from you. Secondly, you are now living in West Texas and these folks tend to do that kind of thing. Thirdly, and most importantly, I will have someone to argue the Scriptures with." (Before all you literate people get agitated about how the Pistolero Padre writes, Winston Churchill had this to say about prepositions, "From now on, ending a sentence with a preposition is something up with which I will not put.") The two men shook hands on it, and Philip hauled Larry back to his car. As Larry was about to get in his car Philip called out, "Larry, I've got a feeling God is working."

Philip high-tailed it into town and made the rounds of those he thought might help. He started with Charlie Marsh, Philip's pastor who assured Philip he could get several more men from the church. Next was Sheriff Warns who Philip laid a guilt trip on, so he was in. Then Johnny Smith the local vet obliged. These along with several others volunteered, then Philip made his way out to Frank Criswell's place. By the end of the day, Philip had rounded up more than a dozen men willing to spend time working at Larry's place.

Philip called Larry to explain the situation, informing him that some of the men would start early Monday morning and several wives had volunteered to provide lunch on the grounds. Philip assured Larry that the men would not work at his place on Saturday, and being Christians they had the same situation on Sunday. Larry said he did have one serious concern. "What about the locked gate and the threat passed on by Mr. Jacob's foreman?" "Larry, there is no guarantee that it will work, but we have changed this from a Jew crossing the Jacob's ranch to a good cross section of the community crossing the Jacob's ranch. Anyway, you have never received that restraining order, and I haven't run out of hack saw blades. See you Monday morning."

Monday morning the gate was locked again, so Philip and Sheriff Warns took turns sawing on the lock. That little task finished, half a dozen men proceeded to the building site and organized into teams. Rabbi Cohen was there dressed in new jeans, long sleeve shirt, work boots, and a straw hat. Excepting for looking like he just stepped out of a Sears catalog, he was just one of the boys. The lumber was cleared away first and burned. Larry had hoped to save some of it, but it was hopelessly rotted. At noon, the women showed up and served fried chicken, potato salad, beans, cold slaw, biscuits and iced tea. Heck, it was worth working just for the grub.

During lunch there was time for the helpers to get to know Larry. One of the wives asked, "Tell us what a Rabbi does?" Larry considered the question carefully, searching for the best way to explain a system that has been in flux for more than 3,000 years. "At the present time there are learned men of good character who are arguing that very point." Philip, having traveled to Israel several times, thought to himself, 'I can't imagine Jews arguing.' There is a saying in Israel, 'Where there are two Jews, there will be at least three opinions.' Philip laughed to himself.

Larry, however, was doing his best to provide a lucid answer. "I tend to take the position explained recently by Dr. Frankel, Chief Rabbi of Dresden, but paraphrased in my words. To explain in biblical terms, Judaism knows no priest in the sense of clergy. There is also the misconception that a Rabbi is a sort of High Priest to the congregation. In the sense of the duties prescribed for the sons of Aaron, a Rabbi cannot discharge those solemn duties. There is no present sanctuary, no sacrifice for atonement from which the blood is sprinkled on the Mercy Seat in the Holy of Holies, no necessary pilgrimage to Jerusalem to celebrate the required feast, or any other priestly duties performed on the Temple Mount in Jerusalem.

Fundamentally, a Rabbi is a teacher. In ancient times there was one other duty of the Rabbi, which was called the Beth-Den. It was the rabbinical court of Judaism, the foundation of the Jews legal system. It still exists, but to a lesser degree, and its authority is limited to Jewish religious life only. It was not until the sixteenth century that the congregation elected their rabbis. Today a Rabbi is a seminary graduate, but that is only the beginning since a Rabbi must be a person who has dedicated his life to studying the Scriptures; as a result they are looked to as the teachers. But one most important point, every Jew is responsible to study and be a learner from the Scriptures."

There was a little excitement that first afternoon. A couple of the men were moving and cleaning rocks when they came across a good size rattler. Apparently they don't have many rattlers in Chicago, so Larry got a little excited. The next thing he knew there were four men and one woman with handguns out ready to settle the issue. Frank, the ex-Texas Ranger always drew first choice on a deal like this, but he deferred to Lester Hayes since he was one of the men cleaning rocks. It took Lester two shots, so there was a fair amount of good natured kidding going on afterwards.

That evening Philip and Emma adjourned to the front porch to enjoy the sunset. The porch ran the entire length of the house, so there was plenty of room for Philip and Emma's rocking chairs, large and medium size, a table with four chairs, and a glider/swing big enough for two to sit comfortably. It was nice just to sit next to each other in the glider. He put his arm around her shoulder. They enjoyed being together (you have to be married to the right person for 40 years to know what that means).

Philip being warm natured tended to radiate heat as Emma snuggled into his side in the cool of the evening. Philip's mind drifted to the first time he saw Emma, at her parent's house in Dallas. She was a vivacious young woman with captivating azure blue eyes, porcelain skin, and long blondish straight hair down to her waist. Having graduated the year before from the University of Oklahoma, she had applied to several school districts. But with the summer vacation coming to an end, she still had no offers. One week after their first date, a last minute opportunity opened at her first preference. So a week later she was teaching school in Tulsa, from which a long distance courtship developed. About three months later, on one of Philip's visits, they went to the Tulsa Opera to see Giacomo Puccini's Madam Butterfly, and fell in love. Little did he know this beautiful young woman would become his lifetime partner. She was a woman of character, whom he had grown to love more each day. Is there a greater blessing than a faithful wife who loves you?

Emma got up to get a sweater and Philip's attention turned to the events of the last couple of days. An unexpected encounter with a stranger (one of God's chosen no less), stiff opposition, potential conflict, faith in God's purpose, the work to be done. Zechariah 4:6 came to mind: *"Not by might nor by power, but by My Spirit, says Yahweh of hosts."* This was going to be as much, or more, a spiritual battle than a physical one. If this is God's plan then the battle belongs to Him, and yet there is neighborly work to be accomplished also. Philip thought how Nehemiah's heart had been broken at hearing the report of destruction in Jerusalem. Jerusalem, the place where Yahweh had chosen to cause His name to dwell; Yahweh, who preserves the covenant of lovingkindness. A little fasting and prayer couldn't hurt.

Still sitting with Emma, his thoughts coursed about the character of God and His *hesed* (lovingkindness). For some reason the old man found himself reminiscing about some children he had observed the week before playing a game. If you ever questioned depravity, just watch children for awhile. A puppy wanted to be in the middle of their games, but they would shove it away. One even picked up a stick and hit the precious ball of fur. It yelped, but came right back in the middle of the action. Yahweh who preserves His covenant of lovingkindness can be something like that puppy. They beat Him almost beyond recognition; cast insults as He hung on a Roman cross. But Jesus loved us enough to pay for our sins with His life.

As was his habit, Philip spent the early morning hours in the Word. A little kindling in the wood stove plus an oak log, and the room warmed pleasantly. Coco, who had followed Philip out of the bedroom, positioned himself on his rug in front of the stove. A sip of coffee would precipitate a visit with his old friend Nehemiah.

The dawn was just beginning to break so Philip roused Coco from a sound sleep so that they could walk and talk with the Lord. The Nehemiah study somewhat paralleled the situation with Rabbi Cohen; the walls were torn down and opposition from a powerful Houston attorney could be intimidating, even when you know who is really in control. Philip certainly didn't think he had the solution to the problem and cutting locks was at best temporary and at worst downright illegal. It is one thing to call someone's bluff; it is entirely another thing if they are not bluffing. Philip spent some time walking and lifting up the situation to the Lord.

Work on the cleanup was going well. The gate was no longer locked but that was only a false sense of security. Philip arrived home one evening tired from working on the cleanup. Emma had been to the post office only to find a certified letter waiting for him from a Houston law firm. In no uncertain terms the letter threatened legal action against Philip if he continued to cross Mr. Jacob's ranch. Philip called an attorney friend in Dallas only to be told that under our system of jurisprudence just about anyone could sue anyone and the one with the deepest pockets usually wins, and no he wouldn't take the case pro-bono. Things just got a little more personal, and I don't mean personal between Philip and the Houston lawyer. Things got personal between Philip and the Lord; now who was he going to believe?

For obvious reasons Philip's study of Nehemiah took on a little more meaning. Now was a small moment of truth. Luckily Philip wasn't a deep thinker so he went with his gut, loaded up Coco and headed for Larry's place to work for the day. Philip decided not to mention the lawyer's letter to anyone figuring that if anyone else received one he would hear about it. About mid-morning Larry pulled Philip off to the side and mentioned that he had received a letter demanding that he not trespass on the Jacob's ranch, but that he was committed to continuing the work. Philip didn't mention that he had received one also, not wanting to put additional pressure on Larry, which is probably what the threat was intended to do. The way Philip figured it, his job was to be faithful to the Lord and encourage Larry.

Many Christians had termed their journey with the Lord as being "a fool for the Lord," which is exactly what Philip and Larry must have felt like as they happily laid out the outline for the house with a string line. It was only a line in the dirt, but it represented a promise of future service to the Lord. Larry got so excited that they also laid out the combination building (conference room, kitchen, etc) and the dorm. Philip could see the wheels turning in Larry's head as he envisioned more than just buildings, but teachers of the Law being encouraged and refreshed.

It would be nice to say Philip's resolution was so strong that the threat of being dragged into court didn't bother him, even if it was by a Houston lawyer who probably made more per hour than Philip did in a month, or a year. Philip had joked with Emma in the past that if he passes on and if she wanted to re-marry he would understand, as long as she did not marry a lawyer. A lot of our so called justice system is in fact a threat system, but there is also such a thing as believing you're right, for which you may very well lose and pay the penalty. Either way Philip had decided he had to follow the Lord as best as he understood, so a Houston lawyer wasn't going to stop him from his normal appointed rounds.

The cleanup of the building site was completed, and Larry contracted with Jeff McClintock to do the foundation, rock work and framing. Philip was busy catching up on work at his own farm, so a couple of months went by without Philip talking with Larry. One afternoon while Philip was working at the barn (or loafing according to Emma), Larry drove up. "Philip, I would like to have you and Emma and the volunteers come to a dedication of the house. Anyone is welcome, but I especially want to be able to officially thank all those who helped. I have a group from the congregation in San Antonio who want to come over, so it will be an ecumenical feast, a celebration to the Lord." Philip expressed how proud he and Emma would be to attend.

At the dedication, the local community was well represented. You didn't have to ask which ones were the guests from San Antonio and who the locals were. The group from San Antonio was dressed like Larry when he first met Philip. Being summer, the locals were dressed in jeans, long sleeve shirts, boots, and straw hats.

Philip was talking to some of the folks that had come over from San Antonio, having just been introduced to a distinguished guest who was part of their party. Philip peered over the shoulder of the woman he was talking with and noticed a silver Suburban coming down the drive at a pretty good clip. Sure enough, none other than Mr. Buford 'Jake' Jacobs from Houston stepped out, acting like he owned that part of Texas. He was wearing dress slacks, blue dress shirt with alligator boots and a belt set off with about a pound of silver. He was the type of big city lawyer that wanted people to think he was a rancher, but who simply was so talented he had to work as a lawyer in Houston. Before he even opened his mouth, Frank Criswell sized him up, whispering in Philip's ear, "Typical dude, big hat no cattle."

Jacobs proceeded to see if he could properly impress this group of common country folks. He demanded to know which one was Lawrence Cohen, kind of an imperative command he must have used when in court. Frankly the whole ostentatious performance made Philip angry. Here was a rich loud mouth from Houston who couldn't hold a candle to Larry intellectually, yet the system allowed him to push people around.

Emma could see what was coming, but wasn't quick enough to stop it. Philip stepped forward, blocking Jacob's way. He punched his index finger into his chest that had to have left a bruise, looked down on the smaller man, and then stuck his hand out to shake and squeezed it hard until he could see Jacobs jaw lock down. He decided to keep shaking and not turn lose for the moment. "Good to finally meet you Mr. Jacobs, and good to have you drop by to welcome your new neighbors. Let me introduce some of the guests to you. There is Sheriff Warns; Frank Criswell retired Ranger and his wife Kathy, Pastor Marsh and his wife, the man of the hour with the vision to bring this place of restoration for teachers, Rabbi Lawrence Cohen. I'm Philip Cole, oh and the distinguished lady I was talking to when you drove up, Texas Supreme Court Justice—the Honorable Rachel Levine. There is also a fine group of citizens from San Antonio and of course our small group of local citizens." Still locked down on Jacob's hand, Philip continued, "It would sure be nice if you could share lunch with us." Jacob had been caught out of his element where he was sure to have the upper hand. He looked around at the diverse group, and then offered: "Maybe another time, just wanted to say welcome. It was good to meet you folks." The Suburban left as suddenly as it had come.

Charlie had asked permission to bring the church choir, which was enough to make the hair on the back of your neck stand up and chills run up and down your spine. They sang a selection of songs, including the following:

"O Come, O come, Emmanuel
And ransom captive Israel,
That mourns in lonely exile here,
Until the Son of God appears,
Rejoice! Rejoice! Emmanuel
Shall come to thee, O Israel!"[13]

It was almost time to have lunch, so there were prayers by Larry and the Rabbi from San Antonio. But then Larry asked Philip to pray. Taking a cue from Nehemiah's prayer, he looked up (Philip was in the habit of praying with his eyes open looking up, but he was also mindful of what his old Prof would say,

"Dinner's not the time to get caught up on your prayer life"):

"Holy God, may Your glorious name be blessed
And exalted above all blessing and praise!
You alone are the Lord, and there is no other
And the heavenly host bows down before You.
You alone can restore what has been torn down.
Next year may we all meet in Jerusalem where You have
chosen to have Your Name dwell? Selah!
Let's eat!"

Some weeks later Philip dropped by to see how the first retreat had gone. Larry was very pleased, but now he was working on refining the program. Philip could stand the suspense no longer, so finally the conversation got around to Mr. Buford Jacobs. "Whatever happened to that injunction?" Larry smiled, placing his hand on his chin. "You were right from the start. This was God's battle to win. It turns out the injunction was never filed, and the word from an acquaintance in Houston is that Mr. Jacob is up to his briefs in legal trouble, something about illegal contributions to politicians." Philip fired up a little 'Thank You Lord.'

"By the way Philip, what was that about when Mr. Jacobs drove up?" "Oh Larry, I guess it's true that the Lord takes care of fools. I shot up an arrow prayer and everything else was just reacting poorly to the circumstances." "Did you pray for wisdom?" "I wish! No, I prayed for strength in my right hand." "What?" "Oh, it's not important other than to explain that I was operating out of what the New Testament calls the flesh, which is never good. That little peacock from Houston strayed over into my sandbox, and I decided to take him down a notch. But I'm not proud of what I did, even if it did work. I was acting no better than Jacobs, just one bully against another. I sent him a hand written apology."

Sometimes the journey is by way of the Lord protecting the foolish, but in that arrow prayer Philip had also reminded the Lord what He had said about Abram and his descendents: "And I will bless those who bless you, and the one who curses you I will curse. And in you all the families of the earth shall be blessed" (Gen 12:3). Selah!

Philip's Study Notes, Nehemiah 1-6

Nehemiah's name means "Yahweh comforts." The books of Ezra and Nehemiah were originally one book, called I Ezra and II Ezra. In Hebrew, II Ezra is entitled "The Words (or history) of Nehemiah." Jerome was the first to distinguish between the two books. Nehemiah covers a time period of about twenty-five years (457-432 B.C.).

Nehemiah is divided into two parts: the restoration of the walls of Jerusalem (chapters 1-6) and the restoration of the people (chapter 7-13). The theme is God's sovereign grace and mercy in restoration.

Originally Yahweh had established a corporate relationship with Israel, promising to bless them as a nation if they were faithful to Him alone and followed His commandments—or judging them if they were unfaithful. The history of even the best kings and the people was a good beginning, but ended in failure. The people were unfaithful, following after false gods. So God allowed the kingdom to be divided in 931 B.C. God's promised judgments were sure, with the northern kingdom falling first to a foreign power by the Assyrians in 722 B.C. Then the Babylonians conquered the southern kingdom, in the process destroying Jerusalem in 586 B.C. The people of the northern kingdom were absorbed into other cultures. With the second deportation (by the Babylonians), the southern kingdom remained generally a unified culture, even when deported to Babylon. The Medes and the Persians conquered the Babylonian empire in 539 B.C., at which time some Jews returned to their homeland. Those returning Jews eventually rebuilt the temple in 515 B.C. In 458

B.C., another group returned led by Ezra. When Ezra arrived, he found the Jews had intermarried with surrounding nations and were also worshiping other gods. Ezra called the people to return to Yahweh and set the spiritual groundwork for Nehemiah's entrance upon the scene. In 444 B.C., Nehemiah returned to rebuild the walls of Jerusalem, despite fierce opposition from surrounding nations.

(You will need to read along in your Bible with the commentary. Remember what my old Prof says, "It is amazing how much light the Bible shines on commentaries.")

(1:1-4) Nehemiah ben Hacaliah ("ben" in Hebrew being "son of." Hacaliah is contracted from "wait for Yahweh; thus Nehemiah's name was "Yahweh comforts, son of wait for Yahweh"). It cannot be overstated that especially in the Old Testament names had great significance.

While in Susa as cupbearer to the Persian king Artaxerxes, Nehemiah received word from his brother Hanani (abbreviated form of "Hananiah" which means "Yahweh is gracious") who had returned from Judah saying, *"The remnant there in the province who survived the captivity are in great distress and reproach, and the wall of Jerusalem is broken down and its gates are burned."* Nehemiah sat down and cried for days… *"fasting and praying before the God of heaven."*

(1:5-11) Nehemiah prays, *"O Yahweh God of heaven, the great and awesome God, who preserves the covenant of lovingkindness for those who love Him and keeps His commandments."* "Awesome" means to fear and revere. The word translated "lovingkindness" is the Hebrew *"hesed"* which has too much meaning just to be translated "love." *"Hesed"* has the meaning of benevolent loyalty, grace, mercy, and steadfast love through thick and thin (usually related to a covenant). Nehemiah quotes Yahweh's promise in Deuteronomy to regather His people, if they will follow His commandments, to *"the place where I have chosen to cause My name to dwell."* The walls had been destroyed by Nebuchadnezzar's army one-hundred forty years earlier. Many scholars believe Nehemiah's distress was because there had been a failed attempt to rebuild the walls earlier (Ezra 4:6-23). But it is more consistent that the reproach Nehemiah felt was because of his devotion to the honor of God, and having the place He had chosen to cause His name to dwell in ruins.

When was the last time you cried because God's name had been disregarded? Nehemiah's prayer was to the "awesome" God (loved, feared, and revered). Jerusalem, the place in which Yahweh chose to have His name dwell, was in ruin. Our God is the One "*who preserves the covenant of lovingkindness for those who love Him.*" He loved us that we might love Him. And where does His name dwell now; inside those who are 'in Christ.'

(2:1-8) About four months passed between the time Nehemiah received the report about the conditions in Jerusalem and this encounter with King Artaxerxes. Nehemiah had been able to conceal his sadness, but now his burden for Jerusalem betrayed him. A servant allowing his feelings to interfere with his duties was not respected, so Nehemiah rightly had great fear when the king took note of his countenance. As would be expected, Nehemiah's answer to the king was straight forward: "*Why should my face not be sad when the city, the place of my fathers' tombs, lies desolate and its gates have been consumed by fire?*" The king asked, "*What would you request?*" '*So I prayed to the God of heaven.*'" (I didn't know they knew about arrow prayers back then, I've had to rely on those for years). Nehemiah never forgot that even though he was standing before the most powerful king on earth, even more he was standing before "*the God of heaven.*" Nehemiah responded, "*Send me to Judah, the city of my fathers' tombs, that I may rebuild it.*" Nehemiah was also a practical manager, so he asked for the necessary authorization for safe passage and materials to rebuild the walls.

(2:11-16) Anyone familiar with the present day 'walled old city' would not recognize the City of David's walls Nehemiah inspected. The walls Nehemiah is describing would have extended south to include the Pool of Siloam, with the southernmost gate, the Dung Gate immediately south of the pool. The city was very narrow north and south, extending on each side of a ridge leading up to the present temple mount. It would have continued north about the width of the present temple mount, but extending north to include only about three-fourths of the present temple mount. The Kidron Valley was to the east and the Tyropeon Valley to the west, the south walls ending at the junction of the two valleys.

(Many years ago Philip bribed a Moslem guide to take him and Emma through Hezekiah's tunnel leading from the Gihon Spring south to the Pool of Siloam. The waters are ice cold and the tunnel is much lower than his six-three frame. That same year he also bribed a guard at the gate to the present Moslem cemetery on the east side of the temple mount. The East Gate, presently walled in, is "forbidden to infidels." But this is the place Jesus Christ will enter the temple mount when He returns. Both areas are now generally accessible to tourist from the outside graveyard, depending on the political situation at the moment).

(2:17-18) Nehemiah's personal testimony was that Yahweh (the self-existing One; God told Moses, 'tell them I AM, that I AM.') was in this project to rebuild the walls. Plus he had the king's personal authority to do so. There is a world of difference between hoping something will happen (one young boy described hope as "wishing for something that ain't going to happen.") and faith that moves the heart to act. God clearly worked in their hearts. They said, *"Let us arise and build." "So they put their hands to the good work."*

(2:19-20) Anytime you are doing God's work, plan on opposition. This is normal; being a servant of God isn't for wimps. Nehemiah's confidence in *"the God of heaven"* would have surely encouraged the leaders and the people. He answered the opposition's challenge that they would not stop them, but that when they finished, *"you have no portion, right, or memorial in Jerusalem."* A leader must never falter in their dependence on God.

(3:1-32) This section is important in that it describes the gates (ten in all), thus giving the rough dimensions of the city. Some scholars have suggested the walls would measure about two and one half miles, so the inner city would be about 220 acres; others suggest the walls were no more than two miles around, enclosing about 90 acres.

(4:1-23) Sanballat and Tobiah, the chief political opponents of Nehemiah, cast insults in the form of five sarcastic questions (vv1-3), but Nehemiah did not stop work to war against them. Instead he prayed because he understood that such opposition was spiritual in nature (v4). As the walls rose, so did the opposition's anger and rhetoric. Therefore Nehemiah posted guards, but he did not stop work. Nehemiah encouraged the builders by reminding them to *"Remember the Lord, who is great and awesome,"* because He alone is to be feared. Throughout the book Nehemiah considers that the project is God's, the challenges are to God, and the victory will be God's. Have you noticed a pattern? Take note that Nehemiah's first response to opposition is prayer!

(5:1-5) Chapter five describes the economic crisis Nehemiah faced. The people were oppressed by taxation on top of a famine, while at the same time the king accumulated vast sums of wealth. One commentary states, "At Susa alone Alexander (the Great) found nine thousand talents of coined gold (about 270 tons) and forty thousand talents of silver (about 1,200 tons) stored up as bullion. As coined money was increasingly taken out of circulation, inflation became rampant."[14]

Did you ever wonder why most of the gold is in Fort Knox? History continues to repeat itself until the Lord returns to rule with a rod of iron. There isn't much difference between old King Artaxerxes and that bunch of politicians and lawyers in Washington DC.

(5:6-19) The Old Testament discourages debt, and since the people had failed in faithfulness to Yahweh, He withdrew His blessings on the land. The consequences were in full bloom. Under taxation, inflation, and famine, the people had gone into debt (does that sound familiar?). If a person could not repay the debt, the family was taken as collateral, and the women were turned into sex slaves (what is the cost of sin?). Even though the Bible forbade it, many were even sold to Gentiles. Nehemiah convinced the loan holders to give back the excess interest they had charged. As governor, Nehemiah had the right to be provided a food allotment. But in order not to be an additional burden on the people, neither he nor his brothers accepted any for the entire twelve years he was governor.

(6:1-19) Sanballat, Bobiah, and Geshem the Arab tried to lure Nehemiah into a trap by offering a meeting, but Nehemiah was too dedicated to finishing the walls to fall into their snare (vv1-9). Next, the opposition paid Shemaiah ben Delaiah to try and deceive Nehemiah to hide in the temple, but he did not fall for that trap either. Only the priest could enter the temple; had Nehemiah gone into the temple his testimony would have been ruined. Because Nehemiah refused to be distracted from God's work, the walls were rebuilt in fifty-two days, September 21, 444 B.C.

CHAPTER 12

THE WOMAN AT THE GAS STATION
JOHN 4:1-38

Philip and Emma had planned on a trip to Big Bend area for some time. This part of Texas is most unusual in its range of scenery; in the morning you can be walking in the Chihuahua desert while the afternoon's adventure affords a hike through a pine forest in the Chisos Mountains.

The surrounding area also provides excellent rock hunting, which was one of Emma's favorite addictions. Emma had planned the trip so naturally it was the most indirect way possible circumventing any reasonable expectation Philip had to "make good time." Emma figured that since we were going that direction anyway, every rock in that part of the world was fair game. Philip, with substantially less enthusiasm, figured if you have seen one rock you have seen them all.

There is a place in West Texas called Balmorhea where rock hunters go to find something called Balmorhea Blue agate. Once again, to Philip it was just a white rock with a little blue in it, but to Emma you would have thought it was the Hope Diamond. It turned out the Balmorhea area was beautiful (if you like West Texas, which Philip and Emma did). Located near by is Balmorhea State Park which includes the San Solomon Spring, producing twenty-two million gallons of sparkling clear spring water per day. In the 1800's the spring was called Mescalero Springs, after the Mescalero Apache who ranged in the area for eons. All of this is located in the foothills of the Davis Mountains, but Emma's heart was in the hills outside of town. They had gotten off to a late start from home, so they over-nighted near that area with the intent to get a fresh start early the next morning. Philip had to admit one thing, there were plenty of rocks. But Balmorhea Blue was going to take some serious rock hunting.

Philip considers himself a hunter (meat hunter that is), but after walking miles with his neck crocked over looking at the ground, finishing his latest book by a Texas Ranger, staring up in the sky, kicking ant beds, using a twig to duel with a spider, etc., enough was enough. Emma on the other hand was happy as a tick on a hound dog. There was one other peculiarity of their rock hunting adventures. Emma could stay still in one place so long, exploring every speck, that invariably buzzards would circle above to see if she might be their lunch. It sounds gross, but it always made her easy to find—not if but when she wandered off.

It was late morning, so Philip decided to venture into town to buy a couple of hamburgers and soda pops for lunch. He didn't mind leaving Emma for a bit, since on such expeditions she carried a Smith and Wesson J frame 357 with a three inch barrel, and loaded it with a good 38+P round. She could outshoot him any day of the week. There were also other rock hunters around, so with Emma's agreement he headed for town. It was a short drive, but when Philip got there the hamburger place was closed with a sign that said "Open 11:45." With a little less than an hour to kill, he decided to top off the gas tank and look for a shady spot to sit and read.

The gas station, the only gas station, was run by a lady with the personality of one of those rocks they were looking for. She was a nice enough looking lady (he guessed in her mid-thirties), but had no expression. Having been in competitive business himself for many years, it always irritated the old man when someone gave less than heartfelt service. The gas pump readout didn't work, so when you finished the lady figured out how much you owed. That was okay with Philip, but he expected a smile or maybe a "thank you," neither of which he got.

Philip had run out of water in his canteen that morning and seeing that the gas station didn't sell bottled water, he asked the lady if she had a drinking fountain. Without even looking up she responded, "No, there's only a faucet in the back office." Again Philip asked if he could use the faucet. She still didn't look up from her magazine. "Why didn't you bring your own water?" For some reason, this sparked in Philip's mind the woman at the well in John chapter four. Had God ordained a divine appointment? There was only one way to find out.

Philip walked over to the counter, reaching in his pocket for cash to pay for the gas. "May I ask you a question?" There wasn't much enthusiasm, but she did say "Okay." Philip shot up one of those arrow prayers. "Are you a Christian?" She replied, flipping pages without looking up, "I am a Baptist!" Philip had tossed the lure out there, but the lady didn't seem that interested. However, Philip continued, "I was a Methodist for years but didn't know Jesus Christ from a telephone pole. It wasn't the Methodists' fault. It was my hard heart. Do you know Him personally?" Somewhat bothered by being forced into a conversation, she sighed and replied, "I don't have to know Him, that's the preacher's job." Remembering how Jesus didn't give up on the woman at the well in Samaria, Philip wasn't going to give up on her. Picking up the change, he stuffed it back in his pocket. "I asked you for water, and if you knew Him like I do you would have asked me for living water." She still wasn't nibbling yet, but she did at least look up. "Mister, you're the one with no water. I have all the water I want." "The water you have will never quench your thirst, but the water I was talking about wells up like those springs out at the park. The water I am talking about gives eternal life."

There was a lot of praying going on from Philip during all this. She finally engaged the conversation. "Well then, give me a drink!" Philip leaned on the counter. "May I ask you a personal question?" The lady didn't say no, so he continued. "Do you have any sin in your life? If Jesus was here He could look in your heart and tell, but I can't do that. The Bible says, '*All have sinned and fallen short of the glory of God.*'" Tears welled up in the woman's eyes. "Why do you care?" Seeing how the questions affected her, Philip's heart was touched with compassion. "Because I know God cares about you and I think He sent me here." The tears now turned into a steady steam. "I wasn't married and got pregnant. I gave up my baby to adoption. I go to church, and I pray, but it doesn't help." Philip never felt so helpless, and by this time he had leaky eyes too. "I cannot imagine the pain you must feel. I am going to say something and you are going to have to believe the truth; God loves you."

He continued, "God is looking for people just like you to worship Him in truth and spirit." Still crying she said, "I don't know how!" Philip took a deep breath, looked her straight in the eyes and in a very slow, deliberate manner shared the gospel. "**Jesus** said to the woman at the well in Samaria, '*an hour is coming, and now is when the **true worshipers** shall worship the Father in **spirit and truth**; for such people the **Father seeks** to be His worshipers.*' I want you to know that it wasn't just a man standing in front of her, it was **Truth and Spirit embodied**.

God knew what would happen to us, but '*God **demonstrated His love** for us in that while we were **still sinners** Jesus died **for us**,*' as a **sin offering**. *He who knew no sin became sin on our behalf that we might become the righteousness of God.* '*Christ **died** for our **sins** . . . He was **buried** . . . He was **raised** on the third day, according to the Scriptures . . . He **appeared** to Peter, then to the eleven. After that He appeared eleven times to more than five hundred . . .*'" '*As many as **received** Him, to them He gave the right to become **children of God**, even to those who **believe** in His name.*' It isn't something you do; salvation is something God does. Jesus said, 'Behold, I stand at the door and knock; if any one **hears** My voice and **opens** the door, I will **come in** to him.'

You can **receive** Him now! Do you want to do that?" There seemed to be a different woman standing in front of him. "Yes!" Philip was awestruck at what God was doing in this woman's heart. Well, it was lucky no one else came in to find an old man and young woman crying tears of joy. Philip went to the truck, got one of his Bibles and gave it to her. "Read this, and I suggest you start in the gospel of John." He wrote his telephone number and email address in the front, telling her to call him anytime.

Philip picked up the hamburgers and drove back to where he had left Emma, listening to the music on the CD,

"To God be the glory, great things he hath done;
So loved he the world that he gave us His Son,
Who yielded His life an atonement for sin,
And opened the life gate that all may go in."[15]

On arriving back he looked for the buzzards and located where Emma had wandered off. When he walked up with the hamburgers she asked, "What took you so long and why are your eyes red?" Philip gave his sweetheart a little smile and said, "I had to go through Samaria!"

That evening they overnighted in a lodge nestled in the Davis Mountains then the following morning turned south for the next adventure. Big Bend National Park is a treasure. Located in West Texas where the Rio Grande, dividing Texas from Mexico, makes a huge southern bend dipping deep into the Chihuahuan Desert, a true sanctuary of nature. It consists of over eight-hundred thousand acres (now that's a real Texas spread) of deserts, rivers and the Chisos Mountains. The park is home to mountain lions, javelinas, black bear, deer, plus all sorts of lizards and birds (including peregrine falcons). If you are a nature loving hiker this is the place to be, but that is another story for another time.

Philip's Study Notes
Commentary, The Woman at the Well, John 4:1-38

(1-3) Jesus' early ministry in Judea was causing concern on the part of the religious rulers (Sadducees and Pharisees) based in Jerusalem. The number of people becoming His disciples was increasing and it was reported that He was baptizing many of them. It was not time to confront these religious and political leaders, so Jesus determined to take His ministry up north to the Galilee region.

(4) *"And He had to pass through Samaria."* Jesus, or any orthodox Jew, would never pass through Samaria unless it was absolutely imperative. Jesus *"had to"* (*dei*, an expression of general necessity) indicates God's will or plan.

"Samaria" was populated by "descendants of two groups: (1) The remnant of native Israelites who were not deported after the fall of the Northern Kingdom in 722 B.C.; (2) and foreign colonists brought in from Babylonia and Media by the Assyrian conquerors to settle the land with inhabitants who would be loyal to Assyria. There was theological opposition between the Samaritans and the Jews because the former refused to worship in Jerusalem."[16] Jews considered even traveling through Samaria to be defiling.

The normal trail a devout Jew would take from Jerusalem to Galilee would be the east road following the Wadi Gulch to near Jericho, then north following the Jordan River up to the Sea of Galilee.

(5-6) Sychar and Jacob's well were located near the base of Mount Gerizim about 50 kilometers north of Jerusalem. Mount Gerizim was the center of Samaritan worship. This area was historically important: near here at the Oak of Moreh, Yahweh promised the land of Canaan to Abram (Gen. 12:6-7); Jacob destroyed the idols brought from Mesopotamia (Gen. 35:2-5);

the Levite priest gave the first reading of the Law in the Promised Land when Joshua lined up half the people towards Mount Gerizim and half towards Mount Ebal to illustrate the mount of blessings or the mount of curses (Josh. 8:30-35); and Joshua gathered the tribes for his farewell address reviewing Israel's history (Josh. 24:1-28).

The sixth hour would have been noon. In that culture the women went to the well together early in the morning, which was a necessity turned into a social gathering. Because of her past, it is likely that this lady was an outcast, not welcome to be part of the other women's early morning social group.

(7-8) Jesus' request was normal for a traveler to ask for a cool drink in the heat of the day. But a Rabbi would not be willing to carry on a conversation with a Samaritan woman, much less drink from her cup.

(9-15) The woman acted offended, but Jesus was more interested in her soul than in winning an argument. Jesus used a normal rabbinic method of applying a secular earthly question to a spiritual problem ("*If you knew*") to help the woman arrive at the right spiritual conclusion. The woman responded that if he wanted to talk spiritually, "we Samaritans claim Jacob as our father."

Jesus' second reply contrasted what the well water offered and what He was offering—temporal versus eternal; physical versus spiritual. To obtain the water in the well required labor; what He was offering would flow naturally. The verb "*springing up*" in v.14 is *hallomenou* which has the meaning of quick movement as in jumping. She still didn't 'get it.'

The woman intends to put Jesus in His place by asking a question that surely He does not consider Himself greater than Jacob. In the Greek a question prefaced with "*un*" anticipates a negative answer, but Jesus has yet much to reveal. Merrill Tenney commented, "Two different words are translated "well" in this incident. The first, in v.6, is *pege* which refers to the source of spring discovered by Jacob. The second word *phrea* used in vv.11-12 denotes the shaft dug into the ground to reach the water. The well tapped a subterranean spring that never ran dry. God supplied the water, but access to it was gained through a man. Now, one greater than Jacob was offering through himself access to water that would satisfy throughout eternity."[17]

(16-18) As the teacher (rabbi), Jesus continues to control the conversation and transitions to the personal, *"Go, call your husband."* His request (even though conforming to social correctness of that day because a man should not talk to a woman without her husband being present) aimed at the woman's greatest need before God which was to recognize her sin. Jesus, knowing the necessity of repentance before salvation continued to drive home the point: *"You have had five husbands and the one you have now is not your husband."*

(19-20) Having had her need exposed and recognizing that the man before her had spiritual insight, the woman asks for the religious solution. She raised the old religious argument between the Jews and Samaritans worshiping on Mount Gerizim or in Jerusalem.

Moses had commanded the people to build an altar on Mount Ebal (immediately adjacent to Mount Gerizim) and that the tribes should divide half on Gerizim and half on Ebal (see comments on vv 5-6); *"these shall stand on Mount Gerizim to bless the people: Simeon, Levi, Judah, Issachar, Joseph, and Benjamin. And for the curse these shall stand on Mount Ebal: Reuben, Gad, Asher, Zebulun, Dan, and Naphtali"* (Deuteronomy 27:12-13). The Jews counterargument was that Yahweh commanded Solomon to build the temple in Jerusalem, and therefore the center of worship must be there. To this day there continues to be sacrificial worship on Mount Gerizim.

(21-24) Jesus elevates the argument even higher by addressing an eternal perspective to her question. God is not in a place. He is spirit, which required more definition. So Jesus tells her,

"*Salvation is from the Jews.*" The Samaritans had worshiped several gods, but first she must understand the absolute "truth" that Yahweh alone is God.

(**v. 23**) "True worshipers shall worship the Father in spirit and truth; *such people the Father seeks to be His worshipers.*" The woman is concerned about where to worship. Jesus is concerned with whom to worship. The woman is looking for religion. Jesus is about to tell her He is the One. He is Truth and Spirit embodied. The solution she needed is a person, not religion.

(**25-26**) The woman expresses what only God could put into her heart, "*I know that Messiah* (both names, the Hebrew Messiah or Greek Christ means the one who has been anointed) *is coming, when that One comes He will declare all things to us.*" Jesus turned hope into faith: "*I who speak to you am He.*" This is the most improbable of circumstances; Jesus had to go (the Father's will) through Samaria for a divine appointment with one woman, an outcast because of her sin. But Jesus transformed her from being an outcast into his first evangelist—extravagant, marvelous, miraculous, unexplainable, unpredictable, wonderful lovingkindness.

(**27-38**) The disciples returned from town with food while the woman hurried into Sychar to tell the people about her encounter. As usual, the disciples were operating from an earthly perspective, concerned about food to give their leader strength. Jesus takes the opportunity to contrast the fulfillment of doing His Father's will.

The Samaritans, wearing their normal cream colored robes, flowed out of Sychar to see if what the woman had said was true. It must have looked like a field of grain ready for harvest. Their receptiveness was a demonstration that the spiritual harvest was ready. Each generation reaps the harvest of God working through believers who came before them; conversely each generation should plant for the next generation.

(**39-42**) "*And from that city many of the Samaritans believed* *in Him because of the word of the woman who testified."* The two key ingredients in evangelism are included; personal relationship with Jesus and the testimony of those who believe to bring them to Jesus. Because of their encounter with Jesus, the Samaritans said to the woman, *"It is no longer because of what you said that we believe, for we have heard for ourselves and know that this One is indeed the Savior of the world."* Do you know why being an evangelist is easy and everyone can do it; it is our job to take them to Jesus by explaining the gospel; it is God's job to save them.

CHAPTER 13

THE END OF THE TRAIL
2 TIMOTHY

The pickup bounded along the gravel road heading for town, as the old man drove with tears leaking from his tired eyes. This would be the last trip for Philip and his beloved dog Coco. His closest friend had been with him fifteen years, long for a dog's life, but far to short for parting with the one who was at his side most of the day and night. For those fifteen years there was never a time when Philip returned home that his faithful friend was not there, anxious to be with him. The two had hunted together, baled hay together, road the fence line together, spent hours upon hours in Philip's study together and generally knew each other's whims without a word being spoken.

The old dog had grown hard of hearing, so in later years he seemed to be oblivious to some of Philip's commands. But that dog could be sound asleep at the other end of the house while Philip sneaked into the kitchen, and with the touch of a safe cracker gently lift the lid off the cookie jar only to find Coco standing at his feet waiting for a treat. When they went to the pasture Coco had developed the habit of running along in front of the pickup, and then abruptly stopping to take a dump in the middle of the road just to see if the old man could stop. This usually caused an outburst from the old man, questioning the dog's heritage. This was all a game to Coco to amuse his companion. But Coco had come to the end of the trail, and Philip felt like he must be at the end of his too! Coco's heart, which had been healthy all of his life, must be giving out. He had seizures all night, the old man at his side praying and holding his companion, hoping to provide some comfort.

The pickup came to a stop in front of Johnny Smith's veterinary clinic, and the old man carried his friend inside. Johnny stopped what he was doing to look at Coco, but there was nothing he could do; Coco's heart was giving out. Johnny did what had to be done, and Philip carried Coco's lifeless body back to the truck, placing him in the seat he always occupied. Emma had enough sense to leave Philip alone, as he buried Coco on the hill overlooking the lake.

Standing there beside the grave, Philip paused a moment. "Father, thank you for the gift of Coco. His race is over. I feel like my race is about over too. Lord, I've been charging hell with a bucket of water for a long time. I'm tired. I feel like the angels are beckoning me to heaven's door, for I have only been a sojourner in this world. If there is anything more you have for me to do on this side, you might oughta show me pretty soon." There will be a time when the curse of death will be no more (Revelation 21:4). But for now, parting is such sweet sorrow.

Johnny waited several days, but made a point to drop by Philip's to see how the old man was doing. They went down to the barn where they sat on a couple bales of hay and talked for a spell, Philip relating some of the adventures he and Coco had together. A year or so earlier, Philip had done marriage counseling with Johnny and Jodi. Philip made sure to ask about Jodi and all was going well. Johnny then mentioned that actually he had come by for two reasons. "Padre, I have watched you for a long time and I admire the fact that you study the Bible. I want to get serious about knowing the Bible, but I don't know how to do it right."

Philip gave Johnny's question due consideration. "Well, you start with a healthy relationship with Jesus Christ. That may sound too simple, but it is easy to get into the Book and lose sight of the life that gives it meaning. It is possible to become an educated idiot, believe me I have done it several times. So if I can help you avoid that pitfall, that would be my first advice. The Bible must be made alive by the Holy Spirit; He must become your teacher and counselor. But there is one other thing. I should think it over before I say anything." "What is that?" Johnny asked. Philip struck out without thinking, "I just said I should think it over first!"

There was a long pregnant pause, Philip realizing his words were cutting. "Look Johnny, I'm sorry. For the first time in memory I feel old; but the truth is I already know the answer. Every child of God should have three people in their life—someone who is a Barnabas to encourage them, a Paul to disciple them, and a Timothy they invest their life into. I have never felt so near the end of my trail as I do now, and I guess the good Lord is telling me to invest in a Timothy before I cross the Jordon. Now you need to be the one to think it over because being a Timothy with me comes with expectations. You think about it and get back with me. It couldn't hurt to pray about it either."

Philip awoke earlier than normal, so rather than fighting the bed he decided to get up, fix a pot of coffee, and adjourn to his study. Coco's little throw rug was still by the wood stove, but it would have to stay there for a while longer. Seeing the rug, Philip couldn't help but hurt down deep, but in self-defense he turned his attention to where to start if Johnny wanted to take on the task of seriously being discipled.

At the moment the old man's feelings were so self-centered, he drifted toward Paul's Second Epistle to Timothy. When Paul wrote this last letter he was confined to a Roman dungeon, in chains cold and dark, awaiting sure execution at the order of

Emperor Nero. His race was all but run. Paul had left Timothy in Ephesus as head of the church there, with instructions to keep sound doctrine and discipline in the face of Satan's twin counter-attack of Judaizers and Gnostics (Judaizers teaching law plus grace and the Gnostics teaching that Christ was not resurrected in bodily form—all material things being evil). Philip decided that this was as good of place to start as any to develop the bonds of discipleship with Johnny.

Johnny waited about an hour past sunup the following day, and then called Philip's house and left a message with Emma. Philip got up early and rode off on Cody, his horse. That evening Philip called Johnny at home, and they agreed to one morning a week to start with. Philip also gave Johnny a little homework. "I want you to start reading 1st and 2nd Timothy and Titus. These three are called the Pastoral Epistles because they address pastoral care for the churches. Just read these slowly two or three times and we will start our detailed study in 2nd Timothy when we meet."

Johnny arrived promptly at 5:30 AM, so the two got a fresh cup of coffee then sat down in Philip's office to begin. "Let's talk for a minute about Bible study in general. You already know I believe the original manuscripts are inspired, without error. However, that does not mean my interpretation is without error, and it doesn't even mean your translation is without error. You will need to learn how to check out what I say for yourself and verify for yourself. But to cut to the chase, with the exception of the disclaimers I just gave you, I believe 2 Timothy 3:16 and 17, '*All Scripture is inspired by God and profitable for teaching, for reproof, for correction, for training in righteousness, so that* (purpose statement to follow) *the man of God may be adequate, equipped for every good work.*'

The historical background for these three letters is that Paul had been released from his first imprisonment in Rome. He traveled to Ephesus where he left Timothy to head up those churches. He traveled to Macedonia where he wrote the first letter to Timothy. He then traveled to Crete where he left Titus to supervise those churches, and then to Nicopolis where he wrote the letter to Titus. Later he was arrested a second time and imprisoned in Rome where he wrote the second letter to Timothy just before he was martyred."

Philip opened his well worn Bible to 2 Timothy and the two began to study. When there was a break after the first few verses, Johnny, with more than a little hesitancy in his voice, interrupted to ask, "This may sound stupid, but why are we starting in Second Timothy instead of his first letter?" "Good question, but the answer is stupid. It is because that is where I need to be at the moment. I feel lonesome and near the end of my journey like Paul was, but my only confinement is a hole in my soul. That's the way I feel, so you get to overview the three letters while I get to study what I need at the moment, kapeesh?

Paul gives thanks to God for putting him and Timothy together. I don't understand God's providence, but I can tell you looking back over my life, which I seem to be doing a lot of lately, I can honestly say everything I have planned so carefully hasn't worked out, and yet the Lord has blessed me every step of the way. But enough about old scars and lost loves." Johnny looked over at Philip, wondering what that was all about. But Philip continued on, never missing a beat. "Paul is grateful to God for bringing Timothy into his life to continue the work he started. Johnny, I commit to praying for you like Paul did for Timothy, but I have often wished I had a tender heart like Paul.

Studying the Bible is important, but Paul and Timothy were more than teacher/student. They were co-laborers in the greatest work ever undertaken. You know they must have talked about more than theology. I talked with Frank Criswell the other day and he said he needed a few does taken off his place to keep the doe to buck ratio in line. What do you say we go over there Saturday afternoon and see if we can't harvest a little meat for the freezer?" Johnny thought that would be a good idea.

Saturday morning Philip took care of chores, and then gathered up his hunting bag. In this part of Texas a long shot can be seventy-five yards, so a 30-30 lever rifle with open sights would be perfect, except for old eyes. Philip had a Winchester Model 94 in 38-55 which he traded for an overdue debt years earlier. But since it was manufactured in 1895, it was a collector more than a shooter, and there was no way Philip was going to mount a scope on it.

Philip reached in his gun case and pulled out a 257 Roberts he had built on a small-ring Mauser 96 action. With a twenty-two inch barrel, it was a quick handling little carbine, and his homemade stock fit Philip just right. He found himself taking in a deep breath, which reminded him one thing was for sure; his spirit was still so low he could walk under a snake with his hat on. Everything would be fine until he turned a corner expecting to see Coco, who wasn't there. Philip didn't want to forget Coco because they spent fifteen good years together. But love is painful! Just ask Jesus about pain because of love.

The veterinary clinic was on the way to Frank's place, so Philip dropped by to pick up Johnny. Johnny had a beautiful 99 Savage in 308; beauty being in the eye of the beholder which was Philip's eye towards the 99 Savage. Emma had made Johnny and Philip sandwiches for a late lunch, which they ate on the way to Frank's house. While driving, Philip remembered what Emma had told him: "Johnny, I'm suppose to tell you Emma suggested that we might switch our study in two weeks from morning to night. We would like to have you and Jodi over for dinner, so Emma can get to know Jodi better." Johnny said he would talk to Jodi and call, but considering Emma's cooking, we could plan on it.

Frank met them at the house and took them to their stands.

Philip's personal preference was not to hunt over bait, so he set up in some brush overlooking the convergence of two trails near some thick underbrush that would make a perfect bedding area. The rut had long since passed, but Philip wasn't hunting a buck anyway. He was a meat hunter and hoped to find a dry doe that was past her prime, but would still make good venison roasts. About forty-five minutes before sundown Philip heard a shot from the direction in which they had dropped Johnny off. Then ten minutes later a big doe walked out. Philip waited to see if a yearling was following, but none appeared. He rested the rifle against his shooting sticks and touched off the trigger. Johnny and Philip prepared their deer for transport side by side. Johnny's was to go to the processing house and Philip's to the barn to be cut into roast and back strap the next morning.

The following week Philip had a surprise for Johnny. Philip had asked that the study be changed from their normal time to Monday and for Johnny to schedule to be off all day. Johnny was able to change his schedule, so the date was set. Philip didn't want to lose sight of this arrangement, being discipled through the Bible study. Philip had arranged through Frank Criswell, retired Texas Ranger, to have access to the city jail in Lubbock. Philip picked up Johnny and Frank extra early and the three headed north at a pretty good clip (I know, it's a sin to speed, but I just confessed it). On the drive up the three went over the Four Spiritual Laws tract. Armed with the gospel and a handful of New Testament Bibles for anyone who received the Lord, the three were ready to do battle with the devil for the souls of men.

On arriving at the jail, they spent awhile just praying for a harvest with special thanks to God for the opportunity to serve His glory. Sergeant McCoy, the chief jailer, met the three at his office to explain the ground-rules, and then each was provided with an escort and they headed out to do battle. These kinds of visits are always unpredictable, but the Lord is always gracious. The three intentionally did not keep count, but at the end of the day they were out of Bibles and had only a few Spiritual Laws tracts left.

I don't think Johnny's feet were touching the ground; he just seemed to be floating. The three had been so busy they had skipped lunch. Sergeant McCoy agreed to have dinner with them and they all ordered the greasiest Chicken Fried Steak smothered in yeller gravy in Lubbock. It was all good. Philip popped in a Steve Green CD and the three headed south with a contented grin on their faces, cholesterol coursing through their veins, and a thankful heart for the opportunity to share Christ.

As usual, there was a lot of work to be done around the farm. A couple of the neighbor's cows had gotten into Philip's pasture, so there was the need to ride the fence line to find the weak spot. For some reason known only to God and little green apples, Philip decided to ride Emma's appaloosa, Porsche (that's right, she gave up the car for the horse, which the best Philip could figure was considerably more expensive to upkeep than the car). Anyway, Porsche was used to little Emma, so when Philip saddled up (who weighed about twice as much as Emma), there was no end to the disgusted looks coming from that horse. This resulted in a wicked grin on Philip's face, kind of a payback for all the times Porsche had stepped on Philip's boot. But, both of them enjoyed the outing and Porsche desperately needed the exercise.

As planned, the following week Jodi and Johnny came to dinner. It was refreshing for Philip to hear a young couple talk about their hopes and dreams. Jodi was looking forward to becoming a mother, and Johnny was scared witless of becoming a father with the added responsibility. The two were settling into becoming one. Emma fixed venison tenderloin, pickled tomatoes, homemade creamed corn, and twice-baked potatoes, topped off with apple pie.

After dinner, Jodi and Emma adjourned to the front porch with tea, while Johnny and Philip had a cup of coffee. Philip had intentionally planned to spend some personal time with Johnny (like Paul and Timothy must have), but he also wanted to know how the home reading was going. "What is your impression of the three pastoral epistles?" Johnny thought for a minute, and then replied, "There was no blueprint to follow like we think of denominations today. But Paul is dealing with the essential elements of what would become the church structure, all in the face of opposition." Johnny may have been young, but he was smart as a whip. "That's a pretty fair observation." The four spent the remainder of the evening playing dominoes and getting to know each other a little better.

Work on a farm is never done. Philip went about his business taking care of the few head of cattle he was raising. The two horses required constant attention and Emma always kept the honey-do list full. Philip decided not to get another dog. The pain of missing Coco as he went about his daily chores did present occasions to reflect on the pain of lost love on a higher level than man and dog, such as the love God must feel for those who will never receive his gift of salvation. Holy God who cannot look on sin so loved us that He gave His Son as a payment for the sins of the world. If we will not accept Jesus, then He will not accept us. But it must pain Him greatly; the pain of love beyond our imagination.

Emma noticed that from time to time she would need Philip for something or another, but he was nowhere to be found. One evening she went looking for him. She took a short walk towards the lake, and from a distance saw Philip's horse tied to a bush and the old man sitting on the side of the hill next to Coco's grave. She guessed the two of them just needed their time together, so she turned around and went back to the house. The journey can be lonely sometimes, but death is not stronger than love.

Philip's Study Notes
Paul's Final Days, Well Done Good and Faithful Servant

"For I am already being poured out as a drink offering, and the time of my departure has come. I have fought the good fight, I have finished the course, I have kept the faith; in the future there is laid up for me the crown of righteousness, which the Lord, the righteous Judge, will award to me on that day; and not only to me, but also to all who have loved His appearing" (2 Timothy 4:6-8).

Bible study is more than parsing verbs, word studies, or reading the Greek text. Sometimes we just need to ponder the subject matter. What was in Paul's soul when he wrote those poignant words above? Paul, the greatest theologian who ever lived, had come to the end of his trail. He had finished his course, and he had kept the faith. Paul quotes phrases from the Jewish burial service as observed by David Stern, "O True and Righteous Judge! Blessed by the True Judge, all of whose judgments are righteous and true."[18]

What memories of obedient service to his Lord must have coursed thought Paul's mind? He was born into a privileged family with both Jewish and Roman citizenship. His home town of Tarsus was the seat of a most highly regarded university with a reputation exceeding even Athens and Alexandria. At thirteen, he was sent to study under the celebrated rabbi Gamaliel in Jerusalem. He was a zealot of the first order, a fanatical partisan for Jewish tradition and against what he considered to be the heresy of Messianic Jews.

The religious zeal of the day against Messianic apostates is illustrated by Richard Longenecker who quotes from a Qumran psalmist, "The nearer I draw to you, the more am I filled with zeal against all that do wickedness and against all men of deceit. For they that draw near to you cannot see your commandments defiled, and they that have knowledge of you can brook no change of your words, seeing that you are the essence of right, and all your elect are the proof of your truth (1QH 14.13-15)."[19]

But then, by God's grace and mercy, Paul came to faith as he journeyed to Damascus for the purpose of arresting those he believed to be Messianic apostates. A blinding light so powerful that it knocked him to the ground appeared, followed by a voice from heaven, a *bat-kol* (in Hebrew literally "daughter of a voice" of God), that of Yeshua HaMachia, saying *"Saul, Saul (Paul's Hebrew name), why are you persecuting Me?"* Then, *"I am Yeshua whom you are persecuting."* It is one thing to have to deal with followers of a dead martyr; it is an entirely different situation to be confronted by the risen Yeshua face to face. Yeshua would use a man named Ananias in Damascus to restore Saul's sight, but first He said to Ananias, *"Go, for he (Saul) is a chosen instrument of Mine, to bear My name before the Gentiles and kings and the sons of Israel; for I will show him how much he must suffer for My name's sake "* (Acts 9).

The primary theme of the remainder of Paul's life was to carry the gospel of grace to the *goyim* (the pagan Gentile nations). Philip thought, after two thousand years of God's mediation to humans through the descendents of Abraham, now Yeshua was establishing His new covenant, the theology of which would be explained by this brilliant Jewish theologian. It is perhaps just as important to put things in perspective, that except for Yeshua's prerogative we would have never heard of this insignificant Jewish zealot from Tarsus.

Paul's biography was certainly impressive, but the power was the fire within that urged him always onward towards the finish line, and not just to complete the course but to finish well. How during his time in Arabia, his mind must have raced 'to connect the theological dots.' God's redemption plan (by grace through faith in Jesus' completed work at the cross, plus nothing) was explained to him. How Jesus must have explained the righteousness of God apart from any religious merit on the sinner's part.

How doubt must have crept into his mind as his outreach was limited to the relative confines of Jerusalem and Damascus for many years. It was Barnabas who invited Paul to go with him to Antioch, not the other way around. But once God set Paul's course to take the gospel to the *goyim* by planting churches, there was no stopping him through three missionary journeys, until he was executed by Rome.

As dramatic as Paul's three missionary journeys were, it was his message of grace that was earthshaking. Doctor Luke, who recorded Paul's journeys in the book of Acts, developed the theme of grace in his own writings when he recorded Jesus reading Isaiah 61:2, but ending mid-sentence (Luke 4:16-21). Jesus read the first half of the sentence about proclaiming the year of the Lord's favor, withholding the second half denoting judgment in the day of vengeance of our Lord. God's Messianic blessing was to be poured out during the age of grace, extended to Jew and Gentile alike, to be followed by a time of judgment still in our future. It would be far too simplistic to say Paul was the apostle of grace only, considering his influence on Christian thinking is a primary theological source for the doctrines of justification, redemption, reconciliation, the church, unity in the body, and the diversity of gifts (just to mention a few). He was ultimately the messenger and defender of grace.

But now, chained to a Roman soldier, Paul awaits certain execution at the order of Nero. Nero, a pervert of the first order would go down in history as a testament to insane egotism. Paul would be remembered as a bondservant of Jesus Christ to the praise of God, of whom it was said, "well done good and faithful servant."

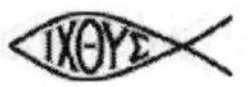

Philip's Study Notes, 2 Timothy

(1:1-5) Paul says he is the author of this book. He may have used a secretary—some say Doc Luke. Paul identified himself in all his epistles by his Greek name *Paulos* (born a Roman citizen to Jewish parents) rather than his Hebrew name *Saul,* because he was an apostle to the Gentiles. An apostle was an office of authority instituted by Christ; who must have been called by Jesus, which Paul was by the risen Christ on the road to Damascus (Acts 9:3-8). The Greek word *apostello* is a compound: *apo,* from; *stello,* to send; or the common word used today, *ambassador.* An ambassador represents the one who sent him. After John died, the last of the apostles, the office did not continue except in the mind of a few vain individuals.

Paul then says, *"by the will of God"* which is a curious Old Testament phrase to use here. Barclay says, "No Christian is ever chosen entirely for his own sake, but for what he can do for others. A Christian is a man lost in wonder, love and praise at what God has done for him and aflame with eagerness to tell others what God can do for them."[20] Paul adds, *"according to the promise of life that is in Christ Jesus."*

'In Christ' is a common theme of Paul's which has the connotation of Christ living His life through the believer, especially as the believer progressively surrenders dominion to the Lordship of Christ. Your journey will be to surrender, not to study. Studying the Bible is a means to an end only. It's all grace; you surrender—He transforms you. Sally Rackets said, "Jesus gave His life for us, that He might give His life to us, that He might live His life through us."[21]

Paul addressed Timothy as *"my beloved son,"* which was how close they had become. Years earlier, on Paul's second missionary journey, Paul met Timothy at Lystra where he asked Timothy to join the mission. It is probable that Timothy was converted as a result of Paul's first missionary journey. It isn't important if it was through Paul's preaching or if Timothy's grandmother and mother came to faith first, and then led Timothy to faith. Either way God had to do the saving. Anyone who is the pastor of a church, such as Timothy was at Ephesus, can use all the "*grace, mercy, and peace from God*" they can get. His words here express a tender love for Timothy as if Timothy was his son.

(1:6) Paul goes on in verse 6 urging Timothy to "*kindle* (fan into flame) *the charisma, the gift of God.*" The word *charisma* comes from the Greek word *charis* which means grace. Paul is telling Timothy that God has given him a special equipping or enablement to minister to the church, and that he should fan that into a burning hot flame.

(1:7) Ralph Earle comments on verse 7: "Paul is fond of making a negative statement and then following it with three positive ideas, thus giving the introduction and three points of the outline for a textual sermon (cf. Rom 14:17). Here he says that God has not given us a spirit of 'timidity' (*deilia*, 'cowardice,' only here in the NT), but rather a spirit of 'power' (*dynamis*), of 'love' (*agape*) and of 'self-discipline' (*sophronismos*, 'self-control,' only here in the NT). This is a significant combination. The effective Christian worker must have the power of the Holy Spirit (cf. Acts 1:8). But that power must be expressed in a loving spirit, or it may do damage. Often the deciding factor between success and failure is the matter of self-discipline."[22] That's a mouthful that Earle just said, and it might be to your advantage to ponder his comments for awhile. I'm not real big on three part sermons, but the remainder of his thoughts are interesting.

In verse 7, the NAS translation has 'Spirit' capitalized. The Ryrie Study Bible has this note, "a spirit, denoting the human personality under the Spirit's influence as in 1 Cor 4:21; Gal 6:1; 1 Pet 3:4. But the reference to the Holy Spirit at the end of this section (1:14) makes it likely that it begins this way also, so that the Holy Spirit is the referent."[23] This seems to fit with what I see as Paul's theology of the meaning of being 'In Christ.'

(1:8-18) Paul now begins a new section from verses 8 to 18. The Ryrie Study Bible outline titles it "The Call of a Soldier of Christ," which is about as good as any. Paul's strength and courage was a result of seeing every circumstance in his life as being part of God's providence. You and I both know that using God's providence can be an excuse for why things didn't go right. But for one who lives by faith in Christ living His life through him, it is a spiritual perspective that empowers and sustains. Paul is literally chained in a dungeon awaiting execution, yet by God's providence you and I are the beneficiaries of this letter.

(1:8-11) The four verses (8-11) are all one sentence in the Greek—crummy English but good Greek syntax. Paul's logical sequential thought process just dumbfounds me. If Timothy is controlled by power, love, and discipline (the proceeding verse 7), then he would be victorious against the opponents of the truth which Paul had preached. Now I know this isn't a scholarly illustration, but the following long sentence reminds me of those old World War II battleships with the twin barrel anti-aircraft guns blazing away at a Kamikaze plane — k-boom, k-boom, k-boom! Watch this, one sentence in rapid fire: "'*do not be ashamed*' (aorist tense, not suggesting he had been ashamed); stand firm with the true gospel of the completed victory of Christ at the cross; nor of me (Paul) even if I am a prisoner; but '*join with me in suffering for the gospel.*'" Paul never sugar-coated the cost of following Jesus: "but you will have '*the power of God*' within to strengthen you; God '*saved us*' to give us '*a holy calling*' by grace through faith in His work in us, not our work. This was His plan for Paul, Timothy, and you and me before time began. What had been hidden is now revealed in Christ; '*who abolished death*' for those taken out of Adam and placed in Christ; '*and brought life*' for those who became partakers of His life, eternal life; and I Paul was appointed as a preacher, and an apostle, and a teacher

—period." Take a moment to catch your breath.

(1:12-18) Paul then mentions that *"all who are in Asia turned away from me, among whom are Phygelus and Hermogens"* (v 15). Paul would not be awaiting execution unless he was charged with a political crime, so to be a friend of Paul's was to put your life on the line, which Phygelus and Hermogens apparently did not do. But there was one, Onesiphorus, who was a true friend, and it probably cost him dearly. It occurred to me that this is the only place in the Bible where these first two are mentioned. What if my name or your name was mentioned? Would it be positive or negative? It's a convicting thought which finishes Chapter 1.

(2:1-10) Paul reminds Timothy of the grace (*charis*) that is '*in Christ Jesus.*" Timothy had traveled with Paul, and he had heard a consistent message given in all types of settings to all types of people. Paul wants Timothy to entrust that true message to others who are qualified to teach (cf 1 Tim 3:2; Titus 1:9). Paul uses the metaphor of a soldier, an athlete, and a farmer to illustrate who suffered hardship to produce the desired results. Paul then switches to the ultimate illustration of endurance in the face of opposition, Jesus Christ. Suffering has always been a part of church growth. Two times when the church grew exponentially was in the first century under the oppression of Rome and in China under the dictator Mao. In both cases Christians were treated as criminals. There were no church buildings. For all practical purposes there were no Bibles. There was no organized above ground church as we know it today. Yet the lost were won for Christ and the church grew. Go figure!

(2:11-13) These verses get a little technical, so I will just quote Duane Litfin: "Once more Paul used the trustworthy-saying formula, so common in the Pastorals (cf. 1 Tim 1:15; 3:1; 4:9; Titus 3:8), to introduce a quotation. The formula serves to place Paul's stamp of approval on the content of the quotation, which may have been part of a baptismal ceremony. The quotation sets forth four couplets, the first two of which are positive:

(1) 'If we died with Him, we will also live with Him' expresses the idea so powerfully portrayed in the rite of baptism and explained in Romans 6:2-23. The reference is not to martyrdom for Christ, but rather to a believer's mystical identification with the death and life of Christ (cf. Col 3:3). (2) If we endure (*hypomenomen;* cf. 2 Tim 2:10), we will also reign with Him furthers the believer's identification with Christ. In the previous couplet the focus is on the contrast between death and life; here the parallel contrast is between suffering and glorification (Rom 8:17). Christ endured and will one day reign (1 Cor 15:25), and those saints who endure will one day reign with Him (Rev 3:21). The last two couplets are negative: (3) 'If we disown Him, He will also disown us' speaks of the possibility of apostasy (cf. 1 Tim 4:1; Heb 10:38-39; 2 John 9) and the Lord's ultimate rejection of those who professed Christ only temporarily (cf. Matt 10:33). Instead of identifying with Christ, the apostate finally dissociates himself with Christ. (4) 'If we are faithless, He will remain faithful' speaks not of the apostate, but of a true child of God who nevertheless proves unfaithful (cf. 2 Tim 1:15). Christ cannot disown Himself; therefore He will not deny even unprofitable members of His own body. True children of God cannot become something other than children, even when disobedient and weak. Christ's faithfulness to Christians is not contingent on their faithfulness to Him. The significance of these couplets could hardly have been lost on Timothy."[24]

The part about '*the resurrection already taken place*' (vv. 8-13) takes a little historical background. Paul is talking to people in a Greek religious culture which thought anything material, such as our body, is sinful while the soul is immortal and good. Paul's teaching is that Christ was bodily resurrected, and that in the future our bodies would also be resurrected. This went contrary to Greek logic.

(2:14) Timothy is told to '*remind them*' (other teachers), which is a present imperative. In other words, tell them over and over. Paul admonished them to *"accurately handle the word of truth,'* which must have been missed by most preachers today. But you best let that one stick in your mind.

(2:20-21) These three verses are problematical, which is a term I use to mean I don't know what Paul is saying. He could be saying some people are chosen to be holy or saved and some are not, which goes along with election which I also do not understand; or he could be saying some people will have a position that looks like greater honor while others have a less desirable looking position. The second one sounds so much nicer than the first, but my gut tells me he is talking about the first one. The point is, I don't know.

(2:22-26) Paul uses another contrast and this one I do understand; the contrast between kind people and quarrelsome people. Remember, Timothy is a young man so Paul gives him some practical advice: *"flee* (present tense verb meaning continue to do it as often as necessary) *from youthful lust"* and *"pursue* (present imperative, must keep doing it) *righteousness, faith, love and peace."* Paul tells the young pastor *'not to become resentful* (*anexikakon*) which means he must learn to bear wrong without resenting the one who wronged him. Now that will take a work of grace, which is one reason I could never have been a pastor. He says to be gentle in your instructions of those who oppose you, in hope that the Lord will do a work of grace in them, which is the only hope that they will ever come to the knowledge of the truth. That 'be gentle' part is another reason I never became a pastor.

(3:1-17) I am not necessarily saying we are technically in *'the last days,'* meaning just before Jesus returns in the air to take believers to heaven. But if we are not, our country and this world is certainly a picture of those days: *"men will be lovers of self, lovers of money, boastful, arrogant, revilers, disobedient to parents, ungrateful, unholy, unloving, irreconcilable, malicious gossips, without self-control, brutal, haters of good, treacherous, reckless, conceited, lovers of pleasure rather than lovers of God, holding to* *a form of godliness, although they have denied its power"* (vv 2-5). These same things were in Israel during the days of the Judges, in Ephesus and Corinth during Paul's time, in Rome and every civilization before their fall. Our nation has one hope; to return to God.

For the remainder of chapter three and the first part of chapter four Paul is going to encourage Timothy to faithfully preach the Word, but in our country I don't think there has ever been better preachers of the Word than we have now. We have men like David Jeremiah, Charles Stanley, Adrian Rogers, Chuck Smith, Chuck Swindoll, John McArthur, and R.C. Sproul. But as a nation we have turned away from the 'truth.' My old Prof used to say, 'Transformation is the name of the game, not information,' and I am afraid we have just become educated sinners. On the other side of the coin, most of today's television preachers are nothing more than blind guides, in a totally dark room, describing a black cat that doesn't exist. You don't need a big name preacher to think they have the 'truth.' You need to know the Word, and you can rightly judge who has the 'truth.' It is the 'truth' in the person of Jesus Christ that you seek. Paul completes chapter 3 with those critically cogent words, *"All scripture is inspired by God and profitable for teaching, for reproof, for correction, for training in righteousness; so that the man of God may be adequate, equipped for every good work"* (vv 16-17).

When I was in seminary I found some old tapes of Lewis Sperry Chafer instructing future pastors on teaching the Word. While listening, I could imagine the tears hitting the pages as the old man talked of his respect for the Word. He told them to teach the truth of God's love and grace; don't beat the sheep with a guilt trip, but show them God's grace, mercy and love. People know they are sinners, but they don't know God loves them. You must reprove and correct sometimes, but do it in love or don't do it at all. Do it in humility and love.

(4:1-22) We ask nothing of ourselves compared with what

Paul laid on Timothy. Listen to this, *"I solemnly charge you in the presence of God and of Christ Jesus, who is to judge the living and the dead, and by His appearing and His kingdom: preach the word; be ready in season and out of season; reprove, rebuke, exhort, with great patience and instruction."* God doesn't have Plan B for salvation and Paul didn't have Plan B for the church at Ephesus. This is Paul's last chance to encourage Timothy for a work that would bring hardship and opposition, even from within. Now that may not sound like a very encouraging message, but Paul finishes by reminding Timothy of God's faithfulness.

I don't think we realize how tough Paul had it, and I don't mean being chained in a dungeon awaiting execution. Paul had seen men he trusted turn from faith under persecution and desert their calling. He mentioned Demas as one of those. I hope you will remember one thing; our trust is never in man but always in God. Paul was helpless to make his life's work go forward. Many had deserted the cause. All he had left in that cold, dark dungeon was his faith that God would finish what he had started. That can be the ultimate lonely place to be, but in reality that is all any of us have. If it was all Jesus had, why would we think it would be any different with us? These are the last words of the greatest theologian (other than Jesus) who considered himself nothing more than a bondservant: *"The Lord be with your spirit. Grace be with you."*

CHAPTER 14

DEBORAH, RAISED UP TO WORSHIP GOD
JUDGES 2:1-3; 4:1 – 5:31

Emma was asleep as peacefully as a baby, but Philip had never been able to sleep on an airplane. He and Emma had missed their connecting flight in London on United because the pilot's union back in the US sabotaged the schedule to put pressure on United's management. Thus, they were lucky to arrange two seats on Kenya Airlines' only flight out of London, flying what must have been one of the last 707s in service. Already deep into their second day traveling and a day behind schedule, it looked like they would make their connecting flight the next morning from Nairobi to Kigali, Rwanda. But the captain pulled off the taxi strip and returned to the gate for repairs. Several hours later, now late at night, the old 707 lumbered off the runway and into the pitch black sky. Air travel on any airline is at best a crap shoot. The remainder of the long flight was uneventful, except that they were seated near the engines. The deafening roar, even with ear plugs, was intolerable.

Upon landing at Nairobi International, they gathered their carry-on luggage and sprinted for the connecting flight. On getting to the proper gate, the clerk told them the plane would not leave for forty-five minutes, but passengers could go aboard (which seemed odd, but this is Africa). The waiting room was crowded, so they opted to find a seat on the airplane. No sooner had they sat down than a flight attendant told them to buckle up. She pulled the door closed and the pilot fired up the turbo-prop engines. Philip exclaimed, "What the…," to which Emma replied, "Hush, at least we made it." Philip decided explanations were impossible in his state of mind, so he spent his time trying to figure out how many days it had been since they left West Texas. With Emma's help, they figured this must be well into the third day, including an eleven hour layover at the airport in London. They worked feverishly for most of that time to trace their luggage and get a flight out. Emma asked rhetorically, "What do you think the chances are our luggage made it this time?" Philip replied, "Zero!" It turned out he was right.

Assuming everyone knows Murphy's Law (If anything can go wrong it will!), then you should also know that traveling in Africa, it is obvious that Murphy was an optimist. Philip had arranged by email for Malachi Surkura to pick them up at the Kigali airport, but that was for Saturday morning, and it was now Sunday afternoon. The pastor's conference, with one hundred plus men and women pastors coming from Rwanda, Burundi, Uganda, and Congo was to start Monday morning. On final approach, Emma turned to Philip and opined, "Well, we're here and nothing else can go wrong." Philip gave her a numb look of "just wait."

It didn't take long to clear customs and find that their luggage was somewhere else in the world. There was one other thing that was missing—Malachi and their transportation to his home. Philip called Malachi's home several times, but every time his young niece would answer the phone and then hang up because she didn't understand English. Philip pulled out a twenty dollar bill and holding it over his head asked in English if any of the taxi drivers would take them to a hotel. He was almost run over by half a dozen young entrepreneurs. On the ride into town, Philip thought about Corrie ten Boom who had a very funny saying: "It's no wonder more people don't follow you Lord, considering how He treats those who do."

The comatose couple arrived at a very nice hotel (the same one used in the movie Hotel Rwanda). They checked in at three times the rate they hoped to pay, but were ushered into a beautiful clean room with the most important thing, a bed. No sooner had Philip stepped from the bath than the hotel manager called the room and said there was a man there asking for them. Sure enough, Malachi had called around and found them. It was decided (and there was no voting on this since Philip had not slept for three days) that Malachi could pick them up in the morning around seven-thirty.

The next morning Emma woke Philip to see the morning glow backlighting the mountains. Apparently she had been sitting on the balcony for some time praying. Central Africa is a visual contradiction; incredibly beautiful landscape but scarred with centuries of tribal wars. Out the balcony overlooking the outdoor dinning area some three floors below was a ficus tree that had to be seventy or eighty feet tall. Bougainvilla covering the walled courtyard, poinsettia trees, and hibiscus hedges. These equatorial highlands are generally a tropical paradise. Off in the distance was the deserted parliament building riddled with cannon shell holes. In front of it were beautiful modern houses, and beyond it the slums where most of the people live. Welcome to central Africa.

Breakfast was served down home style. A good night's sleep made the cost of the room seem like a bargain. Eggs could be ordered any way you wanted them. Philip had three poached with ham, but there was also available sausage, pancakes, fresh fruit, complete cold cuts with cheese selection and hard breads, all European style. Right on time, Malachi was there to pick them up, and after a short ride across the city they were ready to start the conference. Kigali has 'rush minute,' so the traffic was negligible.

These pastors at the conference are starving for Bible training. To see them eat meals also reminds you they don't get three squares a day at home either. Breakfast was eggs on toast. Lunch and dinner was pinto beans on rice. It is amazing how high they can stack pinto beans on rice. As normal, Philip brought along a magnum size bottle of Tabasco which he offered to share, but they liked it plain. The coffee was fantastic; instant coffee, cocoa, and brown granular raw sugar—you just had to be there. Philip found himself feeling ashamed to think it was inconvenient to get here. Some of the pastors had ridden a twelve passenger van, jammed full with more than twelve passengers, Rwanda's type of inter-country bus system. Many had walked to the conference center, not having the money for bus fare.

Each day started and ended with worship. It would be a gross understatement to say these people know how to worship. The song leader would get so ecstatically joyful, he would occasionally jump in the air (no exaggeration here). The bottom of his feet would come up to Philip's waist. The little guy couldn't have been more than five-four, just shorter than Emma, but Philip would have bet the ranch he could dunk a basketball.

Teaching with a translator takes some getting used to, especially if you are used to writing or talking in long sentences. Philip would say part of a sentence in Texican (an amalgamation of English, Texan slang, and Spanish). He would say eight or ten words, hoping to stop at a comma or break in the thought, and then the translator would repeat in Swahili, sometimes having to improvise to give the proper meaning. Obviously God was miraculously at work, and luckily the translator was always smarter than Philip. Emma held her own.

If Philip had any pride, the Lord arranged for that to be taken care of. In their culture, a teacher must wear a coat and tie as a symbol of authority, which would have been okay if Philip had his luggage. Malachi loaned him two shirts and a tie. Malachi is about five-five while Philip is six-three. The shirts were large primary color plaids along with a pastel floral print tie. Emma had to bite her tongue more than once to keep from laughing. Philip had tan slacks, black blazer, and a large hibiscus flowered tie beneath. Naturally, Emma looked great as always in the traditional African wrap which she had been given. Worship started about seven-thirty, and then the teaching would run from about eight-thirty in the morning to seven or eight at night, with lunch and a few fifteen minute breaks in between. Obviously, after a very long day of teaching, it was no trouble going to sleep. Overnight was at Malachi's house.

There still remained one problem. Emma was taking the prescription medication Propranolol. Thinking ahead, she had packed some extra in her overnight bag, and then split the medication in her and Philip's luggage in case one was lost. But with both suitcases still traveling around the world, she ran out.

The second evening Philip asked Malachi to take them to replenish their bottled water supply. The grocery store was about like one of our Seven-Elevens, with a good supply of bottled water. Most of the shopping for food was done at a huge open air market downtown. Next door was what passed for a drug store, about the size of a big walk in closet. On a lark, Emma suggested they see if they could get information on where to get Propranolol. Emma asked the clerk in English about the medication. Apparently the clerk didn't understand, so she slid a piece of paper for Emma to write down what she wanted. The clerk looked at what Emma had written, turned to the relatively bare shelf behind her, searched for a moment, and then pulled the one and only bottle of something down and handed it to Emma. Emma looked at the bottle, and then said, "I can't believe it, our luggage isn't coming because God will provide (Yahweh Jira) the only thing Emma really needed. That's right; it was a bottle of prescription Propranolol (five dollars American).

Back at Malachi's house there was time to catch up on his ministry. There is no telling how many churches Malachi had started in the past forty years. Being one of the few pastors to escape the genocide, he was a rarity in that he had seminary training. More importantly, he was made of the same stuff as the Apostle Paul. Being a humble man, Malachi wanted to talk about his wife Deborah's ministry.

Deborah had to be in her sixties, but she had the vitality of a woman much younger. Being of the Hutu tribe, she was naturally short with a round face. Like Malachi, there was something magnetic about her personality that drew everyone to her. After the war, better described as tribal murders, the family structure was also left in shambles. In addition, as with much of Africa, AIDS was rampant, with most having indiscriminate sex or rape or both. Children soon became children of the street, and there was the beginning of gangs forming. Deborah prayed and fasted about the situation because the Lord laid it on her heart to do something about it. Emma was spellbound! "What did you do?" Deborah had a resolve in her eyes and voice. "I am going to the streets with the Word of God." Someway Philip knew he was watching the genesis of something greater than any of them. "Go on, what is your plan?" In slow measured broken English she talked of the ministry at hand. "You have to catch the fish before you can clean them. God is God of grace and mercy to the faithful; otherwise He judge this nation in righteousness, turn us over to our sin. I am go to pray, fast, repent for Rwanda, then Lord going to raise up an army of evangelist, take gospel to streets and to countryside. That God's plan, not mine."

Philip and Malachi had talked earlier about meetings Malachi had been involved in with older pastors to understand how the genocide was possible in a nation where over ninety percent of the people described themselves as Christian. Earlier, French missionaries had brought the gospel, which under the power of the Holy Spirit had spread like wildfire. But the next generation considered themselves church people, so the sending churches back in Europe pulled their resources, thinking their work was done. As any good evangelist will tell you, God doesn't have any grandchildren. How do Christians, even in a blood lust frenzy, go about hacking other Christians to death? The answer is, they don't. But religious people, even if they call themselves Christians, are capable of the most degenerate sin.

The following day during a break, Philip, Emma and Malachi were talking about Deborah's evangelism ministry. As usual, there were a few others listening in when Emma said, "Deborah's ministry reminds me of the Deborah who was a prophetess and a judge in Israel." Whereupon several of the pastors asked Emma if she knew about this Deborah in the Bible that they had never heard of. No sooner had Emma shook her head affirmative than they called the class to attention and asked Emma to tell them about this judge Deborah. Emma explained that she had not prepared to teach this, but she had studied several women in the Bible and had her notes on Philip's laptop. So she would be willing to try, starting the following morning. To finish out the day, Philip picked up his teaching on Bible Study Methods which was to prepare the pastors to work through the text, asking: 1) what does it say; 2) what does it mean; 3) evaluation and application; and 4) correlation, (all right out of Traina's book and Prof's class in seminary).

Emma worked into the night to prepare her presentation on Deborah, while Philip slept peacefully under the mosquito netting. The following morning, Emma pulled out her Bible Study notes, ready to start in with her translator at her side. But before she could start, one of the pastors raised his hand to ask a question. He was from Uganda, but like all social groups there is a pecking order, and he was one of the recognized and well respected leaders. He addressed the question to Philip and Malachi: "I mean no disrespect, but is it appropriate to have a woman teach men? I read in 1 Corinthians that women to keep silent in churches. What you advise us?" Philip realized the pastor had asked the question in all sincerity, plus it couldn't be passed over lightly since he was one of the leaders. More importantly, it was exactly the kind of engaging question that would give application to their study in Bible Study Methods.

Malachi was about to shut the man down, but Philip walked to the front to take the question. "You have the tools to help you know the answer. We have been working on understanding the Bible by asking the questions: what does it say, what does it mean, and how should it be applied? To know 'what it says' you do have to take into account if it is simple prose, or poetry, or a parable; you will need to understand the components of any language. Next, 'what does it mean?,' keeping in context with the surrounding verses and the general theme of the book. You would also be greatly helped if you knew the culture of the people it was addressed to. You can use other related scripture to see if what you are studying lines up. There should be no contradictions. Then, 'how do you apply it?'

The verses you are referring to are in 1 Corinthians 14:34-35. You don't have the advantage of reading it in Greek, but in your French translation Paul's comments are plain. Women were to keep silent. But secondly, you must ask, 'what does it mean'? Here you must put it in context with what immediately surrounds it. Paul has just admonished the Corinthian church to conduct themselves orderly. Apparently there was confusion as a result of the use of tongues (that only two or three should speak, not everyone at once). So the question you might ask is this: Is Paul speaking specifically to a problem in this one church, or is he giving a broad application to all churches. So you might see what else is said on the same subject, such as Paul's first letter to Timothy where he says, '*But do not allow a woman to teach or exercise authority over a man' (2:12).*

Now you have the same thing verified in two places: 1 Corinthians and 1 Timothy. But, what is the application? As pastor of your church, you must in good conscience determine how you will apply it, and it is a heavy responsibility. I will give you my interpretation and application. A woman may not usurp the place of leadership and authority in the church. That is not a popular belief in America, but I believe that is what the Bible says. However, I believe a woman can teach men in a conference setting such as we have here, as long a she is under the authority of male leadership. In this case I am familiar with what Emma is going to teach. I approve of her homiletics or teaching outline, and she is teaching under my authority. Now if anyone objects to a woman teaching under those conditions, we will respect your beliefs and Emma will teach only those who want to hear her. I am not so interested in you agreeing with my application as realizing that these tools we are teaching you will help you to determine what is Biblical and what is not. Does anyone wish to be excused?" There were no objections, so Philip motioned for Emma to proceed.

Emma was a little shaken, but she regained her composure. "I need to give you some background so that you will understand the context of the book of Judges. The book of Judges is immediately following Joshua in the Old Testament. Joshua, with the Ark of the Covenant and the priests leading the way, crosses the Jordan and into the promise land. Moses has just led them in the desert for 40 years. During the approximately three hundred fifty year time period between Joshua's death and the prophet (king maker) Samuel, Yahweh raised up judges to lead the nation of Israel. A judge was an executive leader, often combining civil, military and judicial authority. Deborah was the only woman judge in the Bible. She was a prophet, a judge, and a military leader. Each judge recorded in the book of Judges was empowered by Yahweh with heroic abilities to deliver Israel from oppression.

During this time, the history of Israel was one of downward

cycles of unfaithfulness (following after other gods): judgment, humiliation through foreign oppression, crying out to Yahweh for deliverance, God's grace in raising up heroic leaders empowered by His Spirit, and then unfortunately backsliding into unfaithfulness again and then the cycle started over.

Israel had three things going for them: theocratic rule (meaning God was their king), the Law, and the Tabernacle. They really only had to do one thing to be blessed—remain faithful to their covenant God, Yahweh. Had they remained faithful, they would have had the spiritual integrity to drive the Canaanites out of the land, and reaped the bountiful harvest of Yahweh's promises. But after Joshua, each succeeding generation forgot their God.

The book of Judges is a portrait of human depravity mated to God's grace and redemption. Chapter four is the story of Deborah's victory over the Canaanite oppression; chapter five is a poem or song of worship about the same event. We are going to look over Chapter 4 to study the historical events of redemption, but then we are also going to study worship, using Chapter 5. You might say our study of Deborah is about a person called by God to lead His people back to Him, resulting in worship of the highest order in Deborah's song. I will tell you up front that one application is the redemption of Rwanda, turning the people back to God after the tribal wars.

First, we will mention the historical events. There was a Canaanite king named Jabin who reigned from a city called Hazor (present day Tell el-Qedah). Philip and I have been to the tel at Hazor which was on the main trade route from Egypt to Mesopotamia, about fifteen kilometers north of the Sea of Kinnereth (the Sea of Galilee). Because of their sin of unfaithfulness Yahweh had allowed Israel to be oppressed severely by the Canaanites for twenty years. Jabin's military commander was Sisera who lived not too far from Megiddo at the west end of the Jezreel valley (Emma had Philip take chalk and draw a map of Israel on the blackboard). Sisera had nine hundred iron covered chariots which is about today like having nine hundred armored vehicles. With his footmen plus the nine hundred chariots Jabin was able to control the whole of northern Israel under the boot of Sisera.

God told Deborah to have her military leader Barak raise an army of 10,000 fighting men to be positioned on Mount Tabor. Then Deborah said to Barak and the army, '*Go! This is the day the* LORD <u>*has given*</u> *Sisera into your hands* ('has given' Hebrew perfect tense verb, completed action from point of speaker). *Has not the* LORD *gone ahead of you?'* Sisera heard about the Israelite army and went out on the plains below Mount Tabor to do battle. God caused a thunderstorm which mired the chariots in mud rendering them useless. Seeing that Yahweh had gone before them the Israeli army swarmed down off the mountain and defeated Sisera and his army.

Now for the second part of our study, Chapter 5. One of the primary lessons of Deborah's writings is worship. Our English word 'worship' comes from the Anglo-Saxon word 'worthscripe.' Worthscripe referred to honoring a member of high society, such as a lord or monarch, or to a particularly esteemed person, such as a loved one. In a secondary sense I worthscripe Philip, but in the primary sense I give honor and worth only to God. Worship has the meaning of 'giving worth to.' We worship or give worth to God by celebrating or remembering things He has done. Deborah's song (chapter 5) is high worship of Yahweh, recounting the great things He did to redeem His people. One other practical application, considering the victory God had won in redeeming Israel, I would ask you to read chapter 5 tonight and be ready to worship tomorrow morning."

Considering that Emma had been up much of the night preparing, she went to sleep immediately after dinner. Philip and Malachi stayed up and talked about Malachi's years of planting churches. Malachi had lived a life of faith and dependence on the

Lord that seemed impossibly strange to Philip, but to Malachi it was a normal part of his journey following Jesus.

The next morning worship was great as always, but maybe a little more meaningful considering Emma's teaching the day before. Emma took the opportunity to talk about an application she had thought about just before drifting off to sleep the night before. "In the book of Judges, each generation forgot their God and turned to false gods. Christian families are the same. An evangelist's work is never done. You must preach the gospel to every generation. God is merciful and gracious when we repent and return to Him. God will judge the unrighteous, but God will also raise up leaders to carry out His will. God will lead the way to win the battle if we are faithful. Deborah said, '*Go! This is the day the LORD <u>has given</u> Sisera* (the lost) *into your hands* (Hebrew perfect tense verb, completed action from point of speaker). *Has not the LORD gone ahead of you?*'

The people during the Judge's time wanted freedom to worship other gods, but only found bondage. But when they repented, God raised up a heroic judge to set them free. Jesus Christ is our ultimate heroic judge to free us from bondage to sin, so that we might worship God in truth and Spirit. It occurs to me that God has raised up Malachi's wife Deborah to call you to go into the streets and into the country and share the gospel—to win back this country for Jesus. Your question about a woman teaching men was justified, but now is the time for you men to stand up and lead the way to take the gospel to the people. The problem in most of the world isn't that women want to assume authority in the churches; the problem is men have abdicated their responsibility.

Some of you may know that for some time Malachi has been meeting with other elders to try and understand why the church in Rwanda had so little influence when the genocide started. It looks like the answer is that the church quit producing authentic Christians and instead produced church members. In the Prophetess Deborah's terminology, *'the Lord has gone ahead of you'* (4:14, the King marches at the head of His army). You are His army, go and make disciples."

At the end of the week there were sorrowful good-byes from everyone. But ahead was the following week in Zambia, a week in the Great Rift Valley west of Lake Victoria, which is where the elder tribal chieftain bestowed upon Philip his African name. But that is another story for another day. Then we wanted to take a short photographic safari in the Masa Mara highlands of Kenya. Leaving Africa is always sad because God causes you to know that those "in Christ" really are brothers and sisters in the journey.

Emma's Study Notes, Judges 4

(1-3) *"After Ehud died, the Israelites once again did evil in the eyes of the LORD. So the LORD sold them into the hands of Jabin, a king of Canaan, who reigned in Hazor. The commander of his army was Sisera, who lived in Harosheth Haggoyim* (Haggoyim meaning of the pagan nations; thus Harosheth of the pagan nations). *Because he had nine hundred iron chariots and had cruelly oppressed the Israelites for twenty years, they cried to the LORD for help."* About 200 years earlier the Lord had freed Israel from slavery in Egypt; but now in judgment for their unfaithfulness He had sold them into the hands of the Canaanites.

(4-7) *"Deborah, a prophetess, the wife of Lappidoth, was leading Israel at that time. She held court under the Palm of Deborah between Ramah and Bethel in the hill country of Ephraim, and the Israelites came to her to have their disputes decided. She sent for Barak son of Abinoam from Kedesh in Naphtali and said to him, The LORD, the God of Israel, commands you: 'Go, take with you ten thousand men of Naphtali and Zebulun and lead the way to Mount Tabor. I will lure Sisera, the commander of Jabin's army, with his chariots and his troops to the Kishon River and give him into your hands.'"*

Deborah's name means 'honey bee.' Can't you just hear two Jews arguing about a plot of land and one says to the other, "If you don't give me what we agreed on, I will take you to honey bee." Her court under the Palm of Deborah was located about 12 kilometers north of Jerusalem, between Ramah and Bethel in the hill country.

I don't know why God called Deborah to be the judge of Israel, but I fear it might be because the men had abandoned their place as leaders of the family and nation. In any case, Yahweh commanded her to call on a man to lead the army against the oppression of Jabin. Deborah challenged Barak to be brave because Yahweh would '*lead the way,*' which the Hebrew words means 'to *lure*' the enemy into a trap. Deborah asked Barak to gather an army of 10,000 men, but Barak said he would only do it if she would go with him into battle.

(8) "*Barak said to her, if you go with me, I will go; but if you don't go with me, I won't go.*" Now I ask you men, don't you just love it when a man stands up and takes control? What kind of a milk toast answer is that? However, it is noteworthy that Barak is listed among the heroes of faith in Hebrews 11:32. When I realized that Barak was among the heroes mentioned in Hebrews, it occurred to me that maybe the list of the faithful in Hebrews is a demonstration of how we with little faith can still follow our God who is always faithful.

(9-10) "*Very well, Deborah said, I will go with you. But because of the way you are going about this, the honor will not be yours, for the LORD will hand Sisera over to a woman. So Deborah went with Barak to Kedesh, where he summoned Zebulun and Naphtali. Ten thousand men followed him, and Deborah also went with him.*" Because of Barak's hesitation to go without Deborah, she prophesied that the honor of killing Sisera will go to a woman.

(11) "*Now Heber the Kenite had left the other Kenites, the descendants of Hobab, Moses' brother-in-law, and pitched his tent by the great tree in Zaanannim near Kedesh.*" Verse 11 is a parenthetical statement, in anticipation of vv 17-22. It is an explanation that the nomad Heber had left his clan in southern Judah to settle near Kedesh in northern Israel.

(12-13) *"When they told Sisera that Barak son of Abinoam had gone up to Mount Tabor, Sisera gathered together his nine hundred iron chariots and all the men with him, from Harosheth Haggoyim to the Kishon River."* Mt. Tabor was situated so that the Jew's position effectively cut off communications or reinforcements from Hazor.

(14-16) *"Then Deborah said to Barak, 'Go! This is the day the LORD <u>has given</u> Sisera into your hands (Hebrew perfect tense verb, completed action from point of speaker). Has not the LORD gone ahead of you?' So Barak went down Mount Tabor, followed by ten thousand men. At Barak's advance, the LORD routed Sisera and all his chariots and army by the sword, and Sisera abandoned his chariot and fled on foot. But Barak pursued the chariots and army as far as Harosheth Haggoyim. All the troops of Sisera fell by the sword; not a man was left."*

Deborah told the army, *'Yahweh has gone ahead of them,'* which in Hebrew was a technical term used of a king marching at the head of his army. Chapter 4 only tells us that Yahweh *'threw Sisera's army into confusion.'* But Deborah's song in Chapter 5 tells us that Yahweh caused a thunderstorm.

There is a lot of symbolism going on here when you realize that all battles were thought of as a contest between the gods. Who would win depended on whose god is the stronger: Baal, the Canaanite god, or Yahweh. Imagine a huge thunderstorm forming over Mount Tabor; the thunder and lighting would surely have reminded the Jews of Moses on Mount Sinai. Then the storm descends into the valley, as though God himself was leading the charge. When the rains came the iron chariots were uselessly mired in the mud, so when ten thousand mad Jews stormed off Mount Tabor, the Canaanite army turned and ran. Not a man was spared.

(17-20) *"Sisera, however, fled on foot to the tent of Jael, the wife of Heber the Kenite, because there were friendly relations between Jabin king of Hazor and the clan of Heber the Kenite. Jael went out to meet Sisera and said to him, 'Come, my Lord, come right in. Don't be afraid.' So he entered her tent, and she put a covering over him. 'I'm thirsty,' he said. 'Please give me some water.' She opened a skin of milk, gave him a drink, and covered him up. 'Stand in the doorway of the tent,' he told her. 'If someone comes by and asks you, 'Is anyone here?' say 'No.'"* Philip says the lesson here is, "never trust a woman with a hammer." In those days the women put up and took down the tents, so Jael knew how to use a tent peg and wooden mallet.

(21) *"But Jael, Heber's wife, picked up a tent peg and a mallet and went quietly to him while he lay fast asleep, exhausted. She drove the peg through his temple into the ground, and he died."* Jael killed Sisera, thus fulfilling Deborah's prophesy. One commentator called this "an unusual breach of Near-Eastern hospitality!" No kidding!

(22-24) *"Barak came by in pursuit of Sisera, and Jael went out to meet him. 'Come,' she said, 'I will show you the man you're looking for.' So he went in with her, and there lay Sisera with the tent peg through his temple - dead. On that day God subdued Jabin, the Canaanite king, before the Israelites. And the hand of the Israelites grew stronger and stronger against Jabin, the Canaanite king, until they destroyed him."*

Well, as our Sunday school teacher might say, 'So what? What are the lessons?' Three basic thoughts come to mind:

1) Sin always leads to bondage, while repentance (turning to God) always leads to freedom.

2) Every generation must hear the gospel and believe, or they will turn away from God.

3) Chapter 5, Deborah's song of worship is an example of how we might give thanks to our God for the things He has done.

I encourage you to read Deborah's song (Chapter 5) to prepare your heart to worship. Consider God's faithfulness to you and worship Him by giving Him worth for who He is and what He has done.

CHAPTER 15

YAHWEH'S APPOINTED TIMES
LEVITICUS 23

The fellow in front of Philip looks distinguished in his black suit, white shirt, black hat, black shoes, and black belt. You get the idea. But it's the beautiful Browning Hi-Power pistol strapped to his hip that caught Philip's attention. Philip always loved the Hi-Power, although he was not crazy about the caliber. This was as elegant a work of weaponry art as ever existed. Philip had just returned home again for a short visit. I say home because if you are a Christian, this is your future address—Jerusalem.

Philip got cornered into leading a small group tour to the Holy Land; 'cornered' only in the sense that he knew a few Christian teachers who have forgotten more about Israel than he knew. However, they are all so popular that they lead big tours, whereas a small group does have some distinct advantages. One of those is not waiting for fifty people to debus at every historical site, and then trying to gather them all up at the same time to leave (which is a lot like herding cats). Philip compensated for his shortcomings by sending everyone a book by Charles Dyer and Gregory Hatteberg, *The Christian Traveler's Guide to the Holy Land*, with instructions to read ahead of time.

Along with the sightseeing, Philip needed a related Bible Study; just a fifteen or twenty minute time in the Word each night before discussing the following day's activities. Leading a tour even with a professional guide could have been a full time job. What to do? As luck would have it, Emma had a great Bible Study she had taught in Africa a few years before, and it would be perfect for a Holy Land visit. All Philip had to do was talk Emma into teaching on the Feasts of Israel listed in Leviticus 23.

The truth be known, Emma always was the best teacher in the family. She never attended seminary, but participated for over twenty years with Bible Study Fellowship. This prepared her well. Also, it is important that the host not be overworked, so that he can be alert to the feelings of each individual in the group. Unfortunately, Philip didn't relate to feelings, so he was simply free to enjoy the trip while Emma stayed up late and got up early to prepare and pray for her study.

We had a great professional guide, if only the group had consisted of unmarried women looking for adventure. Amnon, our guide, was a short version of Bond—James Bond. He had rugged good looks, jet black hair, dark eyes, and even when cleanly shaven a shadow of a beard way before that look came into vogue. Amnon also spoke in that European style broken English that made him even more mysterious. During the '67 War, as a teenager, he was one of the Rangers that slid down ropes hanging from helicopters while taking fierce enemy fire, to secure the Golan Heights from the Syrian cannon emplacements. Incidentally, he was also a knowledgeable guide with an affable personality that fit well with everyone. Abeb was our driver of the small twenty passenger bus, the tour company having the forethought to always provide a Jewish guide and Moslem driver for any eventuality.

Saturday, our first full day in Israel, was spent in and around Tel Aviv just to let everyone get their legs underneath them. But there is too much to see to waste a day. A visit to Independence Hall is first on our agenda. For nearly two thousand years there had been no state of Israel, but on May 14, 1948, just one day before the British mandate over Palestine was due to expire, David Ben-Gurion stood beneath a large portrait of Theodor Herzl (founder of modern Zionism) in the Tel Aviv Museum (today known as Independence Hall) and declared Israel an independent nation.

The hand written draft of the declaration of independence was only finished that afternoon. Ae'ev Sharef, who had the only draft of the declaration, had overlooked one small thing—transportation to the Tel Aviv Museum (the following goes like a Neil Simon comedy with Jack Lemmon playing Mr. Sharef). So he flagged down a passing car, the driver of which at first refused to take Sharef across town to deliver the declaration. Of course the driver had borrowed the car and had no license. The car was stopped for speeding, but when the situation was explained to the police, he was allowed to proceed (without a ticket). He finally delivered Sharef and the document one minute before Ben-Gurion was scheduled to read it over the radio.

Immediately, troops from Lebanon, Syria, Iraq, Egypt, Jordan, Saudi Arabia, Libya and Yemen attacked. Don't you just hate the fact that those Jews are such aggressors (it's a joke, but it wasn't funny on May 15th, 1948)? Every time it looked like the Israeli forces were going to get the upper hand, the UN (known as United Nothing in Israel) would call for an immediate cease-fire, along with a truce plan to stop the advancing Israeli troops. When the attacking Arabs were advancing, the UN got out of the way (and we wonder why Israel doesn't trust the 'fair and balanced' UN).

Next was a visit to the Carmel open air market, with various kinds of foods, clothing and household goods. The quality of the vegetables and fruits available would embarrass our best supermarkets. One of our group bought and ate enough pistachios to founder himself—live and learn. The selection of fresh olives and dates is astounding, but the smell is not so great.

The old port of Joppa (modern Jaffa), where Jonah hopped a boat trying to get away from the Lord's command to go preach to Nineveh, is just south of Tel Aviv. This is a long walk, but a refreshing one after traveling for a day and a half. Some of the group wanted to rest in the hotel, but several took the walk after an early dinner. Going south along the beach walk the sun was setting, highlighting the Mediterranean. Families and vacationers were enjoying being together. Children were playing on the beach. The smell of salt spray was in the air, heavily armed Israeli speed boats were patrolling back and forth, and a military helicopter every ten or fifteen minutes guarding from a terrorist attack. Welcome to Israel!

The old city is like turning the clock back two thousand years. The ladies shopped in the stores, but about 9:00 o'clock as our party was preparing to leave Jaffa, one of those magical moments transpired. In the Clock Square, two recent immigrants from Russia were performing for donations to support themselves. He was playing the guitar and she had the voice of an angel. I have no idea what she was singing, but it was 'drop dead' beautiful (so was she by the way).

Sunday morning the hotel provided a fantastic breakfast spread—no continental breakfast here. Our small party of 14 loaded in the bus, ready for a full day of adventure. A visit to Israel is like having the pages of the Bible come to life in living color; the sights, the smells, the taste, the sounds of the Holy Land. We wanted to consume and experience all of it. To begin our bus pilgrimage, we would be traveling through Samaria in the central highlands on our way north. The central highlands look much like the hill country of central-west Texas, except that the trees are tamarisk and olive instead of scrub oak and mesquite. The morning was cool and the air fresh like back home.

Our first stop was Elon Moreh, the Oak of Moreh where Abraham first dwelled in the land. *"And Abram passed through the land as far as the site of Shechem, to the oak of Moreh. Now the Canaanite was then in the land. And Yahweh appeared to Abram and said, 'To your descendants I will give this land.' So he built an altar there to Yahweh who had appeared to him"* (Genesis 12:6-7). It is impossible to overstate this event at Elon Moreh, because it is in direct line with God's redemption plan for mankind and His eternal theocratic rule. Yahweh's declaration, *"I will give this land,"* is the eternal heritage of Israel.

The fact that Abram built an altar is significant. Some 700 plus years later Joshua would build another altar at this location. These altars were dedications to God—to Abram a promise, to Joshua a prefilling of what will ultimately be fulfilled by Messiah. An altar is a visible symbol, a remembrance that something special happened here. The deeds of the father prefigured the deeds of the sons. The conquest of the land was an accomplished fact when Yahweh made the promise, even though the final conquest is yet in our future.

From our position on what is more properly a hill rather than a mountain, we could view Mt. Gerizim (Blessing) and Mt. Ebal (Curses) where the Law was first read in the Promised Land at Shechem. Below Gerizim and Ebal is the well Jacob dug and the location where Jesus encountered the woman at the well (John 4). Behind us was the mountain where Saul and his son Jonathan were killed, and behind that the valley Elijah ran through to escape Jezebel. Considering the number of Biblical events that occurred in this area, one is struck by how small Israel really is.

All aboard on the road to Shiloh, where during the time recorded in Judges (about 350 years) the Ark of the Covenant was housed in the 'tent of meeting.' *"Then the whole congregation of the sons of Israel assembled themselves at Shiloh, and set up the tent of meeting there"* (Josh 18:1). It was at Shiloh where Eli the high priest lived, and the prophet Samuel, (the king maker), grew up. The word 'Shiloh' is also one of the names of Messiah: "*The scepter shall not depart from Judah, nor the ruler's staff from between his feet, until Shiloh comes, and to Him shall be the obedience of the peoples*" (Gen 49:10).

We then traveled west towards the coast to Mt. Carmel where Elijah defeated the prophets of Baal. "*Now send and gather to me all Israel at Mount Carmel, together with 450 prophets of Baal and 400 prophets of the Asherah, who eat at Jezebel's table*" (1 Kings 18:19). It is at this gathering where Elijah confronted the false gods the people had been following: "*Then you call on the name of your god, and I will call on the name of Yahweh, and the God who answers by fire, He is God*" (1 Kings 18:24).

Then we drove to Megiddo to inspect the ruins there. Megiddo lies in the Plain of Esdraelon (Jezreel Valley) where the final battle with Antichrist will take place. The combatants will be lured to the site by demons (Rev 16:12-16) for that great and terrible day. "*Then I saw an angel standing in the sun, and he cried out with a loud voice, saying to all the birds which fly in the midheaven, 'Come, assemble for the great supper of God, so that you may eat the flesh of kings and the flesh of commanders and the flesh of mighty men and the flesh of horses and of those who sit on them and the flesh of all men, both free men and slaves, and small and great.' And I saw the beast and the kings of the earth and their armies assembled to make war against Him who sat on the horse and against His army*" (Rev 19:17-19). Napoleon stood on this spot and declared it the perfect battle field. Today Megiddo is an archeological dig only. There are twenty layers of building, occupation, and subsequent destruction.

We then transversed east along the Jezreel valley to Mt. Arbel, where we took a short walk for our first breathtaking view of the Sea of Galilee. This almost mythical body of water is only thirteen miles long and seven and one-half miles wide. It lies about 650 feet below sea level (I say about because it is the principal fresh water source for northern and central Israel, and with drought in recent years, it is several feet below normal). In the Bible, this body of water was called the Sea of Kinnereth, the Lake of Gennesaret, the Sea of Tiberias, and the Sea of Galilee.

After a very long day, we dined and spent the night in picturesque Tiberias on the southwest shore of the Sea of Galilee. In the States we think of historical sites in hundreds of years, while here they are measured in millennium. Tiberias was founded by Herod Antipas, named after the Roman emperor Tiberias Caesar who ruled (A.D. 14-37) during Jesus' public ministry.

Emma's Bible Study—The Appointed Times, Leviticus 23

That night Emma began the introduction to her study. "Open your Bibles to Leviticus, chapter 23. About three thousand five hundred years ago, Yahweh spoke to Moses and ordained seven major 'appointed times' as holy convocations (assemblies). The first convocation Yahweh identifies is Shabbat (seventh day of rest), to be observed each week. Lest you forget you are in Israel, on Saturday (Shabbat), the elevators in the hotels are programmed to stop at each floor so as to not defy the law of working on the Sabbath.

The Hebrew calendar year included four spring feasts: Pesach (Passover); The Feast of Unleavened Bread; First Fruits; and Shavuot (Pentecost, The Feast of Weeks); an interval of four months; then three fall feasts: Rosh Hashanah (Trumpets, Jewish Civil New Year); Yom Kippur (The Day of Atonement); and Sukkoth (The Feast of Tabernacles). The purpose of these holy convocations was to teach the people about God's redemption plan through Messiah. These holy convocations were all a pre-filling (a picture) of prophesies to be fulfilled in the Anointed One (Messiah). I say 'in the Anointed One' because the fulfilling is a person, not an event.

The Jewish calendar is also important to understand the prophetic meaning of the various holy convocations, because Yahweh instructed that they be celebrated at specific times of the year. The Hebrew calendar months were determined by the new moon (lunar calendar). In the days of temple worship, three convocations (Pesach, Shavuot and Sukkoth) required every adult male to travel to Jerusalem to celebrate there. Pesach (Passover) is celebrated the first month of the year (Ex 12, Nisan occurs in March or April). Shavuot (Pentecost) is at the beginning of the wheat harvest (Sivan, in May or June), and Sukkoth (Tabernacles) at the end of harvest (Tishri, in September or October).

SHABBAT: The Seventh Day of Rest (23:3) The Lord's instructions to Moses included the Sabbath, even though it is not one of the seven major feasts. All of the feasts are called days of rest, Shabbats, but the other holy convocations come only once a year. The Hebrew word Shabbat (Sabbath—to rest, to cease) is observed from Friday at sundown to Saturday sundown. In Exodus we read, *'Remember the Sabbath day, to keep it holy. Six days you shall labor and do all your work, but the seventh day is a Sabbath of Yahweh your God; in it you shall not do any work, you or your son or your daughter, your male or your female servant or your cattle or your sojourner who stays with you'* (Ex 20:8-11). Shabbat is the only holy convocation that did not include a sacrifice for sin."

At breakfast, Philip took note at the next table over what sounded like a strong New York Jewish accent: "Breakfast, you call this a breakfast with only four types of yogurt, eight varieties of olives, three type of eggs, four hot cereals, fruit, melons, and six selections of cold cuts and cheese? I can tell you about a breakfast—last week at the King David Hotel in Jerusalem, yada, yada, yada. Now that was a breakfast!" But for us who are used to Andy's three varieties of greasy breakfast, the Tiberias hotel was a gastronomical expanse. No fear of losing weight here! After breakfast we loaded onto a boat to sail up the Sea of Galilee to Capernaum, the city of Jesus.

The leisurely boat ride gave us a chance to recover from the previous day's forced march, and to enjoy the sunshine and fresh air while gazing across the lake at the Golan Heights. Sea Gulls hung suspended in air, riding the breeze. Noticing how the lake was situated in a bowl surrounded by highlands, it is easy to see how a storm could descend on the lake without warning. There was time for your mind to drift back two thousand years: *"Jesus and His disciples got into a boat, and He said to them, 'Let us go over to the other side of the lake.' So they launched out. But as they were sailing along He fell asleep; and a fierce gale of wind descended on the lake, and they began to be swamped and to be in danger. They came to Jesus and woke Him up, saying, 'Master, Master, we are perishing!' And He got up and rebuked the wind and the surging waves, and they stopped, and it became calm. And He said to them, 'Where is your faith?'"* (Luke 8:22-25a). The disciples were panicked in desperate fear for their lives, just like we do sometimes. The Prince of Peace was asleep in the boat. Peace isn't a feeling; it is a person—Jesus the Christ. (I think that would preach.)

Capernaum "(kuh PUHR nay whm) is a Greek transliteration of the Hebrew words *"Kephar Nahum—the village of Nahum."*[25] It was here that Jesus chose to set up his ministry headquarters. We view the ancient synagogue like the one where Jesus taught: *"Truly, truly, I say to you, unless you eat the flesh of the Son of Man and drink His blood, you have no life in yourselves. He who eats My flesh and drinks My blood has eternal life, and I will raise him up on the last day"* (John 6:53-54). At that time many of his disciples withdrew and did not walk with Him anymore. Later we viewed the ruins of what is said to be Peter's home.

Our bus met us in Capernaum and we traveled to the traditional site of the Mt. of Beatitudes: *"When Jesus saw the crowds,*

He went up on the mountain; and after He sat down, His disciples came to Him. He opened His mouth and began to teach them, saying, 'Blessed are the poor in spirit, for theirs is the kingdom of heaven. Blessed are those who mourn, for they shall be comforted. Blessed are the gentle, for they shall inherit the earth. Blessed are those who hunger and thirst for righteousness, for they shall be satisfied. Blessed are the merciful, for they shall receive mercy. Blessed are the pure in heart, for they shall see God. Blessed are the peacemakers, for they shall be called sons of God. Blessed are those who have been persecuted for the sake of righteousness, for theirs is the kingdom of heaven. Blessed are you when people insult you and persecute you, and falsely say all kinds of evil against you because of Me. Rejoice and be glad, for your reward in heaven is great; for in the same way they persecuted the prophets who were before you'" (Matthew 5:1-12). The Kingdom of God, arguably the theme of the Bible, is where Jesus begins His teaching; and we are reminded that "because of Me" you are blessed. (v 11)

The traditional site is on a grassy slope overlooking the Sea of Galilee. The acoustics are such that a person can be standing on the slope talking (maybe one or two hundred feet from the road), yet a person on the road can hear the speaker clearly. Tradition in the day of Jesus was that the teacher would sit. No one knows where on this slope the event took place, but it is the message, not the location that is life changing.

Back in the bus we traveled to Chorazin, and then towards the eastern shore of Galilee to tour the northern region of the Decapolis, Kursi, and Bethsaida. Bethsaida means 'house of fishing,' the home town of Andrew, Peter and Philip, located at the northeast end of the lake. Near here, Jesus fed the 5,000 (Luke 9:10) and healed a blind man (Mark 8:22). Jesus rebuked Bethsaida because He performed great miracles there, but the people did not repent (change their mind about who He was: Matthew 11:21). We stayed overnight at a kibbutz on the northwestern shore of the lake. Sleep in the Holy Land came easy after another full day, but there was so much to see and such a short visit. We could rest when we got home.

After dinner, Emma continued her study of the convocations of Leviticus 23.

PESACH: Passover and the Feast of Unleavened Bread (23:4-14)

(4-8) "Pesach is a remembrance of the Exodus story (Ex 12:1-13:10) of freedom from bondage in Egypt. God instructed Moses to have every household select an unblemished male sheep or goat on the tenth of the month of Nisan (lamb selection day; what we call Palm Sunday when Jesus entered Jerusalem to the shouts of Hosanna), and then on the fourteenth to sacrifice it at twilight. They were to apply the blood to the doorpost and lintels, and then the death angel would see it and 'Passover' that house. They were to eat the lamb along with unleavened bread and bitter herbs. Just as Passover foreshadows our redemption, the Feast of Unleavened Bread exemplifies the holy standard of living to which we are called.

There are four cups of wine (Philip says for my Baptist brethren, 'IT'S REAL WINE!'). At a Passover meal, each represented the four promises Yahweh made to His people in Egypt: the first cup, *'I will bring you out from under the tribulation of Egypt,'* the second cup, *'I will deliver you from their slavery,'* the third cup, *'I will redeem you with an arm outstretched and with great judgments,'* and the fourth cup, *'I will take you to Myself as My People.'*

Jesus celebrated the Passover meal (the Last Supper) the night he was betrayed. After the meal, Jesus used the unleavened bread and the third cup of wine as a picture of Himself; a remembrance that like the unleavened bread there was no sin in Him. The third cup is a picture of the third promise of Exodus 6:6, *'I will redeem you.'* This was the perfect picture of what He was about to do—the sinless Lamb of God paying the penalty of sin, making all people savable. Ephesians 1:7 states, *'In Him we have redemption through His blood, the forgiveness of our trespasses, according to the riches of His grace.'* There is no indication He drank from the fourth cup at the Last Supper, but He will at the Marriage Supper of the Lamb when He will rule over Israel as their Lord and King.

The Feast of Unleavened Bread (23:9-14) was celebrated for seven days after Passover. The bread contained no leaven and there was to be no leaven in the home during this time. Using one candle, a search is made for any products containing leaven which must be removed from the house before the Passover lamb is slain; leaven being symbolic of sin. The unleavened bread is called the 'bread of affliction' because the people left Egypt in such a hurry, the dough had no time to rise.

Feast of Firstfruits—Along with the Passover and Feast of Unleavened Bread was the Feast of Firstfruits. Barley is the crop that would have matured first in the spring, so the waving of the sheaves before Yahweh symbolized the first fruits of the total year's harvest. None of the new grain was to be eaten until this presentation to Yahweh took place. An 'ephah' was about three-fifths of a bushel, so two-tenths would amount to about one gallon dry measure of barley. The wine mentioned as an offering was poured over the sacrifice."

Tuesday, we journeyed north of the Sea of Galilee on the ancient trade route to the city of Hazor, located on the main trade route between Egypt and Mesopotamia. "(HOT zor) Hazor was to Israel in the Old Testament what Capernaum was to Israel in the New Testament. It was a strategic city because it was located on a well-defined hill that straddled the International Highway at a spot where it narrowed along the Jordan River. Thus, it served as a first line of defense against armies attacking from the north."[26]

We next visited Tel Dan where Abraham led a force from Hazor to Dan to rescue his nephew Lot. Further up the road we walked through the nature reserve at one of the sources of the Jordan River and visit the Banias Waterfall. We passed by Nimrod's fortress on our way to Caesarea Philippi, at the foot of Mt. Hermon where Peter recognized Jesus as the Christ: *"And it happened that while He was praying alone, the disciples were with Him, and He questioned them, saying, 'Who do the people say I am?' They answered and said, 'John the Baptist, and others say Elijah; but others, that one of the prophets of old has risen again.' And He said to them, 'But who do you say that I am?' And Peter answered and said, The Christ of God.' "* It was here that Jesus said, *"I will build My church and the gates of Hades shall not overpower it."*

Caesarea Philippi marked the northern most location of Jesus' ministry. Jesus' ministry was restricted to no more than a hundred miles from where He was born. He came to live a righteous life and die—propitiation for the sins of the world. The Father's plan was not for Him to go to the world, but for Him to send us with the message that Peter confessed. Jesus is "the Christ of God!" Because of Him, you are blessed. We then traveled the high road up to the Golan Heights on our way back to the kibbutz to overnight.

After dinner we returned to our study of the feasts of Israel:

<u>SHAVUOT</u>: Pentecost and the Feast of Weeks (23:15-21)

(15-21) "The Feast of Weeks represented the first fruits of the wheat harvest. This feast always occurred on the first day of the week, Sunday, fifty days after the Passover Sabbath. It usually fell around the first of June. The offerings were not per household, but as a whole for the nation.

Mankind Separated from God: The Mishkan (Tabernacle; lit. to dwell) and the Temple were built as the earthly resting place for the Ark of the Covenant. The Ark's top was called the Mercy Seat, above which God's presence dwelled, appearing as the Shekinah Glory. But mankind was separated from God; the Mishkan having tent walls and the tent courtyard having rectangular portable walls to keep the people out. The Temple had a series of walls also providing segregation: the outside court being the Court of the Gentiles, inside being the Court of the Women and the Court of the Men, and an area where only the priest could approach the actual temple. The temple had an outside room where the priest ministered with the altar of incense, the seven branched candelabrum, and the table with twelve loves of shewbread. There was a curtain separating the outer temple from the Holy of Holies where only the High Priest could enter one time per year on the Day of Atonement."

Wednesday we headed to the south end of the Sea of Galilee to the baptismal spot on the Jordan River. As the song goes, "The River Jordan is muddy and cold, chills the body but not the soul." After the blessing of experiencing being baptized in the Jordan, we traveled to Beth Shan/Scythopolis. "Beth Shan is located at the strategic juncture of the Jezreel and Jordan Valleys. Like Jericho, Beth Shan was almost continuously occupied throughout history. Today archaeologists are uncovering the extensive ruins of Roman/Byzantine Scythopolis."[27] It's hard to believe that we were looking at a two thousand year old city being unearthed, but under that might be ten or twenty other cities dating back ten thousand years. It makes an old person feel young.

All aboard south we drove past Mt. Tabor where Judge Deborah gathered 10,000 Israelites to fight the king of Hazor's army with 900 iron covered chariots (plus footmen) under the leadership of Sisera. God caused a thunderstorm, which resulted in the chariots becoming hopelessly mired in mud so that Deborah's army won the battle. (Judges 4 and 5). On to the Spring of Herod where Gideon chose his 300 men. God usually works through a remnant, or just a few who are faithful. The number doesn't seem to matter to Him.

We continued south to the Dead Sea for some black mud and water so salty that we bobbed around like a cork. Amnon knew the place to take the ladies to purchase a famous brand of cosmetics made from some concoction found in the area. Having relieved the pent up need to shop for the women, we proceeded to Masada, the magnificent ruins of the fortress where the Jewish defenders made their final stand in their revolt against Rome. In a last desperate act of rebellion against foreign domination, they took their own lives.

We went back north to En Gedi where David refreshed himself by the springs, and then on to Qumran to see the caves where the Dead Sea Scrolls were discovered. We then made a short visit to Jericho. Like all ancient cities, Jericho underwent destruction and rebuilding many times. But some of the old ruins have been dated back to the New Stone Age, about 7,000 B.C., making it one of the world's oldest cities. The walled fortress city represented a formidable obstacle to Joshua leading Israel into the Promised Land (around 1400 B.C.).

It was here that Rahab hid the Israelite spies, and then confessed her faith in their God: "*I know that Yahweh has given you the land, and that the terror of you has fallen on us, and that all the inhabitants of the land have melted away before you. For we have heard how Yahweh dried up the water of the Red Sea before you when you came out of Egypt, and what you did to the two kings of the Amorites who were beyond the Jordan, to Sihon and Og, whom you utterly destroyed. When we heard it, our hearts melted and no courage remained in any man any longer because of you; for Yahweh your God,*

He is God in heaven above and on earth beneath." Rahab's faith in Yahweh saved her and her family when the walls fell. More importantly, she was a Gentile, and is mentioned in Matthew as being in the genealogy of the Christ of God.

After our visit to Jericho we drove up to Jerusalem. The normal route from the Galilee area was to follow the Jordan River south to Jericho, and then turn west up the Wadi Kelt to Jerusalem. Going up, I always think of what is maybe the saddest verses in the Bible when Jesus said, "*Jerusalem, Jerusalem, who kills the prophets and stones those who are sent to her! How often I wanted to gather your children together, the way a hen gathers her chicks under her wings, and you were unwilling*" (Matt 23:37). However, what makes Jerusalem so important is that it is the place where Yahweh chose for His name to dwell: "*but I have chosen Jerusalem that My name might be there*" (2 Chron 6:6). Amnon added a special touch by teaching our group the song Hevenu Shalom Aleichem (we wrought peace upon you) which we sang over and over on our way up to Jerusalem.

Jerusalem has been the spiritual center of Judaism since the 10th century B.C. It was here that the king of Salem, Melchizedek, ruled and worshiped Yahweh. Abram paid tithes to Melchizedek (Gen 14:17-24). It was here, on Mount Moriah, where Abraham prepared to offer up his only son to Yahweh. It was here where David ruled for thirty-three years, and David's son Solomon built the first temple. And it will be here that God's eternal state shall be established: "*Then I saw a new heaven and a new earth; for the first heaven and the first earth passed away, and there is no longer any sea. And I saw the holy city, new Jerusalem, coming down out of heaven from God, made ready as a bride adorned for her husband. And I heard a loud voice from the throne, saying, 'Behold, the tabernacle of God is among men, and He will dwell among them, and they shall be His people, and God Himself will be among them, and He will wipe away every tear from their eyes; and there will no longer be any death; there will no longer be any mourning, or crying, or pain;*

the first things have passed away' "(Revelation 21:1-4).

That night Emma discussed the interval between the spring and late summer convocations. "Verse 22 is interesting in that it is a break from the convocation feast to talk about leaving the corner of the fields for the poor. You may remember that Ruth gleaned from the corners of Boaz's fields. As a result of this instruction, "do not reap to the very edges of your field," a square or rectangular field would be reaped in a circular pattern, thus leaving a triangle of unreaped grain at each corner. For now just remember that this interval of four months is also important in God's redemption plan."

Thursday we awoke in the City of David. No writing, no matter how eloquent, is a substitute for being there. We began our tour of Jerusalem with a survey of the multiple millennium Old City from a panoramic vista on Mt. Scopus. We then followed Jesus' path to the top of the Mt. of Olives where we had the best view of the temple mount. A few of the hardier souls rode the camels provided by a street entrepreneur. Standing there looking across the Kidron Valley we saw the walled-in East Gate (Golden Gate).

Philip's mind wandered back to an audio tape he had which had been recorded immediately after the siege of Jerusalem during the 1967 Six Day War. When Palestine was partitioned, the Old City was controlled by Jordan. But Israel greatly expanded their territory during the Six Day War. An Israeli army officer had advanced his platoon to the east wall of the Temple Mount at the walled-in Eastern Gate. The safest access to the Temple Mount would be to blow the East Gate, but the officer knew his Bible; that Messiah would enter the temple mount through that gate. Instead of taking the safest access, the officer chose to attack the heavily fortified Lion's Gate. The attack was successful, and the recording documents are of a reporter holding the microphone before a Rabbi who is broadcasting to all Israel that the Temple Mount is in Jewish hands after two thousand years. In the background you can hear shouting and the blowing of the shofar and crying as the reporter quotes Isaiah 62:6.

We descended down the Mount of Olives to the Garden of Gethsemane where Jesus often came to pray, including the night before His crucifixion. This was the place where Jesus prayed before his betrayal and arrest, but it is what He prayed that was so significant. He knew what was about to happen, so one might expect him to pray for strength to endure. However, His thoughts on that fateful night were for those the Father had given Him—including you and me: "*I pray for them. I am not praying for the world, but for those you have given me, for they are yours. All I have is yours, and all you have is mine. And glory has come to me through them. I will remain in the world no longer, but they are still in the world, and I am coming to you. Holy Father, protect them by the power of your name, the name you gave me, so that they may be one as we are one. My prayer is not for them alone. I pray also for those who will believe in me through their message, that all of them may be one, Father, just as you are in me and I am in you. May they also be in us so that the world may believe that you have sent me*" (John 17).

We crossed the Kidron Valley floor to visit the traditional site of David's tomb, and then wound through the colorful bazaars of the Old City on our way to Hezekiah's city wall and the Cardo (the main Roman road). Many of the streets of the Old City were only wide enough for pedestrian traffic. The Old City is a beehive of activity, people shoulder to shoulder moving in all directions. One could smell of what might be only described as, the Middle East. Our senses took in shopkeepers cooking their meals in little tourist shops, not to mention the smell of too many people in one place. Street vendors were selling everything from fresh bread to coffee to ram's horns. But this is exactly what the city would have been like in Jesus' day. Most of Jesus' visits were for required holy convocations when every adult male (Bar Mitzvah, one to whom the commandments apply) Jew was to celebrate three feasts in Jerusalem. At those times the city of a couple hundred thousand would swell to a million or more.

One most memorable stop was in Saint Ann's Cathedral. The acoustics of this majestic building are unbelievable, with multiple echoes reverberating back. So when you get several groups of Christians together singing 'Great is Thy Faithfulness,' it is guaranteed the hair will stand up on the back of your neck and every woman had tears running down her face; you will never forget the experience. We sang a couple of more songs, and then we visited the Temple Institute and viewed the treasures produced for the future third Temple.

The next holy convocation Emma addressed was Rosh Hashanah.

Rosh Hashanah: Trumpets, Jewish Civil New Year (23:23-25)

(23-25) "Rosh Hashanah starts the civil new year, while Pesach starts the religious new year (the Jews have a civil and religious calendar). The words Rosh Hashanah mean 'head of the year.' It is also sometimes called 'The Day of the Sounding of the Shofar' (ram's horn). Tradition has it that God sits in judgment of people and nations during this time, but that is not taught in scripture.

Concerning the practice of the festival, Bruce Scott comments, 'Together with Yom Kippur, Rosh Hashanah is part of the high holidays of Judaism. Both Rosh Hashanah and Yom Kippur are referred to as the Days of Awe because during this time an individual's fate is inscribed (on Rosh Hashanah) and sealed (on Yom Kippur) for the coming year. The ten days from Rosh Hashanah to Yom Kippur inclusively are considered The Days of Penitence, during which people are admonished to repent of their sins and perform good deeds in order to merit an inscription in the Book of Life.'[28] It is said that Rosh Hashanah does not determine a person's eternal destiny, but rather their life for the coming year. 'The verdict is settled by opening three books: one listing the righteous, one listing the wicked, and one listing those somewhere in between. Those in the first book are immediately inscribed for life; those in the second book for death; and those in the third book are given ten days to repent and perform enough good deeds to outweigh their bad deeds.'[29]

Scott wrote, 'On Wednesday, June 7, 1967, at the height of the Six-Day War, Israeli forces pushed into Jerusalem and recaptured the Temple Mount. After two thousand years, the Jewish people's holiest place was once again in their possession. At the Western Wall, the last vestige of the walls that once surrounded the ancient Temple, hardened soldiers wept openly in joy. Others gently embraced the rough stones that towered above them. The Chief Army Chaplain, Rabbi Schlomo Goren, then performed a very significant act: He sounded the shofar.' (Same event that was referred to on Thursday, overlooking the Temple mount.)

'People familiar with the prophetic designs of the Feast of Rosh Hashanah immediately recognized the intent of Rabbi Goren. By blowing the shofar, he symbolically announced to the world Israel's return to the home of their forefathers. This is the prophetic message of Rosh Hashanah—the future return, restoration, or regathering of the people of Israel back to the land God has given to them.'[30]"

Friday we were back in the Old City to view the Western (Wailing) Wall and the southern Temple Mount excavations, sometimes simply called the *Kotel* (the wall). The wall is in fact nothing more than the retaining wall expanded by Herod the Great for the building of the Second Temple. A section almost 200 feet long and 60 feet high is exposed, making a kind of plaza where faithful Jews and Pilgrims from all parts of the world come to place a written prayer between the great stones. The entire wall stretches a little over a quarter mile. The wall is made of limestone blocks, most weighing between two and eight tons. One enormous stone weighs 570 tons. Each stone has a finely chiseled border that would make our finest stone masons blush with envy.

Before going up to the Temple Mount, we spent a few minutes at the steps located at the south end of the retaining wall. This is one of the few places where you can accurately say Jesus walked in this area. Next we made our way up to the Temple Mount to view the El Aksa Mosque and the Dome of the Rock. Never being one to beat around the bush, these structures are here as part of Satan's devious claim to a part interest in this holy site for Muslims. But, truth be known, admittedly Philip still has a bur under his saddle after being yelled at by a Muslim guard and having an AK47 pointed in his direction while trying to make his way to the Golden Gate. "Forbidden, forbidden, forbidden!" Somewhere in the area of the Dome of the Rock, the Temple once stood. Orthodox Jews will not walk in this area for fear they may accidentally transgress the site of the Holy of Holies.

We returned to the Western Wall to enter the excavated walk along the wall, making our way to the Via Dolorosa. Not to bust anybody's bubble, but when you walk the Via Dolorosa you certainly are not walking the same street Jesus walked. That street would be somewhere below the present way, but even knowing that it can still be a meaningful symbolic journey. The Via Dolorosa ends at the Church of the Holy Sepulchre, the traditional crucifixion site and burial place of Jesus. It makes you sick when you see the vulgar, tawdry, ostentatious, tasteless way religious idiots have decorated the building. It looks like a crazed lunatic decorated it for Christmas, complete with huge tree ornaments. However, that being said, it is the most likely spot outside the first century walls where Jesus may have been crucified and buried.

Standing outside the church, Amnon pointed out an old wooden ladder in one of the second floor windows, and then related one really amusing story: "The Church of the Holy Sepulchre has shared governance by six Christian sects. That ladder was placed there in the 19th century but has remained there ever since because they cannot agree who has the authority to take it down" (true story, don't you just love religion). The remainder of the afternoon is optional for shopping or revisiting a site in the Old City.

Always present in Philip's thoughts, especially having just visited the Old City, was that this is the place on earth where Yahweh says He would cause His name to dwell, and we will one day dwell with him. Yahweh, who dwells in unapproachable light, such that even the angels cover their eyes, allows us to cry out, "Abba! Father!" (Rom 8:15).

On our bus ride back to the hotel, Amnon had our driver stop at the Jerusalem equivalent of Dunkin Donut. All of us were filling our sacks with sweets when Philip hears over his left shoulder a small voice in the distance. A child (as he was running towards the shop) was calling out, "Abba, Abba, Abba." When that child got to within a few feet of the owner of the shop, he just launched into his father's arms, and his father held him in his arms with tender love. That verse out of Romans crossed Philip's mind when he heard the child crying out, "Abba! Abba! Abba!" He knew that someday we will dwell with God face to face!

After dinner Emma picks up her nightly Bible Study.

<u>Yom Kippur</u>: The Day of Atonement (23:26-32)

(26-32) "Yom Kippur occurs on the tenth of Tishri (September or October), lasting one day only. The significance of this holiday is that tradition has it that a person's fate for the coming year is 'sealed' on this day.

When the Temple existed in Jerusalem, the High Priest alone would enter the Holy of Holies (this one time per year), wearing the breastplate which bore twelve stones representing the names of the twelve tribes, and there make a sin offering for atonement. A bull was chosen as a sin offering for the High Priest. Two goats were chosen as sin offerings for the people, and then lots were drawn to see which goat would be the one sacrificed and which one would be the scapegoat. With two separate quick trips behind the veil, the blood of the bull and the blood of the goat were sprinkled on the Mercy Seat. The people anxiously awaited the appearing of the High Priest, because if God was not satisfied with the sacrifice, He would have struck the High Priest dead behind the veil. After the High Priest came out of the Holy of Holies he would place both hands on the scapegoat's head. He then would confess the sins of the people, and send the goat to be turned loose in the wilderness for removal of sin."

Saturday we boarded the bus to Bethlehem and the Church of the Nativity for a walking tour. Bethlehem means 'house of bread.' Two thousand years ago it was nothing more than what back home we would call a wide spot in the road, on the main north south road through the Judean hill country. The countryside along the short drive between Jerusalem and Bethlehem is much more representative of what it would have looked like when Jesus was born there.

In this area is the tomb of Rachel, Jacob's wife. The story of Ruth took place here where she gleaned in Boaz's barley and wheat fields. David was born in Bethlehem, and in the surrounding countryside he shepherded his father's flock. Micah prophesied that Bethlehem would be the birth place of Messiah: *"But as for you, Bethlehem Ephrathah, too little to be among the clans of Judah, from you One will go forth for Me to be ruler in Israel"* (He will be a human king). "*His going forth are from long ago, from the days of eternity*" (He will be divine/God; Micah 5:2). Sadly, this is also the place where Herod ordered the slaughter of every male child two years old and younger. (Rabbit trail: I dare anyone to read Kay Arthur's *Israel, My Beloved* and try to hold it together when you get to the part about Herod's slaughter. One other thought, Satan has been consistent in the murder of children, from the sacrifices to Baal, Herod's slaughter, and abortion today).

Of course the only reason anyone even knows the name Bethlehem is because of the advent of the Son of Man. Our party visited the traditional site of Christ's birth, the Church of the Nativity, just so we could say we were there, but we spent more time in a nearby cave that represents what the scene would have actually looked like two thousand years ago.

All aboard, we traveled a little further south and east to the Herodium, one of Herod the Great's palace/fortresses which became his burial place. This palace is another testimony to the amazing building projects of Herod. It is built up on a great mound, looking much like a volcano. Walking through the ruins, it is obvious that this was a world class resort, situated to take advantage of the prevailing wind—kind of a first century air-conditioning. However, we could not escape the irony that one of the greatest builders/rulers' legacies were nothing more than a heap of ruins. While Jesus the Christ lived in relative poverty, His legacy is eternal glory.

We traveled west to the Valley of Elah, where David met and killed Goliath. Standing in the valley, we remembered David's response to Goliath's taunting: "*who is this uncircumcised Philistine, that he should taunt the armies of the living God?*" (1 Samuel 17:26b). David would not allow the insolence of anyone, even a giant, when it came to the honor of the God of Israel. David said to Saul, "*Yahweh, who delivered me from the paw of the lion and from the paw of the bear, He will deliver me from the hand of this Philistine*" (1 Samuel 17:37). There is a great Hebrew word that described David's heart attitude toward the honor of God: *chutzpah* (intestinal fortitude). David's words and faith are very convicting.

The seaside resort of Ashkelon was our last stop of the day before returning to Jerusalem to overnight. During the time of the judges, the Philistines expanded their control in Israel. Judges 13-16 tells the story of Samson and the Philistines. The importance of the city is that it was situated on the main road by the sea, along with having clean spring water. It had a major harbor from which was exported wine as far away as Germany. One other interesting fact is that the city was famous for exporting a vegetable which became extremely popular throughout the Mediterranean. The scallion's name is a corruption of Ashkelon. The end of Ashkelon is described by Jeremiah when the Babylonians conquered the land.

Tonight, Emma covers the last of the holy convocations.

Sukkoth: The Feast of Tabernacles (23:33-44)

"Sukkoth was the last of the three pilgrimage feasts where all men were required to celebrate in Jerusalem. It was to begin on the fifteenth day of Tishri (September or October), lasting for seven days. This feast was symbolic of the exodus in Sinai when the people lived in tents. An outside shelter (booth called *sukkah)* was erected to live in for the seven days of the feast. In contrast to the preceding Day of Atonement, Sukkoth was a feast of thanksgiving for the end of the growing season's bountiful harvest; sometimes called the Feast of Ingathering because it was at the end of the harvest season.

Keil and Delitzsch comment: "The leading character of the feast of Tabernacles, which is indicated at the outset by the emphatic (alep kap), was to consist in joy before Jehovah. As a feast, i.e. a feast of joy, it was to be kept for seven days; so that Israel should be only rejoicing, and give itself up entirely to joy (Deut. 16). Now, although the motive assigned in Deuteronomy is this: 'for God will bless thee (Israel) in all thine increase, and in all the work of thine hands;' and although the feast, as a 'feast of in-gathering,' was a feast of thanksgiving for the gathering in of the produce of the land, 'the produce of the floor and wine-press;' and the blessing they had received in the harvested fruits, the oil and wine, which contributed even more to the enjoyment of life than the bread that was needed for daily food, furnished in a very high degree the occasion and stimulus to the utterance of grateful you: the origin and true signification of the feast of Tabernacles are not to be sought for in this natural allusion to the blessing of the harvest, but dwelling in booths was the principal point in the feast; and this was instituted as a law for all future time (ver. 41), that succeeding generations might know that Jehovah had caused the children of Israel to dwell in booths when He led them out of Egypt (ver 43).'[31] Thus, it is in remembering God's grace, care, and His very presence with them in the wilderness that is the central theme of this last convocation.

Richard Booker commented: 'Because the Feast of Taber-nacles was the last of seven feasts, it completed the religious sea-son. The number seven in the Bible represents completion. We learned from this that the Feast of Tabernacles represented the completed or finished work of God in both this present age in which we live and the lives of individual Christian.'[32]"

Sunday, our last full day in Jerusalem, we visited the Shrine of the Book to see the Dead Sea Scrolls. The main building looked like a giant replica of the top of one of the containers which held the scrolls. The prize of the Shrine is two copies of Isaiah which are 1,000 years older than any other Jewish text, written about 150

B.C. There is no other book in the Old Testament that says more about Messiah than Isaiah. We watched in wonder as a young Jewish boy, with his father holding him up in his arms, read the Isaiah scroll. More than 700 manuscripts, biblical and sectarian, were discovered in the eleven caves in the Qumran area. Parts of each Old Testament book, with the exception of Esther, were found among the Qumran scrolls.

We went to the incredibly impactful Yad VaShem, the Holocaust Museum, and the Children of the Holocaust Memorial (I don't care how tough you are, you will cry at the children's memorial). We proceeded to go to the Avenue of the Righteous Among the Nations where there is a plaque and a tree planted for Gentiles who saved Jews during the Holocaust. Philip asked Amnon if he knew where Corrie ten Boom's tree was located. Amnon broke into a big smile and told Philip where to look. He also told him to come back and talk with him afterwards. Philip made his way to the spot, but found a small sapling while all the other trees were mature. When Philip got back to Amnon, he explained, "When Corrie died, her tree died and they had to plant a new one." Philip felt the hair on the back of his neck stand on end.

From there we traveled just outside the north gates of the Old City to the Garden Tomb (Gordon's Calvary) for a worship service and Lord's Supper to celebrate Christ's resurrection. There is a wooden door on the tomb for security, which is folded back during the day. On the inside, when you turn to leave, you will note these words carved in the door: "HE IS NOT HERE, FOR HE IS RISEN." We had several hours remaining in the day, and everyone had free time to visit anyplace they wish. Several of us took the bus to the south side of the old city to visit the area where the city of David had been, which was outside and south of the present walled city. We had run as hard as we could every day seeing this marvelous country, yet had barely scratched the surface.

After dinner Emma provided a summary of her Leviticus study. She handed out a chart to be filled in, and then used a large whiteboard the hotel provided to present the information for the chart (see the chart below).

"In the spring are four convocations: Passover, Unleavened Bread, First Fruits, and Pentecost. They are pictures of what Jesus accomplished in his thirty-three years on earth. Then there is a four month interval, which is the church age, between the time of Christ's ascension and His return to establish His kingdom on earth. In the fall are three convocations: Trumpets, Day of Atonement, and Tabernacles which will be accomplished by Christ on His return. The seven major feasts and the Sabbath day of rest are a complete picture of the work of Christ; past, present, and future.

THE WORKS OF JESUS CHRIST

PAST,   FULFILLED DURING JESUS 33 YEAR MINISTRY

PASSOVER	THE CROSS, LAMB OF GOD
UNLEAVENED BREAD	SINLESS LIFE OF OBEDIENCE
FIRST FRUITS	RESURRECTION LIFE
PENTECOST	GIVING OF THE HOLY SPIRIT

PRESENT INTERIM   CHURCH AGE

FUTURE,   TO BE FULFILLED AT CHRIST'S RETURN

ROSHASHANAH/TRUMPETS	JUDGE AND WAGE WAR
YOM KIPPUR/ATONEMENT	ISRAEL'S MEDIATOR
SUKKOTH/TABERNACLES	JESUS RULES FROM JERUSALEM

These are the PAST WORKS OF CHRIST (Spring Feasts):

Passover and the Feast of Unleavened Bread (23:4-14)
In type, the Passover represents the work of Jesus on the cross, a

substitutionary sin offering acceptable to God for the sins of the world. The emphasis is on our redemption through the blood of the Lamb of God. For fifteen hundred years the Jews had sacrificed at Passover to 'cover' their sins, but only the blood of Jesus could take them away. John the Baptizer testified, '*The next day he saw Jesus coming to him, and said, Behold the Lamb of God who takes away the sin of the world!*' (John 1:29).

Feast of Unleavened Bread (23:9-14)

Leaven was said to represent sin; Jesus was the sinless bread of life (2 Cor 5:21; John 3:5). The day after Jesus had fed the five-thousand, John records this conversation between Jesus and the crowd: '*Our fathers ate the manna in the wilderness; as it is written 'HE GAVE THEM BREAD OUT OF HEAVEN TO EAT.' Jesus answered, 'Truly, truly, I say to you, it is not Moses who has given you the bread out of heaven, but it is My Father who gives you the true bread out of heaven. For the bread of God is that which comes down out of heaven, and gives life to the world.' They said therefore to Him, 'Lord, evermore give us this bread.' Jesus said to them, 'I am the bread of life; he who comes to Me shall not hunger, and he who believes in Me shall never thirst*' (John 6:31-35).

Feast of First Fruits

Jesus was resurrected as the first fruit from the dead, the beginning of the harvest of souls. Paul wrote, '*But now Christ has been raised from the dead, the first fruits of those who are asleep. For since by a man came death, by a man also came the resurrection of the dead. For as in Adam all die, so also in Christ all shall be made alive*' (1 Cor 20-22).

Shavuot - Pentecost and the Feast of Weeks (23:15-21)

In type and time, Shavuot represented Pentecost when Jesus was glorified and ascended into heaven. He then sent the Holy Spirit whom He poured out for all people, Jews and Gentiles alike, fifty days after His resurrection. Jesus said, '*The hour has come for the Son of Man to be glorified. Truly, truly, I say to you, unless a grain of wheat falls into the earth and dies, it remains by itself alone; but if it dies, it bears much fruit*' (John 12:23b-24). With Jesus' substitutionary sacrifice and the giving of the Holy Spirit, all of those segregating walls of the temple were broken down. For the first time since Adam and Eve were cast out of the garden, all people had access through Jesus to the Father.

These are the PRESENT WORKS OF CHRIST
(Interim Church Age)

The New Testament lesson here is the church's responsibility for harvest and a tender heart towards the poor (i.e., those outside God's promises). There is a four month interval between the four spring convocations and the three fall convocations, a time for the church to reach outside its walls to harvest those who glean at the corners of our field. "*And Jesus came up and spoke to them, saying, 'All authority has been given to Me in heaven and on earth. Go therefore and make disciples of all the nations, baptizing them in the name of the Father and the Son and the Holy Spirit, teaching them to observe all that I commanded you; and lo, I am with you always, even to the end of the age'*" (Matthew 28:18-20).

These are the FUTURE WORKS OF CHRIST (Fall Feast)
Rosh Hashanah: Trumpets, Jewish New Year (23:23-25)

Zacharias, John the Baptizer's father, prophesied, "*Blessed be the Lord God of Israel, for He has visited us and accomplished redemption for His people, and has raised up a horn of salvation for us in the house of David His servant*" (Luke 1:68-69). Redemption of the Jewish people as a nation is a future event at the end of the Tribulation. At His coming, Jesus will lead the army of God. John the apostle recorded, "*And I saw heaven opened; and behold, a white horse, and He who sat upon it is called Faithful and True; and in righteousness He judges and wages war*" (Revelation 19:11).

Yom Kippur: The Day of Atonement (23:26-32)

The prophetic significance of Yom Kippur is that Israel has not recognized Jesus as both the atoning sacrifice and their Great High Priest. Judaism today does not recognize the necessity of a mediator between man and God, contrary to their own scriptures. Melchizedek was a mediator for Abram. Israel has always had a mediator: Moses, Aaron, priests, judges, prophets and kings. The NT says, *'For there is one God, and one mediator also between God and men, the man Christ Jesus'* (1 Tim 2:5; also see Heb 8:6; 9:15; 12:24y).

Sukkoth: The Feast of Tabernacles (23:33-44)

As this feast looked back to the days of wandering in the Sinai, it also had an aspect of looking forward to the time when the promised Messiah would rescue Israel. In prophecy, the Feast of Tabernacles is a type of future days when Messiah will rule on David's throne from Jerusalem: *'In that day I will raise up the fallen booth of David, and wall up its breaches; I will also raise up its ruins, and rebuild it as in the days of old; that they may possess the remnant of Edom and all the nations who are called by My name, declares Yahweh who does this'* (Amos 9:11-12; also see 9:13-15).

Richard Booker comments, "As part of the ritual proceeding, a certain priest would draw water from the Pool of Siloam with a golden pitcher. He would then come to the altar at the Temple where the High Priest would take the pitcher and pour the water into a basin at the foot of the altar . . . Just as the fervor of the celebration reaches its peak at the pouring of the water, Jesus makes a bold declaration. John was an eyewitness to it and wrote, *'On the last day, the great day of the feast, Jesus stood and cried out saying, If anyone thirsts, let him come to Me and drink. He who believes in Me, as the Scripture has said, out of his heart will flow rivers of living water. But this He spoke concerning the Spirit, whom those believing in Him would receive; for the Holy Spirit was not yet given, because Jesus was not yet glorified'* (John 7:37-39, NKJV)."[33]

Jesus has fulfilled the first four feasts in His thirty-three year ministry. We are presently in the interval between the spring and fall feasts. This is a time of gathering at the corners of the field, the Church Age. Jesus will fulfill the last three convocations, establishing the Kingdom of God on earth. Selah"

On the flight home we have time to think about the sights and events of this extraordinary historical land; past, present and future. I always look forward to the next visit. Emma's study was particularly impactful for me. The Anointed One (Messiah) has completed the work of redemption for the sins of the world (rendering all people savable). He is presently working in the interval of the church age, and He will return to restore Israel to spiritual faithfulness to Yahweh: *"And I shall give them one heart, and put a new spirit within them. And I shall take the heart of stone out of their flesh and give them a heart of flesh, that they may walk in My statutes and keep My ordinances and do them. Then they will be My people, and I shall be their God"* (Ezekiel 11:19-20).

NEXT YEAR IN JERUSALEM

Psalm 137 relates the Babylonian captive's lament over Jerusalem: *"By the rivers of Babylon, there we sat down and wept, when we remembered Zion. Upon the willows in the midst of it we hung our harps. For there our captors demanded of us songs, and our tormentors mirth, saying, 'Sing us one of the songs of Zion.' How can we sing the LORD'S song in a foreign land? If I forget you, O Jerusalem, may my right hand forget her skill. May my tongue cling to the roof of my mouth if I do not remember you, if I do not exalt Jerusalem above my chief joy."*

But the Temple was destroyed 2,000 years ago. What does "Next Year in Jerusalem" mean today? Those words are said concluding the yearly Seder meal, Passover. It would be a mistake to suppose that most Israelis are religious people in the orthodox form; in fact the majority are not. In the most basic sense, it means redemption—past and future. Most Jews are comfortable expressing the Messianic hope that one day in the future the "Anointed One" will come, destroy the oppressing armies, redeem the nation, and then rebuild the Temple in Jerusalem.

But what would "Next Year in Jerusalem" mean for Christians? Once again it would be a gross exaggeration to suggest that most Christians are evangelical (a theological view emphasizing personal faith and the authority of the Bible). The Greek text reveals a very interesting fact about our future eternal residence. The Temple enclosure is the Greek word '*hieron*.' However, the Greek word used for our future home is '*naos*,' which is the Holy of Holies (the innermost cubical where the presence of God dwelled above the Ark of the Covenant): "*Do you not know that you are a temple (naos) of God and that the Spirit of God dwells in you?*" (1 Corinthians 3:16). "*So then you are no longer strangers and aliens, but you are fellow citizens with the saints, and are of God's household, having been built on the foundation of the apostles and prophets, Christ Jesus Himself being the cornerstone, in whom the whole building, being fitted together, is growing into a holy temple (naos) in the Lord, in whom you also are being built together into a dwelling of God in the Spirit*" (Ephesians 2:19-22). Finally, in Revelation the apostle John describes the New Jerusalem: "*I saw no temple in it, for the Lord God the Almighty and the Lamb are its temple (naos). And the city has no need of the sun or of the moon to shine on it, for the glory of God has illumined it, and its lamp is the Lamb*" (Revelation 21:22-23). Consequently, our journey ends at the future tabernacle (dwelling place), where we will dwell face to face in the presence of The Almighty. So I say to you, "NEXT YEAR IN JERUSALEM."

CHAPTER 16

SOLA FIDE (FAITH ALONE),
GALATIANS 3 & 4

Saturday morning found Philip at his shooting range, testing a 44 hand load for accuracy. The 44 Magnum is a great round, but for West Texas it is more than is needed. Philip had a long running romance with the 44, so he determined to load a round that would be accurate, yet a little easier on the hand and the ears.

Long ago Philip had read about control bear hunters using dogs and a 44 Special load that would drive a 240 grain hard cast bullet to about eleven hundred feet per second, the slightly shorter case with slow burning powder being the key. It didn't make the dogs deaf, but it had enough oomph to penetrate to the vitals of a bear. The general idea was a 44 Magnum case cut down to 44 Special length, loaded with slower burning powder atop a magnum primer to get the desired accuracy and velocity, while at the same time keeping the pressures relatively low (not for experimenting, use only loading manual data).

At his friend's gun shop in Dallas, Philip had seen 44 Magnum revolvers with the cylinder and top strap blown off by hand loads created by idiots with just enough information to be dangerous (the extreme pressures probably resulting from a half- filled case of slow burning powder, or way too much fast burning powder).

Speaking of idiots, one Saturday Philip's friend was shorthanded so he was helping out at the gun shop. The shop was a warranty station for many of the popular brands, plus they had a good reputation as gunsmiths. So they had a lot of guns pass through the shop. About mid-morning, this nimrod came in with a 357 revolver with a lead reload stuck in the barrel. He was hoping we could get the bullet out, but he wasn't real sure about the bulge in the barrel. On questioning, he said the first shot had very little recoil or noise, but the second and third shot "kicked a lot and real loud"—no kidding Sherlock. As unbelievable as it was, this dude had fired a squib load (less than minimum power load) which stuck in the barrel, followed immediately with two more. The quality of the materials used by the manufacturer saved this dude's life—this time.

Being one who did not believe in reinventing the wheel, Philip had found the appropriate loading data in one of his loading books, so the question became one of tinkering with accuracy in his S&W 629 revolver. With a five inch barrel and open sights at twenty-five yards shooting three groups of six rounds, the tests were promising. He grouped a fraction less than an inch, using a sandbag hold and lots and lots of patience between rounds.

Philip was about to switch to his 22 rifle when none other than Rabbi Lawrence Cohen walked up. Philip unloaded and secured his firearm, and then turned his attention to his new friend. "Rabboni, I haven't seen you in months. How is your retreat center going?" The Rabbi, who had become considerably less formal since settling in, walked forward with a welcome smile and firm handshake. "Philip, I have missed you. We have had two groups come through our facilities and it is everything I hoped for. But I have several months before we start the fall retreat schedule, and I have time for some intense personal study. You once said to me that you wanted to take advantage of someone to argue the scriptures with, so I wanted to find out if you are up to giving it a go."

Philip knew he was no intellectual match for Larry, so the sideways look he gave was a little like the sheriff looking over the gunslinger who just drifted into town. "Well Larry, what were you thinking about, maybe something simple like 'The Law?'" Larry, squaring up to Philip to accept the challenge, replied: "That was exactly what I was thinking!" "Say that with a smile stranger." Philip realized the stranger in town had come to do business, so he set his jaw and moved his right hand to his side flexing his fingers, eyes locked, waiting for his challenger to make the first move. He realized that neither man was wearing a 45 strapped low to his hip. "Well stranger, if you want a shootout on the Law you'll have to take it up with my hired gunslinger friend by the name of Saul, a good Jewish boy."

The good thing about Larry was that he was so smart, he could just about read Philip's mind before he said something (I hate that). He played along! "Who is this Saul fellow I have to face to get to you?" Philip squinting, eyes still locked, responded: "He's the fastest gun in the west! No one has ever beaten him and I don't recommend you try, pilgrim." Larry replied: "I came here to study; if I am going to have to shoot it out I want to go against the best, so I accept. In front of the saloon at high noon!" Philip stood just a little taller, and said, "The women and children had better get off the street because this is going to get interesting.

Here's the challenge tenderfoot—the book of Galatians, chapters 3 and 4. I suggest we study during the week, and then meet to discuss. I will give you my study notes, and there is a ton of stuff, good and bad, on the internet." The two men shook on the deal with a little laughter. It turned out Larry was not as much a morning person as Philip, so they agreed to meet after dinner one time a week. Philip suggested Larry come to dinner because there was no way Emma was going to miss this. Philip loaned Larry one of his NAS Bibles with instructions to read the book of Galatians a couple of times.

The following day Philip had to go into town for horse feed and a mineral block, so he left early to visit with the boys at Andy's Cafe. He passed an older fellow walking towards town about a mile and a half out, looked in his rear view mirror, and then pulled to the side. It turned out the fella had a ranch about ten miles out of town, and didn't have enough gas to get into town. He was short on funds to buy gas even if he had tried to drive it.

Philip introduced himself, and the man said his name was Nate Wilson. Nate had run low on groceries, but had enough money to buy what he needed as long as he didn't have to buy gas also. When that happened, and apparently it happens often, he walked or hitched-a-ride into town. Nate was probably in his early fifties, but looked older. He was clean shaven (except for a well kept mustache). He had well-worn clothes and hat, but generally clean and well mannered. Philip asked if he had breakfast, which he hadn't, so considering the grocery store wouldn't be open for about an hour, Philip bought Nate breakfast at Andy's.

During breakfast, Philip explained his schedule. So if Nate didn't want to hang around town, he would meet him back at the grocery store and drive him home. Philip picked up his feed, then met Nate at the appointed time. Out here you don't pry into a man's business, but Nate was the talkative type and explained his life story.

It turned out he was adopted as a baby into a wealthy family in Fort Worth. He had an older sister and brother; the sister was a lawyer in Dallas and the brother was a doctor in Tyler. As Nate put it, he wasn't the sharpest knife in the drawer, so his dad had drawn up legal documents that basically made the family trust controlled by two out of three votes. He was the odd man out every time. His dad had left him fifteen hundred acres of land, with the condition that he could not sell any part of it. The sister was the money keeper in the family, so she paid all the taxes and sent Nate an allowance monthly.

In his earlier days, he had gotten into alcohol, drugs, and minor scraps with the law—each time bailed out by the family. But later on in life he had found an occupation he loved. He got clean and worked for several years in Midland until his dad died. At that time it was occupy the ranch or lose it, so he chose to move in. When they arrived at Nate's house, it was nicer than Philip expected; nothing fancy but a nice two bedroom home, much like the larger ranches provided for a foreman.

Nate insisted Philip come in for just a moment so that he could show Philip his passion. Nate directed Philip to the garage where Nate had a fairly complete gun shop. He had all second hand equipment, but also had a working lathe and mill, plus assorted other equipment. It turned out Nate had studied the gunsmithing trade at Trinidad College in Colorado. Nate explained that this is where his spending money goes. He had a limited number of customers, but did some contract work for a couple of gun shops and kept busy.

He had just finished a trigger job on a 1911 type pistol, locked the slide back and handed it to Philip. Nate nodded at Philip. "Feel that trigger and tell me what you think." Philip had used some pretty good gunsmiths to finish off his pistols, so he knew what a good trigger job felt like. But this one was exceptional; there was no creep and it broke like glass. By this time Nate had Phillip's full attention. "Nate, can you duplicate that trigger job every time?" Nate just smiled, "Not bad, huh?" Philip explained he was in the process of collecting parts to put together another pistol, so when he had it finished he would like to have Nate take a look at it. He then excused himself and headed home, thinking "you just never know what's around the next corner."

—III—

Philip's Study Notes, Galatians 3:1-17

Emailed to Rabbi Cohen for their study

In chapter 1, Paul gives the gospel: "*the Lord Jesus Christ, who gave Himself for our sins, that He might deliver us out of this present evil age, according to the will of our God and Father, to whom be the glory forevermore*" (vv 3b-5). Then in the next verse Paul expresses his amazement, "*that you are so quickly deserting Him who called you by the grace of Christ, for a different gospel; which is really not another; only there are some who are disturbing you, and want to distort the gospel of Christ*" (vv 6-7).

David Stern provides a Messianic Jewish perspective into Paul's use of the term legalism: "It becomes clear in what follows that the particular bad news to which the Galatians have been exposed is *legalism*. Legalism I define as the false principle that God grants acceptance to people, considers them righteous and worthy of being in his presence, on ground of their obedience to a set of rules, apart from putting their trust in God, relying on him, loving him, and accepting his love for them."[34]

In the first two chapters of Galatians, Paul argues that he has apostolic authority, that the gospel he preached was divinely inspired. Thus, he spoke for God and the only true gospel. Salvation by grace through faith alone is not a New Testament idea only. Much of Jewish scripture is prophetic of what Messiah will fulfill. As an example, the Old Testament describes the same type of salvation, by grace, for the regathered nation Israel in the last days:

Jeremiah 24:7: "*And I will give them a heart to know Me, for I am Yahweh; and they will be My people, and I will be their God, for they will return to Me with their whole heart.*" Ezekiel 36:26-27: "*Moreover, I will give you a new heart and put a new spirit within you; and I will remove the heart of stone from your flesh and give you a heart of flesh. And I will put My Spirit within you and cause you to walk in My statutes, and you will be careful to observe My ordinances."* That is a lot of 'I wills' from God; in other words, grace alone.

In the first two chapters, Paul is primarily referring to his experiences in salvation, but now in chapter 3 he turns to the Galatians' experience in salvation. Paul starts out (3:1) asking the Galatians how they had become intellectually inconsistent since the true gospel of grace was preached so clearly to them. Paul then asks them four questions concerning their own experience of salvation to remind them that they believed in Christ by faith apart from works:

1) *"Did you receive the Spirit by the works of the Law, or by hearing with faith?"* BAM! First nail in the coffin of adding works to grace. You received the Holy Spirit by believing alone, not by keeping the law.

2) *"Are you so foolish, having begun by the Spirit, are you now being perfected by the flesh?"* BAM! Second nail in the coffin of works. Logical conclusion; if you were justified by grace through faith, are you so foolish as to think you will be sanctified differently?

3) *"Did you suffer so many things in vain, if indeed it was in vain?"* BAM! Third nail in the coffin of works. Persecution was an everyday event for Christians. Were they enduring the pain of persecution in vain?

4) *"Does He then, who provides you with the Spirit and works miracles among you, do it by the works of the Law, or by hearing with faith?"* BAM! Fourth nail in the coffin of works. Those miracles, recorded in the book of Acts (14:3, 8-11), were by supernatural power alone.

Paul isn't saying the Law is defective; he is saying that keeping it (works and/or religious merit) is not the means of salvation.

Paul leapfrogs Moses and goes back to Abraham as his authoritative example. How was Abraham, the father of the nation Israel, justified? Good question! The answer is in Genesis 15: *"And He took him outside and said, 'Now look toward the heavens, and count the stars, if you are able to count them.' And He said to him, 'So shall your descendants be.' Then he believed in the LORD; and He reckoned it to him as righteousness"* (vv 5-6).

Not only was Abraham justified by grace through faith, it was before he was circumcised (Gen 17:24) or performed any works of the Law. Barclay comments, "Paul declares that to be a true descendant of Abraham is not a matter of flesh and blood; the real descendant is the man who makes the same venture of faith. Therefore, it is not those who seek merit through the law who inherit the promise made to Abraham; but those of every nation who repeat his act of faith in God. It was by an act of faith that the Galatians had begun. Surely they are not going to slip back into legalism—and lose their inheritance."[35] I am not sure of Barclay's position on Israel, but the Gentiles being blessed did not negate the future promises of Israel in the millennium.

Now Paul is going to argue from a negative point to prove that the Law cannot bring righteousness (3:10-12). The Law cannot justify, it can only condemn. Paul quotes Deuteronomy 27:26, *"For as many as are of the works of the Law are under a curse; for it is written, 'CURSED IS EVERYONE WHO DOES NOT ABIDE BY ALL THINGS WRITTEN IN THE BOOK OF THE LAW, TO PERFORM THEM.'"* Paul continues by quoting the law (Scriptures), this time the Prophet Habakkuk: *"THE RIGHTEOUS MAN SHALL LIVE BY FAITH"* (Hab 2:4; my life's verse by the way).

Again David Stern's perspective of the true intent of the Law says, "The key to this paragraph is in sorting out when the Greek word *nomos* means God's Torah and when it means legalistic perversion of it, as discussed in 2:16b and 2:19. In my judgment, most translations fail to make this essential distinction . . . Legalism is the exact opposite of trust. Verse 11 assumes this, but verse 12 proves it. The proof is that legalism uses a wrong hermeneutic. That is, instead of letting the Torah as a whole speak for itself

(2:19) and thus guide behavior, legalism selects one verse, takes it out of context, and elevates it above the rest of the Torah, so that it replaces the Torah as the ultimate authority; it becomes a canon within the canon. . . The heresy of legalism, when applied to the Torah, says that anyone who does these things, that is, anyone who mechanically follows the rules of Shabbat, kashrut, etc., will attain life through them, will be saved, will enter the Kingdom of God, will obtain eternal life. No need to trust God, just obey the rules! The problem with this simplistic ladder to Heaven is that legalism conveniently ignores the rule that trust must underlie all rule—following which that God finds acceptable. But trust necessarily converts mere rule—following into something altogether different, in fact, into its opposite, genuine faithfulness to God. Therefore, legalistic obedience to Torah commands (that is, works of law) is actually disobedience to the Torah!"[36]

Paul anticipates his opponent's objection: Why not both Law and faith? Paul's answer: Have at it; all you have to do is keep the Law perfectly; which is supported by Leviticus 18:5, '*HE WHO PRACTICES THEM SHALL LIVE BY THEM.*' The principles of faith and works are antithetical; you cannot live on both sides of the cross.

Again Barclay comments: "Even at his most involved, and here he is involved, one simple yet tremendous fact is never far from the mind and heart of Paul—the cost of the Christian gospel. He could never forget that the peace, the liberty, the right relationship with God that we possess, cost the life and death of Jesus Christ, for how could men ever have known what God was like unless Jesus Christ had died to tell them of his great love."[37] Jesus lived a perfect life of obedience to the Law, and then He became a curse for us, paying the penalty the Law required for the sins of the world.

Emma's cooking is a testimony to the glory of God. She can set a table about as well as anyone. She prepared a semi-kosher meal of roasted lamb, latkes (Yiddish potatoes pancakes), fresh crisp green beans with almonds, a selection of olives Philip kept in store from Israel, and pita bread with goat cheese to be dipped in olive oil and hyssop. She made the meal in a semi-kosher fashion because admittedly Emma did not have a kosher kitchen. The smells drifting out from her kitchen caused Philip's mouth to water in anticipation.

After dinner the three adjourned to the front porch to begin their study of the Law as recorded by Paul in his letter to the Galatians. Emma fixed herself and Larry a fresh cup of green tea, Philip preferring a cup of stout coffee. Larry began, "Thank you for your hospitality and friendship, and the dinner. It was the best since my mother cooked for me. My intention is to have a look at the Law from a different perspective, and reading this letter of Paul's, it certainly is that. I take it Paul was Saul's Greek name. However, I have to tell you that I think Paul is talking about an abuse of the Law rather than the Law being defective, like David Stern explained in your study notes. But this still looks like a good study. I understand why Paul is your gunslinger. He communicates logically, building his case as if before a jury. I am looking forward to what you have to say, Philip." Philip listened with admiration, realizing the challenge. There are very few biblical scholars he had ever met that could so quickly draw the distinction between the Law being faulty and it being abused.

With a very real sense of respect for Larry's scholarship, Philip opened his Bible and study notes, but decided a little background was necessary. "This book is of particular value to Christians because it is foundational to our understanding of God's redemption plan. It answers the question of how God who is righteous and just can reconcile sinful man, yet at the same time remain righteous Himself. Actually, Romans probably addresses that issue more clearly than Galatians, but Galatians will do for a start. The issues confronted by Paul have been contested because the gospel Paul preached was salvation by grace through faith in Jesus Christ—plus nothing. Grace, by its very definition is unmerited favor. Faith, as Paul is using it here, is trusting in Christ's perfect obedience, death, and resurrection. From the beginning, the church has struggled against error and distortion, even to the point of sometimes perverting the true gospel.

Larry, I would suggest to you that Paul raises the deepest questions in human existence: Is this the one true redemption plan of God the Father? Is Jesus the Anointed One (the Messiah)? If you turn from this one gospel are you in fact deserting God (*'you are so quickly deserting Him'*)? The Galatians' error Paul is addressing was adding works (keeping part of the Jewish law) to faith. Your first point on the law being abused rather than defective I think is right on, but that still doesn't mean the Law was ever intended to be in addition to grace as part of God's plan of redemption.

This is a little bit of a sidebar, but the struggle I have always had with any redemption plan was understanding how God could make a sinner righteous (me in this case), while at the same time remaining totally righteousness Himself. God's very character, His very being is righteous, and I don't believe he would or could compromise His own character. Paul's gospel of grace through faith in Christ has God providing completely for the redemption of mankind, with a person adding nothing except believing in faith what God has done in Christ (faith being the means, but it is the object of faith that saves), without in any way compromising His own righteousness.

Paul describes how God accomplished this spiritual surgery in Galatians 2:20: '*I have been crucified with Christ; and it is no longer I who live, but Christ lives in me; and the life which I now live in the flesh I live by faith in the Son of God, who loved me, and delivered Himself up for me.'* Then with the next verse Paul drives a steak in the heart of legalism, as far as the law being able to justify: *'I do not nullify the grace of God; for if righteousness comes through the Law, then Christ died needlessly.'*

Paul asserts that he died to the law that he might live in Christ. I only comprehended Galatians 2:20 when I realized that biblically I am a spirit with a soul that lives in a temporary earthly suit; a three part being. Before I had always thought of myself as a body with a soul and spirit; those are two very different things. Paul's fundamental identity is spirit. His spirit was co-crucified with Christ. He also rose to new life in Christ. He is living as a new creation (the 'old man' died—Galatians 2:20; Romans 6:4-6; 8:1-2), in resurrection life through the presence of Jesus Christ's life within him. This Galatians 2:20 passage also answers the most perplexing question of how God can accept a sinner, yet still remain righteous. The answer is—He doesn't! That sinner had to die by being co-crucified with Christ, raised to life as a new creation (born again) with Christ's righteousness imputed to his account, and Christ's enabling life within."

Emma spoke up, "Philip has used this illustration many times before. Someone has said, 'Jesus gave His life for us, that He might give His life to us, that He might live His life through us.'[38]" Philip looked up from his notes and paused for a moment. "This is a little bit of a rabbit trail, but when I think of that saying it makes me wonder if this was God's plan for mankind from the beginning; that from before creation in God's mind we were always intended to be vessels to contain and display the life of Christ."

Philip paused for a moment to consider what he had just said, then got back on point. "Paul is saying that when we are placed in Christ, our new spiritual being (new creation) is so identified with Christ that His experiences became ours; His death became our death, His resurrection became our resurrection, His life becomes our life. Galatians was written in Greek, so we have the advantage of being able to see the verb tense. Paul uses the perfect tense (have been crucified), which means that it happened in the past, but with continuing result in the presence."

Philip stopped to see Larry's reaction. Larry was processing the information. "First, with no disrespect intended, it seems to me that Paul takes a decidedly narrower view of the gospel than most Christian leaders I have talked with in the past. Secondly, why should a Jew believe Paul's argument?" "To answer your second question first, Paul was a Jew who believed, but with all due respect to Paul taking a narrow view, the real question is: Is that narrow view God's redemption plan? In chapters 3 and 4 we are studying Paul's doctrinal position on justification by faith apart from the Law. From a Christian perspective, God's salvation plan is in believing in the righteousness of Messiah who was both God and man.

When I think about these passages I remember what Charles Ryrie wrote, 'Only the Lord Jesus, God who became man, could and did resolve that problem by dying for us. He had to be human in order to be able to die, and He had to be God in order for that death to be able to pay for the sins of the world.'[39] As Ryrie states, Christ had to be the man/God. He lived a life of total obedience to the Father, thus qualifying Him to be the Lamb of God. He died to pay for the sins of the world, and He rose as the first fruit of God's redemption plan. It is His righteousness that saves!

I was justified (God's legal declaration) by the means of faith. I received the imputation of Christ's righteousness. God reckoned me righteous by the penalty of my sins being charged to Christ's account—His substitutionary atonement. In addition to paying the penalty of my sins, He imputed to me the positive justness of Christ, beginning the process of sanctification (being progressively set apart unto God). I know that was a mouth full, but I chose those words carefully.

Larry, I want to stop and say again what I believe is fundamental to Paul's argument and to my understanding of Christianity. Christianity is God's work of the old man dying (old man in Adam being crucified with Christ, Romans 5:12 – 6:14; Gal 2:20), being resurrected as a new creation (in Christ), and having the Holy Spirit placed within as the resource or ability to live the new life. This was all by grace through faith, apart from any merit on our part; what Jesus called 'being born again.' It is not conforming to a set of rules, but rather being conformed, by grace through faith, into the image of Christ.

Larry, you'd better cinch up your belt buckle and put on your suspenders, because now Paul is going to pull out the big gun—Abraham. Paul leapfrogs Moses and goes back to Abraham as his authoritative example. How was Abraham, the father of the nation Israel, justified? Good question! You think the answer is in Genesis 15? This is too good not to read." Philip, Larry and Emma all flipped back in their Bibles to Genesis.

5 "And He took him outside and said, 'Now look toward the heavens, and count the stars, if you are able to count them.' And He said to him, 'So shall your descendants be.'"

6 "Then he believed in the LORD; and He reckoned it to him as righteousness."

Not only was Abraham justified by grace through faith, it was before he was circumcised (Gen 17:24) or performed any works of the Law. In our logical assessment, do we detect a trend? Abraham was justified by faith, Paul was justified by faith, and the Galatians were justified by faith. I definitely see a trend here. Paul never lets up, which is why you can't beat him, Larry. *'There-fore* (logical conclusion, my comment), *be sure that it is those who are of faith who are sons of Abraham'* (v 7).

The word 'sons' means 'to be like.' Thus, those who are justified will be justified like Abraham. And can there possibly be more? Yes, Scripture agrees: *"foreseeing that God would justify the Gentiles by faith, preached the gospel beforehand to Abraham, saying, ALL THE NATIONS SHALL BE BLESSED IN YOU. So then those who are of faith are blessed with Abraham, the believers"* (3:8-9).

Now Paul is going to argue from the negative to prove that the

Law cannot bring righteousness (3:10-12), and that is the whole point. A righteous God will not compromise His righteousness by accepting you until you are also righteous. As the Bible says of Abraham, God 'reckoned' righteousness to his account. The Law cannot justify, it can only condemn. Paul quotes the Law in Deuteronomy 27:26: "*For as many as are of the works of the Law are under a curse; for it is written, 'CURSED IS EVERYONE WHO DOES NOT ABIDE BY ALL THINGS WRITTEN IN THE BOOK OF THE LAW, TO PERFORM THEM.'*" Like a good lawyer, Paul continues to quote the law (Scriptures)—this time the Prophet Habakkuk: "*THE RIGHTEOUS MAN SHALL LIVE BY FAITH*" (Hab 2:4;).

Maybe one last point tonight; Paul has just argued from the negative that the Law cannot bring righteousness. Now he is going to argue from the positive that there is a solution, '*Christ redeemed us from the curse of the Law, having become a curse for us.*' The word 'redeemed' means to 'buy out of slavery.' In other words, He paid the penalty required of the Law for our sins; substitutionary redemption, such as the Lamb of God at Passover. In verse 14, 'in order that' means a purpose statement is to follow: so that the Gentiles might receive the blessing of Abraham and all believers might receive the Holy Spirit—all by faith.

Larry, I don't know about you but I am worn plum out." Larry just smiled and said, "Paul makes a point of something I have believed for a long time: faith in God is required. The question is, has the Messiah come or is He coming. I agree with Saul, Messiah will be a person and faith in Him will be required. Next week!"

After breakfast one morning, Emma mentioned that she had some over-ripe bananas, so she was going to bake some banana nut bread. Philip, still thinking about that trigger job Nate had shown him, asked if Emma would bake an extra loaf, just out of kindness to a stranger who has no one to show him God's lovingkindness. That afternoon Philip took the fresh loaf (still warm with the aroma of having just come out of the oven) over to Nate's house. Philip had to open the window to his truck to let the aroma out, or else that bread was going to be gone before he ever got to Nate's.

Nate welcomed Philip, commenting on how he doesn't get many visitors, and fewer gifts. He had just put on a pot of coffee. While in the kitchen, Philip noticed a well-worn Bible lying open on the table. The two sat on the front porch, sipping the coffee and having a slice of Emma's bread, when Philip produced an oily cloth containing a 1911 slide in the white (without a finish). Philip asked Nate if his mill was in good enough condition to make the cut for a low mount Bomar rear sight, to which Nate assured Philip he could do the job. Nate, noting that the slide was still in the white, mentioned that he had been working for several years to duplicate the old Colt royal blue finish and thought that he had come fairly close, at which the hair on the back of Philip's neck stood up. Philip had seen some of those old Colts with the royal blue finish at the Texas Ranger's Museum in Waco, the difference being obvious from across the room.

Philip made note of the well worn Bible on the kitchen table. Nate smiled with a sense of pride. "I read through that once a year. I guess I just got in the habit, but it brings real peace to my soul. I have this chart my pastor in Midland sent me that gives me a certain amount to read each day to get through it in one year." Philip was surprised in that most people, especially those that consider themselves experts on the subject, don't read through it in a lifetime. Nate finished off his coffee, then volunteered, "I guess I am the luckiest guy in the world. All the smarts in the family went to my sister and brother. But when my pastor in Midland shared with me about what Jesus had done for me, you know, His death and resurrection, I trusted in Him to save me right then and there. Philip, how about you, do you read the Bible?" "I read it a lot and understand it a little. Right now

I'm studying about God's salvation plan by faith alone. I'm still missing something that I've got to figure out." Nate thought for a minute. "I am probably missing a lot too, but I just keep it simple. I heard the Good News and I believed it. I don't see any way I could add anything to what Jesus did for me."

After dinner, Philip and Emma were sitting on the front porch reading. Emma asked about Nate, so Philip related their conversation, leaving out the rear sight dovetail and royal blue finish part which he was sure Emma wouldn't be interested in. Emma thought about what Philip had told Nate, about still missing something. "Philip, you know I am starting a study of Romans, and it occurred to me that the first chapter, especially verses 16 and 17 tags right along with our study in Galatians." Philip nodded, without understanding what she was trying to tell him, deciding he had plenty to do just to prepare for their study with Larry.

Philip's Study Notes, Galatians 3:18-29

Emailed to Rabbi Cohen

Paul addresses the character of the Law without invalidating its real purpose, because his intent was never to show disrespect for the Law. Donald Campbell wrote concerning the purpose of the Law: "First, it was given because of transgressions, that is, the Law was given to be a means for checking sins. It served as a restrainer of sins by showing them to be transgressions of God's Law which would incur His wrath (1 Tim 1:8-11). Second, the Law was temporary and served until the Seed (the Messiah; cf. Gal 3:16) came, after which it was no longer needed. Third, the Law was inferior because of the manner of its bestowal. While God made promises to Abraham directly, the Law was established by a mediator. There were in fact two mediators—the angels representing God, and Moses representing the people."[40]

Continuing in verse 21, Paul again anticipates his opponent's objection that if one says the promise of God is superior to the Law, "*is the Law then contrary to the promise?*" Paul's response is '*me ginomai*,' which is translated 'may it never be' (make that in bold letters on a billboard a hundred feet high). This Greek word '*me ginomai*' is the most emphatic way of saying no, never, it must never be. God gave both, but for different purposes. Therefore, if God gave them they must be good. Even though the Law could not give life (make righteous), it is important in the process.

If a person does not know he is a sinner, thus spiritually dead, he would never face the fact that he desperately needs spiritual life. The Law "*has become our tutor to lead us to Christ, so that we may be justified by faith. But now that faith has come, we are no longer under a tutor. For you are all sons of God through faith in Christ Jesus*" (vv 24-26). Paul is saying the believer's status has changed from being under the bondage of the Law to freedom as sons of God.

This idea of a 'tutor' needs a little extra examination because that is what Paul says the Law is like. The Greek word is '*paidagogos*' which means a child-keeper or custodian. These custodians were strict disciplinarians charged with providing the child protection. Barclay notes, "In the Greek world there was a household servant called the *paidagogos*. He was not the schoolmaster. He was usually an old and trusted slave who had been long in the family and whose character was high. He was in charge of the child's moral welfare, and it was his duty to see that he acquired the qualities essential to true manhood. He had one particular duty; every day he had to take the child to and from school. He had nothing to do with the actual teaching of the child, but it was his duty to take him in safely to the school and deliver him to the teacher. That—said Paul—was like the function of the law. It was there to lead a man to Christ. It could not take him into Christ's presence, but it could take him into a position where he himself might enter. It was the function of the law to bring a man to Christ by showing him that by himself he was utterly unable to keep it. But once a man had come to Christ he no longer needed the law, for now he was dependent not on law but on grace."[41]

Paul notes three changes as a result of our status change, by grace, from under the care of a 'tutor' to a son:

1) In Christ you are no longer a child but an adult heir, a son of God; and the Law could never do that.

2) We are all one in Christ, "*neither Jew nor Greek, there is neither slave nor free man, there is neither male nor female; for you are all one in Christ Jesus.*"

3) "*If you belong to Christ, then you are Abraham's descendants, heirs according to promise*" (vv 28-29).

Emma provided another bodacious dinner, topped off with homemade blackberry cobbler from berries Philip had brought back from meeting with a friend in East Texas. As he said, "All you have to do to get to all the berries is kick the copperheads (small poisonous snake with a naturally bad disposition) out of the way." He had in fact killed two on this latest berry gathering expedition.

Philip asked Larry if he had any questions or comments before they got started. "Paul had a tough go of it as he faced opposition from within the church, yet he believed the very efficacy of the gospel depended on not allowing faith to be diluted with legalism." Philip looked genuinely surprised. "Where did you get that?" Philip's surprised look pleased Larry. "I did a little research on my own, but I want to hear what you have to say."

Philip opened his notes. "I'm not so sure who should be teaching this, but I'll stay in the saddle for now. Being a rabbi you are probably more familiar with Paul's style of teaching than Christians today. Last week Paul introduced God's justification of Abraham as proof that salvation has always been by faith. Paul anticipates his opponent's objection; that is, that the law was given after the promise to Abraham. So they reasoned it modified God's plan of salvation. Paul argues that God's promises are immutable, but furthermore the fulfillment of God's promises would not be accomplished until Messiah comes, that is, both the promise and the Law looked forward to the work of Messiah. The Jewish hope had always been in a single individual (seed not seeds of Abraham), the Messiah.

Paul then goes into this whole idea of the Law being our tutor: *'has become our tutor to lead us to Christ, so that we may be justified by faith. But now that faith has come, we are no longer under a tutor. For you are all sons of God through faith in Christ Jesus.'* The Greek word is *paidagogos,* which means a child-keeper or custodian.

What do you think, Larry?" Philip could see the wheels turning in Larry's head as he processed all that had been said. "Paul argues his case well, but it really all comes down to what is God's redemption plan, and more specifically is Jesus the promised Messiah. It is of course possible to make many of these scriptures fit the model Paul has described for Messiah. Paul's argument for 'faith' from Abraham is compelling. It is interesting to see Paul's perspective, especially on the Law as a tutor. Next week, same time?" Philip and Emma agreed.

All during the following week Philip was still bothered by that nagging feeling he would get when he hadn't quite put the puzzle together in his head. He understood that justification was by faith apart from works; as Nate had said, "I don't see any way I could add anything to what Jesus has done for me." But there was still a theological nuance about the whole redemption process that was evading his best efforts to realize the wholeness of God's work.

Then something Emma had said (I just hate that) about Romans 1:16-17 clicked in his head so emphatically that he said out loud, "You idiot, stop looking at it from your position, and look at it from God's!" Naturally, Emma was within earshot so she heard every word. "You say you're an idiot?" "You weren't suppose to hear that!" Emma, not being able to pass up the straight line Philip had just laid out there, stated "Well, if it comes straight from the horse's mouth, it must be true."

Philip sequestered himself in his study. He opened his Greek text to Romans chapter one, verse 16, and began to dig for the answer to justification by faith alone from God's perspective. Talking to himself out loud, he said, "The theme of Romans is 'the righteous of God' first and foremost. It is about what God has done to redeem mankind; unilaterally acting to resolve the issue of how a righteous God buys out of bondage sinful man while at the same time keeping in tact the integrity of His holiness."

Philip reviewed the text, translating the Greek in his head: "16 *For not I am ashamed of the good news, for the power of God it is unto salvation to everyone trusting. Both to Jews first and to Greeks. 17 For the righteousness of God in it is revealed from faith to faith, as it is written, 'but the righteous by faith will live.'*" Philip slowly processed what he has just read. Paul is confident (*not ashamed*) because the good news (*gospel*) reveals the ability (*dynamis*, spiritual ability) of a righteousness of and from God, salvation flowing from His righteous character. The penalty was paid by Christ's blood to everyone trusting.

Philip reverted back to reasoning out loud, "The present tense of the verb '*trusting*' means ongoing activity, not a once-and-for-all event. 'To Jews first' is not merely temporal; it is also one of priority because they are God's chosen people to be custodians of His revelation and the people through whom Messiah would come." Philip thought how God had arranged for Larry, a Jew, to hear the gospel of salvation by grace through faith apart from works. The gospel is for both Jews and Greeks (all non-Jewish), thus there is only one way of salvation."

Reasoning to himself again, he thought, "Now I need just a glimpse of God's redemption plan from my perspective, but not so much as to dim the priority of viewing it from God's perspective. Verse 16 says the gospel reveals the power of God, even though it can seem weak to our fleshly minds; but it is the weak and foolish things of this world that confound the worldly wise, kind of like Nate." For some reason known only to the good Lord, Philip remembered what the eleventh century theologian Anselm had said: "I believe so that I might understand." The prophet Habakkuk took God's Word (*the righteous by faith will live*) in sheer faith, so that (purpose statement to follow) he might comprehend the mind of God. "It is by faith that we begin to understand the depth, and width, and height of God's righteousness in redeeming sinful man."

Philip's Study Notes, Galatians 4:1-20

Emailed to Rabbi Cohen

The logical argument makes a slight transition at this point (chapter 4) as noted by James Boice: "For the final time, Paul contrasts the condition in which believers found themselves before Christ's coming with the position they enjoy now. The difference between these verses and those that conclude chapter 3 is in emphasis. Before, Paul had been stressing the temporal nature of the change, showing what they were then in contrast to what they are now. At this point he dwells on their status, showing that whereas they were previously slaves, they had now become sons of their heavenly Father. This development flows from the thought of the *pedagogue* in vv 23-29."[42]

Background and word study: Paul is going to use the illustration of a child coming of age. In the Jewish culture a boy becomes bar-mitzvah (to whom the commandments apply, a son of the Law) at age twelve or thirteen. In the Greek world a boy became of age at about eighteen; however by Roman law the age of maturity was set by the father. Paul says, *"as long as the heir is a child (nepios, an infant in contrast to huios, son), he does not differ at all from a slave although he is owner of everything, but he is under guardians (epitropous, different from paidagogos) and managers until the date set by the father"* (4:1-2). *"So also we, while we were children (nepios, infants), were held in bondage under the elemental things of the world"* (v3). The *elemental things of the world* would have been their previous heathen religion, since the Galatians were mostly Gentiles and not Jews under the Law. But heathen religion or Law, all were in bondage until Christ set them free.

Boice observes, "Redemption is mentioned here for the first time since 3:13 and is particularly appropriate in view of the imagery Paul is using. Redemption means 'to buy out of slavery.' Men were slaves either to the law, as Jews, or to the elemental spirits of the universe, as Gentiles. Christ paid the price of their redemption and set them free. Moreover, it is through Him that men have the adoption. That is, they move not only from bondage into freedom, they also move into the great household of God where all are free men and all are also 'heirs of God and co-heirs with Christ' (Rom 8:17). Observe the subtle link between the central ideas of this verse and the phrase 'weak and miserable (literally, poor) principles' of v 9. The opposing powers are 'weak' because they are unable to redeem, and 'poor' because they are unable to provide the adoption."[43]

Paul's doctrinal defense of justification by grace through faith in Jesus Christ is completed, but he makes three personal appeals to the Galatians not to return to their former bondage:

1) His first appeal is that they not turn to legalism (vv 8-11). Paul has already established that, as Donald Campbell says, "to supplement the work of Christ is to supplant it." To return to the former things would be to deny the one and only true gospel.

That they were in bondage before believing in Christ is

common to all mankind; but to return is unthinkable. Boice says, "There are three causes for Paul's astonishment: (1) the Galatians were going back to what they had already been through—that is, not to a new error but to an old one; (2) they were turning from reality to non-reality; the absence of the article before the word 'God' stresses a qualitative contrast between the true God revealed in Jesus Christ and 'no gods'; and (3) this was done after they had actually come to 'know' God in a real way. Paul uses the verb *ginosko* (to know intimately and on a personal level) at this point rather than *oida* (to know factually) or *orao* (to know through perceiving something.)"[44] If you ever thought Paul was only a teacher, here (and in the following verses) you see the heart of a shepherd: *"I fear for you, that perhaps I have labored over you in vain"* (v 11).

2) Paul's second appeal (vv 12-16) is that the Galatians remember their relationship with Paul. On Paul's visit to the Galatia region, he had some sort of illness. Yet they received him and his message as *'an angel of God.'* But their opinion of him has apparently changed. Paul had become an offense by telling them the truth and confronting them with their error.

3) Paul's third appeal (vv 17-20) was that they consider his real motive. People don't like to be critiqued, even if it is with a loving heart. Paul's opposition spoke flattering words of praise to the Galatians. In verse 17, Paul says they wish to *'shut you out'* (literally, 'lock you up'), just as legalism would do to them spiritually. Paul assures them that his love for them has not diminished.

The third week after dinner was a warm night, so Emma and Larry opted for iced tea, while Philip stuck to his coffee. Philip looked at Larry, giving the anticipation time to build. Philip's old Prof says, "It is a sin to make the Bible boring."

"In chapters 1 and 2, Paul defends his authority as an apostle and establishes the divine origin of the gospel of justification by grace through faith in Jesus' death and resurrection. In chapters 3 and 4, Paul outlines his doctrinal defense of justification by faith alone. Chapters 5 and 6 give Paul's defense of Christian liberty. Remember that Paul is talking to believers who were justified by faith alone, but now they are being confused by some in the church who insist that salvation includes keeping some of the Mosaic laws.

Paul makes a slight transition (chapter 4) to dwell on their status, showing that whereas they were previously slaves, they had now become sons of their heavenly Father. This development flows from the thought of the *pedagogue*. You may remember from my notes that as long as the heir is a child, he does not differ at all from a slave, although he is owner of everything. But he is under guardians *(paidagogos)* and managers until the date set by the father. Paul's point is that all were in bondage until Christ set them free.

'But God,' without whom no one can be justified, enters history: '*When the fullness of time came, God sent forth His Son, born of a woman, born under the Law, so that* (purpose statement to follow, my comments) *He might redeem those who were under the Law, that we might receive the adoptions as sons*' (vv 4-5).

I have a theory, and if you will allow another rabbit trail I will explain. The '*fullness of time*' has to do with the historical events that had to happen to set the stage for Messiah. First, God called a man of faith to make a promise that would bless all generations. The promise included a seed and a land. Then God grew a family into a nation in Egypt. He freed that nation out of bondage, giving them the Law, the Tabernacle, and the Feasts so that they would understand the gulf between sinful man and holy God. He gave them the Promised Land. But even more importantly, from that nation would come the promised 'Anointed One' (Messiah), their king to rule over the nation. God gave the Old Testament so that we could see the pre-filling of what Messiah would fulfill.

Now here is where my theory gets a little spooky. I believe God raised up Alexander the Great to spread the Greek language across the civilized world. The New Testament was written in Greek, so that the specifics of such things as justification by grace through faith in Christ alone would be clear. To me the Old Testament Hebrew is like a watercolor, passionate and emotional, while the Greek is like a pen and ink, detailed and specific with syntax that leaves no doubt as to the meaning. Then God raised up Rome to build roads so that the gospel could travel from an obscure nation out to the world. Then it was the 'fullness of time' for Messiah to come.

God the Father also sent the Spirit; the whole Trinity is at work here. The Spirit moves our hearts to cry out, 'Abba Father'! Think about that for a moment. Holy God, who dwells in unapproachable light, such that even the angels cover their eyes with their wings, says to us through the Spirit, 'just call me Daddy.'

As you know, 'Abba' is an Aramaic word for the most familiar, personal address to a father. For me that was 'Daddy.' My father's name was Obie, but I never once called him that. He was always Daddy. Even at my advanced age, when I see him in heaven I will call my father Daddy. Can you imagine God the Father allowing us that kind of personal intimacy? Paul concludes the thought: '*Therefore you are no longer a slave, but a son; and if a son, then an heir through God*' (v 7). Paul's doctrinal defense of justification by grace through faith in Jesus Christ is completed, but he makes three personal appeals to the Galatians, as I listed in my notes."

Philip looked at Larry and Emma. "Next week we finish our study. What do you think?" Larry spoke softly with real empathy for Paul. "I can feel Paul's pain for these Christians he looks on as his children. Yet at the same time he believes, like any rabbi worth his salt, he is charged by God to correct error. I can tell you from personal experience that if anyone thought teaching the Scriptures was easy, they have a second thought coming. I look forward to next week."

Nate had asked for about ten days to get to Philip's slide, so one morning after the social hour at Andy's he headed out to Nate's place. Once again Nate had on a pot of coffee, so he stopped work for a visit on the front porch. There is something wholesomely refreshing about the aroma of coffee while visiting with a new friend.

Nate had the slide finished, so Philip inspected the work—which was to perfection. Nate asked if Philip had ever figured out what he was missing in his Bible study. "I've got at least part of it. I needed to look at things from God's position rather than my position." Nate shook his head yes. "I try to always look at it from God's position." Philip was about to get depressed, so he changed the subject back to his pistol which needed a little more polishing on the slide and frame. When that was finished, he sure would like to try Nate's royal blue finish.

On the way home, Philip popped in the CD of his alma mater's men choir singing the school fight song:

"All hail the pow'r of Jesus' name!
Let angels prostrate fall;
Bring forth the royal diadem
And crown him, crown him, crown him, Lord of all."[45]

Philip's Study Notes, Galatians
Emailed to Rabbi Cohen

Some commentators have suggested that what follows is an afterthought. Boice insightfully observes: "However, one may just as well feel that Paul has deliberately saved precisely this argument for his capstone. The advantages are these: (1) The allegory allows Paul to end on a final citation of the law and, in particular, on a passage involving Abraham, who has been his primary example; (2) it allows him to use a method of argument which, we may assume, had been used by the legalizers, thus turning their own style of exegesis against them; (3) it illustrates and reviews all his main points—the radical opposition between the principle of law and the principle of faith, the fact that life under law is a life of bondage and the life of faith is freedom, that the life of faith is a result of the supernatural working of God by means of the Holy Spirit; (4) the story contains an emotional overtone suited both to a wrap-up of the formal argument and to a final personal appeal; and (5) it gives Paul a base upon which to suggest what he had undoubtedly thought, but had apparently been reluctant to say previously—that the Galatians should obey God by casting out the legalizers (v30). Therefore, the allegory effectively ties together both the doctrinal section of the letter and the appeal based on it, while at the same time leading into the ethical section that begins in chapter 5."[46] (That's really insightful.)

Paul recalls an Old Testament story from the life of Abraham to illustrate the contrast between law and grace, between legalism and faith. *"Tell me, you who want to be under the law, do you not listen to the law?"* (v 21). *"For it is written that Abraham had two sons, one by the bondwoman and one by the free woman"* (v 22). Paul reminds the Galatians that their blessing came through Isaac (from Sarah), the free woman, and that Ishmael (from Hagar) was sent away: *"But the son by the bondwoman was born according to the flesh, and the son by the free woman through the promise"* (v 23.) Paul contrasts the two births: Ishmael by man's plan; but Isaac was the miracle of God when Abraham was one-hundred (Gen 21:5) and Sarah was ninety; Isaac, born of the promise.

Paul then interprets the allegory, contrasting the conflict between legalism and grace. The Mosaic covenant from Mount Sinai brought bondage to the law; as Hagar's son was the same as a slave, so were the Jewish people. There are also two Jerusalems; one enslaved by Rome, the other in heaven, the city of the living God. The quote from Isaiah 54:1 depicts Jerusalem before the Babylonian exile: the barren women Jerusalem in captivity.

But later (in the millennium) the city will be blessed again. Paul makes three applications to the allegory:

1) The birth of Isaac is compared to the 'new birth' of Christians. We are the supernatural birth of the promise (v 28);
2) Ishmael's persecution of Isaac is like the Judaizers who are born out of self-willed legalism (v 29); and
3) Just as Abraham cast out the son of the flesh to protect the inheritance of the son of the promise, so the Galatians ought to cast out the false teachers (v 30).

In conclusion, Paul affirms that true believers are not children of the slave woman, but rather children of the free woman, heirs of God and co-heirs with Christ.

The following week during dinner, Philip was reminded that Larry had social graces that he had obviously neglected. "Emma, I appreciate Philip's study, but I don't know how I am going to get along without your excellent dinners." Emma smiled in appreciation of the sincere compliment. "Larry, I hope you have known us long enough to know you are always welcome, and I mean that." After dinner they all adjourned to the front porch to finish their study in Galatians. It was another warm evening, so all settled for a glass of iced tea with mint out of Emma's garden.

Larry mentioned how he had never properly appreciated the Greek New Testament and that he had a real fondness for Paul. He thought he might make a summer project out of refreshing his Greek. Philip struggled with English, much less Greek, so he was not excited about the whole idea. He realized that some folks like Larry were gifted with abilities and talents he would never know this side of the Jordan.

After a sufficient pause, Philip pulled out his Bible. "My old Prof (Howard Hendricks) once wrote, 'Teaching is all about doing battle with shoddy thinking, with upgrading inferior concepts, with spilling cerebral blood to eradicate ignorance.' I don't have the brain potency to operate at the level of the great teachers, but I always remember Prof's challenge to at least give it your best shot.

Now, to put a bow on our study of justification by grace through faith, plus nothing. I might just mention again that Paul has concluded his doctrinal argument for justification by faith alone, but he continues to appeal to the Galatians to remain free from legalism.

Paul recalls an Old Testament story from the life of Abraham to illustrate the contrast between law and grace, between legalism and faith: *'Tell me, you who want to be under the law, do you not listen to the law? For it is written that Abraham had two sons, one by the bondwoman and one by the free woman. But the son by the bondwoman was born according to the flesh, and the son by the free woman through the promise.'* Paul contrasts the two births.

Larry, I think there is something profound here. You are a smart guy. When I read this I see a fundamental difference between traditional Judaism and true Christianity. Paul is describing a 'new life' imputed by God by grace through faith. To me Judaism can say we have the holy Law, given by God to Moses. But Paul argues that is not enough. Paul says faith in Jesus (Yeshua HaMashia) brings new spiritual life, being taken out of Adam and place 'in Christ.' The Law is good, it reveals God's character and is God's minimum standard to be part of His kingdom, but it is faith in His Savior that brings new life. The Law is great, but the Promise is greater. I'll just be truthful and tell you I pray that God will reveal to your heart (call you to repentance), to change your mind about Jesus being your Promised One, because even if you believe Paul's argument intellectually, that is not enough. You must trust in Jesus' life, death and resurrection as payment for your sins. I hope that doesn't offend you."

Everyone sat in silence for a while. Finally Philip spoke up:

"Larry, I say this sincerely. What you do with what you have studied is between you and God. I believe you have at least intellectually understood Paul's defense of justification by grace through faith in Jesus Christ. This was one rabbi talking to another—that is, Paul to you. I hope neither I nor Emma needs to say it, but I want you to know our friendship is based on mutual respect, not on what you do with this information. That truly is between you and God."

Larry responded in kind. "Emma and Philip, I truly value your friendship. I don't know what I will do with Paul's teaching. I know I went into this study four weeks ago hoping to just explore a different view of the Law, but Paul speaks to my head and my heart. Last week you said something that has stuck in my mind, and I promise you I will pray about it. You said, 'But God, the Divine initiative.'"

A few days later Philip had finished polishing the slide and frame of his new pistol. He told Emma, "It's not a new gun Sweetheart; it is just parts I collected." He drove over to Nate's place and handed him the precious 'parts' for bluing. Nate took the parts, then said to Philip, "Trust me, I can do this." Talk about faith alone.

CHAPTER 17

ONE ANOTHER, CHILDREN OF THE LIGHT,
1 THESSALONIANS

"Love to be real must be self-sacrificing. Our love is not genuine unless we are willing to labor earnestly for the blessing of those for whom we profess to have this deep concern" (Harry Ironside, 1947).

Johnny Smith had just finished dinner and was helping Jodi with the clean-up when the telephone rang. It was Charlie Marsh, Johnny's pastor, calling to set up a meeting. Charlie mentioned ahead of the meeting that his wife Peggy was ready to retire from her duties as Sunday school teacher for the teenage group, and Charlie wanted Johnny to pray about taking on the assignment.

After Charlie hung up, Johnny and Jodie discussed the possibility. Was he ready to take on such a serious responsibility? He was a relative beginner at in-depth Bible study, so one of the questions concerned his qualifications to be a teacher of the Word. He was committed to a discipleship relationship with Philip Cole which included Bible study. Was there time to do both? One thing going for him was he and Jodie did not have kids of their own. Yet Johnny had a demanding work schedule, being in partnership with old Doc Hayes, and running the only veterinary clinic in the area while Doc Hayes was in the process of retiring. Jodie said she was alright with it, but suggested Johnny talk with Philip Cole.

The veterinary clinic closed at noon on Saturday, so Johnny was able to get away an hour or so after that. He headed straight for Philip's farm, hoping to catch him there. On arriving, he noted that Philip's pickup was not at the house or barn, so he stopped at the house to ask Emma of Philip's whereabouts. Emma greeted Johnny, and then said, "Philip's down at the target range playing with his new toy." Sure enough when Johnny walked up, Philip was target shooting with a spanking new 1911 type 45.

Philip saw Johnny coming, so he dropped the magazine, locked the slide back, and then set the pistol on a silicone cloth. Philip noticed the questioning look at the pistol and commented, "Just parts I collected. Emma would never put up with me buying another gun. I told you about Nate Wilson, the gunsmith I met. Well, he finished off the trigger job and put that beautiful blue finish on. It's not exactly the same as the old Colt finish, but it's as close as I have seen. I had an old set of ivory grips I traded for years ago, and they spiffed-up the package, but I doubt you drove all the way out here to see my new pistol."

Johnny got right to the point, which was one of the things Philip liked best about him. He explained about Charlie's call and his extended discussion with Jodie. Then he listed all the positive and negative points about accepting the responsibility. Philip listened attentively, and then commented, "That's all fine and good, but you haven't made a single relevant point!" Johnny looked dumbfounded. What else could he have said except to logically process through the facts as he saw them? "Mr. Cole I don't know what you mean. I thought all of these things were relevant."

Philip gave Johnny an understanding look, but replied,

"Well, they're not! There is one and only one principle question when it comes to serving God; are you called to do this? The questions you should be asking are addressed and considered in the heavenlies; these are God's children you are talking about. If you are not called to this work, you will fail!

I have suspected for some time that John Mark was not called to go on Paul's first missionary journey, and he failed, resulting in Paul and Barnabas splitting up. However, at a later time Paul speaks in the highest regard about John Mark, plus of course Mark wrote the earliest gospel account. So John Mark must have been called to a later work. You need to let the Lord show you His will with the focus on your calling, not your situation." Johnny was a willing student, but didn't know how to ask for what he needed. "I don't know how to do that."

Philip thought for a while, and then looked up at Johnny. "It is likely your discernment will come while you are studying the Word, or at least it will be confirmed by the Word. I had thought we would do our next Bible study in the Old Testament, but I think Paul has written the perfect letter to help you discern the Lord's will in this case. Read through First Thessalonians a couple of times before our next meeting." The two men shook on it, Johnny trusting that Philip knew what he was doing.

That evening after dinner, Philip performed his daily duty of checking emails. He noted a communication from Mbusa, a pastor in eastern Congo, asking for prayer. As related before, the Rwandan rebels were driven into far east Congo near the intersection of Rwanda, Uganda and Congo. They live in the bush as outlaws, taking what they wanted and killing anyone who stood in their way.

Emma and Philip first met Mbusa when he acted as a translator on their first teaching mission to Goma, Congo. Mbusa was, and is, one of the most intelligent persons Philip had ever met, demonstrated by the fact that anyone who can translate Philip's disjointed thoughts into an organized presentation of the Word must be brilliant. During that first time together, Philip had encouraged Mbusa to continue his education at seminary in Nairobi. Subsequently, Mbusa moved his family to Nairobi to attend seminary for three years. Seminary doesn't make a pastor, but it doesn't hurt either, and the greatest need in that part of the world is Christian leaders to disciple other pastors who will never have the advantage of college or graduate level preparation. Mbusa has a small frame, standing maybe five feet four inches tall, but he is a gifted giant of a leader the Lord has raised up to oversee His pastors in a forgotten part of the Kingdom. But not forgotten by God Himself!

During seminary, Philip and Mbusa had stayed in touch. Since he moved back to eastern Congo, the contact had been less frequent; one of the things the Lord had been impressing on Philip's heart. Eastern Congo is like West Texas in the eighteen hundreds, only without the Texas Rangers to fight rogue Indians, marauding Mexicans, and outlaws.

Recently, a family in Mbusa's church had been murdered because the father resisted the rebels taking their garden produce. To us, we might think, "give them the vegetables I can go to the store and buy more"; but to them, their children going without food was the alternative. If you ever wondered about the doctrine of 'total depravity,' you only need to see how the 'haves' treat the 'have-nots' anywhere in the world. However, the contact with Mbusa had resulted in deep spiritual conviction in Philip's heart in that he had been remiss in praying steadfastly for Mbusa and the pastors he and Emma had taught. More importantly, they had been accepted as a brother and sister in Christ. This conviction of the Spirit was not a small omission; it was in fact a betrayal of duty to our Lord.

Emma had invited Jodie and Johnny for dinner as part of Johnny's weekly meeting with Philip. Philip was as contented as a flea on a hound dog, since Emma had prepared his favorite; Emma's best ever meatloaf, pinto beans, home made chow-chow, pickled cucumbers, fresh tomatoes out of Emma's garden, and jalapeño cornbread. After their study, they had pineapple cream pie and coffee. The talk around the table was of family, friends, church and work. It is a balm to the soul for two old folks to hear two young folks talk about their life in the future tense.

Finally, Jodie brought up the subject of Johnny teaching the teen class at church. Philip responded, "I have been praying that the Lord would give you two a clear understanding of His will in this matter. As I told Johnny, the only question is one of calling. If you are called, you do it regardless of your feelings one way or another. If you are not, then you should wait patiently.

I did have one thought, but I can't say it is from the Lord, just something that occurred to me. What if both of you were to team teach the class?" Jodie seemed a little taken aback, but not against the idea. Philip went on, "What if the four of us study First Thessalonians together and see what the Lord shows us? The reason I chose this book is because it clearly displays a shepherd's heart—called to care for the Lord's flock. If you have that same calling, note I said calling—not feeling, then this ministry will enrich and deepen your walk with the Lord." It was agreed that the four of them would do the study together.

After dinner they adjourned to the front porch, Emma and Jodie with green tea while Johnny and Philip preferred coffee. Philip normally opened his Bible and got right to it, but he took a moment to consider what he wanted to accomplish. "I think understanding the background is critical to our study, so for tonight we will address the historical setting only, and then cover chapters one and two next week. First Thessalonians is the earliest letter of Paul's, written to a church he had founded on his second missionary journey. But he was driven out of town by opposition, not being there long enough to feel comfortable that the young Christians had been well grounded in practice and theology. What is of particular interest to our inquiry is the insight into Paul's mind and heart for the churches he established. These were brothers and sisters in Christ—not buildings.

Just because this was Paul's first epistle doesn't mean that his theology was incomplete. By the time Paul wrote this letter, he had been a believer for about eighteen years. He had spent three years in the desert graduating Summa Cum Laude from The University of Jesus, and had worked with the other apostles and James in Jerusalem for several years. He had also been on a mission for about eight years. On Paul's second missionary journey, he determined to revisit the churches he had planted earlier to see how they were doing (Acts 15:36), but then go on from there to plant other churches.

It's a little off track, however it is interesting that Barnabas was set to go with Paul and take John Mark along, but Paul was insistent that Mark not go since he had deserted the team on the first missionary journey. The disagreement was so strong that the team split, Barnabas taking John Mark with him to Cyprus while Paul chose Silas to return with him to the Galatians region. I take it that Barnabas was called to encourage and disciple young John Mark, while Paul and Silas were called to plant churches. While at Lystra, in the Galatia region, Paul picked up Timothy to continue with them (Acts 16:1-5).

Then something really interesting happened. Paul had planned to plant churches in Asia, but the Holy Spirit blocked it (Acts 16:6-7). So they went on to Troas where Paul had a vision to go to Macedonia (Acts 16:9). This was the beginning of taking the gospel to Europe. The four evangelists traveled north to Philippi, staying there about two months. Paul was called to more than just plant seeds, so when he departed Philippi, apparently he left young Timothy behind to establish the church there.

As was about to become a pattern in Paul's life, he was asked to leave Philippi (asked in the form of being beaten and jailed). He then traveled west along the Egnatian Way (the great military highway connecting Rome to the east) to Thessalonica. The culture of Thessalonica is important to understand so that we see the circumstances Paul faced in planting a church there and the difficulty the new church was sure to encounter. Thessalonica, with a population of about 200,000, was a free city ruled by a council of citizens. The city had a well-deserved reputation for licentiousness. This was a city where anything immoral or sexual goes, or as the advertising campaign of the today says, 'Whatever happens in Thessalonica stays in Thessalonica.' From these Jews and idol worshiping Greek sinners, God would raise up a new church.

Thessalonica had a natural harbor at the head of the Thermaic Gulf. But it was the Roman road, the Egnatian Way, that made it's location a natural commerce city, and more importantly in our context a natural location from which the gospel would travel. The commerce attracted Jewish businessmen, which accounted for the well established synagogue. The population was made up of well to do businessmen, both Greek and Jewish, plus a large contingent of Greek laborers and slaves.

Paul had only been in Thessalonica a short time (perhaps as little as three weeks, but more likely a few months) when the local Jews incited a riot. Paul had to be smuggled out of the city in peril of his life. However, before Paul was forced out, a thriving church made up of believing Jews, Greeks and Gentiles, was established.

In a sinful city like Thessalonica, you have to know that the pressure on these new converts was tremendous. A Jewish family would disown a Jew that converted to Christianity. The Greek idol worshipers (accustomed to anything goes) would have nothing to do with the 'Bible hugging, gun totting, evangelical, intolerant, fundamentalist babes in Christ.' To become a believer in Thessalonica, one had to expect to be ostracized socially, economically, religiously, occupationally, and in every other way. In most places in the world it cost dearly to become a servant of Christ.

From Thessalonica Paul's party traveled west to Berea, where Paul had a successful audience in the synagogue until the Jewish adversaries from Thessalonica heard about their ministry. They followed him to Berea and caused another disturbance, forcing Paul to leave again. Paul then traveled to Athens. From Athens Paul sent Timothy back to Thessalonica to encourage the church there to hold to the faith. Paul was in Athens to carry on the mission alone, and even worse his ministry in Athens was relatively fruitless. From Athens, Paul traveled to Corinth, from which this first epistle was written.

Paul anguished that he had birthed a new church in Thessalonica and was forced to leave before they could be established in the faith. However, Timothy returned with a glowing report of the fruitfulness of the church which precipitated this letter to the church in Thessalonica. I'll just leave you two with this one thought: What if Charlie had called you to establish a Sunday school class in sin city and your converts were Jews and ex-idol worshiping Greeks?" Philip closed his notes, so Emma inserted, "Well, on that happy thought let's have some pie and coffee."

Surprisingly to Philip, Jodie was really into this study. While enjoying her pie, she excitedly exclaimed, "Next week we get into the meat of the book, right?" Philip and Johnny gave each other a double take, and then Philip shook his head in the affirmative. "Put yourself in Paul's shoes and think about what we talked about tonight. Like most pastors, Paul had to feel the weight of responsibility in his work; after all, he was serving God Almighty. But the question I have is what was Paul's responsibility and what was God's responsibility? Jesus said, 'I will *build My church*' (Matthew 16:18). He also said to Ananias about Paul, '*He is a chosen instrument of Mine, to bear My name before the Gentiles and kings and the sons of Israel; for I will show him how much he must suffer for My name's sake'* (Acts 9:15-16).

If I had been Paul, I would be worried too, because he didn't have time to fully establish all the new churches before he was driven out; all these babes in Christ were left with no shepherd. But the Lord sustained those churches into healthy, fruitful bodies. Maybe that's a lesson for you and Johnny; don't try to do it all. Every part of the body must be fully functional for it to operate properly. If you take this assignment, let the kids be an equally important part of the body.

That's the way it is in parts of Africa where the educated pastors have been killed. The Lord is providing leaders, people are coming to Christ, the Word is being proclaimed, and they know how to worship! Maybe there is a healthy compromise between total dependence on God to do what only He can do, trusting others to do their part, and our responsibility to go and do the best we can. It's something to think about.

Oh, one last thing. I will email you a copy of my study notes each week for you to look over. Read the whole book at least one time per week to keep our study in context to the overall message."

Philip's Study Notes, 1 Thessalonians

William Barclay comments on the importance of the gospel coming to Thessalonica: "It is impossible to overstress the importance of the arrival of Christianity in Thessalonica. If Christianity was settled there, it was bound to spread east along the Egnatian Road until all Asia was conquered, and West until it stormed even the city of Rome. The coming of Christianity to Thessalonica was crucial in the making of it into a world religion."[47]

To paraphrase Charles Ryrie, he lists four purposes of this letter:

1) to express Paul's thankfulness and give encouragement;

2) for Paul to defend himself against untrue accusations;

3) to encourage the new believers to stand fast in their faith in the face of persecution; and

4) a doctrinal question had arisen concerning the fate of Christians who had died before the ushering in of Christ's kingdom[48] (Eschatological doctrine, end times).

When Paul says he gives '*thanks to God always for all of* you,' he means it with all of his heart. Harry Ironside said of verse 3, "Paul linked the three graces . . . faith, hope, and love, and he spoke not simply of these graces themselves, but of the spiritual realities connected with them: the work of faith, the labor of love, the patience of hope."[49] The Thessalonians were continuously in his prayers, which is more than I could say for my intercessory prayer life, but that's another story. Ironside also said, "Love to be real must be self-sacrificing. . . our love is not genuine unless we are willing to labor earnestly for the blessing of those for whom we profess to have this deep concern."[50]

The church at Thessalonica was an 'example' to that entire region, as Ryrie comments: "The word example is *tupos*, from which we get the English word 'type.' It originally meant the mark of a blow (cv. John 20:25); then it came to mean the figure formed by the blow; and thus its resultant meaning is image or pattern (Heb 8:5). The meaning then, is that the conduct of these believers served as a pattern for other Christians in the two provinces of Greece: Macedonia (the northern part of Greece, of which Thessalonica was the chief city) and Achaia (the southern part of Greece, of which Corinth, the place of writing of the letter, was the principal city)."[51]

Barclay observed about this vibrant young church: "Verse 8 speaks of the faith of the Thessalonians sounding forth like a trumpet; the word could also mean crashing out like a roll of thunder. There is something tremendous about the sheer defiance of early Christianity. When all prudence would have dictated a way of life that would escape notice and so avoid danger and persecution, the Christians blazoned forth their faith. They were never ashamed to show whose they were and whom they sought to serve."[52]

There is one little textual problem concerning the word 'gentle' (*epioi* in the Greek). The early Greek writings did not have spaces between the words. The Greek spelling of the word *epioi* (gentle) and *nepioi* (babe) is the same except for the first letter. The last letter of the preceding word is 'n,' so the meaning could be 'gentle' or 'babes' depending on where you divide the words. Either way, Paul was saying they treated the new believers tenderly.

The following week was busy as usual. There was the early morning meeting with the loafers at Andy's a couple of times, daily Bible study, taking care of the horses, replacing the boards in the double-axle utility trailer, changing the oil and filters in the tractor, working on Emma's never ending 'honey do' list, and a few precious moments to shoot. If there was any accuracy work to be done, he used the shooting range. However, Philip was a firm believer that if you ever really needed a gun (poisonous snakes, rabid skunks, one too many coyotes), the target was not likely to be broadside at a known distance, so he tended to shoot from all sorts of positions at knotholes in old logs or pear cactus.

But at the top of Philip's to do list was 'pray for Mbusa and his pastors.' There has to be a special reward in heaven for such men and women who teach the Word and care for the flock under conditions of hunger and threat of life. It must take moment to moment dependence on the Lord just to make it through the day. Just worship with these brothers and sisters and you will know what it really is to 'give God worth.'

Jodie and Johnny were right on time for the next study in

Thessalonians. Everyone got a glass of iced tea, settled in on the front porch, and then Philip opened his Bible and got to it. "From my notes you have the four purposes Charles Ryrie listed for this letter. One of the major themes of 1 Thessalonians is the second coming of Jesus Christ and the resultant effect on the young believers. Paul talks about end times, or to use a two bit theological term, eschatology. The second coming of Christ is referred to in some way in every chapter. But first in chapter one he has much to say about his love and devotion for the brothers and sisters in Christ. Let's keep in mind the application we seek: God calling you to care for this Sunday school class.

Paul's salutation mentions himself, Silas (Silvanus) and Timothy. There was no grand-standing, and no 'I'm the senior pastor'; they were equals in God's eyes. What he says next is a little subtle, but vitally important: *'God the Father and the Lord Jesus Christ'* (the oneness of the Father and Son); *'grace to you'* (which is equivalent to the undeserved favor of God); *'and peace'* (which is the peace—freedom from the wrath of God we have as a result of the reckoning of Christ's righteousness to our account). Ryrie says: 'There can be no real peace until grace has been experienced in the heart.'[53] Paul understood spiritual warfare, so he knew that even more than his Jewish antagonists following him around. Satan had to be hot on his trail as well. How were these babes in Christ holding up against the Evil One who hates the name of Christ being gloried in new believers?

When Paul says he gives *'thanks to God always for all of* you,' he means it with all of his heart. Paul loved them. You might also remember from my notes one of my favorite quotes from Ironside: 'Love to be real must be self-sacrificing. . . our love is not genuine unless we are willing to labor earnestly for the blessing of those for whom we profess to have this deep concern.'[54] I can't tell you how convicting that is to me. Paul genuinely felt love for them, and his steadfast hope was in the ability, the *Dunamus*, of Jesus Christ to hold that which the Father had given Him. They were '*beloved by God*,' which is a perfect participle which indicates past action with continuing force. I'll pause for a second to say something to both of you. If you are called to this work with the teen group, God will create in you this type of love and devotion for those kids—which will be more of a miracle than any of those phony television heisters.

The gospel came to Thessalonica not in eloquent preaching. The Holy Spirit used the simplicity of the message to empower the Word so much so that the evangelist had complete assurance of its intended effectiveness. If God should choose you for this work, you will have the privilege of seeing the Holy Spirit work in young lives through the Word. The word translated 'patience' is the strong Greek word *hupomone* which means perseverance in the battle, in the midst of persecution. This is a little technical, but the Holy Spirit is in the genitive case, which means their joy came from the Spirit—a gift. Let that sink in! They were to persevere in the face of persecution in the joy of serving God in the Spirit.

The church at Thessalonica was an 'example' to that entire region. You may remember what Ryrie said about 'example': "It came to mean the conduct of these believers served as a pattern for other Christians in the two provinces of Greece, Macedonia and Achaia."

Barclay's comment about verse 8 meaning the new believers were like a trumpet sounding defiance is too good to just gloss over. I know of a man in eastern Congo that stands ten feet tall for Jesus in defiance of danger and lawlessness. His name is Mbusa, and except for the providence of God, he would be dead today! But he does not hide from danger. Rather he shepherds all the pastors in the province.

In verse 10 we get the first mention ('*to wait for His Son*') of the return of Christ, which was the foundation of their hope. I want to say here at this first mention that Jesus' return for His own should be a fundamental part of your Christian faith. Unfortunately, many of our churches today don't teach this eternal truth at all. It is my observation that the more this future blessed hope grips a person, the more vital is his present service to the Lord.

Apparently Paul's conduct and motivation had been brought into question by those opposing the new church, so Paul addresses this in chapter 2. We are not told specifically who was opposing Paul's mission and the new church, but it is reasonable to assume that there were at least three: 1) the Jewish opponents who cause the threat to Paul's life while in Thessalonica, then followed him to Berea; 2) the society in general being idol worshipers living in sin city where anything goes, but where a righteous contingent would shine light on their dark deeds; and 3) Satan who opposes every work that glorifies Jesus Christ.

Should God call you to shepherd the teen group, expect opposition. Paul's comments in this letter are not to the opposition, but to the church. So he asks them to recall that his conduct was characterized by just actions, unselfish love, blameless motivation, and without guile. The word translated 'guile' has the meaning of baiting or designed to catch, but that was not Paul's intent or method. Paul also defends his work ethic (labor on their behalf).

We have a whole bunch of applications in this lesson: 1) Paul expressed 'grace and peace' to the church. We should always brandish the dual blessing of living before God in grace and peace as a result of what Christ has done for us. 2) When you are being fruitful for the Lord, opposition is to be expected. But did you notice Paul did not direct his attention to those opposing him, but encouraged those the Lord was molding into a great church. Never put your eyes on the opposition when instead you can shine the light on Jesus. 3) Only God can bring someone to salvation; let God do what only He can do, and be satisfied just doing your part. 4) The church at Thessalonica was an example or pattern of what the true church should be. Always, always,

always keep the biblical pattern in front of you. 5) Paul was unjustly accused of doing wrong. Know that you will also be judged by those outside the church, and unfortunately sometimes by those inside the church, so you will almost certainly end up giving up some freedom. I think that is enough for one night, so we will pick up in chapter 3 next week." Jodie and Johnny looked a little dazed, but shook their head yes.

Philip's Study Notes, 1 Thessalonians 3

Lois Cheney wrote, "I know a pain that passeth all understanding and when I feel that pain, I understand it. I know a truth that defies all understanding and when I live that truth I understand it. I know a love that passeth all understanding and when I feel that love I understand it. I know a God that passeth all understanding and when I love that God I understand God."[55]

(CHAPTER 3) It is unfortunate that the chapter breaks here because the 'Therefore' links this section to the preceding. The purpose of Timothy visiting the church at Thessalonica was to encourage, strengthen, and establish the young believers. Paul lays it on the line; the church is destined to affliction in a fallen world. Paul tells them that Satan will counter-attack, but he has faith in their authentic conversion that they will stand fast.

(6) *"Brought us good news of your faith."* Paul chooses the verb *euangelisamenou* (to bring good news) used in preaching the gospel.

(8) *"Now we really live"* (Gr *zao*, to be warm or to have life). Paul is saying, with Timothy's positive report, He (Paul) has a new lease on life. He is glad to know that his suffering has not been in vain.

(12) Paul uses two verbs: *pleonasai* (to increase or enlarge) and *perisseusai* (abound or abundance) in his prayer, with the meaning that they might 'grow to overflowing' in their love for one another.

(13) "So that" (purpose statement to follow) they may be "unblameable in holiness" at Jesus' return.

Early morning found Philip at Andy's having coffee with Charlie Marsh. They discussed the Thessalonians study with Johnny and Jodie, but eventually Philip turned the conversation to another subject. He wanted to hear Charlie's thoughts. "Charlie, what part of your spiritual journey has been the most difficult?" "P-p-prayer! Hands down the most d-difficult for me, but how a-about you?" "Authentic prayer!" Philip said hesitantly. Both men looked at each other with an expression of "how could that be?"

"P-philip, how c-can you explain the contradiction in f-faith?" "It seems to be a combination of self-centeredness and lack of love for others that affects my harmony with God's thoughts. I know both of us pray, but the gap between what I do and the real possibility of intimate fellowship with the Almighty," Philip paused to rub the back of his neck, "it just seems like I come up short of what it ought to be." "I think it has a component of u-understanding our n-n-necessary desperate dependence on G-God. I think it d-does illustrate the constant b-battle between the f-f-flesh and the spirit." "All I know is I have a friend in Congo who puts his life on the line every day, and sometimes I don't find time to pray for him."

The week went by all too quickly. Johnny and Jodie were back for another lesson. It was a cool evening so everyone decided on hot green tea supplemented with a little spice cake. After a few minutes of polite conversation, Philip opened his Bible to 1 Thessalonians, chapter 3. "If you remember, Paul had made a defense of his conduct before the Thessalonians. I think it is also good to remember the humanness of Paul. God had placed within his heart the same love for these babes in Christ that a devoted mother feels for her child, yet he had been left alone in Athens, left to his own battle of faith. I think we need to feel the loneliness Paul must have felt, and then the joy of Timothy's report that the new babes in Christ were not only surviving in a hostile environment, but were actually prospering. So it appears to me that God was also doing a faith work in Paul's heart.

To the human eye, Paul didn't look like a winner. Paul had been beaten and jailed in Philippi, run out of town in peril of his life in Thessalonica, run out of Berea, and was batting near zero with the philosophers in Athens. But by the grace of God and with Timothy's report, he was strengthened in his spirit. Was Paul satisfied? No! He wanted to see these young believers perfected in Christ.

The Great Commission is not to go and run up big numbers of those confessing Christ; the great commission is to go and make disciples. In verses 12 and 13, Paul says, '*may the Lord cause you to increase and abound in love for one another, and for all men, just as we also do for you.*' He then continues: '*so that He may establish your hearts unblamable in holiness before our God and Father at the coming of our Lord Jesus with all His saints.*' Paul's very prayer is a testimony of his dependence on God, for only God can transform the hearts of men. I might add that only God can transform the hearts of those teens. Paul prays for what is the greatest need of all of us—the outworking of our faith in growing love. And the prime object of our love: vertically God; horizontally one another.

The purpose of God's work is that He might establish them in holiness. A little word study might help. In the Hebrew, the verb '*qadash*' translated 'to be holy' means 'to cut,' something that is separated from another. The meaning or purpose of the cut is to make clean, to dedicate, to purify. In the Greek, the verb is '*hagiazo*' which means 'to keep chaste or pure,' but with the same fundamental idea of separation (from sin). This is the sanctifying work of the Holy Spirit; sanctification meaning 'set apart.' We are set apart to progressive sanctification; holy living being transformed by grace through faith in (you guessed it) the imputed righteousness of Jesus Christ. God uses the same method; salvation is by grace through faith. Sanctification is by grace through faith.

In Paul's prayer he looks to the day of final accounting (not of sin for believers, but of good works) when the Lord returns with all his saints. About now you might ask, 'what is God's intent for that teen Sunday School class?' And the answer?" Johnny knew the answer, but the prospects seemed a little overwhelming. With sober reality he gave the answer: "Loving God and one another as we are all sanctified in holiness looking forward to the coming of our Lord." Philip smiled, "There you go. The job Charlie offered you is impossible for man, but anything is possible for God. Chapters 4 and 5 are practical applications, so we will hold them until next week."

Philip's Notes, Thessalonians 4-5

(CHAPTER 4) Paul views the Christian life as a 'walk' or journey. The first name applied to Christians was 'The Way.' In verses 1 and 2, he reminds the church of his previous instructions and commands. He now summarizes the previous comments in this letter with the single word 'walk.'

(1) In verse 1, the words *"how you ought to walk"* denote moral necessity. Fornication was an every day occurrence in the Roman/Greek culture, but Paul says that being 'set apart' (Gr *hagiasmos,* sanctification, holiness, separated unto God) includes controlling lustful thoughts and actions. These are not abstract thoughts; being 'in Christ' and indwelled by the Holy Spirit is inconsistent with the oneness that comes with fornication, so sexual things must be kept within the marriage.

(9) *"Now"* introduces a new subject; exhortation in brotherly love (Gr *Philadelphia*), but also taught by God to lovingkindness (Gr *agape*) towards one another.

(11) "*Lead a quiet life*" (Gr *hesuchazo*); to be silent, tend to your own business.

(14) Our hope of resurrection is based on the certainty of Jesus Christ's resurrection. Verse 14 says, "*For if we believe that Jesus died and rose again, even so God will bring with Him those who have fallen asleep in Jesus.*" This 'if' clause is a first class condition in Greek, meaning that it assumes the fact; if something is true then the result is also true.

(16) "*For the Lord Himself*" in the emphatic position indicates that He Himself, in all of His glory, will return for His church. He will "*descend from heaven with a shout,*" as in the traditional Jewish bridegroom coming for his bride with a shout and the blowing of the shofar.

The dead in Christ shall rise first, and then (sequence of events, not length of time) we who are alive shall be 'caught up' which means to 'seize' (from which we get the English word 'rapture'). Our hope is in being transported into the presence of our Lord, and our eternal union with Him.

Next in order is the Day of the Lord. Ryrie comments: "The Day of the Lord is a time of judgment and blessing. It is a time when God deals with the world in judgment for its sin; it is the period of great tribulation on the earth. But it is also a time of blessing when the earth shall enjoy the personal reign of Christ during the millennium. Thus, the Day of the Lord as revealed in the Old Testament includes first a time of wrath and judgment on the wicked, followed by the era of peace when Christ will rule over the earth."[56]

Old Testament scriptures concerning the Day of the Lord:

(Amos 5:18-20) "*Alas, you who are longing for the day of Yahweh, for what purpose will the day of Yahweh be to you? It will be darkness and not light; as when a man flees from a lion and a bear meets him, or goes home, leans his hand against the wall, and a snake bites him. Will not the day of Yahweh be darkness instead of light, even gloom with no brightness in it?"*

(Zephaniah 1:14-15) *"Near is the great day of Yahweh, near and coming very quickly; listen, the day of Yahweh! In it the warrior cries out bitterly. A day of wrath is the day, a day of trouble and distress, a day of destruction and desolation, a day of darkness and gloom, a day of clouds and thick darkness."*

(17) There are two important words here: 'caught up' (a thing robbed, one Gr word, *harpagesometha*, a thing robbed, punctiliar future meaning at a specific moment in the future); 'to meet' (Gr *apantesin*, compound of from to meet, or to come into the presence of).

Harry Ironside once said, "While the world sleeps, we should be alert, awake, ever seeking to serve the Lord Jesus. We should be making His truth known to other people and we should be trying to get them ready to welcome Him when He returns. Oh, that Christians everywhere might be awakened out of the lethargy and out of their carelessness and frivolity! Oh, that they might realize the seriousness of the times in which we live! It is a solemn thing to be a Christian in a world like ours, for we will soon have to give an account of our works to the great Judge."[57]

During the week, Philip set aside a little extra time for prayer. The fact is, most of the spiritual battles are fought on our knees addressed in the heavenlies. There was Johnny and Jodie to pray for, Mbusa and his regional pastors, plus Charlie and the church, but prayer is more than intercession. For this episode, it is enough to say Philip had re-engaged the war for the souls of men and the glory of God.

Johnny and Jodie arrived for their last session in First Thessalonians with a little bit of fear and anticipation, both of which can be beneficial as long as they are tempered with trusting God.

Johnny and Philip had coffee while the ladies had tea. Emma set out some friendship cake to munch on. Everyone settled in on the front porch. "We are now in the application and exhortation part of this letter. We have nothing less than the objective of 'loving one another in sanctified holiness until the coming of our Lord in view.' Now Paul exhorts the readers to abound in the things they already know—not just exist, but excel! We have already said that sanctification is a setting apart, in this specific case apart from sexual immorality. Remember, all types of sexual perversions were accepted in that culture, but the culture does not set the standard for the Christian.

When Paul uses the word 'walk,' he is referring to their way of living. In verse 1 the words *how you ought to walk* mean it is a moral necessity. You see how all of this ties into being set apart to holiness, so much so that Paul says in verse 8 that to reject these truths is in fact rejecting God. I respectfully suggest from experience that you do not want to do that. God is holy and you must not treat Him as otherwise. God will not and did not compromise His holiness to reconcile sinners, but the cost of remaining holy while reconciling sinners was the life of His Son.

Paul goes on to exhort them to abound in affection in brotherly love, *'making it your ambition to live a tranquil life.'* All of these things provide the Christian with a testimony to an unsaved world. A soul winner has something different and refreshing about their walk (way of life) that the lost world recognizes. They may not be able to put their finger on it, but they recognize something different (something wholesome), and they want it!

Next, Paul shifts gears to address a topic which had concerned some in the church at Thessalonica. He addresses the subject of end-times doctrines which they had heard when Paul was with them earlier, but were confused. The rapture and the Day of the Lord, both of which play key parts in this letter, are surprisingly enough a stimulus and motivation for the believer. Some had misunderstood Paul's earlier teaching about the return of our Lord for the church, assuming that it was to be almost immediately. Then when some had died before the Lord's return, they were questioning if those who had passed on would miss the Lord's return. The question concerns *'those who sleep,'* which is a present participle, thus continuous sleep or the body has died. *'Sleep'* is in fact a good analogy because those asleep continue to exist and it is temporary; just as we awake from sleep, so shall we be resurrected from death.

This is personal, but when my closest friend's wife died he asked me to assure him that he would see her again. I told him (I believe directed by the Spirit) that if Jesus Christ was resurrected from the dead, then he would certainly see her again. Our hope of the resurrection is based on the certainty of Jesus Christ's resurrection. *'For if we believe that Jesus died and rose again, even so God will bring with Him those who have fallen asleep in Jesus.'* This *'if* clause' says if something is true then the result is also true. Paul goes on to explain the specifics of the Lord's return for His church. The regenerated living shall not (emphatic negative) precede the dead in Christ (those asleep) in the rapture.

The same subject is in view next. What follows has been a motivating factor for every generation who longs for the return of our Lord. *'For the Lord Himself'*—He Himself in all of His glory, will return for His church. He will *'descend from heaven with a shout,'* which reminds me of the traditional Jewish bridegroom coming for his bride with a shout and the blowing of the shofar. The dead in Christ shall rise first, and then we who are alive shall be *'caught up'* (from which we get the English word 'rapture'). Our hope is in eternal union in the presence of our Lord.

Next in order is the 'Day of the Lord.' I hope you noticed Ryrie's comments about 'the Day of the Lord being a time of judgment and blessing.' It is a frightful thing to realize the blindness of the lost: *'While they are saying, Peace and safety! Then destruction will come upon them suddenly like birth pangs upon a woman with child; and they shall not escape'* (5:3).

But we who are being sanctified are children of the light, and more importantly we will be with the Light in the presence of our Lord Jesus Christ. As Christians, we also have the illumination of God's Word. Paul changes from 'you' to 'we' when he writes about living in the light. Paul's admonition has a very practical every day application; since you have by grace been brought into the light, live accordingly. Francis of Assisi's prayer comes to mind:

'Lord, make me an instrument of Thy peace;
Where there is hatred, let me sow love;
Where there is doubt, faith;
Where there is despair, hope;
Where there is darkness, light, and
Where there is sadness, joy.
O Divine Master, grant that I may not so much
Seek to be consoled, as to console;
To be understood as to understand;
To be loved, as to love;
For it is in giving that we receive;
It is in pardoning that we are pardoned; and
It is in dying that we are born to eternal life.'

Since we are children of the light, we should *'be sober, having put on the breastplate of faith and love'* (5:8). 'Be sober' is present tense, meaning sobriety should be our continual attitude, while 'put on' is aorist, meaning momentary action. Thus, always be sober. Put on your armor and leave it on! Because of recent circumstances in my own life, it occurred to me (actually convicts me) that there is no protective armor for my back. This tells me that once I engage in the war, I must not turn from the battle. But Paul gives us a very comforting assurance in verses 8 and 9: *'For God has not destined us for wrath, but for obtaining salvation through our Lord Jesus Christ, who died for us, that whether we are awake or asleep, we may live together with Him.'* Therefore, we are to encourage and buildup one another.

There was apparently dissatisfaction with some of the church leaders, which Timothy reported. God calls people to be His servants, and some He calls to be leaders in the church. If He calls a person, He also equips that person for the work. Even though we are being sanctified (for some reason, and if the Lord had asked me I would have advised against it), He left within us indwelling sin operating through the flesh. Paul discusses this at length in other letters.

If we recognize within us a spirit of contention with our brothers and sisters in Christ, we must immediately go to the Lord in humility and seek His grace to overcome any self-centered thoughts or actions. We are told to *always seek after that which is good for one another and for all men* (5:15). Paul admonishes those under authority to know the true character of your leaders, hold them in high regard, and seek peace with one another. For those in authority, Paul encourages good hard work, being servant leaders, and admonishing when necessary.

Next, Paul turns his attention to individual conduct. *'Rejoice always'* seems out of place for those suffering opposition. But our joy is in being 'in Christ,' not the circumstances of the moment. The only way I know to develop this attitude of joy is to have an eternal perspective. An eternal joy-filled heart attitude is the proper perspective from which to pray, without ceasing. And while you are at it, *'be thankful,'* not for present suffering but for what God has done and is doing through you. The Holy Spirit also comes into play: *'Do not quench the Spirit.'* The verb is present tense; therefore, stop pouring water on the fire of the Spirit.

Also, Paul says for us to not despise prophesy. Of course you know prophesy has two aspects: foretelling and forth-telling. We don't know the details of the problem with prophesy, but we do know that apparently some were idly waiting for the Lord's return. It may be there was confusion about the rapture or the Day of the Lord. But Paul is not telling them to let down their guard and believe everything; '*examine everything carefully; hold fast to that which is good.*' In the context of sanctification, he says, '*abstain from every form of evil.*' Paul ends with an admonition to read this letter carefully. '*I adjure you by the Lord to have this letter read to all the brethren.*' The word 'adjure' (or sometimes translated 'charge') is very strong and means 'to bind with an oath.' Selah!

Well, I don't know about you, but I needed this study to remind me of my duty to the Lord to care for those I should have been praying for without ceasing. Ironside's words questioning genuine, self-sacrificing love for one another was very convicting for me. But enough about me. At some point in the future the two of you have some discerning to do."

Johnny looked at Jodie and said, "On the way over here we talked about this, and both of us are sure what the Lord is telling us. We know we are called to invest our lives in those young people in our church, but it is more than that." Jodie reached over and put her hand in Johnny's. "Something happened in our hearts as we prayed for the Lord's direction. There is a fire to share the love of Christ and the light of the Word with these kids." Then Jodie spoke up, "Now we need something from you, Mr. Cole." Philip looked puzzled and asked, "What could that possibly be?" Johnny and Jodie answered at the same time: "your prayers without ceasing."

Epilogue

The Way

The evening was cool, but without a bite to it. Emma and Philip sat in the glider on their front porch, enjoying another peaceful sunset as it radiated reds with brilliant shafts of silver changing to pinks. His arm was around her to keep her slightly toasty. Philip's thoughts drifted, as they often do, over 40 plus years of sharing the good and the bad with one person. The journey they had started together over 25 years ago had different ambitions, but the same goal—following Jesus. At their age, how long they had on this earth was uncertain. But they had this moment together. Philip had finally just begun to scratch the surface of understanding that the journey is a love story, written before time began.

What Philip remembered most were the people, the ones he would have avoided. But the Lord placed them in his path. They had enriched his understanding of the Word and taught him about the Lord. The light was almost gone, only a soft glow of lilac, the stillness of night approaching, as he recalled to mind something from his study with Johnny and Jodie: The Way.

The locals had tagged him with the absurd handle 'Pistolero Padre,' but the first Christians were simply known as "The Way." He would sleep peacefully tonight, Emma at his side, knowing God is the Lord of the journey. If he is blessed with another day, tomorrow he will follow Him on The Way.

ENDNOTE

1   Charles Ryrie, The Ryrie Study Bible, Moody Press, Chicago, 1995, p 1

2   Stanley D. Toussaint, Behold the King, Kregel Publications, Grand Rapids, MI, 1980, p. 36-37

3   David H. Stern, Jewish New Testament Commentary, Jewish New Testament Publications, Clarksville, MD, 1996, p 2

4   Charles Ryrie, The Ryrie Study Bible, p 491

5   Philip Bliss, Man of Sorrows, What a Name, 1875

6   A. W. Tozer, The Pursuit of God, Christian Publications, Camp Hill, Pennsylvania, p 56

7   C. F. Keil and F. Delitzsch, Commentary on the Old Testament, Volume 1, William B. Eardmans Publishing Company, Grand Rapids, Michigan, pp 33-34

8   NET Bible, www.netbible.com, 2001, p 22

9   Allen P. Ross, The Bible Knowledge Commentary, editors John F. Walvoord and Roy B. Zuck, Victor Books, p 28

10   Charles Caldwell Ryrie, Ryrie Study Bible, p 2061

11   Walter Liefeld, The Expositor's Bible Commentary, Frank Gaebelein editor, Zondervan Publishing House, Grand Rapids, 1984, p 1053

12   William Barclay, The Gospel of Luke, The Westminster Press, PA, 1975, p 293

13   Latin Hymn, Psalteriolum Cantionum Catholicarum, 1710, st 1, 2, John Mason Neale, 1851, st 3, 4, Henry Coffin, 1916

14   Edwin M. Yamauchi, The Expositor's Bible Commentary, volume 4, p707

15   Fanny Crosby, To God be the Glory, 1875

16   NET Bible, p1946

17   Merrill C. Tenney, The Expositor's Bible Commentary, p56

18   David Stern, Jewish New Testament Commentary, Jewish New Testament Publications, Clarksville, MA, 1996, p 653

19 Richard Longeneker, The Expositor's Bible Commentary, Volume 9, p 369

20 William Barclay, The Letters to Timothy, Titus, and Philemon, The Westminster Press, Philadelphia, 1975, p 142

21 Sally Rackets, New Life in Christ, 1996, p29

22 Ralph Earle, The Expositor's Bible Commentary, Volume 11, p 395

23 The NET Bible, First Beta Edition, p 2227

24 A. Duane Litfin, The Bible Knowledge Commentary, Victor Books,1984, pp 753-754

25 Charles H. Dyer and Gregory A. Hatteburg, The Christian Traveler's Guide to the Holy Land, Broadman & Holman Publishers, Nashville, Tennessee, 1998, p60

26 Ibid, p80

27 Ibid, p49

28 Bruce Scott, The Feasts of Israel: Seasons of the Messiah, 1997, p 76-77

29 Ibid, p 77-78

30 Ibid, p 82

31 C.F. Keil and F. Delitzsch, Commentary on the Old Testament, Volume1, p 449

32 Richard Booker, Jesus in the Feasts of Israel, Bridge Publishing, Inc., South Plainfield, NJ, 1987, p 103

33 Ibid, p 108

34 David H. Stern, Jewish New Testament Commentary, p521

35 William Barclay, The Letters to the Galatians and Ephesians, The Westminster Press, Philadelphia, 1976, p24

36 David Stern, p546-547

37 Ibid, p26-27

38 Sally Rackets, p29

39 Charles C. Ryrie, So Great Salvation, Victor Books, 1989, p40

40 Donald Campbell, The Bible Knowledge Commentary, p599

41 William Barclay, p31

42 James Montgomery Boice, The Expositor's Bible Commentary, Volume 10, Zondervan Publishing House, Grand Rapids, MI, 1976, p470

43 James Boice, p473

44 James Boice, pp475-476

45 All Hail the Power of Jesus' Name, Edward Perronet, 1779; st 3, 4, John Rippon, 1787. Tune Diadem, James Ellor, 1838

46 James Boice, p482

47 William Barclay, The Letters to the Philippians, Colossians, and Thessalonians, Westminister Press, 1975. p181

48 Charles Ryrie, First and Second Thessalonians, Moody Press, 1987, p13-14

49 H.A. Ironside, 1 & 2 Thessalonians, Loizezux Brothers, 1947, p19

50 Ibid, p19

51 Charles Ryrie, First and Second Thessalonians, p28-29

52 William Barclay, The Letters to the Philippians, Colossians, and Thessalonians, p187

53 Charles Ryrie, p 23

54 H.A. Ironside, p19

55 Lois Cheney, God Is No Fool, United Writers Press, Tucker Georgia, 2005, p 71

56 Ryrie, First and Second Thessalonians, p69

57 Ironside, p50